SPIRIT OF THE RONIN

THE RONIN TRILOGY: VOLUME III

SPIRIT OF THE RONIN

by

Travis Heermann

Bear Paw Publishing
Denver

Illustrators: Alan M. Clark and Drew Baker
Calligrapher: Naoko Ikeda
Cover Designer: jim pinto

PAPERBACK EDITION

ISBN 978-1-62225-414-9

Bear Paw Publishing
Denver, Colorado, USA

www.bearpawpublishing.com

ACKNOWLEDGMENTS AND THANKS

The author wishes to thank all the folks who made this book possible. In particular, the Pearl Street Gang early readers: Mario Acevedo, Warren Hammond, Angie Hodapp, Aaron Michael Ritchey, and Jeanne Stein. Thanks also to John Helfers and Colleen Kuehne for their enormous help during the editing process.

I am also incredibly thankful to Chanel for her tremendous support in the dark hours of bringing this behemoth into existence, as well as to Kaya for her helpfulness and for putting up with all the missed nights of Harry Potter when deadlines were looking scary.

I am grateful as well to master calligrapher Naoko Ikeda for gracing this volume with her art.

Any omissions are purely the author's fault. Grievances may be filed in person or with the gods.

DEDICATION

For these artists whose work still inspires me

Akira Kurosawa
Toshiro Mifune
Hayao Miyazaki
Eiji Yoshikawa
Takashi Miike
Yukio Mishima
Sonny Chiba
Takeshi Kitano

And all the haiku poets whose work is an endless source of insight and delight.

PART I: THE SIXTH SCROLL

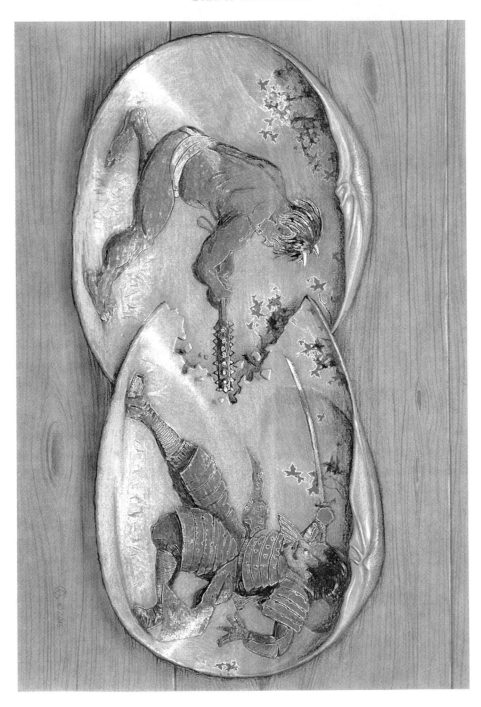

Deftly the new moon
Brushes a silver haiku
On the tips of the waves
　　　—*Kyoshi*

Ken'ishi's first view of the castle of Lord Otomo no Tsunetomo brought his weary feet to a halt on the road. The roofs of its two keeps, one taller than the other, rose majestically over the skirts of the surrounding town. Something swelled behind his ribs, driving out an incoherent sound overcome with profound joy.

His previous visit here, with the itinerant merchant Shirohige, felt like another life, or the account of another's life, so much had changed. A bolt of his life's cloth had been woven with people and experiences and then ripped asunder, leaving only disparate shreds.

Now, the castle was his destination, a place for him to belong, to fulfill his destiny as a warrior. Service with a great lord had been his fondest wish since the day Kaa had set him free to walk the earth with Silver Crane at his hip. For the first time in his life, he would belong somewhere, and that belonging would not be clouded by deceit.

He adjusted his pack, hitched up his trousers, torn and stained as they were from his trek through the forest, and ran down the hill toward the town like an exuberant child. His heaving breath tugged at the stitches of the still healing wound over his heart. As he ran, Ken'ishi marveled again at the majesty of the castle on its hilltop, its stone walls that swept up for five stories, its white-plastered sides, its sweeping roofs, its dark, heavy shutters.

The surrounding lands were a well-tended patchwork of stubbled rice fields, terracing down toward orchards and gardens, all gray and brown and dormant with the onset of winter. In his excitement, even these dismal colors that covered the hibernating world felt as vibrant as the first blooms of *sakura*. He crossed the wooden bridge over the river and trotted into Hita town.

Here in midafternoon, Hita town was alive with far more activity than during his previous visit. Men and oxen pulled carts of grain, timber, and tools. Women and boys toiled with sticks, feathers, and slivers of steel to fill barrels of arrows. The hot, sharp odor of forges and grindstones belched from the dark recesses of smithies. The Mongol invaders had been destroyed, but from the preparations for war going on here, it looked as if the enemy might return at any moment. None of the townsfolk paid Ken'ishi the slightest attention, not even the roving packs of children running bare-legged through patches of cold mud.

His stomach roared at not having eaten yet today—he had wanted to push straight through the last distance to the castle—but he passed several food vendors without stopping. He would not tarry until he had presented himself for duty to Otomo no Tsunemori, brother of the great lord and captain of his forces, and returned to him the little *kozuka* blade he had given Ken'ishi in the aftermath of the Mongol attack. The blade represented an invitation to serve, one of the greatest gifts Ken'ishi had ever received.

Up the cobblestone path terraced with steps toward the castle gates, his legs took on a surer step, each footfall purposeful, determined. His heart skipped a few occasional beats. The gates were open to admit lines of laborers hauling stores on their backs into the castle.

Two guards stood at the gate with *naginata*, clad in armor and helm. They challenged him, but neither appeared surprised to see a *ronin.*

"I am Ken'ishi. I fought with the defense forces against the barbarian invaders. I was told by Captain Otomo no Tsunemori to present myself for service to Lord Otomo. He gave me this." Ken'ishi showed them the *kozuka.*

They raised their eyebrows in surprise at the small blade, engraved with Tsunemori's name.

"Please take me to him," Ken'ishi said.

Both of them eyed him for a long moment, and Ken'ishi began

to grow angry that they seemed to doubt his word. Finally, one said, "Follow me."

He led Ken'ishi through the gates, up through the ways between the castle's concentric fortifications, to a practice yard. Battered striking posts, bales of straw serving as archery targets, and weapons racks surrounded the perimeter of the yard. Ten scruffy-looking warriors with wooden swords sparred in pairs, under the watchful eye of Captain Tsunemori, who sat on a chair upon a raised platform.

Tsunemori was middle-aged, handsome, with eyes revealing a sharp intelligence. Astride his horse in the aftermath of the battle, when he had given Ken'ishi the *kozuka,* Tsunemori had been an imposing figure. Excitement coursed through Ken'ishi at meeting the man again.

Flanking Tsunemori on either side were two other samurai in fine but serviceable attire, upright caps upon their heads like black coxcombs, their faces grim and discriminating. They watched the sparring matches with intense scrutiny. The contestants struck and feinted, yelled fierce *kiai* and grunts of pain as blows struck home.

The sparring warriors, *ronin* all, it seemed, wore various bits of battered armor and carried a wide variety of weapons, some types Ken'ishi had never seen. Chains and sickles, massive axes and hammers, strange, wickedly-spiked spears. Most looked ragged and unkempt. Some of them had crafty, predatory glints in their eyes. How many of them had been bandits? With that question, Ken'ishi felt the guilty weight of his own questionable deeds.

A *ronin* was a unique sort of outsider: a samurai without a master; a man tossed by the waves of life, fitting nowhere—like a wild animal, not to be trusted. Warriors without direction and purpose often turned to banditry to support themselves. Sometimes a warrior became *ronin* because he lost his lord in battle or because he made some grievous error, resulting in banishment from the lord's service. Sometimes a child was born to a *ronin* father, as Ken'ishi had been. Many of the men around him looked like long-time *ronin,* with unshaven pates and beards, threadbare clothing, and unpolished swords.

The guard said, "Wait here until you're called."

Ken'ishi bowed, and the samurai departed. Shrugging off his pack, Ken'ishi noticed three other warriors sitting on the ground nearby, all of varying means, judging by their raiment, all of them sizing him up as well. He sat near them and waited, trying to contain the excitement coursing through him. For the first time in his life, he felt as if he had entered hallowed halls and joined the company of his martial fellows. Joining the defense forces in Dazaifu to stem the invasion, by contrast, had felt like transient good fortune, tinged with the desperation of impending annihilation.

As the sparring matches continued, he surmised that all of these men were new recruits to Lord Otomo's forces. They fought with a wide unevenness of skill and temperament. Some were little more than wild thugs with tenuous control of weapon or self. Others showed edges of sharp training.

Captain Tsunemori scrutinized the matches with a stern, astute eye. Would Tsunemori remember Ken'ishi? Would Ken'ishi have to spar with these men? There was no man he feared in single combat, whether his sword was steel or wood, and he itched to show his powers.

The officer to Tsunemori's right raised a war fan and called a halt to the sparring. The men gathered themselves up, dusted themselves off, and knelt before the dais, pressing their foreheads to the earth.

"Next group!" called the officer with the fan.

Ken'ishi's presence made the next group into four, two even matches.

He stood, and a page boy brought each of them a fresh, white oak *bokken*. Ken'ishi tested its heft and balance.

The officer with the fan gestured them into pairs. Ken'ishi took a deep breath and squared himself against his opponent. His opponent was a man in his thirties, with a vertical scar that twisted his bottom lip and hard-knuckled hands missing the two smallest fingers on his right.

The officer said, "No blows to the head." He raised the fan to commence the sparring, but Tsunemori interrupted him.

"Is that you, Sir Ken'ishi?"

Ken'ishi faced the dais and bowed deeply. Even though Ken'ishi was far below him in rank, Tsunemori had addressed him with respect. "It is, Lord Tsunemori." His face flushed with pride.

"Have you brought my *kozuka*?"

Ken'ishi touched the pouch tied to his *obi*.

"I have, my lord."

Tsunemori nodded. "You may commence."

The eyes of Ken'ishi's opponent flashed with envy and fresh determination. Here was his chance to make his own favorable impression on these Otomo vassals. "You are too pretty to be a warrior," he growled, the words twisting his scarred lip into a sneer.

Ken'ishi faced him, bowed, and raised his *bokken* into the middle guard position. He felt Tsunemori's cool gaze fixed upon him.

Taking a deep breath, Ken'ishi settled into the Void, where there was no victory and no defeat, only the endless slices of moments where all possibilities of the universe remained quiescent, awaiting impetus to be given life.

His opponent's stance was unbalanced, his footwork unrooted in the power of the earth. He was at least ten years older than Ken'ishi, with a chest shrunken and cheeks hollowed by hunger. There was a deviousness in his eyes, calculations within schemes.

They edged closer to one another, gauging distance, the points of their *bokken* inching closer.

Ken'ishi switched to the stance his old *sensei* Kaa had taught him, that reminiscent of a crane's beak, edge up, point extended toward his opponent over his left elbow, body turned sideways. In all his travels, he had never encountered a swordsman familiar with this technique. This *bokken* was not shaped precisely like Silver Crane, but the unfamiliar technique still confused his opponent. The man edged back, and Ken'ishi attacked.

His thrusting point slipped past his opponent's guard and struck his breastbone, as sharp as the blow of a mallet.

The pain from such a blow would be blinding. The man dropped his sword and screamed, clutching his chest. He sank to his knees, gasping, and curled like a withering leaf.

The noise distracted one of the warriors in the other match, giving his adversary the opportunity to drive the *bokken* out of his grip. Weaponless, the man submitted.

The officer raised the war fan. "Stop."

The three standing faced the dais and bowed, and the man on the ground gathered himself up, cheeks wet with the sting of pain and shame. He bowed unsteadily, his eyes avoiding Ken'ishi.

Tsunemori said, "A fine blow, Ken'ishi. You would be a fearsome opponent in a duel. But what about a melee? Say, three against one?"

The face of Ken'ishi's first opponent brightened with hope of redemption. He snatched up his *bokken* and sniffed, rolling up his sleeves.

The three men surrounded him, but fear did not touch him. On the road, he had faced five iron-hard Mongols and killed them. In Hakozaki, he had slain scores of barbarian horsemen. Three years ago, he had faced the terrifying *oni* Hakamadare. In Hita town below, last year, with his *bokken* he had almost killed three of Green Tiger's thugs, all of whom had steel weapons—he would have to be careful here not to cause such injuries to these men.

Finding the Void here was easy, reflexive, so that when these three lunged at him in an uncoordinated attack, he thwarted them easily, counter-striking and gliding between the interstices of opportunity, parrying strikes, slashing them as they stumbled past, leaving stinging bruises and pain in his wake. In a few more heartbeats, it was over, and three men lay upon the ground: one senseless, one weaponless, and the last, Ken'ishi's first opponent, doubled over again and whimpering in agony.

Only in retrospect did Ken'ishi realize he had broken the rules of the match by striking one of them across the pate. Quickly he prostrated himself before the dais. "Please accept my apologies, Lords!"

Tsunemori eased an elbow onto the arm of his chair, a faint smirk on his lips. "In combat, when an enemy offers a target, one strikes. And look, Yukiiye is already coming around. It is difficult to restrain oneself in the fog of battle. When good technique is so ingrained, it becomes as one's very flesh. An admirable display of skill, Sir Ken'ishi. Was it not, Lieutenant Nagata?"

The man with the fan nodded. "Admirable indeed. Have you just arrived, Sir Ken'ishi?"

"Yes, Lords," Ken'ishi said. "Lord Tsunemori, it is my honor to return to you your *kozuka*." He withdrew it from a pouch attached to his *obi* and offered it up with both hands.

Tsunemori gestured, and a steward standing beside the dais rushed forward to retrieve it.

"I regret that there were no sword polishers along my journey," Ken'ishi said.

Tsunemori accepted it from the steward. "I thank you for keeping it safe." Then he raised his voice. "All of you will be given the opportunity to serve as retainers to the powerful, glorious, and honorable Lord Otomo no Tsunetomo. Many of you were *ronin* before the barbarians came, a few of you cast adrift by your masters' deaths. But my brother needs men, and you fought the barbarians as befits true samurai. The life you led before you came to this is unimportant. What happens from this moment forward *is* important. After tonight, you will be the sworn servants of Otomo no Tsunetomo, and you are expected to behave as such. Our lord is fair and generous to those who serve with honor and distinction. Those men whose conduct shames his house will receive swift justice. If you dishonor yourself, you dishonor your lord." His voice deepened, guttural. "If you disappoint him, you dishonor me, who chose you."

Ken'ishi knelt again. In spite of his controlled jubilation, however, the invisible, ethereal spirits of the wind and earth, the *kami,* buzzed at him like a mosquito behind his ear. There were eyes upon him that wished him harm. His awareness sharpened in that moment, and he stood, surveying each of the men around him. His first opponent fixed him with an expression of puzzled consternation and hostility. The other two dusted themselves off and regarded Ken'ishi with stunned respect.

"Everyone, follow Captain Yoshimura to your quarters," Tsunemori said. "Tonight, at the Hour of the Cock, you will report to the castle keep for your fealty ceremony."

The officer on Tsunemori's left stepped down from the dais and gestured to them to follow.

"[I]t can be said that bows and arrows, swords, and halberds are...instruments of bad fortune and ill-omen. The reason for this is that the Way of Heaven is a Way that brings life,  while instruments that kill are, on the contrary, truly ill-omened. Thus they are considered repugnant because they are contrary to the Way of Heaven.... [However, there] are times when ten thousand people suffer because of the evil of one man. Therefore, in killing one man's evil, you give ten thousand people life. In such ways, truly, the sword that kills one man will be the blade that gives others life."

—*Yagyu Munenori, The Life Giving Sword*

Shoulders hunched, Hatsumi shuffled into the chamber of Lady Otomo no Kazuko, clutching her belly. Here in the high room of Lord Tsunetomo's central keep, the winter wind slunk among the heavy ceiling beams like a thief, stealing all warmth and wringing a shiver from her, even in her quilted winter robes. She wondered if it were this cold in the other, smaller keep, where dwelt Tsunemori and his wife, Lady Yukino. Even the *tatami* was cold through her slippers. She was only twenty-seven, but she too often felt like a doddering old woman these days.

When Hatsumi saw that Kazuko was brushing her own hair, she gasped in annoyance. "My lady! You must allow me!" She hurried forward, reaching for the brush.

Kazuko flashed her a brilliant, beautiful smile and kept brushing. Hatsumi was struck by how the young woman had matured in the three years since her marriage. When they had first come to Lord Tsunetomo's castle, Kazuko was but seventeen, her features still soft and girlish. Now, however, her face had taken on a regal elegance, the kind of beauty found once in ten thousand women. Why she did not blacken her teeth as proper, married ladies of means should, Hatsumi would never understand—baring one's teeth, especially when Kazuko's were so perfect and Hatsumi's were not, was so rude. Besides, beautifully lacquered teeth allowed a lady to keep them longer. "It is no trouble, Hatsumi. You are not feeling well today. And I can hardly ask you to do something I can do for myself."

In truth, Hatsumi was not well today. Her innards clenched and writhed and had sent her to the privy far too often. But even there she found no relief. Her belly was full of rats trying to gnaw their way out. And there was a strange lump on her scalp, just above her hairline, painful like an incipient boil. It itched, but she resisted the urge to scratch. "It is not proper for a lady to do such things. That has always been my place. Now, please give me the brush."

Kazuko smiled indulgently and handed it over.

Hatsumi took the brush in one hand, a handful of Kazuko's long, lustrous, raven hair in the other, and began to brush. She had always enjoyed this when Kazuko was a girl. Nowadays, in the aftermath of the Mongol attack, with Lord Tsunetomo still recovering from his wound, Kazuko had taken more of these tasks upon herself. Hatsumi did her best to conceal the hurt she felt at being swept aside, her purpose diminished, for it was not her place to complain. Kazuko was the lady, Hatsumi the servant. It had always been so.

Hatsumi said, "And how fares your husband today? His wound is healing well, yes?"

Kazuko nodded. "At breakfast this morning he said he will try to draw a bow today."

"Ah, good! That's good!" Hatsumi continued brushing. "A comfort that he mends so well. Such a strong husband your father found for you."

A wistful look crossed Kazuko's face. "A comfort, yes. Such a strong man." The look hazed into some memory for several moments until her face flushed. "Open the shutter please, Hatsumi. It grows warm in here."

"But, my lady, it is winter!" The nearby brazier of coals barely warmed the room.

Kazuko's eyes hardened as she peered back over her shoulder, and Hatsumi drew back. *Fine, let us open the window and grow chilled again.* She bit back this angry retort, crossed to the nearest shutter, swung it up, and propped it open to admit a blast of cold air.

Below, in the practice yard, Tsunemori and his officers watched a group of four men sparring. Since Lord Tsunetomo and Captain Tsunemori had returned a few weeks prior, *ronin* and other vagabonds had been trickling daily into the castle, new recruits to replenish the ranks of troops slaughtered in the barbarian attack. A ragged-looking bunch to be sure, but perhaps they could be polished into proper samurai.

Her gaze drifted over the faces from on high. Then she thought she saw something. A familiar face. A familiar, shaggy topknot. She fixed her attention upon the man. Standing one among many, oblivious to her presence as Tsunemori addressed them.

No...

It could not be him.

Not here.

Not now.

Not ever!

"What is it, Hatsumi? Do you see something?"

There was no mistake. The man below was Ken'ishi.

Hatsumi backed away, gripping her hands to keep them from shaking. "No, I was just trying to get a better look."

"Another batch of recruits today? Are they all hale and strong?" Kazuko's voice was playful, and she rose to come to the window.

Hatsumi cleared her throat and intercepted her. *By all the gods and buddhas, no, not him, not here. He'll ruin everything.* "They look like a bunch of unwashed scoundrels."

Hatsumi's mind, all of her will, focused on one thought. Kazuko must not see him. She must not know *he* was here. Hatsumi's mind raced. She must get rid of him! The *ronin* Ken'ishi must be driven from the castle like a dog. Or killed. He must never trouble Kazuko again. He must remain forever only a memory. Three years had passed since they had last seen each other, and only recently had Kazuko seemed to stop pining for him.

If Kazuko saw him, she would throw away everything.

"Come, my lady, sit back down," Hatsumi said. "The wind is freezing. Please let me close the window."

Kazuko sighed. "Very well."

Hatsumi hurriedly closed and latched the shutter. As she did, another stabbing pain doubled her over, like a bite into her lower belly, into her womb. She gasped and clutched her middle, biting back a scream.

Kazuko voice rose. "What is it? What's wrong?"

Hatsumi tried to speak. "I...am not well today."

"Oh, Hatsumi, again?"

Hatsumi went to her knees.

"I must call for my husband's physician!"

Hatsumi groaned, "Yes! Please!" Fear cinched a rope around her heart.

The pain coalesced again in her womb, as it always did, like the *oni* Hakamadare's enormous member tearing into her, its savage claws puncturing her flesh.

Kazuko gathered her robes and hurried out.

Hatsumi knelt on the floor, praying for the wave of pain to subside. It always did, but the agony of its presence was a thing of terror.

Her brain reeled with what to do. If Kazuko saw Ken'ishi, she would fall in love with him all over again, and Tsunetomo would see it.

She staggered to her feet, straightened herself as best she could, and went to find the only man who could fix this situation.

Yasutoki sipped his afternoon tea and hated the world.

Since his return to Lord Tsunetomo's estate, after the destruction of everything he had built in the guise of Green Tiger over almost twenty years, after the loss of his house near Hakata Bay, after the loss of the sword Silver Crane, for which he had spent years searching, after the utter failure of the invasion in which he colluded with the illustrious Khan of Khans, after so many schemes within schemes had been wiped out in one great swipe by the hand of the gods, he wanted to kill something. He wanted to snuff the life from some hapless creature put in his path to settle his nerves.

The afternoon light was gray and cold here at the beginning of winter, seeping through the slats in the shutter to steal the warmth from his office and his bones. His aging bones. So much lost. His body was no longer as strong as it had once been, nor as resilient, the curse of age that eats away the efforts of conqueror and commoner alike.

In the weeks since the typhoon had wiped out the barbarian fleet, Yasutoki had taken stock of what he had lost, and it pained him even more now. Immense wealth, washed away. Underworld contacts, slain or lost. His henchmen, Masoku and Fang Shi, slain. In the onslaught of burning and destruction, his gambling parlors and whorehouses in Hakata and Hakozaki, all destroyed. Silver Crane, fallen into the hands of some strange, masked figure with a trained bear at his side, according to Tiger Lily's account of that night.

The only good news was that, in such an emptiness left by the immense destruction of the invasion and the storm, new opportunities could be prised from the wreckage. One of these days, he would finish licking his wounds and stand ready to rebuild Green Tiger's underworld empire. He would fight for the re-ascendance of the Taira clan.

Amid endless whorls of black thoughts, he sipped his tea and contemplated death. Death to the Shogun and the Minamoto clan. Death to the Hojo clan that propped up a corrupt and useless government. Death to anyone who opposed him from this day forward. One bit of good news was that sweet, tender, obedient Tiger Lily awaited him every night in a small hovel he had arranged for her in town. Their secret meetings had become the poultice for his wounds.

A timid knock at his door almost roused a snarl from him, but he restrained it. Best not to reveal his black mood.

"Enter."

The door slid open, and there stood one of the people he least wanted to see in all the world.

Hatsumi knelt at the door jamb and bowed. "I'm very sorry to disturb you..."

His voice was cold. "Hatsumi. You may come in."

She swallowed hard and entered. Her face was pale, taut, sheened with sweat despite the chill, fringes of her hair falling loose around her ears. When had she started to gray? She kept her eyes downcast, her lips pursed over her horse-like teeth. She knelt before him like an upright sack of grain settling into place, then winced as if in pain.

How he had ever stomached bedding her, he could not fathom. "What is it?"

She cleared her throat. "This is a delicate matter, dearest—"

"Do not call me that," he snapped.

"But—"

"Listen to me, Hatsumi. I do not love you. Our liaisons are at an end. No more letters. No more poems. Do you understand?"

She flinched as if struck, her face crumpling, eyes tearing. She spun away from him and collapsed onto her hands and knees, shoulders convulsing.

He waited for her to compose herself.

She inched away from him as if every sob was driven out of her by a lash in his hand.

Finally, after the interminable, shameful spectacle, she pressed herself upright on her knees and turned halfway to face him. Her face was even paler now, eyes rimmed with blood. "I am very sorry, Lord Yasutoki, but I did not come here to talk to you about...us."

"Then do continue, and be quick about it," he said. "I am certain your mistress requires your services."

"It is my mistress I wish to discuss with you. Well, not her directly, but a...difficulty involving her. There is a man, a *ronin*. Before she was betrothed to Lord Tsunetomo, she loved this man. I believe she still loves him."

Hatsumi's presence suddenly became less tiresome.

On the night Lord Nishimuta no Jiro had announced his daughter Kazuko's betrothal, at a banquet with Yasutoki in attendance, the flames of love had risen clearly between Kazuko and the *ronin* Ken'ishi. By a chance encounter, Ken'ishi had delivered her from the hands of the *oni* bandit, Hakamadare. Kazuko had stolen from the castle in the dead of night, presumably to meet her lover, and in the morning, the *ronin* had fled the province on pain of death for the killing of a village constable in a duel. For three years, Yasutoki had nursed this knowledge, saved it for the time when he might have to exert some leverage against Lady Kazuko. Did Hatsumi not know Kazuko had stolen out for a tryst that night? Ken'ishi had been a more-than-capable warrior, with a spirit the likes of which Yasutoki had rarely encountered. Unfortunate that he had escaped Green Tiger's clutches. Being devoured by sharks or drowned in Hakata Bay was too ignominious a death for such a man.

Hatsumi continued, "This *ronin* is among the new recruits. I saw him in the courtyard—"

Yasutoki jumped to his feet, his teeth clamped down upon an exclamation. The *ronin* lived!

"What is it?" Hatsumi asked, cringing. "Have I offended?"

He took a long, deep breath and let it out, slowly. And then another. Then he spoke. "No, Hatsumi. It is not that. I know of this man. I was there at Lord Nishimuta's announcement, do you remember?"

Hatsumi nodded. "I remember."

"The stories of his fight with the *oni* have become the stuff of songs. What a strange happenstance."

Hatsumi cleared her throat again, and tears trickled down her cheeks. "Lord Yasutoki. You must drive him out."

The knowledge that Ken'ishi lived was still too fresh, too shocking for him to have considered his next move, but, given their frequent contact in the bowels of the torturer's den, Ken'ishi was one of the few men in the world who might recognize Yasutoki as Green Tiger. Such an exposure would be disastrous. In all of their meetings, whenever Green Tiger had visited Ken'ishi in his underground torture chamber, he had kept his face concealed by mask and basket hat, but there were other ways to recognize a man.

All he said to Hatsumi was, "Why?"

Hatsumi's voice quavered, and in her face Yasutoki recognized her awareness of the betrayal her next words represented. "She still loves him. For the good of our lord's house, for the good of his honor, the *ronin* must be destroyed. For the love of this *ronin*, Kazuko will bring dishonor to the Otomo clan."

"And why do you think I can accomplish this? I am but Lord Tsunetomo's advisor."

Her gaze flicked to him and held there for a hard, bitter moment.

"You forget, 'dearest,' that I *know* you."

A smile curled the corner of his lip. Perhaps she was not so stupid after all.

She said, "My lady must not know of the *ronin*'s presence here. Whatever you do, it must be done quickly."

"Tonight is the fealty ceremony for these recruits. Our ladyship enjoys attending these. After being left in charge of the castle, she fancies herself a warrior-lady."

Hatsumi's voice lost its quaver. "I will keep her away from the ceremony tonight. What are you going to do?"

"That is not your concern. You may go."

Hatsumi stiffened at the dismissal, but gathered herself and departed, walking with a pained, uncertain gait.

Yasutoki sipped at his tea again, the buzz within of nascent machinations helping to ease the former blackness of his mood.

So the *ronin* had escaped after all, which made a bald-faced lie of Fang Shi's account of his disappearance from the cell in the tidal cave. Unfortunate that the Chinaman had been slain in the White Lotus Gang's attack. The death of a betrayer like Fang Shi would have gone far to scratch Yasutoki's murderous itch today.

Was it possible that the *ronin* had been the one to steal Silver Crane from Yasutoki's house near Hakata? Unlikely—his body had been too ravaged by torture and confinement—but Ken'ishi had a greater motive than anyone. His attachment to the sword was plain; he had searched northern Kyushu for it. At the time Ken'ishi had escaped, he could not have defeated a skilled ruffian like Masoku. How could he have recovered in so little time? How could he have known where to find Silver Crane, hidden as it was under Yasutoki's house shrine? Had someone told him of its location? Who among Yasutoki's retainers would betray him so? Only Masoku and Tiger Lily knew of the sword's location. So many questions without answers. Which was precisely why he would not kill the *ronin*...not just yet.

"A certain general said, 'For soldiers other than officers, if they would test their armor, they should test only the front. Furthermore, while ornamentation on armor is unnecessary, one should be very careful about the appearance of his helmet. It is something that accompanies his head to the enemy's camp."

—*Hagakure, Book of the Samurai*

C aptain Yoshimura was a man of about thirty years, with a round face, a barrel body, and tufts of mustache at the corners of his mouth. In the surety of his gait, Ken'ishi recognized a warrior's strength. Once set into motion, Yoshimura would not be diverted from any chosen path.

He led the newcomers to a long, whitewashed structure built into the wall of the castle. Beside the door hung a wooden placard that read "Barrack Six." Inside was a row of fifteen two-tiered bunks. In each bunk was a narrow *futon* and a blanket, both carefully folded. About half of the bunks appeared to be occupied, with boxes and gear stowed nearby.

One side of the barrack was interspersed with small, shuttered windows. Through one open window, Ken'ishi peered below to the terraced incline of one of the castle approaches. These windows were built to serve as a firing position for archers against any attack from that direction.

Captain Yoshimura called the men around him. "I am the commander of the castle garrison. Through your chain of command, all of you report to me, and I to Captain Tsunemori, and he to Lord Otomo. Claim your bunks. Each bunk has a trunk for your possessions. By the look of some of you, I should tell you that in Lord Tsunetomo's service, thievery warrants execution. The privy is down at the end over there." He pointed. "The bath house is just beyond. The induction ceremony is, as Captain Tsunemori said, at the Hour of the Cock. If you're late, you may as well pack your things and leave. Training begins tomorrow."

Ken'ishi and the other recruits bowed deferentially, and Captain Yoshimura departed with the same abruptness as when leading them here.

The recruits filtered among the bunks, placing their packs on the floor, and began to introduce themselves. More than one grumbled, "When do we eat?"

The man with the scarred lip, Ken'ishi's former sparring partner, thumbed his chest. "I'm Ushihara, from Shimazu country."

"You're far from home," another man said, one of the better appointed of the new recruits, about Ken'ishi's age, with the shaven pate and topknot of a samurai.

"I came to join the defense," Ushihara said. "By the time I got here, the fighting was over."

"You're not samurai," the man said, gesturing toward Ushihara's bedraggled mane.

Ushihara bristled. "And what of it? I'm here to prove myself. What have you proven with your topknot there?"

"I fought in Hakozaki," the man said, standing straighter. "I am Michizane, of the Ishii family, vassals to the Otomo clan."

"You *fought*," Ushihara scoffed. "From the tales I hear, it was more likely you ran like a rabbit."

Michizane lunged for him, fist cocking back and then forward. It landed hard across Ushihara's nose with a meaty crack. In a flurry of arms and sleeves, grasping and scuffling, more blows fell.

Ken'ishi stood back and watched. Two other men jumped in and prised the fighters apart. Ushihara landed a parting kick to

Michizane's belly, doubling him over.

"My brother died in Hakozaki, you peasant scum!" Michizane gasped.

"At least he didn't run!" Ushihara snarled back, his nose gushing blood.

"*Enough!*" A deep voice boomed over them.

The recruits turned toward the speaker. Standing with fists on hips, clad in a light breastplate and iron skullcap, a burly man filled the doorway, even though he stood shorter than all of them. His arms were like knotted boughs and his chin like an anvil. Deep-set eyes glared at them all in turn. His voice was like the rasp of a blade on a whetstone. "You should know that the penalty for brawling is flogging. Care to continue?" His gaze speared each of them for a long moment. "No? I am Sergeant Hiromasa, and this is my barrack. I don't care what it was about, but if it happens again, it'll be my hand on the cane."

Twice already Ken'ishi had been witness to talk of penalties for various infractions or crimes. Such things should not be necessary for men of honor, for samurai. But many of these men were not even *ronin.* That such rules existed bespoke stories of unruliness and other poor behavior that necessitated such things.

Hiromasa's eyes turned upon Ken'ishi. "What's that there, *ronin?* You think this penalty harsh?"

"No, Sergeant. I am...surprised it's necessary. Are we not all blessed by fortune for the opportunity to serve under such a master as Lord Otomo? Who in his right mind would put that at risk?"

Hand pressed against his nose, Ushihara snorted, spraying a fine mist of crimson across his arm.

Sergeant Hiromasa burst into laughter, which continued until he finally composed himself and wiped his eyes. "In times like these, every peasant and *eta* gravedigger from here to Kamakura shows up at our gates thinking they can rise above their birth or seek a glorious death." His gaze fixed upon Ushihara, who averted his eyes. "Perhaps some even can. Hold a spear, swing a sword, draw a bow, do it all bravely and there might be rewards for you. For those things, the barbarians won't care whether your father is a leatherer or your mother a whore. You don't have to be born a samurai, but under Lord Otomo, you will learn to die like one." His gaze raked back and forth over them. "Now, get yourselves cleaned up. The lot of you smell like the trench of a shithouse."

Sergeant Hiromasa strode away.

Ushihara grumbled, "Bastard." Seeing Ken'ishi's eyes upon him, he snapped, "What are you looking at?"

"A fool," Ken'ishi said.

Ushihara stabbed a blunt finger at Ken'ishi's face. "Now listen here, I've had about enough of you!"

"I think you have not had enough, else you would be more respectful." He gripped Silver Crane at his hip with his left hand.

Ushihara took a deep breath to shout again, but Michizane said to Ken'ishi, "That was indeed quite a blow you struck in the trial bouts, Sir Ken'ishi. I have never seen such a technique before."

Ken'ishi bowed, glancing at Ushihara rubbing his chest with a scowl.

"Tell me," Michizane said, "how did you come to acquire Lord Tsunemori's *kozuka*?"

"He gave it to me in Hakozaki, after the typhoon."

"What were your exploits? The granting of such a gift goes beyond the mere foot-soldier."

"I killed some of the barbarians." If he told them the truth of how many, would they believe him? "I saved the life of Otomo no Ishitaka."

"Tsunemori's son!" Michizane said.

"He was in my scout unit. We met a group of enemy horsemen. Ishitaka was wounded. We saved his life and killed the barbarians."

Ushihara listened, his eyes hooded and wary.

"Where do you come from?" Michizane said. "Your accent is strange to me."

"I grew up on a mountain in the far north of Honshu, a land of forests and loneliness."

Michizane smiled. "A poetic soul."

"You have a country accent yourself."

"It is true. My village is small, but the Ishii family is proud," Michizane said. "Ken'ishi, you may share my bunk." He laid his hand on one of the racks.

Ushihara snorted, wiped blood from his face with the back of his hand, and stalked away.

Small bird, forgive me,
I'll hear the end of your
    song
In some other world
          —*Anonymous*

T he serving girl knelt with the tea tray next to Kazuko, beside where Hatsumi lay on a *futon*. The earthenware pot steamed as the girl poured two cups of emerald green tea.

Hatsumi lay with her head on a pillow of buckwheat husks, her face pale and drawn, both hands still clutched over her belly. A strange odor emanated from her robes, one Kazuko could not identify; similar to the sickly-sweet smell of rotten fruit, but there was something else as well, something deep and pervasive. She kept a scented kerchief at hand for the moments when it became too much.

"It is wrong of you to care for me, my lady," Hatsumi said, squeezing Kazuko's arm.

"How many times have you cared for me, Hatsumi, over the course of my life? How could I not? You have been with me for as long as I can remember," Kazuko said. She had never seen anyone so ill before, and it frightened her. Even when her husband returned wounded from the battlefront, the worst of his fever had passed. Hatsumi's bouts of strange illness had grown more frequent and more painful. But in all the other instances, they had ebbed.

Her husband's physician had not yet arrived. Where was he?

Furthermore, she had not seen her husband since breakfast. Likely he was preparing for the induction ceremony tonight, the third in as many weeks as potential recruits filtered into the castle. With an imminent threat just across the sea, the *bakufu* had ordered the samurai lords of Kyushu to redouble their defense preparations and build their fighting forces. Word had come that representatives from the Hojo clan, the regents of the ten-year-old shogun, Minamoto no Koreyasu, would be arriving soon from Kamakura. He would bestow gifts upon the samurai lords and their vassals who had repelled the invaders.

No one believed that the Mongol emperor of China, Khubilai Khan, would attack again any time soon after the loss of so many ships and men, but the consensus among the Imperial Court and *bakufu* was that he was too ambitious and tenacious to give up easily. The Mongol Empire would not have spread all the way to the lands of the setting sun without such ambition.

Kazuko sighed and squeezed Hatsumi's hand. Tsunetomo had invited Kazuko to observe the previous fealty ceremonies and afterward asked her impressions of the men, taking her insights into consideration before assigning them specific duties. In the weeks of his recovery, she had taken to reading a book on the art of war by a Chinese general, a book he had left for her when he departed for the battlefront. She could only admit to herself that she found this realm of men a fascinating one. She found no reason for it to be only the men's pursuit. She hated the violence of war, but she loved the strategy of it. The insights into human nature of this ancient Chinese general were as astute today as they had been more than fifteen hundred years before. That she was one of the few women in the world not just permitted but encouraged to delve into the realm of men filled her with pride and trust in Tsunetomo. She could tell from her husband's actions that he had diligently studied this book and others like it.

She regretted missing the ceremony, but she could hardly leave Hatsumi alone at a time like this. No one else would care for her. The other servants all hated her, and Kazuko could hardly fault them. To them, Hatsumi was haughty and often cruel, with inexplicable bursts of anger that had been growing more frequent in recent months. She had no friends beside Kazuko, and her affair with Yasutoki—how detestable the mere thought!—had been foundering for months. Even so, Kazuko could not bear the thought of someone suffering alone.

Hatsumi groaned and convulsed.

Kazuko stroked her hand. It was hot and coarse. "Poor, poor thing." It was then Kazuko noticed the strange, bruised color of Hatsumi's fingernails, shading to a disconcerting reddish purple at the base. They looked thicker than she remembered them, coarser, hardly a lady's fingernails at all.

"Kazuko, my dear, will you..." Hatsumi rasped. "Will you promise me something?"

"Oh, Hatsumi, you are not dying!" Kazuko said. "You must brace up!"

"As I lie here, something tells me I will not die, that this will pass as it always has. But something in me...I won't be the same after this. Like an old woman whose fingers turn into gnarled twigs. My spirit is knotting up...." Hatsumi sounded almost delirious.

"You will be fine. The physician will come. He will find a way to ease your suffering. Here, drink some tea. The warmth will ease your belly."

"Yes, tea.... But no physician! Please, no physician! This is no one else's business.... This is between you and me...."

Kazuko lifted the cup and held it to Hatsumi's lips while she supported Hatsumi's head with the other hand. Hatsumi's last utterance had sounded almost delirious.

A gusting breath burst from Hatsumi. "Ah, it's such good tea! That is what I most enjoy about living here, you know. The tea fields. The best on Kyushu, they say."

Kazuko smiled. A point of pride for the people of this province was that this area boasted the highest quality tea, rivaled only by the fields in the mountains near the old capital, Kyoto.

"Kazuko, you know I love you like a little sister, yes?"

Kazuko blushed at such a direct and heartfelt sentiment. "I know, Hatsumi. And you are the sister I never had. Ease your mind! Rest now! I command it." She smiled at the last.

Hatsumi sighed again, straining and groaning to find a comfortable position. "Yes, rest." Her voice grew fainter. "You must promise me, don't leave me tonight. I...could not bear it. Please, promise. I will be better in the morning, I think."

Oh, where was that physician? Kazuko would call him to task the moment his bald head appeared.

"Please, promise.... Don't leave me tonight," Hatsumi said.

"I promise. I will not leave your side."

A labored sigh escaped Hatsumi, and she sagged against the floor as if all the tension had just drained from her.

"Perhaps I'll be able to sleep now, yes," Hatsumi breathed. "You are too good to me, Kazuko...." Her voice trailed off.

In the ensuing silence, Kazuko listened to Hatsumi's breath grow shallower, steadier, descending into sleep. She stroked her servant's hand with gentle fingers, stoked the coals in the brazier for more warmth, sipped at the tea. Whenever she took her hand away, Hatsumi's eyes fluttered, turning toward her as if to ascertain that she was still present.

Hatsumi's fists relaxed, little by little, until they hung slack.

Kazuko's gaze kept sliding toward Hatsumi's fingernails. What malady caused such an effect? She had no notion, but if that cursed physician ever appeared, she would ask him.

"[F]rom the time one has been taken into a *daimyo*'s service, of the clothes on his back, the sword he wears at his side, his footgear, his palanquin, his horse and all of his materiel, there is no single item that is not due to  the favor of his lord. Family, wife, child and his own retainers—all of them and their relations—not one can be said not to receive the lord's favor. Having these favors well impressed on his mind, a man will face his lord's opponents on the battlefield and cast away his one life. This is dying for right-mindedness."

—*Takuan Soho, "The Clear Sound of Jewels"*

K en'ishi spent the remainder of the afternoon meticulously preparing himself for tonight's ceremony. After a stint in the *ofuro*, where he scrubbed off weeks of sweat and road dust and shaved his face, he shared the bath with several other men, luxuriating in its heat as respite from the winter. Meanwhile, several servants laundered their clothes. When he received his own again, they were warm and dry, smelling of smoke. The bloodstains were gone, but he lamented the holes and frayed hems. He had no other clothes.

Everything he owned had been burned along with his house in Aoka during the barbarian attack, including the fine set of clothes Kazuko had given him three years before when he had fled her father's domain. Those clothes would be helpful now, on this, one of the biggest nights of his life. Instead, tonight he would look like a vagabond *ronin* again, and the thought filled him with shame.

He caught snatches of conversation throughout the afternoon, learning that recruits had been coming steadily in the past weeks. Tsunemori and his officers had been liberally refilling the ranks depleted by Mongol arrows. Previous newcomers eyed Ken'ishi's group with skepticism and disdain, which seemed foolish to him, considering that not so long ago they had been in the very same position.

At the Hour of the Cock, about sunset, the recruits were summoned to a banquet in the lord's audience hall. They sat in precise rows along either side of the room, with Lord Tsunetomo's place awaiting his arrival on a raised dais at the head of the room. Tsunemori, Yoshimura, and several of the other high-ranked commanders sat at the ends of the rows nearest the lord's dais.

Ken'ishi's belly quivered with nervousness. The last such formal gathering he had attended had nearly destroyed him. He slammed a cage down around the wildly fluttering hope in his heart that his dreams could be achieved, lest they be crushed again by unforeseen circumstances.

If the *kami* would just quiet down, he might be able to enjoy these moments, but the spirits of the air and earth, of the castle itself, were howling in multitudes of little voices as if he were sitting in a den of hungry, invisible wolves.

Finally, Otomo no Tsunetomo entered the room, without fanfare, and the assemblage pressed their foreheads to the floor in obeisance until he settled himself on the dais. He moved with a sure, unhurried grace, and his presence filled the room with power, as if he were larger than the dimensions of his flesh. The lord settled himself on the dais and took a moment to survey the recruits. His eyes settled on Ken'ishi and held for a moment. Under the great man's gaze, his ears felt like burning coals astride his head. The yearning to be found worthy formed an impassable gobbet in his throat, and breathing became difficult.

Looking at the warlord directly would be rude, so Ken'ishi tried to size him up with surreptitious glances. He was tall, perhaps forty years old, a few lines of gray streaking his hair, but his eyes were sharp and deep. Compared to Tsunemori, the brotherly resemblance was plain, but Tsunetomo was the larger man, thicker in the chest and shoulders.

"Welcome to my domain, warriors all," Tsunetomo said. "I am pleased that my brother continues to find such strong, capable recruits." Tsunemori bowed at this. "Let us commence." His voice was as strong and sure as everything else about him, and it carried the weight of complete command. He was a man to be obeyed, without question or hesitation. Tsunetomo showed no evidence that he had been wounded during the invasion. He clapped his hands and several servants sprang out as if from nowhere, bearing trays of food for the assemblage.

The servants brought course after course of rice, soup, fish, fruit, cakes, and some rich, mellow *saké*. Tsunetomo and his officers spoke about news from Hakata, Dazaifu, Hakozaki, and from the *bakufu*. Their conversation was good-natured and pleasant. Sometimes Tsunetomo smiled at someone's anecdote, revealing for a moment a pleasant gleam in his eye, an easy good-humor. However, the gravity of the occasion held Ken'ishi and most of the recruits in silence. Besides, warriors did not typically indulge in frivolous chatter.

Throughout the evening, Ken'ishi found the hope inside him threatening to burst from its cage, and he became more inclined to let it. After tonight, he would have *a place*. He would *belong*.

The peculiar whisper of the *kami* sent gooseflesh up his arms, stood the hairs on end. Someone was watching him. The *kami* were screaming so loudly now he could not ignore them. Wariness tightened his muscles, prompted his gaze to scrutinize everyone around him, over and over. What danger could there be here?

One of the doors in the back of the audience hall was ajar. He thought someone might be there behind the rice paper, but he could not see for certain. Why should anyone be watching him? He had done nothing wrong here. He chided himself for a fool. What did he have to fear? Nevertheless, he stared at the crack, trying to discern a presence there. After one moment where he took a bite from his bowl of rice, the crack was closed.

* * *

From behind Tsunetomo's dais, Yasutoki observed the audience hall through the crack between rice-paper doors, scratching his chin, feeling the delicious beginnings of new schemes spawning in his imagination.

How strange that the *ronin* had turned up at his very doorstep!

Concealing himself from the man, at least for now, felt like the proper path. As Yasutoki was not among Tsunetomo's military advisors, it had been easy for him to beg off from the evening's ceremony, citing an excess of work. New requirements for the amount of food to be stored in castle towns, as preparation against the eventuality of another barbarian invasion, had just come down from the *bakufu*.

What tangled web of fate had brought Ken'ishi here now, to join the service of the lord who had married Kazuko? Had the *ronin* forgotten the affair? Did he hate Kazuko now at her father's betrayal? He did not look like the sort of man who bedded a different peasant's daughter in every domain. He had been beside himself with anguish when Lord Nishimuta no Jiro had announced his daughter's betrothal to Tsunetomo. Was he here seeking some secret revenge? Was it possible that he did not know or remember who she married? No, that could not be. The *ronin* must know. The motive had to be simple revenge. If that were the case, having him implicated in some illicit scheme would be too easy.

Yasutoki felt a grim, perverse fascination. My, wasn't this interesting. Oh, the ways this could be twisted. What a wonderful pawn this man would be, more than he ever would have been as a servant sworn to Green Tiger. All he had had to do was wait for the threads of their destinies to cross once again. Lord Tsunetomo would soon have a would-be assassin in his very house. An assassin who might have been intimate with the lord's wife before their marriage.

Yasutoki practically clapped his hands with glee. This was exactly what he needed to deliver him from the depths of his blackest mood. Oh, the sport!

Throughout the evening, the buzz of the *kami* was a persistent annoyance, but Ken'ishi could not identify the spur for their warnings. His thoughts lingered on who had been at the crack and what harm they might mean for him.

After the banquet was finished, the servants cleared away its remnants. Ken'ishi wondered at how many servants populated the quiet depths of the castle. A lord of this stature would keep a large household.

Anticipation rose within his belly, a nervous fluttering.

Finally Tsunetomo addressed them.

"Gentlemen, you will now come forward to sign your name to documents swearing your fealty to me. Yoshimura..."

He gestured and Captain Yoshimura came forward with a sheaf of documents and a small writing desk. He set them down before Tsunetomo.

Yoshimura addressed the men. "This document contains your oath of fealty. There is one for each of you. Once you sign this document, you are dead." He paused for a moment, letting his statement sink in to the ominous silence that fell between words. "From this day, your spirit is merely counting the days until your body must be given for your lord. Your death and the deaths of your family are bound to the house of Otomo no Tsunetomo. You swear to serve him with the deepest loyalty and the greatest courage. Your death is his to command. Those who cannot or will not take this vow, leave now." He waited for a moment to see if anyone would leave, but no man did. No man would. "Very well. Come forward."

Ken'ishi watched the first man approach Tsunetomo's dais, kneel, and press his forehead to the floor. Then the man turned to Yoshimura, who slid a document forward. The man took the brush and signed his name. Tsunetomo handed Yoshimura a *kozuka* much like the one that Ken'ishi had received from Tsunemori. Yoshimura bowed and took it with both hands. He handed the *kozuka* to the man and said, "Your blood upon the oath, Masamoto." The man took the knife, made a quick slice across his thumb, and dripped his blood onto his signature.

They bowed to each other, then Masamoto slid to the side, allowing the next man to approach. One by one, each of them approached the dais to sign his oath of fealty.

When Ken'ishi's turn came, he felt the sharp buzz of warning again, so strongly he felt the urge to duck. But how could there be danger here? He took the small blade and sliced his finger. As his blood dripped onto the paper, another surge of joy and pride washed through him.

He was *ronin* no more.

After all the new retainers had signed their oaths, Captain Tsunemori addressed them. "I am pleased. Welcome to the house of Otomo. To show my gratitude, I have gifts for all of you from our generous lord." He clapped his hands once, and the doors at the rear of the audience hall slid open. Another procession of servants marched into the room, carrying armloads of lacquered cases of various shapes and sizes, which he recognized as containing suits of armor, helmets, and proper stands upon which to rest them.

Ken'ishi could hardly contain his elation and awe when a servant placed a wooden box before him and opened it to display the armor within. Gleaming, interlocked scales of black-lacquered steel. The thick, silken cords of brilliant scarlet, highlighted in beautiful yellow accents. Showing the pride he felt would not be seemly, so he kept his excitement in check. He could hardly resist the urge to run his fingers over the armor's contours and laces.

Tears stung his eyes and the lump in his throat thickened. Only one moment in his life had been happier—the night he had lain beside Kazuko. This was a night of too much emotion, so much that he felt like an overfull cup brimming with tears.

Then the servants returned carrying long, black-lacquered boxes that Ken'ishi recognized as sword cases. A servant placed one in Ken'ishi's hands and bowed deeply. Ken'ishi took it and placed it reverently before him, then untied the clasps. Inside, wrapped in fine, black silk, lay a pair of swords, the long and the short, the *katana* and the *wakizashi*. His head felt light, and the swords swam in his vision as if in a dream.

No.

Silver Crane's voice echoed through his mind with that single, resounding sentiment.

He shook away the intrusion.

Judging by the hilt-wrappings, he surmised that the swords were newly made. The modern *katana*-style blade possessed less curvature than the antique *tachi*-style of Silver Crane, with a meatier spine. Unlike the naked ray skin of Silver Crane's grip, this katana sported black silken cords crisscrossed over the ray skin. The circular guard, the *tsuba*, bore a motif of the Otomo clan *mon,* two apricot leaves, rendered in the steel with silver inlay. The scabbards were ornamented and fitted in a modern style, meant to be thrust through the *obi* rather than hanging from it.

Again, a sharp intrusion into his thoughts. *No.*

Ken'ishi considered his position.

To leave behind Silver Crane, his father's weapon, the sword that had saved his life many times, the sword that had twisted the threads of fate to return to him, would dishonor his father, his ancestors, and the sword itself. But to refuse Lord Tsunetomo's gift would be an insult.

For many long moments he thought about what to do, but he could not come to a satisfactory conclusion. Finally, he said, "Honorable Lord, may I entreat to ask you a humble question?"

The mutter of quiet conversation in the room ceased.

Lord Tsunetomo leaned forward. "Eh? Of course, Ken'ishi. What is your question?"

"Great and honorable Lord, words cannot express the joy I feel at the generosity of your gifts. I am but a humble warrior, from humble beginnings. The honor you have bestowed upon me I can only repay with my life, so my life is yours to do with as you will. But...you have given me swords to wear in your service. Since I reached manhood, I have worn only my father's sword. How can I wear your sword without dishonoring my father's memory? How can I wear his sword without dishonoring you? I beg of you, please tell me what to do. I do not have the knowledge of such things." He pressed his forehead to the floor.

Yoshimura bristled. "How insulting! That you would even consider spurning such a gift—!"

Tsunetomo raised his hand, cutting Yoshimura off. "Filial piety is one of the greatest of all virtues. This young man worships his father's memory, as well he should. Ken'ishi, you would serve me just as well with the weapon you have made your own. I know as well as anyone the comfort of a familiar hilt. This is my answer. You will wear your father's sword, and the wakizashi of the house of Otomo."

An acceptable compromise. Silver Crane's voice was a bell in the caverns of Ken'ishi's thoughts.

Another flush of joy and fresh tears burst from Ken'ishi's eyes as he pressed his forehead to the floor once again. "Lord, you have my never-ending thanks, and my undying loyalty."

"You honor us both, Ken'ishi," Tsunetomo said. "I am grateful to have such an earnest and forthright retainer. My younger brother has chosen well!" He nodded to Tsunemori. "And now, let us conclude. The time grows late, sunrise comes early, and training begins at the Hour of the Rabbit."

Lying in his bunk in the barrack, staring into the rafters, Ken'ishi hardly needed the blanket to warm him, such was the fervor of his excitement. Here he was, having accomplished the most fervent desire of his life.

Only one other desire rivaled even remotely the yearning for this one, and he would likely never see Kazuko again. But what would he do if he did? She was married to some samurai lord now—the pain of that night had stolen the memory of his name—probably having borne the lord an heir or two by now. But nothing would ever steal the memories of their night together. The fervor, the softness, the beauty, the ecstasy, the tears of parting, and the threat that if they were caught it would have meant certain death for him, perhaps even for her.

What if, during his service to his new master, he encountered her? The samurai lords of northern Kyushu numbered perhaps a score. Would she recognize him? He did not doubt that he could spot her instantly in a crowd of a thousand women. Her beauty would outshine the sun.

No matter what happened, he could show no recognition, or both of their lives would be in danger. If her new husband knew that Kazuko had not been a virgin when she was wed, he might well spurn her, send her back to her father, and set fire to a new feud among often fractious men. Not since the night she came to him had he doubted that she loved him. But theirs was a dangerous love, one that must never be. That ferry had already crossed the River of Tears and would not return.

And why was Kazuko still the first woman in his thoughts? He had spent three years with Kiosé. She had earned more of his loyalty than Kazuko had. Kiosé had *loved* him, with a depth and breadth he could never return. She had known this, yet she had done it anyway. She had warmed his bed, cleaned his house, and filled his belly. And she had died trying to protect their son from barbarian swords.

In the midst of the invasion, when Ken'ishi had returned to Aoka village and found the terrible corpses of Kiosé and Little Frog, the stallion Thunder had taken a single sniff of Little Frog and known him to be of Ken'ishi's blood.

Ken'ishi had failed poor Little Frog in innumerable ways. Every day that Ken'ishi had not claimed the boy as a son condemned Little Frog to another day as one of the Unclean, the bastard child of a common whore. It did not matter that Ken'ishi could not have known the boy was his. He *should have* known.

For a time, Ken'ishi's thoughts spun in such circles until he finally reached a moment where he chided himself. Too long on these paths led only to black despair, and tonight was a night of celebration. Kiosé was gone. Little Frog was gone. The chances that Ken'ishi would encounter Kazuko again were so small that it hardly warranted further thought.

As he tightened his thick blanket around him, drifting toward sleep, he thought he heard the distant ring of Silver Crane's voice, but he could not be certain if it was only a dream.

Destiny.

Into a cold night
I spoke aloud...but the
　voice was
No voice I knew
　　　　—*Otsuji*

K azuko awoke with a start, aroused by a pe-culiar noise: a rumbling, part thunder, part growl. The quiescent coals in the brazier glowed red-orange, casting shadows deep into the rafters.

She had wrapped herself in a blanket and sat at Hatsumi's side as night descended, listening to the older woman fret and whimper and cry out in fitful sleep. Sweat glistened on Hatsumi's face. Kazuko's legs, back, and neck ached from sitting. Beyond the ring of brazier glow, the darkness coupled with the winter chill, driving Kazuko to clutch her quilted blanket tighter around her.

What had she heard? It was too late in the year for thunder. The sound had come from inside the room, but its timbre could not have come from Hatsumi. Could it? Its absence nevertheless left a reverberation on her soul.

"Is someone there?" she whispered.

A cricket's chirp broke the deafening silence.

Kazuko had declined her husband's bed tonight, and he had been somewhat displeased. It was the first time she had ever refused him. That she was staying with Hatsumi rankled him even more. He had long desired to send Hatsumi away. Her erratic behavior had become too troublesome, bordering on dangerous. Nevertheless, Kazuko had begged him to allow Hatsumi to stay and he had acceded, on the condition that if there were any more outbursts or mistreatment of the servants, Kazuko would be the one to send Hatsumi away.

She had finally received word that her husband's physician had been injured by a runaway cart and could not come. He sent his regrets, saying that he would try to come tomorrow. But if he were injured, how could he come tomorrow?

There was no one tonight who could ease Hatsumi's suffering.

Hatsumi groaned and drew a deep, shuddering breath.

And then a great, wet, resounding belch erupted from her mouth, lasting for several heartbeats, followed by a groan of relief.

Kazuko flinched away in surprise, almost with a sense of amusement at its absurd vulgarity. Until the miasma of putrid decay washed over her.

One summer, when she was a child, she had been passing through a village on the way to visit her father's younger brother, lord of another portion of the Nishimuta clan's domain. Two peasant men were attempting to load the rotten carcass of a pig into a cart. The men's faces were wrapped in cloth, their eyes watery and desperate. The errant pig had ventured into a bog, gotten stuck, and drowned in the summer heat. The bloated purple carcass was such an unwieldy blob it was as if most of its bones had liquefied. Just as the palanquin bearing her and her father was passing, the men lost control of the carcass, and it spilled from the back of the cart and burst open on the ground. The expulsion of rancid putrescence sent the men flailing away, retching and wailing. The palanquin bearers lurched into a quicker pace. The bodyguards stopped and admonished the men for doing such work when a lord was passing by. Kazuko simply cried. She cried for the enormity of the stench her mind had difficulty encompassing. She cried for the misfortune of the peasant men. She cried for the pig that had died in such a terrible fashion.

And she cried now for Hatsumi, whose body had just emitted the closest thing to that stench Kazuko had encountered since that day.

The stench hung in the air like a living thing. She jumped up and hurried to the window, clutching her blanket to her face. Her watering eyes fractured her vision, catching the coals' light and darkness together. She reached the shutter and flung it open, leaning out as the chill air rushed inside, washing over her like a fresh, sweet waterfall.

How could a human being emit such foulness? Was Hatsumi dead?

But Hatsumi stirred again, and something in her breathing and movement suggested the return of comfort as if some threshold of suffering had been crossed and survived.

Kazuko steeled herself and returned to Hatsumi's side, covering her nose and mouth with one hand and waving frantically with her other sleeve to disperse the foul air.

Then, Kazuko saw the expression on Hatsumi's face.

Hatsumi's eyes were closed in sleep, but she was smiling. It was not a smile of pleasure, or happiness, or contentment.

It was a smile of savage glee, blackened teeth clenched, lips parted and spread wide into her cheeks.

And still she did not awaken.

Something worked inside her face, behind her face, as if sleep allowed the opportunity for this force to reveal itself, to revel in newfound freedom.

The fear that washed through Kazuko was akin to the first time she had looked into the face of the *oni* bandit, Hakamadare. He and his gang had attacked her entourage, slaughtered all her servants and bodyguards, and snatched Hatsumi from the overturned palanquin and raped her. The same would have happened to Kazuko, had not a *ronin* named Ken'ishi wandered into her life, saved her, and changed her forever.

She thought about awakening Hatsumi, but what person would look out from her eyes? The Hatsumi she had known her whole life? The Hatsumi she loved like an older sister? Or this...creature?

Kazuko edged away, wary, her heart pounding. Then she hurried to the cabinet where she kept a dagger, a gift from her father. She removed the dagger and hid it in her voluminous sleeve.

The image of that awful smile, seared into her memory, kept her from sleep until dawn.

"In the words of the ancients, one should make his decisions within the space of seven breaths. Lord Takanobu said, 'If discrimination is  long, it will spoil.' Lord Naoshige said, 'When matters are done leisurely, seven out of ten will turn out badly. A warrior is a person who does things quickly.'"

—*Hagakure, Book of the Samurai*

Yasutoki settled himself before Lord Tsunetomo, distastefully close to Tsunemori, draping his voluminous sleeves over his thighs. He already knew the nature of this meeting.

Lord Tsunetomo sat straight and strong as a bridge pillar unmoved by the passing of the river. It was a trait that made him a powerful leader of men. Tsunemori possessed a similar mien, but with a more mercurial nature, a bit more prone to fly into action on waves of emotion rather than stepping back to consider all possible facets of a situation. This made him easier to manipulate, but also unpredictable.

Tsunemori said, "What is the news of our cousin and his prisoners?"

Otomo no Yoriyasu kept rich holdings and rice farms to the west. Younger cousin to Tsunetomo and Tsunemori, he was still feeling his way into political and martial power. His forces had captured fifty barbarians and Koryo sailors in a ship dashed against the shore by the storm.

Lord Tsunetomo said, "Yoriyasu and his fifty prisoners are traveling to Kyoto. No doubt, the barbarians will be interrogated and executed by the *bakufu*."

Yasutoki said, "And no doubt he will be richly rewarded for so great a prize."

Lord Tsunetomo said, "No doubt." He produced a scroll and offered it to Yasutoki to read. "We are to be rewarded as well. The Shogun and the Emperor send their thanks and their congratulations once again on holding back the barbarians long enough for the gods to destroy them. A hundred prize stallions and a hundred mares. Ten thousand bags of rice. Ten thousand pieces of gold. These rewards are to be distributed to those warriors who fought the most bravely, and to the families of those who died in battle."

Yasutoki raised an eyebrow. "His Excellency the Shogun is most generous."

"And so is His Highness the Emperor. Two Shinto shrines are also to be rewarded for their part in winning the gods' favor. They claim their prayers brought about the storm."

Yasutoki snorted. One of the traits he shared with Tsunetomo was a disdain for religion as anything but a tool of control.

"Read on," Tsunetomo said, with a hint of tension in his voice.

Yasutoki's gaze slid over the letter until he reached a portion describing the number of troops from northern provinces being relocated to Kyushu, with expectations of hospitality from the Western Defense Commissioner and the lords of Kyushu. This was information for which the Great Khan would pay handsomely.

Yasutoki languidly offered the letter back to Lord Tsunetomo. "So we must prepare quarters for their arrival."

Tsunemori scowled. "It chafes, Brother. So many northerners on our soil."

"I expect this news will not sit well with any of the other lords," Tsunetomo said. "There is also the expectation that new fortifications will be built, but as yet there is no further word about that. Who will pay for them? Where are the engineers going to come from? They are in scant supply in these parts."

"A wall around the perimeter of Hakata Bay would have been

most welcome during the attack," Tsunemori said.

Tsunetomo inclined his head in concession, "Of course, but the effort will be enormous. It will take peasants away from farming and from our *ashigaru* ranks, and turn warriors into laborers. And who knows when the barbarians will attack again? The barbarian emperor is tenacious. He has been trying to conquer the Sung of southern China for twenty years. They will come again. So what are we to do?"

"The fact that the Sung have been able to resist for so long proves the Mongols are not invincible. And we have the gods on our side," Tsunemori said. "If they come again, we will fight them again. And now that we know how they fight, we will not be caught off-guard."

Tsunetomo said, "I have been in touch with the Shogun's wisest strategist. The *bakufu* is developing battle tactics to counter theirs. Next time they come, it will be different."

Placidly listening to these two talk about the utter destruction of every one of Yasutoki's machinations of the last decade required more self-control than most men possessed. Nevertheless, he knew he played his part well, listening attentively, nodding appreciatively at the appropriate moments.

Tsunetomo turned to him. "You will, of course, oversee the distribution of the rice and see to the preparations of the arrival of the northern troops."

"They will not travel in winter," Yasutoki said, "which is just as well. We will have time to prepare quarters and find laborers."

"In the meantime, little brother," Lord Tsunetomo said, "Write a list of names of warriors who distinguished themselves, living and dead."

Tsunemori bowed. "I have already prepared a partial list." He offered a folded paper. "The other officers will submit their recommendations to me by tomorrow."

Lord Tsunetomo took the paper and perused it. "This one, Ken'ishi. You give him the highest distinction. This is the man who saved Ishitaka's life, yes? Does he have other exploits?"

Tsunemori leaned forward. "He saved not only Ishitaka's life, but also the lives of all the men in his unit, if the stories are to be believed. Some say he single-handedly charged into the teeth of an entire unit of barbarian horsemen, with only a breastplate and an antique *tachi*, and slaughtered them all, men and horses. Some say there were a dozen. Some say a hundred."

A tingle passed through Yasutoki so profound that he thought it must be visible to the other men. There could be little doubt that Silver Crane was back in Ken'ishi's possession. But he had to be sure. If it were so, what a stroke of fortune. Furthermore, it meant that he had vastly underestimated Ken'ishi, because it meant the former *ronin* had been the masked man who broke into his house near Hakata, somehow found the sword's hiding place, and stole the sword back. And using the threat of war with the White Lotus Gang as a diversion had been a stroke of genius. And Ken'ishi also knew that Green Tiger was somehow connected to the Otomo clan. Yasutoki's house in Hakata bore the markings of the Otomo clan, and if Ken'ishi asked questions of the right people, he would know precisely who owned the house in which Silver Crane had been stashed.

Oh, but the game had just grown considerably more dangerous.

Lord Tsunetomo raised his eyebrows. "That is the first I have heard of this tale. I presume this is the ancestral blade he mentioned during the fealty ceremony."

"Without question, Brother. Having seen the way he defeated three opponents during the sparring trials, I believe the stories are no exaggeration."

"What do you know of his background?"

"Only that he was a *ronin*, said to be from the mountains of northern Honshu. He has never mentioned a family name. Ishitaka speaks well of his skill with a bow. However, he needs training on horseback. His knowledge of military strategy and tactics is unknown."

"Watch him closely, little brother. I want to see how he develops. If he is as formidable as they say, we are fortunate to have him. If he proves himself not just a capable warrior, but a leader as well, we shall see that he receives military instruction under Yamazaki-sensei."

Oh, yes, Yasutoki thought, *watch him closely indeed.*

I am sad this morning.
The fog was so dense,
I could not see your
    shadow
As you passed my shoji.
    —*The Love Poems of*
        Marichiko

"If you will forgive me for saying so, my lady," said Lady Yukino, "you look frightfully weary."

Kazuko smiled faintly at her elder sister-in-law. "I can hardly take offense. I must look such a mess. I feared to look into the mirror this morning."

Here in the second tower, which housed Tsunemori and his family, the rooms bore the same cold walls of white plaster as the other tower, but were smaller and less grand than in the main keep, and a hominess here bespoke a long-settled family. The family shrine held funeral plaques for Lady Yukino's ancestors and offerings for the house *kami* of a rice ball and a cup of *saké*. Servants came with a tray of tea and rice cakes.

"It would be rude of me to ask why...." Nevertheless, Lady Yukino seemed to hope for an explanation as she slid the Go board between them, the precision of its two perpendicular sets of nineteen lines mirroring the precision with which she arranged it, and then smoothed her beautifully embroidered robes. As always, Tsunemori's wife's hair was immaculately brushed and styled, her face powdered to conceal the lines of age encroaching on her mouth and eyes. Her oval-shaped eyebrows were drawn high on her forehead, as was the fashion for noble ladies. Kazuko hoped that if she lived another twenty years to be Yukino's age, she would be as graceful.

Gnawed by grief and fear, Kazuko tried not to think about the horrors of sitting at Hatsumi's side the night before. "My handmaiden, Hatsumi, fell ill, and I took care of her."

Yukino's brow crinkled. "You must love her very much."

"She has been like my sister since I was a child...."

Silence hung between them, filled with grasping for meaning in words best left unspoken. Directness was vulgar and rude. Together, they opened the gilded drawers on the lacquered Go board and revealed the stones, black and white.

Kazuko and Yukino had been meeting regularly over tea and a game or two of Go since Kazuko had taken up residence here. In those early days, when pining for Ken'ishi had been an icy spike through Kazuko's heart, she had taken great comfort in Yukino's quiet, womanly wisdom. Nevertheless, she had kept Ken'ishi a secret. Other noblewomen—especially those so much older—might have been jealous of Kazuko's superior position as the wife of the lord, but Kazuko had never seen evidence of it, despite Hatsumi's whispers to beware of the "scorpion in the other tower."

Lady Yukino must have been stunningly lovely in her youth. Now she had assumed a handsome, well-groomed beauty that her husband and son doted upon. "She falls ill quite often these days." Her face and voice were neutral as she spoke.

"It is true. I fear for her. Last night was the worst I have seen. This morning she seems quite recovered, but..."

"You fear the sickness, whatever plagues her, will return again?"

Kazuko nodded.

"And perhaps that disease will spread to others?" Yukino placed her first stone, black, near the center of the board of vertical and horizontal intersecting lines, nineteen in each direction, the battlefield upon which each of them would try to claim the most territory while preventing the other from doing the same.

Kazuko shook her head. "I did fear that, in the early bouts, but...it has not spread to me or the other servants. I called for my husband's physician yesterday, but he is injured and could not come."

"A stroke of ill fortune. He is the best healer in the province.

Perhaps she has been infected by evil *kami*. A rite of purification, perhaps?"

Kazuko considered this, remembering the purification a priest had performed on Hatsumi, Kazuko, and Ken'ishi after the attack of the *oni*. "It could not hurt," she mused, placing her first stone.

Lady Yukino gestured a nearby handmaiden to pour the tea. Kazuko took the cup when it was offered, but the memory of what she had experienced last night at Hatsumi's side turned her belly into a cold swamp.

Before she realized what was happening, she blurted, "Tsunetomo thinks I should send her away."

Lady Yukino's hand hovered above the board with its stone. "A difficult decision." She slowly placed the stone with her index and middle fingers.

"It is difficult to—" Kazuko choked off a sob and the rest of what almost came out. It was difficult to watch a loved one go mad.

Lady Yukino straightened herself. "Have you ever heard the story of the Princess of the Full Moon?"

Kazuko shook her head. She had read pillow books and the tales of the famous nobleman Genji, with his adventures and liaisons, but she had not heard the story of the Princess of the Full Moon.

"In centuries past, in Kyoto, there was a captain of the Imperial Guard. The Imperial Court then, as now, was a glowing brazier of schemes, intrigue, and romantic liaisons. Lovers drifted between ministers, nobles, and courtesans on waves of poetry, the most popular means of wooing the object of one's affection.

"The captain was handsome and honorable, and a number of the court ladies were quite enamored of him. But he was in love with a mysterious noble lady. This noble lady was known to leave the Imperial Palace on the nights of the full moon, concealed in her palanquin, and visit the Heian Jingu shrine. On such nights, the captain would accompany her as her chief *yojimbo*. He never saw her face, as she never left her palanquin. But through the slats in her blinds she would view the majesty of the full moon and grow despondent, which the captain knew from hearing her quiet weeping. His heart went out to her. Every night he pleaded with her to tell him why she was so sad. Every night, she refused.

"One night, he heard her speaking a poem about the full moon, but it was clearly a poem from a lover. With his heart full in his chest, he wrote his own poem to her on a fan, decrying the cruelty of the lover who had deserted her, and passed it within the palanquin. She took the poem, and before long he heard her say, 'Captain, you are the kindest man I have ever encountered.'

"He responded, 'And you are my Princess of the Full Moon.'"

Kazuko's heart stirred, and wondered if Ken'ishi, rough, uncultured, uneducated as he was, could woo with such eloquence as the nobles of old.

"And then she called her bearers to return her to the Imperial Palace.

"Meanwhile, over several months, a series of strange apparitions had turned the Imperial Palace almost upside down with fright, even in the midst of what should have been a joyous time. You see, one of the Emperor's concubines, the daughter of the Minister of the Right, was with child, and everyone hoped that she would bear his first heir. But little by little, over several months, strange moanings and cries began to fill the palace halls in the dead of night, voices so unearthly and terrifying that no one had the courage to seek the source. They spent their nights huddled in their chambers, praying that the evil would not fall upon them. Servants and court ladies told stories of seeing a shadowy, slumped figure with long, black hair. Whispers spread that the palace had been cursed to be haunted by a *yurei*. *Onmyouji* were summoned, but even the most skilled augurers, exorcists, and masters of yin-yang sorcery could not assuage the fear that permeated the palace. Some even feared for the welfare of the baby soon to be born."

The strange sounds in the tower at night, coupled with Hatsumi's increasingly erratic and incomprehensible behavior, echoed with Lady Yukino's words.

"The new mother's time came nigh on the night of a full moon. She secluded herself in the specially appointed house away from the palace grounds so that the birth blood would not pollute the palace any further than the curse had already done.

"The captain, as chief of the palace guard, accompanied her entourage to the place of birth, and stood guard outside the house with several of his best men. They patrolled the fence and the surrounding streets.

"The lady's labor commenced at sunset and continued for several hours, her cries of pain and exertion emanating from within the birthing house until finally, after midnight, the cries of the baby joined those of the mother. Immediately one of the ladies-in-waiting announced that the child was a boy. The Emperor had an heir!

"But then, in the darkest hours of the night, frightful moans and distant shrieks of agony, echoing from several directions, put the captain and his men on high alert. The sounds grew nearer.

"With the full moon high above, bathing the garden in milky moonglow, a figure with long black hair that seemed to move like living shadow appeared in the garden, moving toward the house where the newborn baby lay. One of the guards attempted to apprehend the figure, but it slew him in the most unspeakable way. The noise of the guard's demise drew the captain thither, and then he heard a voice call out from the figure, quiet and sad and yearning, 'Your Majesty, are you there, my love? I hear our child crying.'

"It was a voice the captain knew well, the voice of his Princess of the Full Moon.

"But when he saw her now, her countenance was frightfully changed. She had become an *oni*, and even in her corrupted beauty, he recognized her as the daughter of the Minister of the Left, whom the emperor had also taken as a lover at the urging of her father. The Minister of the Left had been hungry to secure his place in the Imperial Line by providing the Emperor an heir and was furious when his daughter would not become the Empress Dowager. Palace gossip said that His Majesty had lost interest in her, in favor of the daughter of the Minister of the Right. But she had loved His Majesty deeply and yearned to give him an heir. The chance to bear his child had been denied her by the vicissitudes of love. For months she had prowled the halls of the palace, little by little losing herself to jealousy and grief, until her emotions consumed her, and nothing was left but a demon."

Kazuko's eyes teared. Had she not encountered a living, breathing *oni* herself, she might have dismissed this as just a story. How far had she herself gone down this road with so much time spent yearning for Ken'ishi? Was it too late for her? Was it too late for Hatsumi?

Lady Yukino's gaze penetrated Kazuko. "The captain tried to stop her, but she flung him aside and charged toward the house. She ripped open the doors, ran inside, and seized the newborn heir from his mother's arms. She had her hand around its tender throat when the captain caught up with her. He took her head in one swift stroke.

"In her hand he found a fan, upon which was written a poem:

The full moon of spring rises high,

The portal to my heart,

To the land where dew glistens

Upon the exquisite lily

"This poem to which she had clung for so long was not the poem the captain had written to her. Alas, his poem, doubtless filled with his own eloquent words of love, has been lost to the dust of time.

"The captain was lauded as a great hero by the entire Imperial Court and His Majesty himself, and he was showered with rewards. But soon afterward, he took his monastic vows and retired from public life."

The familiarity in this tale pulled tight around Kazuko's thoughts, threatening to choke her, making her squirm. She took several deep breaths, realizing her heart was beating fast. Her hands were clenched in her lap.

Lady Yukino placidly placed another stone on the board. "It is your move."

"When Lord Katsushige was young, he was instructed by his father, Lord Naoshige, 'For practice in cutting, execute some men who have been condemned to death.' Thus, in the place that is now within the western gate, ten men were lined up, and Katsushige continued to decapitate one after another until he had executed nine of them. When he came to the tenth, he saw that the man was young and healthy and said, 'I'm tired of cutting now. I'll spare this man's life.' And the man's life was saved."

—*Hagakure, Book of the Samurai*

The morning dawned like every morning of the last several days, chill and gray, frost thick on the well heads, on the tufts of grass ambitious enough to grow here, on the pebbles and the hard-packed earth of the yards, on the ceramic tiles of the roofs, becoming an extra sheen of glittering diamonds on the whitewashed walls.

Ken'ishi had found that life in the barrack was simple. A *futon* and a blanket were preferable to the cold ground. Braziers of coals heated the barrack, but here on the castle hill, the cold wind whipped with a fervor like the highest mountain slopes. His old master, Kaa, would have admonished him for growing soft, over-accustomed to the comforts of human civilization.

Other similar barracks were situated around the perimeter of the walls, housing more than two hundred men in total. Some were veterans, skilled warriors; others were new recruits, varying from long-time *ronin* to former peasants.

Being thrown in with so many peasants would have once bothered Ken'ishi, so proud had he been of his samurai heritage, but it was a heritage about which he knew nothing. Having no real knowledge of his pedigree, it seemed unfair to look down on anyone. No doubt his father had been a true warrior—Kaa had told him as much—but he had given up the life of a warrior to work a plot of land. What life would Ken'ishi's father have wanted for him? What name would he have been given? He did not even know what his baby name had been. Throughout his time with Kaa, he had just been called Boy. When Kaa had sent him out into the world, Ken'ishi had chosen his own name, Sword meets Stone.

Each morning, under the supervision of Sergeant Hiromasa, they formed ranks in the practice yard and drilled with spears, practiced how to march, how to move in formation, learned the meaning of orders given by drum and conch and war fan. They were being trained for the castle garrison, which demanded proficiency with spear and bow, sword and *naginata*. Captain Yoshimura had declared that if they showed promise, they might be dispersed into units suited to their individual strengths.

Ken'ishi's hands grew ever more familiar with the feel of the wooden spear haft, of its weight, reach, and balance. Of course, it was infinitely inferior to Silver Crane, but there were some purposes and circumstances for which a spear might be a superior weapon. Insight into its utility gave him a strong appreciation for it.

Sergeant Hiromasa told him, "You gain skill quickly."

Ken'ishi bowed. "Thank you, Sergeant."

"Have you ever used a spear before?"

"No, Sergeant."

Hiromasa gave him a look of thoughtful appraisal. "I think tomorrow I will make you unit leader."

Elation washed through him. "Thank you, Sergeant!" He bowed

again. "My duty is to serve with all my ability."

Hiromasa cracked a faint smile, then moved on.

But Ken'ishi was not made a unit leader the following day, and he wondered if he had failed somehow to make Hiromasa change his mind. He redoubled his efforts and trained harder.

And then Hiromasa would approach Ken'ishi and say again, "I think tomorrow I will make you unit leader." But still no promotion came.

Day after day, the constant movement helped keep the cold at bay, so that when breakfast came in the form of a fresh egg cracked upon hot rice, the meal became among the most appreciated he had experienced since his days as a starving *ronin*.

For Ken'ishi, the drills were easy, if taxing. Working with a spear required a different style of movement and poise, but still required balance and control of one's body. Perhaps he should not have been astonished at how many of the new retainers lacked the kind of control Kaa had drilled into him since he was five years old. Footwork, balance, and timing were the foundations of martial practice of any discipline, and many of the men lacked these skills in such profundity he wondered how they had managed to survive this long without suffering a tragic accident walking out of their houses. On the other hand, many of them were warriors trained and bred, hard-muscled, flint-eyed, and steady. They knew what it was to kill and to face one's own death.

Bred in a samurai family, Michizane exhibited this sort of martial training. He moved with a steadfast stoicism Ken'ishi admired. They sometimes sat together at meals. Michizane once complimented Ken'ishi's footwork and balance. It was clear, he said, that Ken'ishi had been taught well, and that his skills formed the basis of real strength, no matter what weapon or fighting style he chose. Ken'ishi thanked him, upon which Michizane began to ask about his upbringing and training. Ken'ishi demurred. He knew almost nothing of his heritage, and tales of his upbringing were not something most men would believe.

During one such conversation, he detected a wistful longing when Michizane asked about Ken'ishi's family, prompting him to return the question.

"Ah, my family," he answered with dreamy delight in his eyes.

"My wife Satsuki is as beautiful as wisteria in spring, and kindness drips from her like the petals of those blossoms."

Ken'ishi smiled. "Now who is the poetic soul?"

Michizane said, "And my daughter, Omitsu, is as fragile as a hatchling, but so adventurous, so inquisitive. Everything she sees brings a question." His face glowed with pride. "Of course, I wish I had a son as well, but perhaps I'll get to see Satsuki again and we can work on that."

Ken'ishi felt a bit of surprise that Michizane's family could not be with him. "Where are they?"

"Yame village. About four days' walk from here. My stipend is modest, for now. Until I can rise in rank, they must live with my parents in Yame, which is fortunate. I cannot put them in the kind of house they deserve."

"So you are the eldest son."

"Of five brothers. And my father does not have wealth to divide among us. But our home is a happy one. Little Omitsu's smile is like the sun." A tear formed at the corner of his eye. "And Satsuki... Satsuki..."

Kiosé and Little Frog leaped into Ken'ishi's mind. "You miss them very much."

Michizane nodded. "I have not been home since before the invasion. My father told me to seek greater fortunes than can be found in Yame village. I've been sending all of my pay home...."

In contrast to Michizane, Ushihara was a clumsy bull. Stubborn and dim-witted, he had little but vague intuition where grace and poise should have been, but he was also strong and earnest, with a powerful desire to walk the path of a true warrior.

Michizane snorted that would it be a long journey, and Ushihara would likely die in the attempt. Ushihara spat and called him an over-groomed fop.

One day, Captain Yoshimura came at the noon meal and pulled Ushihara, along with Takuya, another man of peasant origin, out of the barracks. Lord Tsunetomo's chamberlain had requested them for a specific duty within the castle keep. Ushihara grumbled at first, but shut his mouth after a stern look from Captain Yoshimura.

After the midday meal, the recruits were given a short time to rest. Ken'ishi returned to the yard to practice sword drills. Silver Crane moved like fluid metal in his hands, cutting the air with hungry slashes of sound.

Drills and practice resumed in the afternoon. A couple of hours later, Takuya returned, and some time after that, Ushihara as well.

Ushihara had never been particularly gregarious or light-hearted, but for the rest of the afternoon his frequent glances toward Ken'ishi were fraught with a kind of dark intent and calculation. As the day went on, whispers of the *kami* grew louder in Ken'ishi's awareness.

That night, after the soldiers' muscles were wrung out, their hands and feet sporting fresh rounds of blisters, and their bellies full of rice, smoked fish, and pickled plums, the men huddled around the braziers in the barracks. Faces were painted yellow-orange in the pools of glow. Some groups boasted and laughed. Others sang songs. Ken'ishi's group—Ushihara, Michizane, and seven others—hunched quietly.

Ken'ishi opened his trunk and pulled out his bamboo flute, given to him when he was just a boy by the first human being he could remember meeting, an itinerant monk, high in the mountains of northern Honshu. Raising it to his lips, he began to play. The notes flowed like mournful birdsong, wavered and trilled and echoed, like a nightingale calling for its mate. The men fell silent. The group around him grew.

Ushihara sat near him with hooded eyes, scowling. "Damn you, quit that infernal racket. It makes my heart hurt."

Ken'ishi had played this song for the girl he fell in love with on a long-ago forest road. The unquenchable yearning for her surged within him, like the scar in his thigh that ached when the weather was about to change, familiar as an old shoe, part of him. He closed his eyes and let it take him, pouring it into the song.

The flute was snatched out of his hands.

He opened his eyes.

Ushihara snapped the flute in two against his knee. "I said stop!"

The shock boiled up in Ken'ishi like lava from a fire mountain, turning to rage as it spilled over the top. He launched himself at Ushihara.

Ushihara met him with a fist against his teeth and fingers gouging for his eyes.

Ken'ishi bowled him over, rage stealing his reason, blood in his mouth. They rolled on the floor, a straining, shouting, punching knot.

Cries erupted around them. Hands reached for them, trying to pry them apart. Ken'ishi reared back a fist meant to slam Ushihara's head into the floor, but someone caught it and used it to peel him loose.

Moments later, Sergeant Hiromasa appeared, roaring, along with armed guards of the night's watch. Ken'ishi caught a glimpse of a truncheon moments before it slammed into his head. And then blackness.

Ken'ishi awoke surrounded by night, his outstretched arms aching from being bound, face-first, by coarse ropes to a cross. His head pounded from the truncheon blow. The winter wind sliced through clothing and stole all warmth from him. He gathered his feet under him to stand and relieve the tension on his shoulders, but the ground was too close for him to stand up, too far for him to kneel. He could only hang there from his arms, straining his shoulders.

The wood was rough and hard and merciless against his face. His breath misted from his mouth and formed a frost on the wood of the cross. The yard was silent, except for the quiet footsteps of the watch passing somewhere behind him.

His only thought was: How strange to be in a position of torture again so soon.

Green Tiger's torturer had subjected him to such eternities of agony that, in the march of the real world's time, he had no memory or imagination of how long it had lasted. Only an infinitude of hells.

He was not alone. On a nearby cross hung a dark shape. From the ragged shock of hair, Ken'ishi recognized Ushihara.

The crescent moon slid across heaven with its entourage of silken stars, silent and aloof, painting two sullen shadows onto the castle wall.

Eventually the ropes and strain and cold numbed his arms, and he hung in a half-daze, dipping in an out of a black stupor and visions of snarling *oni* coming to devour him. And with the practice he had learned in Green Tiger's torturous hell, he let himself descend into the stupor, where things were quiet and dark and the pain only a distant beast clawing at the door.

Then a sound roused him.

Weeping.

Ken'ishi cranked his knotted neck to look at Ushihara, whose cheeks were wet with tears, lips glistening with snot and spittle.

After a time, Ushihara noticed Ken'ishi's eyes on him. He sniffed and tried to compose himself, but his eyes still glowed with terror. "They're gonna kill us!"

"No," Ken'ishi said, "we're to be flogged."

"It hurts!"

"Shut up, coward." It was only pain.

Ushihara wept. "It hurts, it hurts...."

Ken'ishi sighed and shook his head. "You cry like a peasant. You are no better than a gravedigger."

At the last word, Ushihara flinched and began to struggle at his bonds, but it was no good.

From across the yard, a guard's voice called out, "Shut up, you shit heads!"

Ushihara settled back against his ropes.

The shadows crept along the wall and exhaustion crept through Ken'ishi's body, drawing fingers of blackness through his mind.

Then he heard Ushihara's ragged whisper. "He made me!"

Several moments passed before Ken'ishi absorbed those words. "Who made you?"

"He said he'll do to me a hundred times worse than a simple flogging if I tell!"

"Then why tell me anything at all?"

Long moments passed. Ushihara sniffled. "I don't know." Something in his voice—remorse?—suggested Ushihara spoke the truth.

Several times, Ken'ishi pressed for a name, and every time he met with fearful refusal.

The night dug deeper into itself, and Ushihara wept again.

For some reason he could not explain, Ken'ishi pitied the lout.

Allowing himself to drift in the currents of pain and cold, his consciousness dimmed until the shadows on the wall diffused into the gray of early dawn. Before long, the morning conch sounded, roused him fully, and brought the men out of the barracks.

All the recruits of Barrack Six shuffled out onto the practice yard, yawning and rubbing their eyes.

Sergeant Hiromasa's voice roared, "*Attention!*"

The men leaped into line and stood straight, motionless, and silent.

Two guards approached the crosses where Ken'ishi and Ushihara hung.

Sergeant Hiromasa's voice called out, "Are they alive?"

One of guards checked them. "Yes."

"Then perhaps there's hope for them," Hiromasa said. He raised his voice toward the men standing at attention, speaking with gruff emphasis on each word. "I will explain this to you only once. *Brawling is forbidden!* Your flesh, your bone, your blood, your lives belong to your lord, and only to your lord! You die when he tells you to die! You fight when he tells you to fight! If you fight with another of his retainers, you are fighting with Lord Tsunetomo himself! If you injure or kill one of his retainers, you are doing harm to your lord! You may as well have cut off one of his fingers! He has given you a sword, comrades, a bed, food. Serve him well and he will care for you well. Until that day he deems it your time to die." He paused, striding slowly before the line, glaring at each man in turn. In his hand, he carried a bamboo cane as thick as two fingers.

At the sight of the cane, a shiver of memory whispered through Ken'ishi. How many times in his boyhood had Kaa used a cane on him? Memory of its bite raised tingles on his buttocks and thighs.

"These two men harmed your lord!" Hiromasa shouted. "Should we show them mercy?"

Cries of *"No!"* came from the ranks.

Sergeant Hiromasa approached Ken'ishi and Ushihara. "Do you understand why you are here?"

Both croaked in affirmative.

"Now, let us get to the bottom of this. Who started it?"

"I did, Sergeant," Ken'ishi said.

Ushihara gasped and stared at him.

Ken'ishi continued, "Ushihara offended me greatly, but I should have held my temper. I attacked him. Please give me his strokes."

Hiromasa grunted with surprise. "And why would you accept his strokes? Has he not made himself your enemy?"

"We are brothers in service to Lord Tsunetomo, Sergeant."

Ushihara's mouth worked, but no sound came out.

"Very well," Hiromasa said. "But he will not be let off without punishment. When he should have been building comradeship, he rudely, blatantly offended one of his comrades. Ken'ishi will have half of Ushihara's strokes. Ten strokes for Ushihara. Thirty strokes for Ken'ishi." He squared himself behind Ushihara. "Strip him."

The two guards came forward and tore Ushihara's clothes from him, leaving him naked but for a loincloth. Ushihara clamped teeth hard onto his bottom lip.

"You will count," Hiromasa said. "If you cannot count, I will continue until you can."

Terror twisted Ushihara's face. When the first blow fell, hissing, sharp, and meaty across his back, he clenched his teeth and shouted, "One!" When the second blow fell, a whimper found its way into the word, "Two!" Like the slow beat of a drum, the cane snapped into his back, driving the count from him. He convulsed around each blow like a worm touched with burning twig. The shout of "Ten!" came out with an explosive bleat of relief.

Two flicks of the tip of Hiromasa's *wakizashi* severed Ushihara's bonds, and he spilled onto the ground, clutching his arms to his chest like nerveless stumps.

"When you can get up," Hiromasa said, "breakfast awaits."

Trembling, gasping, Ushihara rolled onto his knees. His arms shifted shades of red and blue and purple. Stripes of blood seeping from the crimson weals on his back and buttocks, Ushihara rolled onto his knees.

Hiromasa turned toward Ken'ishi. "Strip him."

The guards tore Ken'ishi's clothes from him.

He breathed deeply and steeled himself for the first blow.

It came, shocking in its depth of pain, as if a strip of flesh had been ripped from him. Perhaps the chill that reached to his bones reduced the pain. He swallowed hard and said, "One."

A silvery tendril reached into his mind, threaded between his thoughts, cooled the hot agony of the first blow.

After this, everything changes, Silver Crane said.

"Two."

In a flash of staggering despair, Ken'ishi envisioned himself being cast out in disgrace.

That is not the man's destiny.

"Three."

Even such pain as this was bearable. It would pass, as all things bad and good.

Was his destiny further humiliation? Would he have to cut his belly open to escape it?

This is not the man's humiliation. It is the threshold.

Is it just the wind
In the bamboo grass,
Or are you coming?
At the least sound
My heart skips a beat.
I try to suppress my
    torment
And get a little sleep,
But I only become more restless.

            —*The Love Poems of Marichiko*

A terrible nothingness stalked Kazuko like a lone wolf stalking a fawn. The nothingness was not a pleasant, floating void, but a vile, diabolical thing that ate at the substance of everything she was. Sometimes it took form and peeled memories from her like stale, sticky noodles, dipped them in her moon's blood, and ate them with delight.

One by one, the nothingness flayed her memories away: her childhood, her coming of age, her studies of Chinese classics, her education in the ways of noble ladies and of how to pleasure a husband, and then, the memories of her night with—

A ragged gasp dragged her upright in bed, chest heaving. Chicken skin sprang up on both arms, across her shoulders, and up her neck.

Tsunetomo snored quietly beside her, his broad chest rising and falling. He stirred at her movement, then settled himself back into slumber.

The thought of losing who she was, of having her very self stripped away piece by piece, the sensation of it happening *right now,* of being replaced by *nothingness,* unsettled her so profoundly that she rose out of bed and stood above her husband, the grayness of early dawn seeping around the shutters. Frozen by shock, she stood for a long time until she roused herself and did the only thing she knew to drive away the most unpleasant of thoughts: she donned her practice garb, took down her *naginata* from its rack on the wall, and descended the narrow staircases through the floors of the keep, heading toward the practice yard. Physical exertion would fan the flames she knew to be within her and drive back the darkness of her dreams. She was Otomo no Kazuko, a samurai lady, and no mere visitation from the Land of Dreams would steal that from her.

Two drill yards, those of Barracks Five and Six, stood between her and the practice yard where Master Higuchi schooled her in the ways of the *naginata.* The men of Barrack Five stood outside, slapping their arms against the cold, preparing for their morning exercises.

Around a bend of the central keep, she entered the domain of Barrack Six, but here there was a punishment in progress.

The warriors stood at attention as another man, who was lashed to a cross, was flogged with a bamboo cane. She could not see his face. A pool of sick dread formed in her belly. With so many new recruits, many of them from lowly backgrounds and thus not schooled in the behavior and expectations of true samurai, such punishments had become almost commonplace in recent weeks. Her husband had assured her that once a few examples were made, the recruits would shape up. She could hardly disapprove if the alternatives were casting them out or demanding their *seppuku.*

Crossing the yard now would interrupt the proceedings, so she waited off to the side, unnoticed.

The man on the cross bore each resounding blow with a quiet, unfathomable stoicism. His voice counted out the strokes, calm and quiet and steady, as if he were in a trance, as if the pain did not touch him. Angry, scarlet welts crisscrossed his muscled back, weeping blood.

The burgeoning amazement was plain on the sergeant's face.

"Twenty-seven," the man called.

Something was familiar about his voice.

His forehead pressed against the wood. From her vantage point behind and to the left of him, she could not see his face.

Then he turned his face toward her. "Twenty-eight."

Her heart burst through her ribcage and fell at her feet.

Some sound must have escaped her.

His gaze swept toward her.

Their eyes met.

The next blow fell.

Ken'ishi's mouth opened, but no sound came forth.

The sergeant administering the blows paused for a heartbeat in his terrible rhythm. But the look of amazement on his face changed to something else, something harder. He struck again.

Still, Ken'ishi did not speak.

From this distance she could read nothing in the implacable mask of his face.

Another blow fell, and his body convulsed with pain as if for the first time.

Several of the men glanced toward her. She dared not reveal she knew this man, or the potential ripples of effect could be disastrous for him. She gave not a moment's thought toward herself. Only for him. If it became apparent to anyone that she knew him, his life would be in danger.

She wiped all expression from her face and looked away. Willed the tears not to come, she stood taller, straighter, held her *naginata* with greater solemnity.

Finally, after four more blows, Ken'ishi found his voice again. But now its gasp made it barely audible. "Twenty-nine!"

His face turned away and he slammed his forehead into the wood—once, twice, thrice.

The sergeant struck again.

"Thirty!" Ken'ishi called, and then he sagged unconscious against the ropes.

With a deliberate pace that she hoped painted a picture of calm disinterest, she began to cross the yard.

At the sight of her, the sergeant called out, "Honor to Lady Otomo!"

All the men hurriedly prostrated themselves, pressing their foreheads to the earth as she passed. She hurried her step and kept

her gaze steadfastly forward, so that she would not have to see Ken'ishi's ravaged body lying in the dirt.

An eternity of stricken heartbeats later, she rounded the corner, out of sight, and then she fled. Once she reached her own practice yard, she leaned against the whitewashed plaster and slid to the ground, trembling.

"Within this body solidified by desire is concealed the absolutely desireless and upright core of the mind. This mind is not in the body of the Five Skandhas, has no color or form, and is not desire. It is unwaveringly correct, it is absolutely straight. When this mind is used  as a plumbline, anything done at all will be right-mindedness. This absolutely straight thing is the substance of right-mindedness."

—*Takuan Soho, "The Clear Sound of Jewels"*

Ken'ishi sat near the fire inside his barrack. The bowl of rice cupped in his hands had long since gone cold. Sensation had returned to his arms. Strangely, parts of him warmed, allowing him to feel the cold again. The night's chill had permeated his bones, made them feel like frozen boughs buried in his flesh.

He stared into the coals, unable to muster a coherent thought. His mind was an empty room, like the abandoned hovel he had found in the forest before arriving here, filled with nothing but dust and forgotten detritus.

Outside in the practice yard, the rest of Barrack Six drilled.

Ushihara sat across from him, his bowl of rice empty. "Aren't you going to eat yours?" he asked.

Ken'ishi blinked and offered him the bowl.

Surprise flashed on Ushihara's face. "Truly?" Then he snatched it.

Ken'ishi's back burned as if covered in hot coals, but he did not care. This kind of pain would heal.

An old wound had been opened, one that cut deeper than any wound of the flesh.

A storm of emotions hung ready to crash over him, but squelched somehow, as if he had put the storm in a kettle and covered it with a lid. A strange moment passed over him, that he must be watching some other poor fool's life unfolding before him. Such a cruel twist of fate could hardly be believed.

"When we were bound," Ken'ishi said, "you told me that someone had put you up to it."

Ushihara stopped chewing. "I-I didn't say anything like that. You must have been dreaming."

Abject terror blanched his face, but Ken'ishi lacked the strength to force the truth from Ushihara.

Around midday, the men in the yard filed inside with fresh bowls of rice and roasted fish on skewers.

Michizane sat down next to Ken'ishi, giving Ushihara a hateful look. Ushihara could not meet his gaze. "How are you feeling, Ken'ishi?"

Ken'ishi said, "I have not yet crossed to the realm of the dead."

"Everyone is talking about how you withstood the pain. Thirty-five strokes as if they were nothing at all! How did you do it?"

Ken'ishi took a deep, painful breath and let it out.

When Michizane saw no answer forthcoming, he said, "Tomorrow we begin archery practice. How are you with a bow?"

"I can shoot."

"What about on horseback?"

"I have only ridden one horse. We did not shoot."

"They say Captain Tsunemori is a master horsebowman. Perhaps he'll instruct us. I expect some of us barely know how to sit astride a horse, much less fire a bow at the same time." He glared pointedly at Ushihara.

Ushihara turned to face the wall, shoulders hunched.

Sergeant Hiromasa approached, his face hard, eyes like chips of basalt. "Ken'ishi, tomorrow you will be a unit leader. Do not disappoint me again."

Ken'ishi tried to jump to his feet, but his muscles allowed only a painful unfolding. He stood at attention. "Thank you, Sergeant. I will bring honor to Lord Tsunetomo."

"See me before morning drill for your command roster."

Hiromasa turned and left them all gaping in shock.

Ken'ishi sank back down beside Michizane, the lid on the cauldron of his emotions threatening to blow off. But this was a different sort of shock.

Michizane smiled. "It seems you have made an impression."

Ken'ishi roused himself before dawn the next morning, preparing himself for anything that might come. In spite of what should have been a great success in being promoted to unit leader, he felt as if an invisible sword hovered just over his head. Someone in the castle had put Ushihara up to goading Ken'ishi into a fight. If anyone discovered that he and Lady Kazuko had been lovers before her marriage, both their lives would be destroyed. He did not care about his, but she would be disgraced, possibly cast out.

The enormity of the web of circumstances that had brought them both to this place at this time staggered him. He could sense the innumerable gossamer threads weaving him into the fabric of the universe, twining him with Kazuko, Kiosé, plus others he had encountered, but now those threads seemed hidden from him. Silver Crane had ignored his pleas for answers. The sword kept its mysteries well hidden.

The expression on Kazuko's face was as indelible as a woodblock print in his mind. There had been surprise, but more than anything she looked like someone who had just encountered her worst enemy, the person who could destroy everything. Perhaps in that she was right, at least. The thought of causing her any harm, purposefully or inadvertently, sickened him. Surprise and fear on her face, and then... nothing. Her expression had become a blank wall, a Noh mask.

His muscles still felt like knotted, overstretched ropes, and the touch of the robe on his back chafed at the bruised, scabbed weals. At least he had blankets to warm him, even though sleep fled his every attempt to grasp it.

He stood outside the tiny room of the barrack sergeant with two other newly appointed unit leaders and Sergeant Hiromasa. Hiromasa gave each of them a list of the ten men under their command. Ken'ishi noted that Michizane and Ushihara were among his men.

As Hiromasa outlined the duties of unit leaders, Ken'ishi found himself grateful for this distraction. His body wracked by pain, his torso a sizzling cavern, he had lain on his side or his belly in his bunk all night, wide-awake. The more he yearned for sleep, the more it eluded him. His eyes felt puffy and full of grit, but none of that would deter him.

When he had found himself in command of an imperiled group of scouts during the invasion, thrust into that position by his own exploits, assuming command had felt natural. But all of that had been little more than an attempt to organize a desperate patch of order in a sea of chaos and death. Here, his mind floundered between attentiveness to everything that Hiromasa was telling him and fear that he would fail to remember any of it.

As night faded and he stood at the forefront of his ten men, leading them in exercises that warmed the sleep out of them, he spied a lone hawk sitting on the peak of the barrack roof. Its gray feathers blended with the morning sky, and its sharp eyes watched the proceedings with unusual interest.

A moment later, he recognized the hawk as the same one that had spoken to him in the rain, at a crossroads, as the typhoon descended upon the battlefields of northern Kyushu. The hawk was his old master and teacher, the *tengu,* Kaa. In its gaze was the mixture of exasperated impatience and incredulous amusement Ken'ishi knew so well. The *tengu* came and went at the strangest times. Seeing him here now made Ken'ishi stumble, disrupting the cadence of the drill.

For an hour, the hawk watched. Before long, several of the men of Barrack Six had noticed its presence and called to it. Its unwavering gaze seemed to judge them as a horse trader might examine a crop of foals. Ken'ishi did not see the hawk fly away. One moment it was simply gone, and he could only continue with the spear drills and wonder at the purpose for Kaa's presence. The *tengu* did nothing without a purpose.

The afternoon brought a cart full of bows and arrows. Straw targets were erected. Since some of his men were peasant-born, like Ushihara, he had to instruct them in the most basic knowledge of how to string a bow, how to nock an arrow, and how to shoot without hitting their comrades.

By the end of the day, a modicum of satisfaction had chewed a few holes in his black mood. His skill with the bow remained undiminished, and in the instruction, the men found a new way to respect him.

Ushihara was still sullen, but he worked as hard as anyone, even though the pain must still have been crippling. Ken'ishi suppressed his own pain, much as he had done under the efforts of Green Tiger's torturer. Ken'ishi thought Ushihara would not try to cause trouble for him again.

But who had put the man up to making trouble in the first place? How could Ken'ishi have enemies here already? Could he trust anyone? Even Michizane? Until he knew more, however, he would give Ushihara the widest berth.

"Calculating people are contemptible. The reason for this is that calculation deals with loss and gain, and the loss and gain mind never stops. Death is considered loss, and life is considered gain. Thus, death is something such a person does not care for, and he is contemptible."
—*Hagakure, Book of the Samurai*

Yasutoki regarded the two men—Ushihara and Takuya—as they deposited their buckets of charcoal in the corner of his office.

"Have you any further work for us, Lord?" Takuya said.

"That will be all," Yasutoki said. "You may return to your barrack."

The two of them bowed and turned to leave. Ushihara's expression was nervous, expectant. As Takuya slid open the door, Yasutoki said, "Oh, I do have one more thing. Ushihara, please stay a moment longer. This will not take long, I assure you."

Takuya bowed and departed.

As soon as the door slid shut, Ushihara prostrated himself before Yasutoki, trembling with fear, whispering, "Forgive me, Lord! I tried!"

"Then how is it that he has been promoted?" Yasutoki asked, his voice steady and measured.

Ushihara shook his head. "I don't know, Lord!"

"What am I to do? I am a loyal servant of Lord Tsunetomo. It is my duty to ensure the smooth workings of my lord's estates and pass forward to him any information that might be deemed...unpleasant. I thought it strange to find a man named Ushihara—an unusual name, to be sure—on the rolls of my lord's new recruits. I had heard recently of an *eta,* one of the unclean, a gravedigger by the name of Ushihara, a man wanted for the murder of a wealthy Kagoshima merchant." A man with whom Green Tiger had had numerous profitable business dealings. "This other Ushihara is not you, I am quite certain. At least, for now. Of course, if I believed you and this other Ushihara to be the same man, I would have to have you arrested immediately, after which doubtless you would be tortured to death."

Ushihara trembled, sweat trickling down his face.

Yasutoki said, "So I must ask the question. What can you do for me now?"

"I can't bear another flogging, Lord."

"Flogging is the most lenient punishment you are likely to experience ever again," Yasutoki said. What kind of fool would still answer to a name that had been so tainted with a death sentence? Was he actually stupid enough to think that he would be safe here, hundreds of *ri* from the crime?

Ushihara cringed.

Yasutoki said, "I will ask you again, what can you do for me now?"

"A dagger across his throat in the dead of night, Lord?"

Yasutoki had considered the possibility of having Ken'ishi murdered. But such a brazen assassination would raise uncomfortable questions, such as why Ushihara had met twice, privately, with the lord's chamberlain. Tsunemori already despised Yasutoki; he would be quick to point an accusing finger, and he was one of the few men with the status and rank to get away with it.

No, Yasutoki would have to find another instrument if Ken'ishi were to be killed. First he must determine if Ken'ishi possessed Silver Crane. He had already attempted to bring the man into his employ, many times, and been refused, many times, even under the coercion of torture. Would Ken'ishi be more willing to work for the lord's chamberlain than for Green Tiger? Again, too many chances for Green Tiger to be recognized. Best to continue watching Ken'ishi from a distance. As long as Silver Crane was close, available for snatching at any moment, Yasutoki could tolerate his presence. Besides, now that Ken'ishi was here, he would make a perfect lever with which to pry Kazuko into doing his will.

"For now, I want you to pay attention to his sword. Study it. In a few days, you will tell me what you know of it."

"I don't know anything about swords, Lord. What do you want me to study?"

Yasutoki let out a controlled breath between tightened lips. "Tell me of any designs on the scabbard. Tell me what the hilt looks like. Tell me what the guard looks like." Those details would tell him everything he needed to know. And then he could act from that knowledge. "Serve me well, and you will be rewarded. Betray me, and you'll wish for that other Ushihara's punishment."

Frost covers the reeds of
   the marsh.
A fine haze blows
   through them,
Crackling the long
   leaves.
My full heart throbs
   with bliss.
     —The Love Poems of
          Marichiko

A fter so many days of training, a day of rest was declared. The men were free to venture out of the castle. It was a chill, windy day, with a sky swathed in gray clouds.

Ken'ishi's back still pained him, but it was no longer a field of raw flames. Everyone else had gone to town for hot *saké* to warm their bones. Ken'ishi practiced sword drills alone, trying to focus his scattered mind, when a familiar voice called out to him.

"Always practicing, eh, Sir Ken'ishi?" Ishitaka said as he approached.

Ken'ishi sheathed Silver Crane, and they bowed to each other. Ken'ishi had not seen Ishitaka since that day in Hakozaki some weeks before, in the aftermath of the typhoon. Doubtless being the son of Captain Tsunemori entailed many duties far above the heads of lowly spearmen. Ishitaka's beaming face and infectious grin betrayed his youth. He was only sixteen, but had been trained from birth to be a warrior of the Otomo clan. Their experiences in battle against the Mongols had turned them into comrades, despite the vast difference in their respective status.

Ishitaka threw an arm around Ken'ishi's shoulders. "You are coming with me! After everything you've been through, you need to find some enjoyment."

Ken'ishi stiffened. "You heard about the—"

"The flogging? Of course. I was very sad about that. Especially when it was the other man's fault. What an uncouth bag of filth."

The thought of his friend hearing about his disgrace made Ken'ishi lower his head.

"Brace up, Ken'ishi!" Ishitaka said, guiding him into movement. "The way you withstood the flogging is more on people's tongues than the reason. And you took half his strokes! I've heard that forty strokes can kill a man. You look so glum, it's as if you've resigned yourself to another round of torture. Let us look toward the future! A future where *saké* and girls await us!"

"Girls?"

"Of course! You don't see any around here, do you? What better way to lift one's spirits than the attention of a pretty girl?"

Ishitaka's boyish zeal scratched at the black shell of Ken'ishi's mood. He smiled. "Very well."

The Roasted Acorn was the largest *saké* house in town, with a spacious common room on the ground floor, and two floors above for private meals and meetings. Tonight, the common room was alive with boisterous company, the men from the castle mixing with townsfolk and farmers. The aromas of hot *saké*, smoke from cooking fires, roasting chicken and fish, and steaming broth and steaming rice awoke fires of hunger in Ken'ishi's belly. He and Ishitaka enjoyed course after course of simple food in sumptuous quantities. Jar after jar of hot *saké* poured warm honey into their veins.

Some of the men broke into drinking songs, and one of them stood up and began to dance with comical exaggeration, contorting his face into farcical expressions. Before long, he dropped his trousers and continued the dance with the utmost earnestness, trousers around his ankles, amidst roars of laughter.

The villagers of Aoka, where Ken'ishi had lived most of the last three years, had seldom been this boisterous except at New Year. The village's fishermen had been a taciturn bunch. Ken'ishi had never had the opportunity to share the company of so many warriors, and he found himself enjoying their camaraderie and good humor.

Some of them, however, looked at him and whispered to each other. He often felt eyes upon him, but the *kami* were silent, so he was able to relax. Let them gossip. He need prove himself to no one except his lord. *The man married to—*

He slashed that thought short, sharply, and tossed back another cup of *saké,* letting the warmth assuage the cold buzz in his belly.

Ishitaka clutched Ken'ishi's arm. A new serving girl had just brought a tray of fresh jars to a nearby table. She moved with incredible grace and a delicate, fetching sway. Ishitaka stared, rapt. Her hair was long and lustrous, hanging free over her shoulders.

"Ken'ishi!" Ishitaka gasped. "By the gods and buddhas!"

She glanced at them, then turned away and hurried into the back.

"She was the most beautiful girl I have ever seen!" Ishitaka breathed.

Ken'ishi said, "She was very pretty, but so young. Hardly fourteen." But in spite of her youth, there was something older about her, a loss of innocence in her lips and eyes, the way she looked at all these men without a trace of fear, as if she knew precisely how to handle herself around them, heedless of all the ways they could hurt her. The *kami* niggled at his awareness like tadpoles.

"The perfect age! I am sixteen! A man should always be older than his wife!"

Ken'ishi laughed. "Wife? The son of a high-ranking samurai marrying a peasant girl?"

"Well, perhaps just concubine then," Ishitaka chuckled. "I must speak to her!"

"I'm sure she will return."

"I cannot wait that long! I must ask the proprietor if she's available." Ishitaka tried to stand and found himself somewhat unsteady.

Ken'ishi pulled him back down with a thump. "Calm yourself. Let us just observe."

She did indeed return with another tray of *saké* jars and came to their table.

Ishitaka needed no more *saké*; his eyes drank only her. "What's your name?" His words slurred together.

She smiled at him. "Yuri, Lord."

"What kind of 'yuri?' What are your characters?"

"I'm sorry, I don't know, Lord. I cannot read or write."

Ishitaka's brows furrowed in concentration. "Surely your parents told you why they gave you that name?"

"I..." Something passed behind her eyes, and the *kami* voices grew louder in Ken'ishi's mind. "It is a kind of flower, I think."

"Ah, yes, the lily!" Ishitaka's face bloomed with pleasure. "What a perfect name for the most beautiful girl I have ever seen."

She bowed and began to back away. "I am just a serving girl, Lord. Please excuse me."

"No, wait! Stop, you must sit and drink with us!"

"Why me, Lord?"

"Because I desire it, and it is my intention to woo you until your heart is mine forever!"

Her cheeks flushed ever so slightly. "I am sorry, Lord, I must—"

Ishitaka lifted himself higher and gently took her hand. "You must stay."

Ken'ishi raised an eyebrow. Such a gesture in public was incredibly forward.

She tried to speak, but half the eyes in the room were upon them, brimming with amusement.

"No, wait," Ishitaka said. "Send your master to me."

"Yes, Lord," she said, then bowed and hurried away.

As soon as she disappeared, the room erupted with cheers and laughter.

The music continued. Another man got up to dance with the first, this one striking exaggerated feminine poses in Ishitaka's direction. Ishitaka ignored them and said to Ken'ishi, "Did you see, my friend? A goddess walking among mortal men! Have you ever experienced that before?"

Ken'ishi emitted a wry chuckle. "I have."

"I swear I will have her, or else my heart shall break into ten thousand bleeding shards."

A short, balding man with a thin face came out of the back, wiping his hands on a towel, with Yuri just behind him, looking toward where Ken'ishi and Ishitaka sat. Recognition flickered in the man's eyes when he saw Ishitaka. He slapped on a smile and approached their table. Ishitaka gestured the man to sit, poured a cup of *saké,* and offered it.

"I am Otomo no Ishitaka, sir. And you are the owner of this splendid establishment?"

"Heikichi is my name, and yes, Lord, this is my place. It is a pleasure to make your acquaintance, Lord. Your exploits in battle precede you. Please look with favor on my humble establishment."

Ishitaka waved a dismissive hand. "How is it that you have such an exquisite creature working here as a simple serving girl? She should be a princess! An empress!"

"She is new, Lord, only started this week—"

"Is she for sale?"

"Her bed is her own, Lord." The man spoke haltingly, as if a number of conflicting urges tangled his words. "I do not offer her to customers. I do not own her—"

"Good! Because she is far too good to be a common whore. Is she a hard worker? Do you pay her well?"

Ken'ishi covered the amusement on his lips with a hand.

"She does passably fine, and customers seem to like her—"

"Excellent! How much are you paying her today? No, never mind that. Whatever it is, I will double it."

"But, Lord—"

"Very well, sir, you drive a hard bargain! I will *triple* it if you consent to allow her to join my companion and myself for the rest of the evening."

The proprietor's mouth hung open for a moment. "Very well, Lord. You are most generous. May I interest you in a private room upstairs?"

"That sounds splendid! Just splendid!" Ishitaka's words were losing their intelligibility. He beamed at Ken'ishi. "Now we must find you a girl, too!"

"But, sirs—"

Ken'ishi raised a hand. "That won't be necessary, Heikichi. We don't want to put you to any more trouble."

The proprietor bowed to them. "Thank you, sirs, for your generosity and patronage." He pointed to a beaded curtain in the corner leading to a stairway. "Up the stairs, second door on the right. I'll send Yuri up with fresh *saké* and some *mochi* cakes with my compliments."

"The No-Mind is the same as the Right Mind. It neither congeals nor fixes itself in one place. It is No-Mind when the mind has neither discrimination nor thought but wanders about the entire body and extends throughout the entire self....
"When this No-Mind has been well developed, the mind does not stop with one thing, nor does it lack any one thing. It is like water overflowing and exists within itself. It appears appropriately when facing a time of need."

—*Takuan Soho, "The Mysterious Record of Immovable Wisdom"*

Upstairs in a small private room, Ishitaka and Ken'ishi settled themselves—somewhat unsteadily. Conversations and boisterous laughter seeped through the rice-paper screens, mostly masculine voices, but a few feminine as well. A servant boy brought a brazier and a bucket of coals and set them up to warm the room.

Ishitaka was still beaming. "The gods are smiling upon me today, Ken'ishi, I can feel it. How could such a beautiful creature be found in a place like this? Did you see the way she looked at me?" His eyes glowed.

Ken'ishi could not help but smile at his excitement. "Perhaps we should switch to tea. Too much *saké*, and your little warrior will not stand at attention."

"Bah!" Ishitaka laughed. "She could make a dead man rise to greet her."

The door slid open, and Yuri entered with a tray of fresh jars. She tucked a lock of hair behind a delicate ear. Ishitaka's eyes devoured her. Ken'ishi could appreciate his friend's infatuation, but she was so young, with womanly curves only beginning to show.

She smiled graciously at them both. "I am at your service, gentlemen."

Now, with her sitting right there, Ishitaka seemed to have been struck mute. His face flushed scarlet, and his mouth was frozen. Ken'ishi leaned back with an amused smirk at his friend's discomfiture.

She said, "May I pour?"

Ishitaka said, "Of...of course." He raised his earthenware cup.

She raised a jar and with dexterous grace did not spill a drop, even though she was aiming for a moving target.

Ken'ishi decided to let his companion catch his breath and asked the girl, "Aren't you a bit young to work here? Have you any brothers and sisters?"

"No, sir, I am an only child. My father is a...a merchant. He travels a lot." Her clothing was not the faded threadbare of peasants, but a fine weave, crisp and new.

Ken'ishi watched for a reaction from Ishitaka. Merchants held the lowest social standing of anyone besides whores and *eta,* as they produced no food, built nothing, crafted nothing, served no one but themselves, and made money solely on the efforts of others.

Ishitaka seemed not to care. "And your mother?"

Her head bowed. "Alas, she is dead."

Ishitaka said, "That is a pity. You must be very lonely when your father is gone."

She nodded sadly. "He tells me he is trying to find me a fine husband."

"Is he traveling now?"

"Yes, sir. I like coming here to work when he is gone."

Ishitaka's eyes sparkled.

Ken'ishi watched her over the rim of his cup, measuring Ishitaka's chances. If Ishitaka were a certain kind of man, his status as the nephew of Lord Otomo might allow him to force her into his bed, regardless of her wishes. Thus far, Ken'ishi could not discern whether she truly liked Ishitaka, or was simply indulging his infatuation with politeness. And there was something else about her. As if he had seen her somewhere before...

They whiled away another hour. A few cups of *saké* and her cheeks flushed and smiles bloomed on her lips. There was a darkness in her eyes, however, that the smiles could not disperse, some part of her spirit that had been lopped off or stuffed away. Ken'ishi had seen the same in Kiosé, after several years working as a common whore. But this girl was younger even than Kiosé had been. She asked many questions and looked interested in hearing them talk about life in the castle. She said, "I look up at the castle and wonder what it must be like up there, looking down on us poor creatures in the town."

Ishitaka did his best to regale her with tales of his exploits, but the *saké* seemed to mix up the details. Nevertheless, Ken'ishi just leaned back, offered occasional corroboration, and watched. She listened with fascination, prompting Ishitaka with smiles and surprise.

Over time, she edged closer to him, until their shoulders brushed.

Ken'ishi finally excused himself to use the privy, and when he came back, found them leaning close, looking brazenly into each other's eyes. At the sight of him, Ishitaka's eyes flashed with frustration. Taking this cue, Ken'ishi said, "The night grows late, and I feel I must retire. Thank you, Yuri, for being such a charming companion. Perhaps we shall see each other again. Lord Otomo, by your leave."

Ishitaka beamed a drunken smile at him. "Yes, yes, Ken'ishi, you must be very tired. I will see you again tomorrow."

With that, Ken'ishi bid them goodnight, settled the bill with the innkeeper—a surprisingly large sum, considering the innkeeper had offered refreshments on the house—and walked out into the night. He could not afford another night like this anytime soon.

The sky had cleared for the frosty stars. He slipped his arms into his robes for warmth. His step meandered slightly. The town was quiet, redolent with the smells of wood smoke. A lantern man walked the streets, striking his bell four times to call out the Hour of the Pig. The hour would soon be midnight.

Ken'ishi chuckled at Ishitaka's moony-eyed ardor, remembering how it felt. He yearned to feel such feelings again, unencumbered by the bitterness of loss. But he swore he never would.

At least now, he knew the answers to many of his questions about Kazuko. She had borne Lord Tsunetomo no heirs, and Ken'ishi wondered why. Had the gods cursed her for giving up her virginity to him?

He wanted to hate the man who had stolen her. But Tsunetomo had shown him incredible generosity and fairness in many ways. High- and low-ranked alike, the men respected their lord. The higher their rank, the greater their reverence and devotion. It was not just a matter of duty. Tsunetomo's presence and bearing commanded this devotion, called men to follow him. It seemed an even worse torture that Ken'ishi could not hate him. Lord Nishimuta no Jiro, Kazuko's father, on the other hand, Ken'ishi had plenty of reason to hate. But not the man to whom Kazuko had been given.

Perhaps, as long as Ken'ishi did not have to see her, he could accept her being just on the other side of a few walls, where at least she was safe and well. He wondered if Hatsumi was still with her, and how she was faring after what Hakamadare had done to her.

He drew a deep breath of frosty, invigorating air and gazed up at the castle silhouetted against the tapestry of stars. A needle-thin streak of fire shot halfway across the sky and then sparkled into non-existence, all in silence. He stared in wonder. The stars swam in his vision, misting with iridescent halos. He blinked and rubbed his eyes.

"Hey, samurai!" a voice called.

Ken'ishi paused.

A man's outline stood bathed in the glow from within a shop. A fringe of graying hair glowed around a head backlit by a lantern. "Care to have your soul polished?" A wooden placard above the door read *Souls of samurai polished here.* As samurai believed their souls to be their swords, such signs were customary for sword polishers.

"Isn't it a bit late for you to be working, Uncle?"

The man gave a moist chuckle. "It's never too late. I'm a bit of a night bird. My name is Tametsugu, and I polish a great many swords for Lord Otomo's retainers. You might say I'm famous in these parts. That looks like an interesting sword. One doesn't see *tachi* much anymore. Is it a family weapon?"

"It is."

"May I examine it?"

Ken'ishi untied it from his *obi* and offered it to the man with both hands.

Tametsugu bowed and accepted it with both of his long-fingered hands. Then he turned his rheumy-eyed scrutiny upon it. "If you'll forgive my rudeness, I must say the scabbard needs some sprucing up. Perhaps some new ray skin on the hilt. But the silver fittings are not tarnished at all. Very unusual for a piece this old. Do you polish the silver yourself?"

Ken'ishi shook his head.

"Very interesting." The old man drew two hand-spans of blade from the scabbard and peered closer. His eyes widened. "No! It cannot be!"

"What is it?" Ken'ishi said with growing alarm. The sword had not been polished in years, not since he had passed through the capital and a high-ranked samurai had had it polished for him as a kindness. It had since bathed in buckets of barbarian blood. In spite of its use, however, its edge remained unmarred.

"Pray, sir, tell me if this sword has a name."

After having Silver Crane stolen from him, after what he had suffered to reclaim it, he lied, "Not to my knowledge."

The old man deflated slightly. "Ah."

"Why do you ask?"

"Well, do you see the *hamen*? See how the temper line along the cutting edge looks like feathers? This is the work of one of the old Heian mastersmiths. There is no one left who knows how to do this. With the cranes on the guard and the silver fittings, it matches the description of a sword named Silver Crane."

"What do you know of it?"

"Silver Crane was a treasure of the Taira clan. Taira no Tomomori was the last to possess it, and he died at the Battle of Dan-no-Ura, over a hundred years ago. The Minamoto clan caught the Taira fleet in the straits and wiped it out, destroyed most of the clan and even His Highness, the eight-year-old boy emperor, Antoku. The stories say Tomomori tied an anchor rope around his own waist and let it drag him to the bottom of the sea."

Memories exploded like a bomb in Ken'ishi's mind of dreams he had seen describing just such events, and of the tales Minamoto no Hirosuke, the historian, had told him while they were imprisoned in Green Tiger's sea cave. Silver Crane had been at that battle, lost, and then found. Silver Crane had once told him, *I follow the bloodline.*

The sword polisher shrugged. "Yes, this is probably not Silver Crane. It's doubtless still at the bottom of the sea. But once I remove the hilt, perhaps the name of the smith engraved on the tang will be a clue to its origin. If Silver Crane had been found and the remnants of the Taira clan got wind of it, they would not allow such a treasure to remain in the hands of someone not of Taira blood. If you'll indulge an old man's curiosity, sir, where did you get it?"

"From my father."

"And who is your father?"

"Alas, I do not know. My parents were murdered when I was a baby."

"A sad tale." The sword polisher clucked his tongue, but curiosity still filled his face. "But you should know that this sword is beyond the work of a present-day swordsmith's art. It would be my great honor to polish it for you."

Ken'ishi stilled his mind and listened for the *kami*. Would this man steal the sword? Was he an agent of Green Tiger? Had Green Tiger survived the invasion? The answering silence of the *kami* put him at ease. "I would be honored for you to polish it."

The old sword polisher beamed with gap-toothed pleasure. "Very well, come back in three days, at sunset, and your sword will be ready."

"That is the New Year's celebration."

"Make sure you come at sunset, or you won't find me." The old man bowed deeply. "Thank you for the chance to polish your magnificent weapon. It is an honor I will not forget. And remember, come only at sunset."

Ken'ishi returned the bow. They bid each other goodnight, and he walked up the street. As he was not yet familiar with all the town's streets, he paid special attention to the neighborhood, making sure that he would be able to find the shop again.

A shudder of worry brought him around. The glow of the shop door had disappeared. Last year he had suffered unthinkable agony to recover Silver Crane, and now he had just given it into the hands of a sword polisher he had never met. Had he just made a horrendous mistake? But the *kami* were silent. He had to trust they would warn him. But would they?

We cover fragile bones
In our festive best to
    view
Immortal flowers
                    —*Onitsura*

The climb up the castle hill apparently dissipated the effects of the *saké*, because by the time Ken'ishi reached the first castle gate, the stars had resolved themselves back into brilliant silver dust. At the orchard below the first gate, naked cherry trees entwined their black branches toward the glittering sky like fingers.

He sat upon a stone and gazed up through the spidery branches at the stars. Six months ago, while he had waited for the itinerant merchant Shirohige to return from an errand inside the castle, he had thought he recognized Kazuko walking in this orchard. As it turned out, his eyes had not lied to him, but his mind had refused to grasp it then.

Kiosé had granted him three years of her life to distract him from his pain, but now she was dead, and the pain not only remained, but now bore the added weight of his guilt. Would Kiosé have forgiven him? Would it have been best to let her go? She had been oblivious, under an enchantment to erase her memories of him, of pain he had caused her. Would he have been able to win her back, as he had promised? Would it have been fair of him even to try?

A bellyful of *saké* did not make such musings easier.

A group of drunken samurai headed up the hill through the gates, laughing, singing, carrying two comrades unable to walk.

Then a familiar voice, coming from not two *ken* away, said, "You're doing well for yourself, old sot."

Ken'ishi gasped and spun. "Hage!"

"Observant as ever." A round-bellied old man, a tuft of white beard dangling from his chin, wisps of unruly hair sticking out from his head, settled himself onto another rock with a gust of breath, wooden staff between his knobby knees.

Ken'ishi could not help but grin. "I am glad to see you."

Hage smirked, eyes twinkling. "Been diddling the *saké* without me, I see."

"And you survived the barbarians, I see."

"A bit of a tussle there. They were as thick as lice and twice as stubborn. But I did find your leathery old benefactors after the storm passed."

"How are Shirohige and Junko?" Ken'ishi still felt he owed a debt to the old merchant and his vile-mouthed sister for nursing him back to health after he escaped from Green Tiger's clutches.

"Ill-tempered as ever, but they were alive when I left them."

"Thank you, Sensei, for looking after them." Ken'ishi bowed to him.

Hage waved a gnarled hand. "Bah! You are too soft-hearted for the likes of them."

"How did you find me?"

"The same way I always do. You leave a stench trail a *ri* across. But you found what you sought. Service with a fine lord!"

Ken'ishi nodded, slowly. "I have."

"What, 'tis not everything you hoped for?"

"It is...complicated."

Hage rolled his eyes. "By Hachiman's hairy balls, there's *another* woman!"

"Sensei—"

Hage stood and waved his arms in exasperation. "Always a

woman with you! Has there ever been a human more addled by love and loins? What did you do, fall in love with some nobleman's wife?"

Ken'ishi's faced heated.

Hage rolled his eyes again.

"It's not like you think!" Ken'ishi said.

"I very much doubt 'tis like *you* think!"

"I knew her...before."

Hage's eyes narrowed for a moment. "Oh, you mean *her.* The one you would never tell me about."

"Yes."

"Well, I refuse to help you again like I did back in Aoka village."

"Enchanting Kiosé's memories was not 'helping!'"

"I daresay you know not what help is!"

"Sensei," Ken'ishi said. He had to draw a deep breath to push out the next words. "Little Frog was my son. And now he is dead. Killed by the barbarians. Kiosé, too."

Hage's eyebrows rose like white caterpillars, then he shrank with a heavy, sorrowful sigh. "Ah, I am very sorry to hear that. What a terrible pity."

"I was a fool, a great, blind fool."

"Without question."

Stricken, Ken'ishi stared at him.

"Apologies, old sot. I was just agreeing with you."

Ken'ishi stood. "Have you come to do anything but taunt me?"

"Don't twist up your loincloth, sit down. I came to tell you what I've heard. About Green Tiger."

Ken'ishi sat.

Hage untied a gourd from his rope belt, uncorked it, and took a drink. Ken'ishi caught the scent of *saké.* Hage offered it, and when Ken'ishi declined, shrugged and put it away. "The barbarians wiped out most of Hakata and Hakozaki. A few people managed to get away, but it will be some time before either town is rebuilt. Green Tiger's organization was rooted in the Hakata Underworld. Gambling parlors, brothels, most of them built near the docks and seashore. Those were the areas mostly burned. Nothing of Green Tiger's Hakata wealth remains. As for Green Tiger himself, he has disappeared."

"Was he killed in the invasion?"

"Unlikely. Do you remember the house where we found your boar-poker?"

"Yes."

"Do you remember the clan?"

"No. Most of that night is a fog in my memory."

"*I* remember. Dual apricot blossoms."

Ken'ishi let out a long, slow breath, his teeth clamped tight. "The Otomo clan!"

"We must consider a couple of possibilities, especially in light of your new situation."

"Green Tiger is involved with the Otomo clan."

"One of many possibilities." He raised a hand and counted each point on his fingers. "Green Tiger is secretly a member of the Otomo clan. Or, he is closely allied with a member of the Otomo clan, close enough that Green Tiger can say, 'Hide something for me' and expect agreement. Or, perhaps a low-ranking servant or retainer of that house's owner is working for Green Tiger. The connection is plain." Hage scratched his beard with a dirty fingernail.

A chill went up Ken'ishi's spine. Every bit of news, every revelation, gouged away at his happiness. He had once thought this was the greatest good fortune of his life. In fact, he may have fallen into a nest of vipers.

"Cheer up, old sot! Count your victories. You killed both of Green Tiger's chief henchmen. He may well lie in a mass grave, riddled with Mongol arrows."

"Or his web may still stretch through all the Otomo lands of northern Kyushu."

"Well, there is that. Of all the Otomo lords, Tsunetomo casts the longest shadow of power and prestige, the perfect shadow in which one such as Green Tiger might hide."

"This is not 'cheering up!' I should lose my appetite if I thought as you do." Ken'ishi gestured at Hage's bulging belly. "Appetite has never been a problem for you."

"And thank the gods!" Hage hefted his paunch and heaved himself upright with a grunt. "I shall see you around, old sot. I have a few more visitations to accomplish tonight. There's an inn with a well-stocked larder calling out to me to be pillaged. Fear not, I will pay attention for you. It would cause me sadness for Green Tiger to get his claws into you again. A *tanuki*'s ears can listen at more knotholes than yours."

With that, Hage's form shrank into the hunched, low-slung, furry shape of a *tanuki*. It winked at him and then ran off through the trees.

Stumbling up the hill came a lone figure. In spite of the figure's drunken shamble, Ken'ishi recognized Ishitaka, so he waited.

Before long, Ishitaka spotted him and rushed forward, his eyes glowing with moonlight. "Ken'ishi! Ken'ishi! You won't believe it! She...she..." The joy on his face evaporated, and he staggered to the side of the road, doubled over, and vomited.

Ken'ishi steadied him, looking up and down the path for anyone who might see. He hoped the sentries at the gate were too far away. He would have to be more careful with Ishitaka next time. Drinking could be a great pleasure, but for the son of Captain Tsunemori to exhibit such a state of excess would be an embarrassment. He guided Ishitaka into the orchard, sat him down upon a rock beside a tree, and let him hang his head between his knees. The heaving eventually stopped, and Ishitaka leaned back against the tree, eyes fluttering closed.

Ken'ishi patted his cheek. "Wake up, Ishitaka. We're not home yet."

Ishitaka's eyes snapped open. "Oh! Yes! You won't believe it, Ken'ishi! She told me to meet her beside the north bridge tomorrow night! Oh, by the gods and buddhas, I have never felt this before! After you left, she spoke such kind words to me. She said I was handsome! And gentlemanly! And brave! Her name is Yuri, the lily, the lily..."

"She is a fine judge of character." Ken'ishi flung one of Ishitaka's arms around his shoulders and lifted him upright. "Now, it is time to get you home."

"To the tower, good sir!" Ishitaka cried, pointing to the shorter tower. "And we mustn't wake father. Shhh!"

In spite of Ishitaka's drunken gaiety, a chill had seeped into Ken'ishi's bones. Had he landed himself squarely in Green Tiger's very den? Had Green Tiger instigated Ushihara's attempt to have Ken'ishi disgraced? And he had just given up his sword. He stopped for a moment, thinking to go back for it. But Ishitaka stumbled, dragging Ken'ishi forward, and he had a feeling that the polisher would not be found again tonight.

Regardless, he was finished being Green Tiger's pawn.

"The appearance of pain in grasses and trees is no different than the countenance of suffering among human beings. When they are watered and the like, they grow and appear happy. When they are cut and fall, the withering of their leaves is no different from the death of a human being.

"Their pain and sadness are not known to human beings. And when grasses and trees look at the sadness of human beings, it is just like human beings looking at them, and they probably think we have no pain or sadness either. Simply, it seems that we do not know the affairs of grasses and trees, nor do they know ours."

—*Takuan Soho, "The Clear Sound of Jewels"*

K azuko pushed away the tray bearing her breakfast of honey-sweetened rice and tea. Another sleepless night, another dreary, gray morning, and another day of pain in her heart that could only be assuaged by working herself to near exhaustion in the practice yard. Her grip on the haft of her *naginata* had roughed her palms like a man's.

Tsunetomo sipped his tea, raising an eyebrow. "Has something happened, my dear? You have not been eating. And I have not seen you this way since...well, for some time."

He was talking about how she had withered away in the months after their marriage, secretly crushed by her forlorn longing for another.

"I am worried. About Hatsumi." Not exactly a lie, but the secondary cause of her distress.

His voice hardened. "Has she done something else?"

"No, but...I fear for her. I fear her malady will return."

"I have sent word to some of my kinsmen, asking about new handmaidens for you. Without question, there are young ladies of rank all over Kyushu who would be delighted to serve you. Besides, having only one handmaid is insufficient for a lady of your position."

"Thank you, husband. You are very kind." The thought of Hatsumi's reaction to such news filled Kazuko with fear. Hatsumi had cowed the entire household of servants until she was the only one allowed to see to Kazuko's daily needs. It was not a pleasant situation. She relished the idea of surrounding herself with good-natured young women, yet at the same time she was sickened with guilt at the thought of putting Hatsumi out. They had been together for almost as long as Kazuko could remember. Was Hatsumi eavesdropping even now from behind the thin rice-paper wall? Kazuko no longer trusted her to maintain the most rudimentary courtesies.

She waited for her husband to finish his rice so that she could call the servants. He sucked the last kernel from his chopsticks, drained his teacup, and prepared to leave. His valet offered him a cap and a jacket against the chill, and then tied his sword onto his *obi*. "Where are you off to today, husband?"

"The new horses are arriving today, all the way from the slopes of Mount Aso. A hundred stallions and a hundred bred mares, gifts from the Shogun. Tsunemori and I must appraise them."

"Oh, that is good news!"

"I will pick out a good one for you."

She clapped her hands in surprise. "Me? Learn to ride?"

He smiled indulgently. "Tomoe Gozen was a great rider. Why not you?"

"I am not Tomoe Gozen." Her cheeks flushed at the mention of the legendary samurai woman, dead now some thirty years. With ivory skin and beautiful features, Tomoe was not only beautiful, but a remarkable archer and swordswoman. Her deeds of valor during the war between the Minamoto and Taira clans had become the stuff of songs, calling her a warrior worth a thousand men. She would challenge demon or god, mounted or afoot, handling even unbroken horses with consummate skill.

"She was a legend," Tsunetomo said, "and so shall you be. We may not have children, but our names will echo through the ages." He stood and gave her an affectionate kiss on the forehead.

The flush deepened at the resignation in his voice. He had meant those words as a comfort to her, to show that he did not resent her for not producing an heir, but in them she felt her failure like the stab of a dagger. She clutched his hand and gazed up into his eyes. "I will give you an heir, husband. I swear it."

He tried to smile for her, but it did not travel far on his lips. He left her there to descend into her well of despair once again.

How long before he divorced her and took a new wife? How long before he chose a concubine and planted a son in her womb? Even a bastard son was better than no son at all.

Moments after he departed, the sound of movement from behind a nearby door caught her ear.

"Hatsumi, is that you?" she called.

No response.

"Hatsumi?"

Silence.

Kazuko stood and crossed toward the door where she was certain she had heard the movement. The sudden sound of cloth whispering against flesh and floor quickened her pace until she reached the door and flung it open.

Hatsumi hurriedly gathered her robes about her, gaze downcast.

"What is the meaning of this?" Kazuko said. "You are to come when I call!"

Hatsumi's eyes blazed with hot rage, driving Kazuko back a step.

"You're going to send me away!"

The feeling of ice-water dashed over Kazuko's shoulders, and she raised a hand as if to fend off an attack. "No...no, Hatsumi, I—"

"I heard you plotting against me!" Hatsumi's voice was a grating sneer, her hair a disheveled mane of tangles. A haphazard effort at powdering her face failed to cover strange reddish blotches on her cheeks and throat. "After all I've done for you!" She stalked forward, and Kazuko retreated.

The chill became a spike of fear in Kazuko's belly.

Hatsumi's fingers curled into ragged claws. "You can't send me away! I won't let you! You'll never find anyone as loyal to you as me! No one will ever love you as much as I do!"

"Stay away from me!" Kazuko cried. She snatched up her breakfast tray, the only thing close at hand.

"But you are my little sister! Why are you afraid of me?" Hatsumi's blackened teeth looked wrong somehow, as if they had grown sharper. She crept closer on bare feet. Her toenails were strangely discolored.

A door slid open behind Kazuko, and the voice of Lord Tsunetomo's valet came forth, "My lady, is everything—"

Hatsumi shrieked and flung herself at him, seized him around the throat with both hands, and squeezed off his cry of alarm. Blood-red lines shooting through her bulging eyes, Hatsumi swung him like a doll. Something meaty popped in the man's neck, and he sagged in her grip like a rag.

Hatsumi let him fall at her feet and turned back to Kazuko. "Look at what you made me do!"

In Hatsumi's wake, she had left a terrible, cloying miasma. Like the stench of the ichor that had once flowed in Hakamadare's veins.

Kazuko cast about for some sort of weapon, but Tsunetomo had taken his swords. Her dagger, a beautiful gift from her father, was wrapped in silk in a black-lacquered box in a cabinet on the far side of the room, replaced after the night Kazuko had sat by Hatsumi's side.

"It's all because of *him*!" Hatsumi shrieked.

Kazuko backed away from the other woman, toward the cabinet. Her voice trembled. "Who?"

Hatsumi followed, step by step. That grating sneer again, "The *ronin!*"

Kazuko gasped.

"Yes, I saw him the day he arrived with all those other scurrilous vagabonds! And you have seen him, too! Out there pretending he'll ever be anything but a filthy bandit! Oh, I heard your cute little sighs back then, the way you wanted to sell your honor for less worth than a ball of rice. You slut!"

Hatsumi knew of Ken'ishi's presence, and she knew that Kazuko had loved him, in her heart at least. Did she know they had consummated her love? What would she do with that knowledge? Kazuko bumped up against the cabinet. Hatsumi advanced, claws clenching at her sides.

"Please, Hatsumi," Kazuko said, "Calm yourself! Let us talk about this like sisters! Please!"

"No more lies!" Hatsumi's voice rose to a ragged wail. "We were never sisters, no matter how much I wished it!"

"What do you want?" Kazuko reached behind her, slowly, fingers seeking the bronze clasp of the gilded cabinet doors.

"Renounce the filthy *ronin* forever! Better yet, have him executed! Only his death will satisfy me!" Hatsumi stood two paces away now.

"How can I do that? He has done neither of us any harm. He saved your life, Hatsumi!" Her hand was on the latch. The flick of a finger spun it open.

Hatsumi's eyes blazed. "No harm? *No harm!* He destroyed us! He took your heart away from me! He let *you* escape! And I...I..."

Kazuko slipped a fingernail into the crack between the doors, pried them open ever so slightly. The box with the dagger lay on the bottom shelf. "I don't love him anymore. I love my husband."

Hatsumi stepped so close, her wretched breath washed over Kazuko. "You lie. I see it in your face. No one in the world knows you better than I do, little Kazuko. You will tell your husband of the *ronin*'s crimes and have him executed. Or else I will tell your husband!"

Rage flared in Kazuko, drowning all caution. She shoved Hatsumi back with both hands, with all her strength. Pushing Hatsumi felt like trying to shove a tree away, but Hatsumi floundered backward a step. Kazuko spun, whipped open the cabinet door, snatched the box, and whirled back just in time to catch Hatsumi lunging for her throat.

Hatsumi's eyes blazed with heat like flaring coals. Her rough-clawed hands clamped around Kazuko's neck, cutting off her air. With both hands, Kazuko smashed the lacquered box, emblazoned with the Nishimuta clan *mon,* against Hatsumi's face. The box splintered. Hatsumi staggered back, shrieking more in surprise than pain, releasing Kazuko's tender throat.

A silk-wrapped cylinder thumped onto the *tatami.* Kazuko lunged for it. Hatsumi lunged for her. Through the silk, Kazuko felt the hilt of the *tanto.* Hatsumi's hand closed around the scabbard. Kazuko pulled hard. The silk slipped out of Hatsumi's grasp, and Kazuko managed to unfurl it. Hatsumi plowed into her.

Kazuko jerked the *tanto* free of its scabbard and thrust it into Hatsumi's chest.

Hatsumi halted, her claws a mere finger's breadth from Kazuko's face, a look of profound surprise on her twisted visage. She stepped back, and the dagger slid out of her with a tight slurp. What dripped from the blade was not crimson blood, but a venomous black ichor, a rancid putrescence that filled the air with noxious malignance.

Hatsumi's face melted into anguish, like a child who had just been slapped by her mother for the first time. Her bottom lip quivered. "No..."

Kazuko brandished the dagger. "Stay back!"

Hatsumi looked back and forth several times between the dagger and Kazuko's face, then at the blackness staining her fingers from the wound in her chest.

Loosing a horrific scream so loud that Kazuko fell back and covered her ears, Hatsumi launched herself at the nearest window. She crashed through the shutters like an ox plowing through a rotten fence. Kazuko gasped and leaped to the window. They were five stories above the courtyard.

Below, Hatsumi's body lay amidst splintered wood on the hard-packed earth, her limbs twisted at grotesque angles.

Tears burst into Kazuko's eyes. Was it finally over? Why did she feel only relief?

Cries of consternation and surprise from nearby warriors echoed up toward Kazuko. Several men began to converge on Hatsumi's twisted shape.

Hatsumi's foot twitched.

A bolt of dread shot through Kazuko. "No, get away from her!" she tried to shout, but it came out as a whisper.

Before Kazuko could gather her voice, Hatsumi sprang to her feet, pounced upon the nearest man, and tore out his throat with her claws, sending a fan-shaped spray of crimson across the earth. He collapsed with a gurgling scream.

The other men jumped back and drew their swords. Hatsumi's blood-red glare swung once more up toward the window where she must have felt Kazuko's eyes upon her. The look of rage and betrayal and anguish on Hatsumi's face would be burned into Kazuko's memory forever.

Then Hatsumi rushed through the ring of samurai, bounded over the wall to the next ring of fortifications below, and disappeared from sight.

Kazuko listened at the window for as long as she could as the cries and shouts left in the wake of Hatsumi's flight echoed into nothingness.

Oh the anguish of these
   secret meetings
In the depth of night,
I wait with the *shoji* open.
You come late, and I see
   your shadow
Move through the foliage
At the bottom of the garden.
We embrace—hidden from
   my family.
I weep into my hands.
My sleeves are already damp.
We make love, and suddenly
The fire watch loom up
With clappers and lantern.
How cruel they are
To appear at such a moment.
Upset by their apparition,
I babble nonsense
And can't stop talking
Words with no connection.

           —*The Love Poems of Marichiko*

The deaths of the two men, one of them Lord Tsunetomo's personal valet, shattered the castle's spirit like a discordant gong. The tales grew wilder at every telling. Some said Lady Kazuko's handmaid had been possessed by an evil spirit; others said Kazuko herself had become an *oni*; still others said the *oni* had been a servant. But many witnesses agreed how the demon woman leaped over the castle's concentric fortifications in great bounds, with a terrible keening that could have been laughing or weeping. After murdering six townspeople and spreading a great panic through the rest of town, she disappeared into the forest.

Ken'ishi had not witnessed the incident, as he had been drilling with his men that morning, but his ear had caught the horrific wail echoing through the castle environs, a wail that had raised the hairs at the nape of his neck.

Later that day, Captain Tsunemori and the other officers addressed the men, assuring them that Lord Tsunetomo and Lady Kazuko were in good health, and explained that the culprit, the lady's handmaid, Hatsumi, had been going mad over the course of several months.

Tsunemori said, "We seek volunteers to go after her. She must be found and stopped."

From the ranks of troops seated around Tsunemori's dais, Ken'ishi was the first to stand. He did not know Hatsumi well, but somehow he felt connected to what had happened to her. Responsible for her, maybe. After all, it had been his arrival on the scene three years past that interrupted the rape and stopped Hakamadare from killing Hatsumi. Perhaps Hakamadare's evil had tainted her somehow. He was doubtless the only man here who had ever killed an *oni* as well.

Fifty men volunteered. It seemed a lot of men to capture one woman, but the forested hills around Hita town afforded bountiful places to hide. The searchers clad themselves in light armor and carried bows, nets, and ropes. They were ordered to capture her if possible, but not at the expense of any more lives.

Ken'ishi took his Otomo clan katana with him. Others carried lances.

One man said, "I saw what she did to Matsunari. These nets will not hold her."

Captain Tsunemori took charge, a fact that surprised most, as he was too high-ranked to lead so small a party. Nevertheless, the determination on his face was earnest, and suggested he knew more than what the men had been told. "She must not be allowed to stain the honor of the family, or of the clan," was all he said.

While Tsunemori and a dozen of Tsunetomo's personal guards set out on horseback, Ken'ishi joined one of the groups on foot, searching the hills to the north and west.

Those on foot carried gongs and drums and shouted as they tramped through brown, waist-high grass, across terraced rice fields, through patches of forest, higher into the pine-swathed mountainsides and bamboo groves. Birds fled the clamor in cloud-like flocks. Ken'ishi sought a chance to speak to one of them, as Kaa had taught him to do as a boy. He wanted to ask for word of Hatsumi but could not get close enough. The dreary gray sky and close-hanging clouds created a sense of foreboding, and drained all sense of life from the land.

Snow began to fall in heavy, wet flakes, and the search went from dreary and exhausting to freezing and damp. At nightfall, they called off the hunt and returned to the castle.

Over the next two days, search parties scoured the countryside but returned to the castle empty-handed each night.

The pall that fell over the town and the castle dimmed the gaiety of the coming New Year festival. Preparations continued, but smiles were thin as people did their work to distract themselves from the worry about any terrible curse. Brightly colored banners, painted with images of *koi* and prayers and wishes for the coming year, fluttered from poles as usual, but many of the banners included talismans inscribed to ward off evil and protect people from harm.

The town shone with lights at night, and people walked the streets with wary expressions as if one of their neighbors could be suddenly possessed. Shinto and Buddhist priests collected offerings and filled the town with the scent of incense and the ringing of bells.

On the morning of New Year's Day, a servant woman came into Barrack Six bearing a box of rice-paper packets for each of the men, a gift from the lady of the castle. Ken'ishi unwrapped his carefully, noting the elegant, feminine hand in which his name had been written on the scarlet ribbon. Inside he found three *mochi* cakes colored pink, green, and white. The men cheered the lady of the castle and devoured the cakes. Different flavors and colors of sweet bean paste filled each one.

And when his last cake was gone, Ken'ishi found, half-obscured by rice flour, meticulously written in tiny script on a slip of paper underneath, a poem:

> *The nightingale listens from her cage*
> *At the Sanmon Gate*
> *For footsteps at dusk*
> *Caught between darkness and light*
> *She calls,*
> *"Will he come? Will he come?"*

A bolt of simultaneous joy and suspicion shot through him. The words wormed into him, kicking his heart into a faster rhythm.

He crumpled the paper and tossed it into the brazier.

The coals licked orange along the crumpled edges, and fire bloomed and blackened.

He watched it burn until it was nothing but ash.

Ken'ishi thought about his dilemma. He could not meet Kazuko when he was appointed to retrieve Silver Crane. The sword polisher had said that he must come at the exact appointed time, or he would not find him.

But this could be his only chance to speak to Kazuko, ever. Warriors of his rank were not allowed to speak to ladies of hers. Any secret liaison invited discovery. If he failed to go to her, what then? And if he could speak to her, what would he say? That his heart had not been his own since the day they met?

He trusted no one else to retrieve Silver Crane from the sword polisher, nor could he send anyone in his place to meet Kazuko.

Besides, the Sanmon Gate at the temple and the shop of the sword polisher were on opposite sides of town. If he did not meet the sword polisher, he might never see Silver Crane again.

Around him, the men dispersed from the barracks to join the festival in the town, from which the sound of merrily beating drums echoed up to the castle.

Michizane sauntered up and said, "What say you, Ken'ishi? Let us join the merriment and forget our troubles until tomorrow."

Ken'ishi acquiesced. The festival lay nearer both destinations anyhow. Together they walked into town to where brightly colored tents had been erected. Villagers pounded cooked rice into *mochi* with great, wooden hammers and hollowed out tree stumps as bowls. The streets were redolent with smells of roasting chestnuts, boiling seaweed, and roasting fish. Gongs and jangles rang and jounced. Knots of giggling children ran past. In spite of the gaiety, the *kami* still whispered to him of the tension in everyone's hearts. Perhaps they sang and laughed a bit too boisterously. Perhaps they drank just a little too much.

A group of performers had gathered before the Roasted Acorn, jugglers and dancers and singers, collecting a large crowd of laughing onlookers. The performers were dressed in brightly colored clothes, some sewn with tattered rags that bounced and twirled as they moved.

One of the jugglers was a tall man with a hatchet-like nose, wearing a suit of fluttering, rainbow-like rags, who kept a veritable cloud of multi-colored balls arcing over his head. The Raggedy Man. Kaa, the *tengu,* in the same guise he had used to seduce Kiosé the previous year. How shocked Ken'ishi had been to discover them, soon after Hage had enchanted away her memories.

"What is it?" Michizane said. "Did something just bite you?"

Ken'ishi cleared the lump from his throat. "There's someone I must speak to, right now. I'll find you later."

He hurriedly circled the crowd to where the Raggedy Man juggled for a pack of children, who squealed with laughter at his preposterous expressions and incredible dexterity. Before Ken'ishi could get close, however, the Raggedy Man turned his dark eyes upon him like spear points, and tracked Ken'ishi for several long, painful moments as he wormed through the crowd. The balls fell into the Raggedy Man's hands. Then he bowed with exaggerated aplomb, turned, and disappeared into the gap between the Roasted Acorn and the paper-maker's shop next door.

Ken'ishi circled the paper-maker's shop at a run, hoping to catch the Raggedy Man in the alley behind.

But no one was there.

"Sensei!" Ken'ishi called. "Where are you?"

The reply was a burst of cheering from the street. The only other occupants of the alley were three chickens in a bamboo cage, huddled together against the cold. He tried to talk to the chickens, but they were all so terrified of human beings that they flung themselves into a squawking, feather-flapping frenzy until he sighed and moved on.

He searched the alley and finally gave up, returning to the street, where a man in a fearsome *oni* mask cavorted with a comically bulbous club. Initially, the crowd was hesitant to embrace his efforts, but he won them over with ribald songs whilst slapping his own backside.

Before long, the resonant tones of a great bell rang up and down the street, growing louder with each slow chime. Monotone chanting joined the sound of the bell as a group of thirty shaven-headed monks rounded a corner, carrying a large shrine on poles hefted on their shoulders. They chanted and rang the bell with a great, padded wooden clapper.

The crowds in the street parted and bowed as they passed, hands pressed together in prayer. As one sutra came to a close, the abbot, riding upon the shrine as if it were a palanquin, extended his arms and then bowed his head in fervent prayer for all the buddhas and bodhisattvas to deliver the town from evil influences. By the time the shrine and its attendants passed, the crowd was already resuming its former boisterousness.

Michizane brought hot *saké* for each of them, which they drank straight from the jar.

"Is it possible to understand religion?" Ken'ishi asked Michizane. "All those gods and buddhas. It is so complicated."

"This procession is meant to bless the town through the coming year. They will pass by here twice more before sunset."

"That's simple enough, I suppose...."

"If you want to know more, I'm not the man to ask," Michizane said. "My father always said that the Shinto priests and the Buddhists are simply two sides of the same false coin. I'm with him."

"You don't believe in the *kami*?"

"I have never seen a *kami*, nor had a prayer answered to my satisfaction. The gods are either cruel or careless. I'll have truck with neither." Michizane took a drink. "You look as if you disagree."

"I don't know about gods and buddhas, but I know the *kami* to be real."

"How?"

"They talk to me every day. And I talk to them."

Michizane raised an eyebrow with a slight smirk. "And how do you manage that?"

"My teacher taught me how to listen for them when I was a boy. They are there, if you know how to listen."

Michizane shrugged. "I'd rather listen to my wife's sighs in my ear. I wish she were here."

The clouds parted, allowing the sun to warm the festivities and turn the snow into slush. Amid flurries of giggles from village children, snowballs flew in random directions. Villagers danced and sang to the music of drums and gongs and flutes.

The afternoon of merriment wore Ken'ishi's mood into roughness, however, because he had not yet resolved his dilemma. His mind kept going back to the look the Kaa had given him through the Raggedy Man's eyes. It had been angry, almost challenging him, daring him to do something foolish. Why had he chosen to appear now, in the same guise with which he had fooled Ken'ishi and seduced Kiosé? With Kaa's otherworldly powers, should Ken'ishi bother to wonder whether the *tengu* knew of the note?

As the afternoon progressed, his demeanor lost all affability, and Michizane wandered off to join another group of men from Barrack Six.

The only decision Ken'ishi could accept was that he would try his utmost to reach both meetings in time.

First, he would go to the sword polisher's shop. And then he would run as fast as he could to the Sanmon Gate, and hope that whoever sent the note would still be waiting for him.

At sunset, he went to the sword polisher's shop. On his way, he spotted the gray hawk perched on the thatched peak of a roof against a sky so splashed with orange and purple that it filtered down onto the snow-dusted mountaintops, turning the entire landscape into exquisite stillness. The sunset gleamed on the bird's feathers, and its eyes followed him with cool judgment.

"Sensei!" Ken'ishi called. "Please, I have questions!"

The hawk ruffled its feathers and looked away.

Ken'ishi sighed and scanned up and down the street for the sword polisher's placard above the door. He scratched his head. This was without doubt the correct street. After walking further up the lane again, he paused and looked behind him. Had he gone too far? He walked up and down, searching for the placard.

The hawk remained upon his perch.

The shining fingernail of the sun slipped away behind the distant hills, and the shadows deepened.

A light emerged from a doorway some distance down the street. It did not match his memory of the sword polisher's location, but perhaps whoever was there would know where to find it.

Approaching the door, he peeked inside and found the sword polisher, wiping Silver Crane's scabbard with a soft cloth. A dim, gray eye flicked toward the door, caught sight of Ken'ishi, and a gap-toothed grin emerged. "Ah, Sir Ken'ishi. Please, do come in. I am just finishing up."

Ken'ishi slipped off his *zori* and stepped up into the shop. The sword polisher shuffled over to greet him and bowed.

"It was indeed a privilege to polish so fine a blade. May I show you?"

Ken'ishi bowed. "Of course."

The sword polisher drew the sword, and its blade caught the lantern light like liquid silver, almost as if it glowed with the light of the moon itself. He pulled a handful of long, gray hairs from his unruly fringe and laid them across the upturned edge, light as whispers, and they fell, divided, on either side. He grinned with pride at Ken'ishi.

"That is the greatest work, sir," Ken'ishi said. "Your skill does me honor."

"Let it never be said that Tametsugu does not know his business." He slid the blade back into the scabbard with a swift clack. Then he bowed and offered it up to Ken'ishi.

Ken'ishi accepted it and tied the scabbard to his *obi*. Then he took out his coin purse, having some heft nowadays thanks to his lord's generosity.

The sword polisher held up a hand. "Oh, no, I could not take something as vulgar as gold for polishing a sword such as this. I must ask a different kind of price."

"Oh?" Ken'ishi's wariness trickled over his back. He had encountered too many mystical creatures, and this sounded like a dangerous kind of price. At the same time, he itched to be away, to meet the mysterious poet at the Sanmon Gate.

The sword polisher's face darkened. "This is a weapon as demonic as it is magnificent. Guard your soul, samurai."

"What do you mean?"

"There is a tremendous, unseen weight upon it. It has drunk blood like the waves of the ocean. I see you know this. Good! You are not a fool. What does it say to you?"

Ken'ishi did not know how to answer.

"Oh, it has power, this one," Tametsugu said. "Power like the rivers that can eat a mountain away. My thoughts are too small to encompass what it has told me. It *is* Silver Crane. And it made its way from the bottom of the sea back into the hands of a great warrior of the Taira clan, a man who thought that becoming a farmer would make men forget. But powerful men never forget. All that blood, all that weight of souls set free by its cutting edge. It is a terrible burden. You have spilled much blood for it, have you not?"

"I have, during battle—"

"Oh, but it loves battle. The only moments when it is truly free to fulfill its purpose. Sir Ken'ishi, look to your soul. The soul of the samurai lives in his blade, but this blade already has a soul of its own. Do not doubt your own soul. There may come a day when yours will be tested, when you must answer the question of who is the servant and who is the master. And remember, the more blood you spill at its behest, the greater your burden."

"I—"

"There is already a burden upon you, I see. But alas, that is not for me to polish away. My price is this."

The sword polisher raised his hands and placed them on Ken'ishi's shoulders. "At the moment you most desire to use Silver Crane, when deepest peril and greatest triumph are suspended in balance, you must put the sword away. If you do not, your immortal soul will be in danger."

"H-How?"

"Go now. My time grows short."

Ken'ishi turned and stepped outside the shop into his sandals.

The sun had disappeared, and it was darker now than it should be. The sky should still be painted with dusk. How long had he been inside?

The old man's silhouette wagged a finger at him from the glowing doorway. "Guard your soul, samurai."

Ken'ishi bowed. "Thank you." He walked a few paces away, his mind churning with all the old man had said, and then he remembered the Sanmon Gate. He broke into a run. Reaching the next intersection, he glanced back.

The glow of the shop was gone.

I waited all night.
By midnight I was on
   fire.
In the dawn, hoping
To find a dream of you,
I laid my weary head
On my folded arms,
But the songs of the
   waking
Birds tormented me.
   —*The Love Poems of*
      Marichiko

Ken'ishi's breath huffed in and out as he sped across town toward the temple. His *zori* slipped and slid and collected mud from the melting snow. He ran through aromas of food and sounds of revelry. His heart beat so fast that he felt lightheaded, and not because of his pace. The heavens appeared too dark, as if the sunset had been hours previous. Had he stumbled into another realm of enchantment, where the loom of time moved differently? How long would Kazuko wait for him?

At the outskirts of town, the temple hill reared above him, its summit a froth of black treetops against the stars. Up the manicured mountain path he ran. The ancient forest formed a moss-draped tunnel, limned in lantern glow, and the forest floor had been carved into steps. The only sounds were the clap of his sandals on the stone steps and his heaving breath. His sandals pounded off bits of caked mud as he climbed, and the lines of a gate at the temple entrance came into view, the single-story Somon Gate, its roof swooping upward at the tips.

Beyond, bathed in globes of lantern light, lay the two-tiered Sanmon Gate. Through its three openings, people could enter the temple proper. Each opening allowed the pilgrim to free himself from the sins of greed, hatred, and foolishness.

In the lantern light, he cast about for signs of anyone, but silence lay like a blanket. The portable shrine the monks had carried through town now resided in the center of the temple yard. If any monks were not abed, they were nowhere in sight.

His beating heart grew cold.

The earth around the gate and through the central opening had been torn up by hundreds of fresh footprints. But around the sides... Would she have waited out of sight?

He took down one of the paper lanterns, careful not to extinguish the lone candle inside, and used it to light his path as he examined the areas around the sides of the gate.

There, in the soft, moist earth. The tracks of *geta,* small enough, perhaps, to belong to a woman. A bit farther on, he found those *geta* impressions gathered in great profusion. Someone had waited there, pacing, for some time.

His heart sank even lower.

This might have been his only chance to speak to her. If she had waited for him for a long time, what must she think of him now? If the note was indeed from Kazuko, she had put herself at great risk to meet him. And he had failed her. He wanted to apologize somehow, but how could he send a message to her? Low-ranked *bushi* did not simply send letters to the lady of the castle. Should he pretend he had not received the message? What had she come here to say?

Too many questions. Too many worries. Too many failures.

He sat down upon the ancient foot-smoothed planks of the porch that encircled the gate. Then he took a deep breath and quieted himself.

Silver Crane's luminous bell rang in his mind. *Many threads coming together, weaving and interweaving.*

Snow still rested upon the gate's eaves above. Water dripped before his feet. He sat there for a long time, envying Hage's *tanuki* nature, and wishing he could simply scamper off into the forest.

Kazuko barely felt the cold mud around her toes from having trudged through a slush-puddle. She clutched her straw peasant's coat tighter, more out of instinct than awareness of the chill. She had acquired a torn, threadbare set of robes from one of her servants, without offering explanation of why she wanted them. Her long hair was still raised in a haphazard bun, like that of a beleaguered servant woman, her face smudged by soot. She kept her gaze squarely downcast, lest she be recognized. As night advanced, such an event was unlikely. And on New Year's Night, the castle gates would be open until dawn to admit revelers, so she would be able to slip back inside, unnoticed.

Her wild, forlorn attempt to contact Ken'ishi had been a failure. He had not come. Possible explanations twisted her insides like a cyclone. He had not received the note in time, or at all. He had not realized that it was from her. He suspected a trick and stayed away. He did not want to see her. He wanted to come, but was delayed....

He did not love her anymore.

The last possibility was a curdled tincture of relief and bitterness.

In her shock and grief over Hatsumi, her heart had yearned until the only way to assuage it had been to reach out to the only person who would understand. Perhaps Ken'ishi would know what to do.

Was that all she wanted? Or was it something more? A torrid, romantic liaison? Or an opening of her heart once again and for all time?

She was certainly not starved for carnal attention. Her husband bedded her more nights than not, still seeking an heir, and this modicum of fleshly pleasure had sustained her through long, dark times. Growing to love Tsunetomo for his goodness, his strength, his fairness had saved her from a lifetime of despair, but he had never set her loins aflame the way Ken'ishi had.

But those were negligible concerns in the face of the devastation that might be wreaked if she succumbed to those desires. To be a samurai lady meant steadfastness, loyalty, duty, honor. To be with Ken'ishi was the antithesis of those ideals.

Nevertheless, to simply talk to him again, to have him tell her that all was forgiven...

Perhaps that was it.

She wanted his forgiveness.

For allowing her father to cast him out of the province on threat of death. For marrying Tsunetomo. For not running away with Ken'ishi, regardless of his refusal to allow it. For being unable to even speak to him.

She had wronged him in so many ways, none of which he deserved.

And she wanted to know where he had been these three long years. Had he a wife somewhere? Children?

She walked up and down the streets, the winter night leeching all warmth from her. Tsunetomo was carousing tonight with his brothers and high-ranked retainers at a special party for the men, hosted at the estate of Hoshino no Katsumitsu, head of one of the Otomo clan's prominent vassal families. The estate lay just to the west, and boasted a hot spring revered for its healing properties. With his shoulder still on the mend, he had been grateful to accept the invitation, taking Tsunemori, Ishitaka, and Yasutoki with him. It was these absences that had emboldened her to attempt to reach Ken'ishi.

A band of drunken village men came down the street, arms around each other's shoulders, singing ridiculously out of tune. She stepped out of the light of the street lanterns and slipped into the shadows between two houses.

The singing grew louder, and she shrank deeper into the shadows.

Then a quiet, crunching, snapping sound behind her spun her around with a gasp.

Two yellow eyes swung toward her, hanging close to the ground, catching the lantern light from deep in darkness. The creature stopped chewing.

Their eyes met.

Its silhouette, barely discernible in the darkness, was low-slung, mound-like, and indistinct. It was not a dog. A *tanuki*.

The revelers passed by in the street.

The *tanuki* looked past her.

An unexpected, irrational fear clutched her. If the *tanuki* made any noise, it would give her away. If the men saw her, they might recognize her. What might a gang of drunken peasants do to a lone, unprotected woman? Even if she got away from them, what sorts of rumors might begin to fly? The uneasiness and gossip about Hatsumi had already darkened the town's mood, with talk of curses and evil influences.

The *tanuki* kept silent, but its eyes never left her, sparkling with mischievous intelligence.

The singing moved off down the street, and she began to breathe again. The men stumbled on into the dark. When she turned back toward the *tanuki,* it was gone.

Kazuko hurried back into the street and quickened her pace toward home.

A frosty moon emerged from behind a cloud, bathing the street in luminescence so bright it cast her shadow at her feet. Through the streets of town she went, until the road reached up toward the castle gates.

As she passed by the orchard, a distant sound caught her ear and she stopped to listen. It had been like the forlorn howl of a dog. It could not be a wolf, as there had been no wolves on Kyushu for generations. And yet, in the ululation lurked primal emotion, a bestial cry of anguish.

"She is out there," a small, child-like voice said, "So full of pain."

She jumped with shock and cast about for who had spoken. She saw no one.

"She will draw strength from the mountains, become more powerful.... He's going to have to go after her, I'm afraid," the voice said from the moon-shadow of a stone. "Ken'ishi. She'll come after him. He'll have to kill her."

The words chilled her, as if the speaker knew everything.

A hoarse whisper was all the voice she could muster. "Who are you?"

Sharp, yellow eyes turned upon her with a chuckle. A furry shadow emerged from the shadow of the stone. Another tanuki? Or the same one?

"Are...are you truly...a *tanuki?*"

"Glad to see you're no fool, Lady Otomo," said the *tanuki* wryly.

She flinched back with a gasp.

"And I am not 'mound-like,'" the *tanuki* said with a sniff of umbrage.

She clapped a hand over her mouth.

"No, you are not dreaming. But you should return to the castle before you're missed. 'Twould be quite a shame to stir up even more trouble."

"Do you...do you know Sir Ken'ishi?"

"Do *you*?"

"I...I...yes."

"Well, I see honesty is one of your virtues. So that makes two of us who know our former *ronin*. What shall we do about that?"

"I do not know. I have never spoken to a *tanuki* before."

"And the richer you are for the experience." Then another distant howl drew his attention again. "Such suffering is a blight upon the natural world." He fixed her once again with his luminous gaze. "You must be careful, lady. Or else go the way of that creature."

"What are you saying?"

"Love, hate. Laughter, rage. Clinging too tightly to any of them is a disease. Ah, I see something ringing true for you, lady."

"I am not blind to my own failings." Her voice turned bitter, and she clutched her coat tighter around her.

"Well, then, that is a fine beginning. The world moves. All living creatures, even the gods, must move with it or perish in our own self-made hells. Like *her*."

Kazuko's eyes teared. "Dear Hatsumi..."

"Evil is everywhere. We make our own. It sticks to us. It sticks to others. It sticks to the world. It all feeds upon itself, and it twists everything." A long moment passed, and the *tanuki* licked a front paw. Then he said, "Perhaps it would interest you that I knew Hakamadare, back when he was a man."

Terrifying memories shot through her of the *oni*'s horrific face, yellow tusks, and three horns and lantern eyes, the way it had leered at her, the way it had feasted upon the flesh of her slaughtered bodyguards, what it did to Hatsumi...and what it would have done to her, if not for Ken'ishi. She said, "How could you talk to such a beast?"

"He was not a mindless beast. Given to fits of rage, lust, greed, all of those great passions, perhaps, but so are humans. But he was never any less clever, or else he would have been caught and killed long before he met his demise. Oh, but what a black, twisted sense of humor he had! A fine drinking companion! Now, if I may continue my spellbinding tale?"

"Please, do continue."

The *tanuki* said, "Hakamadare got his name from the droopy way he wore his trousers. He was clever, tenacious, bold—all excellent traits for a robber. And a robber he was. He loved it so. I encountered him and his gang on a number of occasions. He tried to rob me once, thinking I was a mendicant monk. A man must have a terribly hard life to steal from a monk. But Hakamadare's life was given to wild swings of fortune. As rich as an emperor one week, a starving beggar the next. Humans most often have some chief downfall within them, a favorite kind of trap, different for everyone. For Hakamadare, it was greed. He could never steal enough to satisfy his appetites. And it was also fear.

"The beginning of his downfall was his encounter with a nobleman named Yasumasa, I forget the family name. Yasumasa was walking down the street one night, playing his flute, carefree as can be, and Hakamadare decided he wanted the nobleman's fine clothes. He ran up to the nobleman, thinking to jump him. But the man simply turned around and looked at him, unperturbed. The robber found that he could not attack, so he ran away, confounded.

"Twice more he tried to ambush the nobleman, but each time the man just stopped playing his flute and said, 'What in the world are you doing?' Hakamadare lost all his courage when faced with Yasumasa's gaze.

"The nobleman asked him again what he was doing. He replied, 'I'm trying to steal your clothes.'

"The nobleman said, 'Come along.' Then he went on his way, playing the flute.

"Hakamadare followed him all the way to the rear gate of a wealthy estate. The nobleman said, 'Wait here.' For some reason— and Hakamadare told me this himself—"

She gasped. "He told you himself!"

"I already said we tipped a jar now and then." He rolled his eyes and sighed. "Anyway, while he waited at the gate, Hakamadare realized he was dealing with an extraordinary man.

"The nobleman returned carrying an armload of clothes of the richest kind and said, 'If ever you need clothes again, come here and tell me. If you keep going around jumping people, you might get hurt.'

"And in meeting that nobleman, all of Hakamadare's failures, every misdeed, every weakness came home to him, and he wept at the nobleman's gate until the night watch found him and arrested him. This knowledge, that he could never become such a man as Yasumasa, no matter how much he stole, no matter how fine the robes he acquired, ate at him like rats in the belly of a carcass. And that is how he became an *oni*."

Kazuko said, "You are very wise, Mr. *Tanuki*."

"Sometimes. But mostly I talk too much. And now, the hour grows late. Proper ladies should be abed, and proper *tanuki* should be seeking victuals and amusement."

"But what about Ken'ishi?"

"What about him?"

"What shall I do?"

"Wake up to the sunrise. Go to bed at night. Breathe. Eat food you like. Anything else is a boon." With that, the *tanuki* scampered off into the darkness.

As she headed back into the castle, she was thankful at least that the howling had ceased.

How many lives ago
I first entered the
   torrent of love,
At last to discover
There is no further
   shore.
Yet I know I will enter
   again and again.
       —*The Love Poems of*
              Marichiko

The day after New Year's Day was the first of many days of celebration. Lord Tsunetomo returned and led a great procession of his retainers, including Ken'ishi, to the temple. Joined by the abbot and all the monks, Tsunetomo knelt with hundreds of his men in the temple courtyard, gave thanks to the Buddha and bodhisattvas for the defeat of the barbarian invaders, and entreated them for aid in the trials certain to come.

The abbot blessed them, and many sutras were sung to a profusion of bowed heads. Incense filled the air in melodious, fragrant clouds.

The abbot gave a sermon in which he extolled the bravery of the fighting men gathered there, talked of virtues and evils, of the Three Treasures, kharma and dharma and sangha. Ken'ishi found his thoughts wandering back to the events of the night before.

Was he a member of the Taira clan by birth? The sword claimed to follow the Taira bloodline, but until now such an idea had been ephemeral, uncertain. Should he claim his birthright and seek out others of his blood?

But the Taira had been all but destroyed by the Minamoto-founded shogunate for supporting the Emperor. They were all but an outlaw clan.

Would he put himself in danger by trumpeting his lineage to the world? Should he care about any possible danger to himself? Was he any different as a man today, now that he knew more of the truth, than he had been a month ago? Would the remnants of the Taira clan embrace him? Would they even believe him?

He still did not know who had killed his parents. Had the Taira clan turned on them? Or had they been purged by the Minamoto?

Then something the abbot said broke his reverie.

"—Warriors are unique in the halls of the universe. Your purpose is to fight for those who command you. But to cause the death of living things brings a heavy kharmic burden. Our actions in this life ripple throughout all our lives into eternity, until we finally embrace the Way and join the Buddha in Nirvana. But if the warrior kills for his lord, for duty and honor, for right, for justice, is he then to be punished in subsequent incarnations?"

A sudden realization crashed over Ken'ishi like a storm surge. How many deaths were on his hands?

The dozens of Mongols he had killed? They had obeyed the orders of their lord. Was their adherence to duty and honor any less than his? The fact that they drank blood sickened him, but Kaa's admonishment to consider their origins had clung to his thoughts. Underestimating them, making them any less brave or fierce or earnest than him, was to invite defeat.

And what about the tens of thousands of Mongols and the Koryo sailors drowned and smashed by the typhoon? Was he responsible for their deaths?

A typhoon brought to life by Silver Crane's power to weave the threads of fate. Power granted by the slaughter Ken'ishi had wreaked upon the Mongols in that desperate Hakozaki street.

Were all those tens of thousands of deaths now an enormous kharmic weight upon his soul? If that were true, his next hundred lives would be spent as an earthworm.

Queasiness settled in his gut.

The end of the abbot's sermon brought him back to the moment again. More sutras were chanted. Lord Tsunetomo offered a gift of many bags of rice, casks of *saké*, and pieces of gold to the temple, which the abbot accepted with dignified thanks. After this, the ceremonies were concluded.

As the chill descended that evening, Tsunetomo hosted a great feast for all of his retainers in the main courtyard of the castle. Hundreds of lanterns festooned the walls and hung from strings crisscrossing the sky, bathing the entire courtyard as if in daylight. Several bonfires provided warmth. It was a sumptuous feast such as Ken'ishi had never experienced, even grander than the fealty ceremony. Servants carried woven bamboo platters bearing great mounds of steaming rice. Cauldrons of soup warmed their bones against the winter chill that the bonfires could not defeat. Trays of sweet rice cakes were emptied with astonishing gusto. The *kami* of the wind and sky smiled upon them and opened up the heavens, allowing the stars to sparkle above like the inside of a cosmic bowl.

It was a beautiful evening for a feast.

Lady Kazuko sat upon the dais with her husband, resplendent in quilted robes of golden brocade, quite the contrary vision to the warrior woman Ken'ishi had seen in the courtyard, and thankfully far enough away that he could pretend to pay little attention to her. With this being his first real chance to look at her since they parted ways three years before, however, he could not help but notice how she had changed. Her face now was thinner, more angular, with more maturity in it, but it had lost not a *momme* of its beauty. He admonished his heart for beating faster whenever he looked at her.

Ken'ishi sat among the men of Barrack Six and tried not to let his troubles dim the merriment of those around him.

The performers from the village the night before—without the Raggedy Man, however—made another appearance here, and created the same sort of gaiety with their antics and songs. The audience was more gruff in its appreciation, but, as the *saké* flowed, their applause increased.

Captain Tsunemori, seated with his wife and Ishitaka on a lower dais to Tsunetomo's right, caught Ken'ishi's eye at one point and raised his *saké* cup.

Ken'ishi blushed and raised his, too.

Eventually the eating flagged, servants gathered up the bowls and plates, and the performers dispersed.

The lord's chamberlain, Yasutoki, stood up from his place on Tsunetomo's right, held aloft a gong, and struck it three times.

Conversation ceased by the third percussion.

Lord Tsunetomo raised his voice. "There has been much talk of the barbarian invaders and the stroke of fortune that destroyed their fleet. It is true that the gods smiled on us that day, or it would have gone much worse for us. The men of Kyushu suffered many defeats that day. The Mongol ways of battle were unfamiliar, dishonorable. They put us back on our heels. But here is something that needs to be said again and again: They blackened our eyes, but we *held*. They cut us, and we *held*. They pierced us with storms of arrows, but we *held!* And then we struck back, and contained them until the power of the gods could do its work. This could not have happened without deeds of bravery and prowess that will soon become legendary. Songs will be sung about how the Wolves of Kyushu caught the invaders in their teeth and crushed them."

Several of the men raised fists and howled, to great rounds of laughter and applause.

"I am fortunate indeed to have so many of the fiercest wolves here before me on this night of celebration, where we look to the coming year. The Mongols might not come again this year, or the next, but there is one thing certain—they *will* come. Next time, we will be ready, and the gods will smile and know there is nothing left for them to do but sit back and watch us destroy the barbarians."

This brought another round of howls and applause.

"The Shogun knows there are heroes among us, and he wants us to reward them. It is only meet and right to thank them. I have here a list of those who distinguished themselves during the fighting. If your name is called, come forward and receive your reward. If your name is not called, recognize that it may be your turn next time, if you can rise to the deeds of your valiant brothers."

Tsunetomo unfurled a scroll and began to read the list of names, along with the deeds that distinguished them. First upon it were Captain Tsunemori and Captain Yoshimura, who had organized the remnants of fleeing troops and marshaled counterattacks. Each left his respective seat and went to kneel before Lord Tsunetomo. He gave them each a carefully wrapped packet of rice paper, which they accepted with great humility.

The entire crowd waited in silence and solemnity as the names were read. Ishitaka was among them, and tears of joy were in his eyes as he accepted the packet from his uncle, who extolled his bravery in the scout force where he had been gravely wounded, the scout force in which Ken'ishi had found himself the leader. A dozen more names were read, including Sergeant Hiromasa for holding a strategic bridge through Hakata in the face of waves of enemy attack. Hiromasa approached the dais like a swaggering block of granite and accepted his reward with taciturn gravity.

"Ken'ishi," Tsunetomo called. "For slaying five Mongol scouts, for saving the life of Otomo no Ishitaka and the others of his unit, and for killing more than a score of the barbarians singlehandedly in the streets of Hakozaki."

Ken'ishi's heart leaped. He had not dared hope to be recognized here. He stood, and felt his legs turn to wood at the thought of approaching the dais where Kazuko sat, demure and quiet, without a trace of emotion on her face. Weaving through the crowd, he feared his thrashing heart might break free of his ribs. Scores of eyes followed him, wide with amazement at his exploits. Sweat formed on his face. Voices whispered around him.

Ken'ishi kept his gaze downcast. He did not glance at Kazuko, but she remained in his peripheral vision. If she glanced at him, he did not see it. Tsunetomo offered the packet and he accepted it, feeling a lump in his throat choking off his breath. He pressed his forehead to the ground, spun, and retreated, his insides churning. With every step, anger grew in him at her utter indifference. She had treated him like a common stranger. But if the note had been from her, how must she be feeling that he had not come? How could he be angry with her, when the cost for her would just as high as for him? His emotions whipped into a storm of confusion.

He returned to his seat among the men of Barrack Six, where Michizane and others clapped him on the back and raised their cups in honor. Even Ushihara, sullen as he was, raised a cup to Ken'ishi.

Ken'ishi and Ushihara had not spoken since their flogging, except to give and receive orders during drill. Ushihara's furtive glances caused whispers from the *kami*, but Ken'ishi did not know what to do with him, other than to treat it all as a past unworthy of worry. Ushihara had never thanked Ken'ishi for taking half the strokes, but he seemed embarrassed about it. As long as Ushihara caused no more trouble, Ken'ishi saw no reason to think poorly of him. Ushihara earnestly applied himself to weapons and marching drills, even though he lacked agility.

Finally Lord Tsunetomo folded up his list and said, "I am honored by your service. I will strive to be worthy of it. And now, good night to all. May your revels please the *kami* and bring us good fortune in the coming year."

Servants returned bearing baskets of fresh *onigiri*, rice balls stuffed with pickled plums and wrapped in sheets of *nori*. They distributed several of these to each of the men.

With heads swimming from *saké*, Lord Tsunetomo's retainers dispersed. Some of the men of Barrack Six returned there, while others headed down into the town to join the villagers' celebration.

Ken'ishi knew not what to expect when he opened the packet. Inside he found a series of documents.

First was a certificate of ownership for a trained stallion, bred on the slopes of Mount Aso. He thought back to Thunder, the stallion he had befriended during the invasion. They had fought together against the invaders, and nearly died together upon the tusks of a wild boar in the forest. Having to put down the brave stallion, mortally wounded as he was, had been a terrible thing.

Second was a certificate to an account in Ken'ishi's name in Lord Tsunetomo's treasury. The account held one hundred pieces of gold, available for him to use however he saw fit. He had never conceived he would possess such a sum. In truth, he had no idea what to do with so much money.

And lastly, there was a letter of personal thanks from Captain Tsunemori for saving Ishitaka's life. Ken'ishi's face warmed with a mix of pride and embarrassment at the praise heaped upon him.

Until he began to fold it all back up together.

It was then he spotted the innocuous slip of paper tucked between Tsunemori's letter and the wrapping. On the paper, another poem brushed in the same graceful hand as before.

At the Sanmon Gate, pricked by greed,
At the Sanmon Gate, haunted by hate,
At the Sanmon Gate, drowning in foolishness,
The nightingale awaits the moon
But it does not come.
When it deigns to appear
Its glow does not touch her
At the Sanmon Gate

Ken'ishi crumpled up the note, approached the brazier, but stopped himself from throwing the note in. It hung there in his fist, fingers locked around it. The men of Barrack Six bustled around him, sang songs.

He did not need to read the note again. The words still blazed in his memory, brighter than the coals before him. For a long time, he stood there and chewed on the words. *Pricked by greed, haunted by hate, drowning in foolishness.* Greed, hate, and foolishness, the three sins absolved by passing through the gate.

When the heat from the coals stung his fist, he pulled it back and thrust the paper into his robes. He sucked the reddened skin of his knuckles.

With a bellyful of too much revelry, he unfolded his futon atop his bunk. As mechanically as a mill wheel, he climbed into the bunk above Michizane and lay atop his blanket, staring at the ceiling.

The coals dimmed to a dull orange, deepening the shadows. A chorus of snores rose. His eyes would not close. His stomach, so full from the lavish feast, roiled and clenched. Too many thoughts. Too many uncertainties. Too many injustices. Did she hate him? Did she think him cruel?

He sat up in his bunk. There was something he must do if he wanted to sleep ever again.

If I thought I could get
   away
And come to you,
Ten thousand miles
   would be like one mile.
But we are both in the
   same city
And I dare not see you,
And a mile is longer than a
   million miles.
   —*The Love Poems of Marichiko*

Ken'ishi sat on the stone in the orchard and placed two warmed onigiri beside him. Then he poured a cup of warm saké and placed that beside the rice balls. Faint wisps of steam rose from the saké and onigiri, lifting into the night breeze.

And thus, he waited. Occasionally he fanned the food and drink into the breeze.

In the distance, a strange howl echoed and moved away, like the cry of a lost soul. Its bereft keening sent a chill up his spine, until the sound disappeared among the black slopes of the mountains.

"You know me too well, old sot," said the *tanuki*.

Ken'ishi jumped.

"A warrior should hone his alertness, else he lose his head." Hage sat back on his haunches, *onigiri* clutched between his front paws. He took a luxuriant sniff and then an enormous bite.

"I need your help."

"What is it?" said Hage, cheeks bulging with rice. "Do you require another woman bewitched?"

"No—"

"I met her last night, you know. She was here. Probably pining for you. Foolish girl."

"I may well be the greater fool. You must help me get inside the keep. I must give her a message."

Hage sighed and finished chewing his mouthful. He put down the rice ball, took up the cup of *saké* in both paws, and drained it in one gulp. He burped and held the cup aloft. Ken'ishi refilled it for him.

"Old sot, normally I would give you a shove toward such a woman, loins foremost, but even a randy old badger such as I can see great danger here. What are you going to do?"

"I must speak to her."

"And what are you going to say?"

"I-I don't know."

"'Tis frightful fire you're playing with."

"Yes, Sensei."

"I must think about this. Allow me to finish these delightful *onigiri*, and I will give you my answer."

Ken'ishi sat listening to Hage's little jaws chomping and licking, the small grunts of satisfaction, filling the *saké* cup when it was raised, trying to gauge the *tanuki*'s response from the tenor of his noises.

Finally, Hage took a deep breath and settled himself. "Very well. I will help you." He burped again, and his furry jewel sack swelled between his rear legs until it raised him from the earth. He balanced perfectly upon it. "Give me your hand."

Ken'ishi extended his hand, and Hage took it in his front paw. A crackle of lightning passed between them, coursing through him from the skin of his fingertips to the deepest bones of his hips and thighs. Ripples washed through the tiny hairs all over him. His skin smoothed and softened. Parts of him plumped and rounded. Others shrank until they disappeared. His hair lengthened and fell around his face, down his back. His robes changed to the coarser weave of a servant's, but with festive pink camellia blossoms woven into the fabric. His feet and hands became small and dainty.

"You do make a fine-looking woman." Hage grinned with satisfaction.

"Sensei—!" Hage had turned him into a woman once before, but only for a moment. The loss of physical strength, of stature, of power sent his spirit into a brief panic.

"No arguments this time! You have until sunrise."

Yasutoki prowled the halls of the castle with a small lamp in hand, as he often did when his mind would not settle. Echoing among the polished wood floors, latticed rice paper walls, heavy wood ceiling beams, the narrow staircases of this great edifice, were sounds of continuing revelry. In their modest chambers, the servants were still drinking and singing to small skin drums and bamboo flutes. Walking allowed his mind to fall still, wherein he could sort and weave threads of information and possibility. The distractions of the servants did not bother him. If he wanted absolute silence, he would descend into the earthen storerooms built into the castle's foundations.

Seeing Ken'ishi there at the banquet, all hale and strong again after being tortured and starved into a skeletal shadow of his former self, had pleased Yasutoki. The man had extraordinary powers of recuperation—and the luck of the gods—to be standing there tonight before Lord Tsunetomo and accepting such generous gifts. After everything the *ronin* had suffered at the ministrations of Goumonshi the torturer, Ken'ishi had been able to recover in time not only to defeat Masoku and steal back Silver Crane, but also to join the battle against the invaders. Extraordinary indeed.

Green Tiger would never be able to recruit him. Yasutoki knew that now. Ken'ishi would never bend. But could he be recruited by Yasutoki? And the question still remained: how had he first acquired Silver Crane? From his father, he said. But who was Ken'ishi's father, and how had *he* come by the sword?

A furtive step in the hallway ahead of him caught his attention. A servant girl rounded the corner, carrying a tray and a teapot.

Yasutoki raised an eyebrow. She was strikingly pretty for a lowborn girl, dressed in a fetching *kimono* woven with delicate pink camellia flowers. She was as pretty as she was familiar, but he could not remember seeing her before. As he occasionally availed himself of the pleasures of the young servant girls, he would have noticed this one.

Spotting him, the girl started, and turned away.

"Stop," he said. "Turn around."

"I am sorry, Yasutoki-*sama*," she said with a deep bow. "You... you startled me. I must take this special tea to Lady Otomo."

"I have not seen you before. What is your name?"

She hesitated, eyes downcast. "Oiwa, Lord."

A stolid, robust peasant woman's name, and this lithe, pretty thing was none of that. Clearly, her parents had been among the less imaginative. "Come here."

Others might not have noticed her steel herself, but Yasutoki had made a life-long study of reading people as if they were calligraphy on a scroll.

"Is something wrong, Lord?" she said.

"How long have you worked in the castle?"

"About a week. My lady added me to the staff in preparation for the New Year celebrations."

"Why have I not seen you before? You are very pretty."

Her cheeks flamed scarlet, and she tensed. "Begging my lord's pardon, but I have seen you before. I knew you instantly. Perhaps you *have* seen me before."

"You are indeed so familiar. Have you a brother?"

"No, Lord."

Yasutoki approached her. He would enjoy a bit of feminine distraction tonight.

He could not visit Tiger Lily tonight. Besides, in the last few days, she had been behaving strangely. He wondered if some aspect of working in the Roasted Acorn disagreed with her. She moved to obey a heartbeat less quickly. After the last two occasions when he bedded her, she had turned sullen and taciturn. In Hakata, she had embraced her life as his flesh puppet, but here, something was changing. Perhaps it was because she did not live in his house. With odious Hatsumi out of the way, his reason for keeping Tiger Lily hidden away had disappeared. Perhaps it was time to bring her into the castle. Would she not make a splendid replacement for Hatsumi? It could be an incredible stroke of fortune for him to replace the hag with one of his most loyal playthings.

He began to circle Oiwa, admiring her shape and her grace, the curve of her soft neck. He slid a hand up the back of her leg to cup her buttock.

She gasped and tensed. Her gaze flashed back at him, but it was not with fear. It was anger, quickly squelched by submissiveness. "Please, Lord..." Her voice trembled. "My lady awaits the tea." Her hands clenched the black lacquered tray.

He smiled. This one had spirit. He considered how he should respond. Should he break her immediately? Or should he toy with her for a while?

He stood before her, cupped her chin in his hand, and raised her gaze to meet his. "We must not keep the Lady Otomo waiting. When you have delivered your tea, you will come to my quarters."

What happened next was the strangest series of moments he could recall. First of all, her eyes held no fear. He had never encountered any female whose gaze did not betray a number of closely nursed fears. Being the weaker sex and at the mercy of men, none but the most extraordinary women managed to hold any control over their lives. This girl looked at him as a man would, as an equal.

Second, the moment he lowered the tone of his voice to harness its authoritative power and looked down into her eyes, he saw recognition bloom in them, then a flash of shock, then a blazing roar of suppressed fury.

He drew back, seized her chin, and studied her face. "Do I know you?"

At that moment, two castle guards rounded the corner, and froze in deep bows. "Apologies, Yasutoki-*sama*."

Then she twisted her face out of his hand and looked back at her tray, trembling with something that was not fear. "May I go, Yasutoki-*sama*? I swear on my honor...that I will find you."

What a strange thing for a woman to say. "You may go. I will await your return."

She bowed. "Yes, Lord." Her face now was strangely white, with flushed spots on each cheek. Then she hurried away, the tea pot clattering on the tray.

As he watched her go, her reaction, her recognition of him wormed into his thoughts and lodged there. Some stark realization had struck her in that moment. But how was it then that he could not remember her at all? He would have recalled a girl so comely.

Were it not for the guards' presence, he would have halted her. In any case, he would have those answers when she came to his chamber. And if she failed to obey, she would rue that failure.

Nothing in the world is
    worth
One sixteenth part of the
    love
Which sets free our
    hearts.
Just as the morning star
    in
The dark before dawn
Lights up the world with its
    ray,
So love shines in our hearts
    and
Fills us with glory.
            —*The Love Poems of*
                Marichiko

Kazuko held the seashell for a long time, the meticulously painted samurai on the interior of the shell seeming to perform the movements of a dance. The shell's mother-of-pearl glowed in the lamplight, and her fingers stroked its milky smoothness, so gently sliding over the faint ridges of paint that formed the samurai's face.

Lady Yukino cleared her throat. "Which shell do you have?"

Her three handmaidens shifted in their places around the beautifully woven silk cloth, where lay several other shells face-down. Beside the cloth sat two elegantly lacquered and gilded buckets, both filled with more shells waiting to be drawn.

Kazuko blinked and wondered how long she had been lost in her own mind. She laid the palm-sized shell on the silk. "A proud, dashing warrior."

One of the handmaidens clapped her hands with gentle glee. "Oh! I know where the match is, my lady!"

Kazuko knew the matching shell to which the handmaiden referred, a painting of a demure, noble maiden, awaiting her lover's return under *sakura* branches. Instead, she reached across nearer to where Lady Yukino sat and turned over the image of an *oni* about to be vanquished. "This one." The two shells placed side-by-side formed the picture of the samurai facing the fearsome demon in a battle of life and death.

A handmaiden said, "Forgive me, my lady, but is the proper match for the *oni* not the Buddha, defeating evil through kindness and compassion?"

Lady Yukino smiled faintly. "An appropriate match for Lady Kazuko." The rules of *kai-awase* allowed the players to form their own associations.

Everybody knew how Kazuko had been saved from Hakamadare by a *ronin* who happened along at the critical moment. She had told none of them his name.

"Of course, my lady," the handmaiden said, bowing.

The game went on, with each of them taking turns drawing from the containers and seeking matches from there, or from the shells already in play.

Kazuko's hand stroked the shell before her, the image of the fierce, proud samurai, while the other women tittered and chatted.

The shadow of a servant in the hallway darkened the rice-paper wall. A light knock sounded at the door.

"Tea, my lady," came a servant girl's voice.

"I did not request any," she said absently.

"Oh, but tea would be lovely now," Lady Yukino said, beaming. "I would love something to warm these old bones."

"My lady!" said one of the handmaidens, "You are not old!"

"Bring the tea," Kazuko said.

The servant girl slid the door open and brought in a tray. "I am sorry! I did not know you had guests."

"Then who sent the tea?" Kazuko asked. She had never seen this girl before. There was a powerful familiarity in the servant's face. Kazuko had also never seen a servant dressed in such a pretty robe before, woven with delicate pink camellia blossoms. It was not the kind of fabric within the means of a servant.

"The servants, my lady. Offering you thanks for being such a good mistress."

"Are you new here?" she asked.

"Yes, my lady."

"Where do you come from? Your accent is...unique." Kazuko had heard its like only once before.

"I am far from home, my lady. Please, the tea. I promise to return with more for your guests."

"How did you come into service here? Did Yasutoki find you?" Her voice took on a suspicious edge. As the overseer of the daily workings of the castle, Yasutoki always seemed to hire the prettiest servant girls, regardless of their competence. His motivations had more to do with his carnal pleasures.

"Yes, my lady. Have I displeased you?"

Kazuko sighed. "Bring more tea and all will be well."

"Yes, my lady." The girl pressed her forehead to the *tatami* and departed with peculiar haste.

Kazuko said, "I will pour for you first, Lady Yukino."

"You are too gracious, little sister," Yukino said with real affection.

Kazuko took up the teapot and poured a cup of emerald green tea. Tucked between the pot and the cup was a slip of folded paper. She offered the cup to Lady Yukino, then picked up the paper.

Written on it in charcoal, in a rough hand, was a poem.

The moon walks too far below
The Lady of the Stars
To heed her call.
He cannot reach her.
His path is marked.
Her voice is law.

The Sanmon Gate is where
Heaven and Earth might meet
The next time
Day and night greet.

"What is it?" Lady Yukino said, sipping her tea.

Kazuko's hand was trembling. "It is...a poem from my husband."

A handmaiden clapped her hands and bounced where she sat. "Oh, how romantic! Look how she is overcome with emotion! Oh, my lady, your beauty has inspired him!"

Kazuko smiled and cleared her throat. "So it seems." She slipped the paper into her robes. "Well, whose turn is it?" She focused her attention on the shells, avoiding the gentle pressure of Lady Yukino's gaze.

The most difficult part was the waiting. "Oiwa" would never again appear in the halls of the castle. She would be a ghost, a curiosity, an enigma to which only Ken'ishi would ever know the explanation. He did not dare return to Barrack Six in his womanly guise, so he slipped out of the castle in the midst of the revelries and made his way through town to the temple.

But he had no coat or blanket and the winter night was cold, so he slipped into the central temple. The golden glow of the Buddha filled the alcove, painted with candlelight. The Buddha's eyes radiated kindness, and seemed to watch Oiwa as she knelt there and prayed.

It was a peculiar sensation, having nothing hanging between her thighs, and soft, sensitive mounds on her chest that her arms continually bumped. Damn Hage for the extra-plump bosom.

Walking across town to the temple had been frightening. Her vulnerability to the crowds of drunken men meandering the town had been a stark fear. Hage had not seen fit to provide Oiwa any weapons. A peasant girl with so much as a dagger would rouse instant suspicion.

It was the bit of shocking new knowledge, however, that was most perilous. Green Tiger was alive and well, and serving as chamberlain to Ken'ishi's new master!

Ken'ishi had never seen anything of Green Tiger's face except the eyes, but that was enough. There was no question, no mistake. In the

eyes, in the voice, in the manner that he had used to try to intimidate
Oiwa, Green Tiger had revealed himself. What could be done about
it? Yasutoki was a high-ranked member of the Otomo clan, one of
Lord Tsunetomo's most trusted vassals. He could not be accused by a
low-ranked samurai, only by someone of comparable or higher rank,
and then the testimony of witnesses must be substantial. Of that,
Ken'ishi had none. He could attack Yasutoki outright, attempt to kill
him, but the most likely outcome, even if he was successful, was that
he would forfeit his own life for the murder of a high-ranked Otomo
vassal. Would his death be worth it to rid the world of a monster
like Green Tiger? Could he stalk Yasutoki on some excursion and
kill him when he was vulnerable? Ken'ishi was no assassin. Yasutoki
was no warrior who could be challenged to a duel of honor. The
difference in their rank meant that Ken'ishi simply could not touch
him.

When his mind had exhausted itself on Green Tiger, it churned
onto what he would say if Kazuko appeared. Since their parting, he
had had so many conversations with her in his mind, some of them
angry, some recriminatory, others because he wanted to show her
something, or tell her about something. She had walked his dreams
in a hundred different forms. When he had taken up with Kiosé,
such thoughts had diminished, but never disappeared. He had often
wondered if Kazuko would approve of him, think well of him, or
help him if he were in dire need. And so much of the last year had
been the direst of need. In his darkest moments, his thoughts had
gone to Kazuko, not Kiosé.

But this was all tiresome, well-trod ground.

Little Oiwa huddled there before the Buddha on the polished
wooden floor of the temple, warming her hands over candles and
rubbing warmth back into the rest of her.

Her eyes felt full of sand by the time the sky began to gray. She
wanted nothing more than to sleep, but there would be none of that.
Not until after.

She was tired of admonishments and danger. This all had to end,
or she could not go on. Ken'ishi might as well become *ronin* again
and flee to Shikoku or Honshu, where the Otomo clan could not
reach. But running away was the most dishonorable of paths. When
could he ever stop running then? He had spent too much of his life

running.

It all had to end. Somehow.

Here in the temple, wearing this female form, Ken'ishi entreated the gods to lift the burden of death from his soul. There were too many deaths haunting him. But had he not done only what he must? He had not been cruel, or vicious, or unjust to the barbarians he had slain. He had done only what men must do in war; he had protected his comrades and fought the enemy.

In the pre-dawn stillness, monks stirred from their slumber and entered the temple for their morning prayers and chants and meditation. They greeted her with warm smiles and asked if she would like anything to eat. One of them draped a blanket over her shoulders, and it was one of the most welcome kindnesses Ken'ishi could remember. Such kindnesses were few in a world where the currency was strength and prowess. Ken'ishi expected them to ask questions about why they found a woman alone in their temple, but there were none.

With dawn drawing nigh, Oiwa thanked the monks for their compassion and ventured out to the Sanmon Gate, where she waited, wondering if Kazuko would find a way to come.

After a time, a gray shadow hurried up the long series of steps, a woman, judging by her shape and gait, not dressed in the rich robes of a lady, but in the threadbare tatters of a desperately poor peasant. Soot besmirched her face and hands.

Breath heaving, she rushed to the level of the first gate, the Somon Gate, and ran through it, the pale beads of her eyes wide.

Spotting Oiwa there, standing near the gate, wrapped in a blanket, the gasping woman stopped short. "Oh. It is you." Kazuko's beauty shone through the soot like the breathing coals of a forge. "I thought..."

Oiwa swallowed hard. "You were right to come. I'm glad you're here, although I'm afraid we won't have much time to talk."

"Who are you?"

"We have...a mutual friend. You know who I speak of."

A flurry of emotions flashed across Kazuko's face. "Are you...his lover? His wife?" There was a forlorn bitterness in her voice.

Oiwa shook her head. "No. Would you prefer that I was?"

"No."

"Is that all? No?"

"What would he have me say? We are both slaves to our duty. We are not free to love whom we will." Kazuko peered around the area, into the bushes, as if wondering if someone was listening. "Where is he?"

"He'll be here soon." Oiwa's breath made a steaming pennant into the brightening morning. "Tell me, my lady. What would you have him do? If it could be anything in the world."

Kazuko's brow furrowed for a long moment, then smoothed again. "I would wish him to serve as befits the heroes of legend, because that is what I think he would want. I want for him everything that befits a warrior's dreams. Strength, honor, glory. If it were within my power, I would make him the greatest general in the world or the most renowned swordmaster, whichever is his wish. I would give him the moon and stars."

"But you would not give him your heart."

"He already has that." The sigh that came out of her was long and shuddering. "But I cannot give him the rest of me. That belongs to someone else. And if my husband were a cruel man, a vicious man, a slothful man, a foolish man, a greedy man, any of those things, then putting aside my duty would be easier. But he is none of those things. My husband deserves better than I am. So I aspire to be worthy of him. But what about Ken'ishi? What would he have *me* do, if it could be anything in the world?"

"He would have you do what honor demands. Because while the love is great between you, to succumb to its temptations would make you unworthy of it. He loves the lady not just for the beauty of her face, but the beauty in her heart, which shines out of her like the moon behind clouds. He loves her for her strength and honor. But if she joins her dew with his, thus forsaking her husband, both of them become unworthy of the lord who trusts them. In his darkest moments, he dreams of taking you away to China, as you once suggested."

Kazuko's face flushed behind the soot as she gasped. "How is it that you know this? I have told no one of the words we spoke together...that night. Not even my handmaid Hatsumi, who has been like my sister since I was a little girl. What are you to him?"

"I am the only woman in the world who knows him better than

you."

"But you are not lovers?"

"No."

"Has he...loved anyone else?"

The sky was shifting from purple to red.

"There was another. But she is dead now. They had a son. Killed by the barbarians."

Kazuko sat on the porch surrounding the gate, stricken, tears bursting. "Oh, that is a pity. How terrible for him. To lose a son so cruelly... When some of us want one so desperately."

A ray of sunlight touched the topmost branches of the massive camphor tree nearby.

Kazuko sniffed and wiped her eyes. "And what of his dog? He had the cutest, smartest dog with him. Akao was his name. He looked at me with more wisdom than many human beings I have met."

"Akao was killed, three years ago. He saved...four lives that night, facing down an *oni*. He was so brave, so valiant. I shall never encounter his equal again."

"You knew him even back th—?" Kazuko cut off her own question.

Oiwa's voice had begun to deepen.

The camellia robe was now the garb of a man, and legs and arms were lengthening to fit it, shoulders thickening.

A quiet, astonished "ohhh..." escaped from Kazuko's open mouth.

Hands hardened. Jaw squared. Chest broadened.

Kazuko swallowed hard, comprehension filling her face, and her voice was a mere whisper. "How...?"

"A gift from Hage."

"Who is Hage? A *shugenja*, that he can make you change form?"

"A *tanuki*." Ken'ishi could not help but smile at how foolish it sounded.

"Oh, him." She smiled at a memory. "How is it that you have such interesting friends?"

"I am not certain I can call him a friend. Mostly I think I amuse him."

"I have no friends at all." As soon as she uttered the words, she seemed to realize how pitiful they sounded. "But it matters little.

Sometimes all that can be hoped is that nobody wishes one ill."

Seeing her there, radiant in spite of her exhaustion and disguise, remembering the way she had felt in his arms, remembering every curve of her breasts and thighs, every swoop of her soft belly, every curl of petal-soft down between her legs, the taste of her, the feel of her, the smell of her, brought it all roaring to life again.

But the chasm between them yawned wider than ever. And to cross it—as they had done on the night of her betrothal—meant dishonor and death.

"I will tell you what I will do," Ken'ishi said.

Looking up at him, her cheeks glistened with tears, her eyes brimmed with silent entreaty.

He said, "You said that I have your heart. I tell you now and for all time that you have mine. I shall serve you with a loyalty born of that love, in the only way I can. We shall remain worthy of our lord, faithful to our duty, and loyal to the love we share." He knelt before her, pressed his forehead to the ground at her feet, then straightened again. "By my sword, by my blood, by all the strength in me, I am yours, Lady Kazuko. Until the end."

"It is a fact that fish will not live where the water is too clear. But if there is duckweed or something, the fish will hide under its shadow and thrive. Thus, the lower classes will live in tranquility if certain matters are a bit overlooked or left unheard. This fact should be understood with regard to people's conduct."
—*Hagakure, Book of the Samurai*

"There is no doubt, Lord," Ushihara said. "The sword he bears is the one you're after."

The peasant who would become samurai knelt before Yasutoki in his office. On this, the third day of New Year festivities, all the warriors were still at liberty, so there was little questioning of movements and associations.

Yasutoki had already surmised this, but it was time to stroke his new pet. "You have done well, *Sir* Ushihara." He laid a tightly wrapped paper bundle, stamped with the *mon* of the Otomo clan and the character *gin*, for silver, before Ushihara.

Ushihara's eyes bulged. His hands trembled as he reached for the bundle. Yasutoki thought for a moment that the man might drool.

"Do I have your attention now, Sir Ushihara?"

"Yes, Lord!"

"I can be as generous to those loyal to me as I am cruel to those who fail me."

"Yes, Lord!"

"And I shall sweeten the cup. Take this slip to the Roasted Acorn and give it to the proprietor." Yasutoki produced a rice paper card from a drawer in his bureau. On the card were written the three characters that made up the word *whore,* stamped with an official seal.

"What's it for?" Ushihara said.

Yasutoki kept his breath steady. Maintaining patience for illiterates taxed him. "He will bring you a whore. It would be a pity for you to spend all of that silver right away. Enjoy yourself."

Ushihara's face beamed. "Thank you, Lord! Thank you!" He pressed his forehead to the floor over and over.

"You may go."

Ushihara scooped up the bundle of coins, clutched them in both hands, and retreated.

After Ushihara had gone, a woman's phlegmatic voice came from the doorway. "You called for me, Yasutoki-*sama*."

"Come, Oguri," Yasutoki said.

The servant woman bowed her way in. Decades of hard work had slumped Oguri's shoulders, callused her hands, grayed her hair. A broad mouth, thick lips, and deeply lined features gave her the appearance of an old, wrinkled frog. She knelt before him. "What do you require?"

"There is a new servant in the castle. I wish to interview her. Her name is Oiwa."

"Eh? Forgive me, Lord, but there have been no new servants since the eighth month."

"But I saw her last night. She was carrying a tea service for Lady Kazuko. She claimed her name was Oiwa."

Oguri rubbed a bit of sweat from her wrinkled brow. "Very sorry, Lord. But there is no one by that name in the castle's employ."

A spy? This unexpected turn put a cold blade against his spine. "She was wearing a robe with pink camellia flowers. Very pretty." A whore from town smuggled into the castle? Not implausible. But by whom? Tsunetomo was not a man given to bedding whores and tavern girls. Such clandestine dealings without Yasutoki's knowledge was an affront soon to be corrected.

"I did not see her, my lord," Oguri said. "Shall I ask around?"

"Yes. And report back to me by the end of the day."

Oguri bowed her way out.

Now, perhaps he could finish some work—

A figure filled his door and strode in without a word or the slightest gesture of respect. Yasutoki opened his mouth to unleash a torrent of recrimination, but then reached for the *shuriken* concealed in his sleeve.

Ken'ishi slammed the door shut behind him. He was armed with the *tachi* Yasutoki knew so well hanging from his *obi*.

The *bushi* stood over him, his eyes dark and full of purpose. "I know who you are."

Yasutoki gauged the distance between them. His office was small enough that the tip of Silver Crane's blade could reach him with the draw. But if Ken'ishi intended to attack, he would have already done so. Yasutoki remained poised to act, like a spring cranked to highest tension, a handful of poisoned *shuriken* in his right hand, concealed within his sleeve. "And I know who *you* are."

Their eyes met like spear points clashing, tip on tip. Yasutoki held his gaze. "I must commend you on your escape. No one else has ever managed it. Sit. We must talk."

Ken'ishi gripped the hilt of Silver Crane. He did not sit. "Is this what you've been looking for? Again?"

Gauging the distance, Yasutoki knew the warrior could draw and strike him down almost instantaneously.

"What are you going to do with that?" Yasutoki nodded at the *tachi*.

"You are a fool to employ Ushihara. The man is as subtle as a three-legged ox."

Yasutoki allowed a small smile. "One uses the tools at one's disposal. How were you able to enter the castle armed? Only guards are permitted weapons. If you are caught, it could mean your head."

"My head is less important than why I am here."

"What do you intend to do? Strike me down? That would be most unwise."

Ken'ishi's hand had not yet left his hilt. "Leave the castle now. Beg Lord Tsunetomo's forgiveness for abandoning his service and take your vows as a monk. Go into retirement."

"Are you planning to take your revenge if I refuse? You see, I know who *you* are, Ken'ishi the Oni-Slayer. Ken'ishi, the *ronin* who murdered Nishimuta no Takenaga, a duly appointed constable of the Nishimuta clan. Ken'ishi the *ronin* who saved Nishimuta no Kazuko from the bandit Hakamadare, thus depriving me of a valuable associate, I might add. The same *ronin* who despoiled the honor of the girl betrothed to Lord Otomo no Tsunetomo."

Ken'ishi's eyebrows jumped.

"Oh, yes, I do know about that. I have suspected this moment might come since you appeared on the rolls of Tsunemori's new recruits. Thus, I have written a letter that describes in detail everything I know about your relationship with Lady Kazuko. I was there to see much of it for myself, you will recall, and I had even more from the lady's servant Hatsumi before she went mad. If anything happens to me, if I am killed by brigands or die of infection from a splinter, this letter will be delivered by someone loyal to me into the hands of Lord Tsunetomo. You are samurai. I do not doubt for a moment that you would spend your life to take your revenge on me. You could do it now. But the more interesting question is whether you care about what happens to our Lady Kazuko. If this knowledge were exposed, her shame and humiliation would be the least of the consequences. Lord Tsunetomo would be within his authority to have her executed. But I have no interest in that. I have no interest in rocking the boat, as they say. Thanks in part to you, I have lost almost everything. The tiger must repair to his cave and lick his wounds."

"I have written a similar letter."

"A bit childish to say, as I doubt that very much. If I allow you to leave this office, however, I do not doubt that you will soon write one."

Ken'ishi scowled. "Or perhaps you're lying. Perhaps no such letter has been written."

"Are you willing to take that chance?" Yasutoki's gaze remained fixed on Ken'ishi's face. If the man's right hand so much as twitched, Yasutoki would send a storm of poisoned blades at his naked face.

Ken'ishi growled, "You tortured me. Imprisoned me. Starved me. The gods would thank me for sending you to Hell."

"Doubtless you're correct. But I don't intend to meet them any time soon."

"If Silver Crane 'disappears' again, the gods themselves will not save you," Ken'ishi said.

"I am content to let you have it. I know now that it was wrong to take it from you. Besides, now I know where to find you if I have need of it."

"I'll never bow to your will."

"But you already have. We are talking, rather than hacking off bits of each other. Do you know that sword's history?"

"I do. But I don't know why it matters so much to you."

Yasutoki considered for a moment. Throughout his life, he had honed the art of weaving secrets and lies in the most advantageous ways. "It belonged to my great-grandfather, Taira no Tomomori, who died at the Battle of Dan-no-Ura, protecting the Emperor Antoku."

Another flash of surprise on Ken'ishi's face.

"You *do* know its history," Yasutoki said. "Then you know it was lost at sea. And yet, somehow, it has been found. It is a treasure of the Taira clan, priceless beyond measure."

"*You* are Taira clan?"

"An illustrious heritage, to be sure, but one that it is no longer expedient to claim. Only those who swore fealty to Minamoto no Yoritomo were allowed to keep their family name. The rest were expunged, but a few, my grandfather, managed to escape into anonymity. So, as you see, the sword has great value to me, both sentimental and monetary. There are those who would pay an emperor's ransom for it. There is a legend as well that the sword grants power to one of Taira blood who wields it."

Thoughts flickered behind Ken'ishi's eyes.

"With that sword," Yasutoki said, "you defeated an *oni,* five Mongols on the road to Dazaifu, and untold dozens more in Hakozaki. That sounds like great power. This inclines me to consider that you might be of Taira blood yourself. You claim no knowledge of your heritage. Your parents were murdered when you were a baby. That may well have been in one of the purges by the Hojo clan to make sure that no scattered seed of the Taira clan ever takes root again. We may well share the same enemies."

Ken'ishi's face quivered with suppressed emotion.

"Now then, as we may well be kinsmen," Yasutoki said, "we must decide what to do. Rather than forcing you to work for me, a proposal to which I know you will *never* agree, I suggest a truce."

"A truce." Ken'ishi spat the word like it was poison.

"Neither of us can kill the other outright, as neither of us relishes the idea of our secrets being exposed. But we are both ambitious, more than willing to kill those in the way of what we want. Perhaps one day you will come to appreciate my powers, as Lord Tsunetomo does."

"Never!"

Yasutoki waved a hand. "As you will. But it is such resolve that makes you powerful. I predict that you will go far in Lord Tsunetomo's employ. If you can manage to keep your secret."

"Stay away from me," Ken'ishi said. "Stay away from her." Then he spun and stalked out of the office.

Yasutoki released his breath slowly, let the tension ease out of him. He had been not at all certain this confrontation would pass without bloodshed. Unfortunately, Yasutoki now had a vulnerability, even if he still held the advantage.

Better still, he now knew the key to moving Ken'ishi, the lever by which to move a mountain.

Kazuko.

SO ENDS THE SIXTH SCROLL

PART II: THE SEVENTH SCROLL

"There is a saying, 'Sever the edge between before and after.' Not ridding the mind of previous moments, allowing traces of the present mind to  remain—both are bad. This means one should cut through the interval between the previous and the present. Its significance is in cutting off the edge between before and after, between now and then. It means not detaining the mind."

—*Takuan Soho, "The Mysterious Record of Immovable Wisdom"*

K en'ishi took a deep breath to still his thundering heart.
 He settled himself into the Void, felt the morning sun and spring breeze on his face, the rigidity of the saddle, the warmth of the horse between his legs, and kicked the flanks of his stallion, Storm. Storm tossed his pale head and thundercloud-colored mane, and leaped forward.

Raising himself in the saddle to steady his aim, Ken'ishi nocked an arrow and drew his bow. Rushing closer was the first diamond-shaped wooden plank, about the size of a breastplate, his target. Storm's hooves pounded the packed earth between the rope fences of the arrow-straight *yabusame* course, picking up speed with each bound.

Since *yabusame* training had begun three months ago, Ken'ishi had practiced from the back of a wooden horse as it rotated in place. Endless repetitions of rising from the saddle in a half-crouch, balancing on taut thighs, clutching the horse's sides with his feet in the stirrups, releasing the reins to draw an arrow from where it was tucked into the back of his *obi*, nocking the arrow as the wooden horse rotated, all unhurried, raising the bow with the arrow, drawing the bow as he pulled it down and rotated his whole body toward the stationary target, releasing the arrow into the target at the precise moment the target passed his arrow point—and missing more often than not. It was all carefully timed—the rotation, the nock, the draw, the release. All was One. All was Void. And then he would nock and draw another arrow, and the target would come around again, and he would fire again.

Today was his first try at horse archery from horseback.

Ken'ishi had fired thousands of arrows from the back of that wooden horse, as his comrades pushed the yoke that rotated the horse, until he could perform the movements in his sleep. In truth, perfect arrow shots filled his dreams, like that of Nasu no Yoichi.

A century before, the Taira clan, in their flight from the Minamoto clan in the Great War, were caught at the edge of the sea, but managed to escape with the Emperor Antoku aboard a great many ships. The Taira clan placed a fan atop the mast of their tallest ship and taunted the Minamoto to shoot it. Nasu no Yoichi rode his horse into the sea as the ships were moving out of range and fired a single arrow straight through the center of the fan. The Minamoto had taken it as a good omen. A month later, the Minamoto overtook Antoku and most of the Taira clan at Dan-no-Ura and slaughtered them.

As Ken'ishi's skill with a bow had put him ahead of most of the men, he was among the first allowed a live run with a real horse. If he succeeded, his reputation and status would grow. If he failed, the shame would be too much to bear, and threaten his standing in Lord Tsunetomo's forces. In five short months, he had gone from a unit leader to sergeant in charge of Barrack Six, replacing Hiromasa, who was promoted and placed in charge of the west quarter, consisting of Barracks Four, Five, and Six.

The first cedar-wood target pounded nearer. Storm charged down the run between the rope fences.

Ken'ishi raised himself in the saddle, released the reins, reached for an arrow, passed it around under his right arm, placed it in the bow, raised the bow, lowered it with the draw, and fired at the target four paces to his left. The *thud* of the arrow into the straw backstop told him he had missed.

Another target, eighty paces ahead. Another arrow. Maintain his place in the Void. Another draw. Another release.

Another *thud*.

The final target rushed nearer. A deep breath. A settling into the quiet. The thunder of Storm's hooves faded. The eyes of his teachers and superiors disappeared. Just as the infinite moments to be found in the Void, the target came, and he had plenty of time to help the arrow to its target. Nock, raise, draw, release.

This time, the sound was not a thud, but the satisfying *crack* of the turnip-shaped arrowhead snapping the cedar-wood target into three pieces.

With immense satisfaction and a tingling calm, Ken'ishi took up the reins again and drew Storm to a halt. He caught himself grinning with joy as he reined his mount and rode back toward the middle of the run, where a dais had been erected, upon which sat Captains Tsunemori and Yoshimura, along with Captain Ishii no Soun and his two assistants, the horse archery instructors.

"Well done, Sergeant Ken'ishi," Tsunemori said. "Few manage to hit a target on their first attempt upon a real horse."

Ken'ishi bowed. "Thank you, Lord."

Captain Soun said, "Wait here and watch the next attempts."

"Yes, Captain," Ken'ishi said.

Storm snorted and tossed his head. His mottled coat was a beautiful pale gray, with dark gray mane and tail. On the day the stallions had been chosen, Ken'ishi had awaited his turn with growing nervousness, certain that someone else would choose the stallion before he had his chance. But when his turn came, he did not hesitate to name this horse as his reward. In the months since, they had gotten to know each other well.

Ken'ishi leaned over to Storm's ear and whispered, "If you stop fussing, I'll see to it you get extra brushing later."

"Bah!" the horse snorted. "All this standing around chafes me! I want to run!"

"Behave for now," Ken'ishi said. "We shall run again soon enough."

Ken'ishi's comrades had mostly grown accustomed to his way with animals, the way he appeared to speak to them with mutual understanding, but this still resulted in puzzled looks.

Nine more riders from Ken'ishi's training group made their runs. Seven of them failed to hit the target at all. Of the other two, one hit a single target, the other hit two.

Page boys replaced the broken targets, and the riders went through their runs again. So it went throughout that morning.

In the rice fields surrounding the town, the paddies had been flooded and the seedlings planted. The patches of still water caught the sunlight like mirrors, stippled with perfect rows of spindly rice stalks. Peasants worked irrigation machines that carried water up the mountain slopes to terraced fields. The land bloomed again, lush and vibrant with a hundred shades of green. Perhaps a *ri* distant, the castle's white walls caught the sun like chalk, a thing of beauty and power.

As men and horses rested with the midday meal, a rider came hurtling down from town and met the officers within their cloth compound. Immediately after, Tsunemori and Yoshimura departed with the messenger, leaving Ken'ishi and the others to continue their training.

By the end of the day, the saddle had turned Ken'ishi's backside into a mass of tender sores, and his legs felt like overcooked *ramen*.

That evening, Lord Tsunetomo called a meeting of all senior and junior-ranked officers in the castle's hall.

Lord Tsunetomo, Captain Tsunemori, and Yasutoki sat at the head of the room in solemn array.

"We received word today," Lord Tsunetomo said, "that a ship has arrived in port in Murotsu, in Nagato province. The ship bears emissaries from barbarian emperor of China, Khubilai Khan."

Rustles of reaction rippled around the room.

"It has been six months since the invasion. We do not know what missive they bring from their Khan, but they have demanded to speak to the 'king' of our 'small country.'" He spat derision into the last two words. "The emissaries are to be escorted to Kamakura, where the Shogun will hear their message and decide what to do with them. I daresay they will not be welcomed."

Yasutoki cleared his throat and leaned forward. "Begging my lord's pardon, may I offer a humble suggestion?"

"Please do, Lord Yasutoki," Tsunetomo said.

"I should like to offer myself to be your eyes and ears in Kamakura. I would accompany these emissaries and report directly back to you. After all, if you are expected to spearhead the defense efforts, would it not be most useful to receive...unfiltered information?"

Tsunetomo stroked the point of his beard.

Ken'ishi kept his gaze squarely on the back of the man before him. At the sound of Yasutoki's voice, knowledge and hatred roiled in Ken'ishi's guts like molten slag.

Tsunemori's face was tight with distaste. His contempt for Yasutoki was written in broad brush strokes. Did he know Yasutoki's secret? Was he also held to inaction by some dark secret? Did Tsunetomo know? Did he somehow condone the actions of Green Tiger?

Tsunetomo nodded. "A fine idea, Lord Yasutoki. You will depart for Kamakura as soon as preparations are made. Meanwhile, we have also received orders that the Hakata fortifications are to begin within the month. Engineers are en route from the capital. The construction efforts are being coordinated through the office of the Western Defense Commissioner in Dazaifu. Lord Yasutoki, your skills will be missed in this effort, but it is more important that we know what is happening first-hand in Kamakura."

That night, Ken'ishi had drawn guard duty, so he stood at the front gate, clad in armor and holding a spear, listening to the songs of the night creatures around him. The *sakura* in the orchard had shed their exquisite blossoms about ten days prior, and their profusions of new dark leaves now lay bathed in silent moonlight. In the land below, flooded rice fields glowed like sheets of silver, stitched together in a patchwork by the levies and paths among them.

It was the Hour of the Rat, midnight. The man beside him was from Barrack Three, a taciturn fellow, which suited Ken'ishi's temperament just fine. Michizane and Ishitaka both chided Ken'ishi occasionally for his lack of social graces, but he doubted he would ever be comfortable talking for its own sake. He liked silence, and he liked listening to the sounds of night creatures, and he liked that he alone among human beings could catch snatches of understanding. The world was full of life, all of it communicating in a myriad of worlds matching the size of the creatures speaking.

Footsteps from behind him caught his attention. A figure in a basket hat turned his muscles into taut ropes. The last time he had seen a basket hat was on Green Tiger's head.

He barred the way with his spear, and the other guard followed suit. "Who goes there?"

The figure stopped. "Oh, it's you, Ken'ishi. I am Ishitaka."

Ken'ishi and the guard stepped aside. Ishitaka's rank was such they could not challenge his purpose for leaving the castle at such an hour, although they would note on the morning report who came and went. Ken'ishi, however, knew Ishitaka's purpose.

"Sergeant Ken'ishi, may I have a word with you?" Ishitaka said.

"Of course, Lord," Ken'ishi said.

The two of them moved down the hill away from the gate.

Ken'ishi said, "So your parents still forbid it?"

Ishitaka sighed within the basket hat. "To them she will never be anything but a simple tavern wench. But to me, she is the sun, the moon, and the stars!"

Ken'ishi pitied his friend. "I know what it is to love a woman I could not have. But I must caution you. If you think she will ever be more than a lover, you must be prepared for a great deal of trouble. Unless Lady Kazuko is blessed with a son, you are the only male heir of this bloodline. There is talk that Lord Tsunetomo will have to adopt you, or else pass everything to your father. Your marrying a peasant girl would have grave repercussions for the entire clan."

"Don't you think I know that?" Ishitaka snapped, then eased his bitterness. "I am sorry, my friend. Half of my time is filled with thoughts like this, and the other half is spent yearning to return to her arms. I fear I will be torn in two!"

Ken'ishi clasped his shoulder. He knew that feeling too well. "And how does she feel?"

"She is so guarded, but she says she cares for me. When I spill my heart for her like a love-sopped courtier, she just goes quiet, and I would swear I see sadness there."

"Perhaps she sees the possible outcomes if this continues. You might forsake her, and she might be left with a bastard child that you will not claim. Or you will cleave to her, destroy your life, and throw your family into upheaval."

"I know! And every time I think about it... A few weeks ago, I suggested that it would be too painful to continue, that we should end it. She panicked and convinced me to relent. This tells me her love for me is true."

"And what of her father?"

"I have never seen him. She will meet me only on nights when he is gone. But now, I have secured a quiet house in the District Six where we meet."

"District Six. That is near the sword polisher's shop, near the outskirts, yes?"

"Sword polisher? There is no sword polisher in District Six."

"Yes, there is. I met him, just before New Year. He did first-rate work. Very knowledgeable."

Through the grill in the face of the basket hat, Ken'ishi saw Ishitaka's eyes narrow. "In my whole life there has never been a sword polisher in District Six. What is his name?"

"Tametsugu."

"I know of him, but you must be mistaken."

"Why?"

"Tametsugu was a sword polisher of great renown, a treasure of the Otomo clan, as my father said of him. He died when I was a baby."

The hairs on the nape of Ken'ishi's neck stood up.

"I can see that you were quite sure of the name," Ishitaka said. "It seems that you are the center of many strange occurrences." The young man chuckled, but with a touch of uncertainty. "But fear not. Your heart is brave and good. The *kami* will protect you. And now I must go. Good night, my friend."

Ah, bold nightingale
Even before his lordship
You won't mend your
　　song

　　　　　　　—Issa

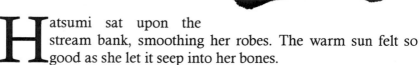

H atsumi sat upon the stream bank, smoothing her robes. The warm sun felt so good as she let it seep into her bones.

The hem of her robes had grown ragged. She would have to see about finding a seamstress to fix it when Kazuko allowed Hatsumi back into the castle. And her clothes needed a good laundering, but she seemed to have so little time for such things. All of her hours seemed to be spent searching for things to eat. The peasants would not share their rice with her, not even millet. The selfish fools seemed to be afraid of her, but she could not fathom why. When she used the same tone on the peasants that she used on the castle servants, they fled rather than obeyed. This angered her. Selfish, ignorant, low-born pigs, all of them.

She opened the sack she had made from the skin of a filthy stray dog foolish enough to expect her to pet it, and rummaged through her remaining food. She had gnawed the monkey skull clean and there was no succulent marrow in a skull, so she tossed it into the river. Monkeys were tasty, but difficult to catch. Nevertheless, she did manage one occasionally. The squirrel had been in her sack too long, so she tossed it aside as well. That left a few bones, the origin of which she could not remember. With a sigh, she pulled one out, crunched the end off, and sucked at the delectable marrow.

Someday, when Kazuko forgave her and let her back into the castle, she would be able to have proper food again. She would eat monkeys only on special occasions. Kazuko would love fresh monkey meat. They squealed so delightfully when one starting biting parts off. But they sometimes scratched at one's eyes, so it was best to start with their little, human-like fingers. The finger bones were small enough to be easily chewable.

Bits of dry pine needles clung to her robe, and she fussed until it was all brushed clean. It was time to replenish her bed with fresh, soft grass. There was a nice patch on the opposite bank, so she slung the sack over her shoulder, crossed the stream, and began to tear out swaths of grass, ignoring clumps of earthy roots still attached to some handfuls. With a nice, big armful, she climbed up the slope to her cave, crawled inside, kicked a few bones and scraps of hair and desiccated skin from the mound where she rested, and freshened her bed.

With a sigh of satisfaction at her handiwork, she considered taking a lovely nap upon it.

Until a scent wafted through the narrow jag of cave entrance.

The scent seemed to take her by the nose, turn her around, and draw her outside. The scent of fresh food on the foot. She peered out and down the forested slope.

With a gust of relief, a woodsman eased his rack full of chopped wood from his back onto the stream bank and sat down upon a stone. His limbs were wiry and tough—probably with more gristle than she liked—but her protuberant belly, hanging between her squatting thighs, rumbled with hunger nevertheless. Gray streaked his hair, but he was not yet an old man. And he carried a hatchet.

Then she shook her head. If she kept eating people, Kazuko would never let her back into the castle. She would be nice to this one. But she must not give away her hiding place. No men had come to kill her lately—she had eluded them, thankfully—but revealing her cave seemed like a bad thing. So she crept out, circled around him while he dangled his feet in the stream. As he rested, munching a rice ball, she approached him from the foliage of the opposite bank.

"Hello?" she called in her sweetest, most plaintive voice. "Is someone there?"

He jumped to his feet, splashing water everywhere. "Who's

there?"

"Oh, no one," she said. "Can you help me? I'm so lost."

He peered into the foliage toward the sound of her voice. "Where are you?"

"I'm behind this bush, but I'm so dirty from being lost in the woods, I cannot bear anyone to see me."

"Where are you from?"

"Hita town."

"Oh, well, that's easy. It's about ten *ri* that way." He pointed down the slope. "How are you so far from home?"

"I traveled to visit my mother in Dazaifu. She is very ill."

"But Dazaifu is that way." He pointed in a different direction.

"I told you, I am lost."

"You must be very lost. Here now, I'm sure it's all right if you come out. I won't hurt you. If your clothes are bit dirty, that's nothing I ain't seen before. My neighbor's wife is a terrible housekeeper, does laundry maybe once a month. I always tell him—"

"You promise you will take me to the road?"

"I'll show you to the road and send you on your way."

"Very well."

She stepped out of the bushes.

Across the stream, his mouth fell open. He snatched up his hatchet and fled, leaving his rack of wood where it lay.

"Where are you going?" she said. "You promised!"

He scrambled up the bank, flinging great clumps of earth and fallen leaves and frenzied gasps behind him. He sounded like a small forest creature.

She leaped across the stream and landed beside him.

"You promised!" she screamed.

He swung his hatchet at her face, but it was a terrible swing, and she dodged easily.

Incoherent protests came out of him, and he swung the hatchet over and over, missing every time.

She squatted back and watched him.

"It's you!" he shrieked, trying to claw his way backward up the stream bank, facing her with the hatchet brandished. "The Wild Woman!"

"Wild woman? I'm a cultured, educated woman, the handmaiden

of a noble lady."

Confusion played across his face. "Get away!"

"You promised to show me to the road! I must go home."

She grabbed him and squeezed until parts of him fell off and he stopped screaming.

"Now, look what you made me do!" She bashed his skull a few times with a rock until it cracked open like a melon. She scooped out some juicy pulp and ate it.

Then she sat down and sobbed for a while, because she could not remember which direction he said Hita town was.

Eventually hunger overcame the bout of sobbing, but at least she had something to eat now. Unfortunately the leftovers would not fit in her sack, but she stuffed as much in there as she could, gorged herself on the rest, patted her overstuffed belly, and then returned to her cave for a long nap. It would be days before she was hungry again.

"A monk cannot fulfill the Buddhist Way if he does not manifest compassion without and persistently store up courage within. And if a warrior does not manifest courage on the  outside and hold enough compassion within his heart to burst his chest, he cannot become a [lord's] retainer. Therefore, the monk pursues courage with the warrior as his model, and the warrior pursues the compassion of the monk."

—*Zen priest Tannen, Hagakure, Book of the Samurai*

A great procession assembled at the gates of the castle as Yasutoki made preparations to depart for Kamakura, home of the *bakufu*. Twelve mounted *yojimbo*, some of the most elite warriors of Tsunetomo's house, including Captain Yamada, captain of the house guard, all clad in their most ornate armor, plus bearers for Yasutoki's palanquin, attendants, and servants, all formed a dual column.

Kazuko watched this from a high window. Yasutoki's presence made the servants fearful and furtive, as if a dark fog permeated the air itself. Perhaps his departure—with Hatsumi gone as well—would allow the castle to breathe again.

The detachment of bodyguards for Yasutoki's journey seemed a bit extravagant, but Yasutoki was the third-ranked man in the largest Otomo house on Kyushu, and Kamakura was a long journey. It was as much about appearances as practical protection. If they traveled overland, the journey would take the procession through domains unfriendly to the Otomo clan. Instead, they had chosen to travel by sea, embarking from Moji to sail east toward Kamakura. A dozen hardened warriors should be enough to defend against the pirates known to haunt the seas around Shikoku and eastward. She did not wish the *yojimbo* harm, but she would not lament any fatal mishap befalling Yasutoki.

"My lady," came the voice of the new valet from a polite distance behind her. "Please forgive the intrusion." Naozane had come from one of the clan's loyal servant families, with ancestors who had served the Otomo for generations.

She faced him.

Naozane said, "There is a woman from Takeshita village who requests an audience with you. I would have conveyed her message to you myself, but she looks very earnest, and says she has news of..." The man had to swallow something to produce the name. "... of Miss Hatsumi."

A chill sickness trickled into her belly. "Very well. See her into the meeting hall."

The steward departed, and Kazuko took a moment to collect herself.

She had wished more than anything that Hatsumi be caught by one of the many search parties, or that she be killed somehow. Every time a search party returned unsuccessful, Kazuko remembered the horror of Hakamadare. Stories filtered in from the countryside about the Wild Woman who stole food and terrorized villagers. She was blamed for several unexplained deaths, but no witnesses still lived. The descriptions of her varied widely. Some said she had horns; others, great gnashing fangs; others, four arms and four legs. It was all so outlandish, except that Kazuko had once seen such a creature with her own eyes. Ever since, she did not like to think about where the boundaries were between truth and fabrication.

In the great hall, she found a middle-aged peasant woman waiting, graying hair tied into a simple bun, wearing simple gray-brown homespun, with hands gnarled and shoulders hunched by labor. At Kazuko's entrance, the peasant woman pressed her forehead to the floor.

Kazuko settled herself on the dais, and Naozane sat between the peasant woman and the dais.

The steward addressed the peasant woman. "You may speak."

"Oh, Lady Otomo," the woman breathed, "your beauty far surpasses the wildest stories!"

"Your kindness does me honor, good woman, but today I more resemble an old *geta*."

"Lady Otomo is too modest."

"What is your name? What is your village?"

"I am Otsugi from Takeshita village. My husband was a woodsman."

"Was?"

The woman's lips trembled. "Yes, my lady. He was...killed."

"Is this why you have come?"

The woman bowed low again. "Yes, my lady. I...I saw *her*!"

"Whom did you see?"

"The Wild Woman! She killed my Shuntaro. And she ate him like a beast!"

Kazuko's memory of Hakamadare biting a great clunk of flesh from the severed arm of one of her *yojimbo* leaped into her mind, and the cold dread in her belly began to froth. "Tell me your story."

"My Shuntaro was gone a little too long. He was a woodsman, as I said, and he was up on the mountain. Night came, and he did not return. I was not too worried right away. Sometimes he liked to fill his rack and go drinking at night after he came back to the village. But he was gone all night, and that was very strange, so I went looking for him. I asked after him all over town, and no one knew of his whereabouts. So I took my brother and we went looking for him up on the mountain. People had been hearing howls up there late, late at night. They said it was the Wild Woman. We looked all up and down the mountain for three days, and..." Her voice choked, but she cleared her throat and recovered. "And then we found him.... We thought it was him. But there was so little.... It was like...what a fox leaves of a rabbit. I thought, this could not be him, this could not be my Shuntaro. But then I saw his rack sitting by the stream. I know it was his rack, because I helped him make it, and he would never just leave it like that."

Kazuko said. "Such a terrible pity! I am very sorry to hear about your husband."

The woman bowed low again, and tears streamed down her cheeks. "He was just a woodsman, my lady, but he was the best man I ever knew."

"What makes you think the Wild Woman is to blame, and not a bear or some other wild creature?" Naozane asked.

The woman's eyes blazed wide. "Because I saw her! You will think my head touched by the gods if I tell you what she looked like, but I *saw* her!"

"What did you see?" Kazuko's heart skipped into a faster rhythm.

"We were there by the riverbank, looking at...everything, when I happened to look up the slope. And I saw this shape looking at me from inside a small cave. I thought, 'Who is that person up there?' And the more I looked, the more I thought the shape looked like a woman, with long hair and such, and fine robes. I know good weaving, my lady, yes, I do. And those clothes were...not peasant clothes. Very soiled, but fine threads and bright colors. The stories about the Wild Woman say..."

"You may speak freely," Kazuko said.

"They say the Wild Woman was your servant who went mad. Some say she was cursed. That's why I came to you, my lady. I thought you would want to know. I know there were searches before, but..."

A pang of guilt shot through Kazuko's breast. "If the Wild Woman had been found, your husband would still be alive. Be assured, the hunt for her will recommence. Takeshita village is far, so I thank you for traveling this far to bring me this tale—"

The woman's eyes bulged again. "But that is not all, my lady! Oh, I pray to all the gods that it were!" Sobs seized her speech.

Naozane opened his mouth to spur her tale onward, but Kazuko raised a hand and shook her head.

When Otsugi regained control of herself. "My poor brother, you see... She...she...came...down..." Sobs wracked her. "In one big jump. Like a monkey jumping from a tree. And...he screamed at me to run, my poor brother did. And...and so...I did. I ran for the road as fast as I could. I thought he would be behind me. But she came out of the sky and landed on him like a hawk on a mouse, squashed him. And I saw her. And she...killed him. And I ran. I *left him there!*" Her barely intelligible words erupted into a keening wail.

Kazuko and Naozane waited quietly, awkwardly, as the woman's anguish spilled out of her, until it finally spent itself.

The woman sniffled and wiped her face with both hands, composing herself. "Please forgive my outburst. My lady, you are kind, and you are just. I beg of you. Destroy her before she kills anyone else. Send an army after her. I can show you the cave."

Kazuko wiped at her own tears with her sleeve and swallowed hard. "Are you certain of this cave?"

"Yes, my lady. I have lived my entire life in the shadow of that mountain. My grandfather used to say that cave was an old bear's den. It is her den now. There was a well-beaten track on the slope up to the cave."

"Very well," Kazuko said. "I will see that this is done. And please, accept my deepest sympathies."

The woman shuddered with relief. "Thank you, my lady. You are nothing less than an Empress." The woman bowed her way out, guided by the steward's hand.

When Naozane returned, Kazuko told him, "Give her money enough to sustain her. She has lost her entire family. I must speak with Lord Tsunetomo."

The steward's face was pale, his eyes haunted. "Yes, my lady."

"For a samurai, a single word is important no matter where he may be. By just one single word martial valor can be made apparent. In peaceful  times words show one's bravery. In troubled times, too, one knows that by a single word his strength or cowardice can be seen. This single word is the flower of one's heart. It is not something said simply with one's mouth."

—*Hagakure, Book of the Samurai*

"She is an *oni* now," Kazuko said. "There can be no doubt, husband. And she must be stopped. We must not relent this time."

Over their dinner together, arranged between them on a black-lacquered meal service, Kazuko poured him a fresh cup of tea. Sparrows sang in the eaves right outside the open windows. A sweet-smelling spring breeze wafted through the castle's uppermost chamber.

"I understand, my dear," Tsunetomo said, "and I agree. She must be destroyed. However, the difficult part is this. Finding one person, even an *oni*, up in the mountains is not the same as sending twenty men on a boar hunt, because we are looking for a particular boar. And she is far more cunning than any boar. She can move faster and hide in places a party of men cannot easily look. This is why old Hakamadare was able to run free for so long. Horses are useless up there. It must be done by men on foot. I was forced to call off the search in the winter because I have too many new recruits in need of proper training. Many of them are not true samurai, but I need their feet on the ground and spears in their hands. And I need my best warriors to train them."

"The villagers are too frightened to hunt her themselves. Might we send only two or three experienced hunters? They could steal upon the cave, wait for her to appear...."

He put down his rice bowl and took a drink of tea. "Perhaps that would be more effective than an entire regiment."

"I feel responsible, husband," Kazuko said, her voice quavering. "I should have sent her away long ago. Then perhaps this would not have happened."

"You must not feel responsible. It is Hatsumi's evil that has become her undoing. She was a foul creature from the moment I first met her, though I am sorry to say that to you. You were blinded by your love for her. Sometimes we grow to love someone, truly and rightfully, and then they become something else. Love takes away our ability to see their evil." His voice grew quiet and earnest, his gaze turning inward, the voice of experience.

She knew almost nothing of his life before he had married her. What lost loves and failed ambitions lurked in his past? In this moment, she sensed her advantage. "Would you mind terribly, husband, if I saw to this personally?"

"You are not going into the forest after her."

"I have killed an *oni* before. I am much more skilled with the *naginata* now."

"But you had aid. Would that that *ronin* were around to help you again. He would be the perfect hunter. Besides, do you think Hatsumi will come running to embrace you if you have a *naginata* in hand?"

"I could offer myself as bait. My presence could draw her out."

"Bait? Absolutely not!"

"Husband, am I not trained to be a warrior? Am I not born of a warrior house? Do you not tell me I am Tomoe Gozen reborn? Are you saying that I am less of a warrior because I am a woman? Must the villagers in the mountains continue to be prey for her? She is *eating* them, husband!'"

Tsunetomo's brow furrowed. "Your life is worth more to me than a host of peasants."

"No, Husband, that is not the Way. To be samurai means to put oneself in the path of evil and protect those weaker. You are a great lord, and I am your wife. Hatsumi has become a blight upon the land, a canker that reflects upon you. For many years, the people of this province have revered you. You are strong and just. You are a kind husband to me. But now they are whispering that a curse has fallen upon our house. That I am the source of this curse. I cannot bear you an heir, and my handmaid has gone mad. I will not be an anchor around your neck, Husband. If Hatsumi kills me, you are free to find a fertile wife. Your lands will not have to pass to Ishitaka. If I succeed, then the blight has been wiped away."

Tsunetomo stood abruptly. "No." Then he stalked out of the room, his face pinched, fists clenched.

After another long day of practice in horse archery, Ken'ishi's muscles were in need of rest, and the men of Barrack Six felt the same. Even though he had moved into the quarters formerly occupied by Sergeant Hiromasa, he still made a point to observe the men. Tonight they were subdued, already preparing their bunks.

Ushihara sat on his bunk, head in his hands, a stricken, fearful look in his eyes.

Ken'ishi stopped near Ushihara's bunk and addressed him. "Do you have a problem?"

Ushihara wiped his face, attempting to distract from his expression, but without success. "It's nothing, Sergeant."

If something was amiss, responsibility lay with Ken'ishi, so he asked again more sternly.

Ushihara's posture and face hardened. "Nothing, Sergeant."

Michizane, Ushihara's unit leader, approached. "He fell off his horse today, Sergeant Ken'ishi."

Ushihara's face blazed with anger at Michizane, then the stricken expression re-emerged. "And broke my bow."

No wonder, then, that Ushihara was so troubled. Without real samurai rank, he lived and died by his own prowess, and his supply of prowess was meager.

"Then perhaps you belong among the spearmen," Ken'ishi said, "It is an honorable post."

"Yes, Sergeant," Ushihara said, but his tone suggested disagreement.

"Sergeant Ken'ishi! A word, please," a voice called from the door of the barracks. Ishitaka stood there at attention, his pate freshly shaved and his topknot immaculately arranged. But there was something dire in his gaze, his face pale. The nearby troops bowed to him.

"Ushihara," Ken'ishi said, "you'll have another bow, and more practice, for now."

Ushihara dropped to his knees and bowed low. "Thank you, Sergeant!"

Ken'ishi excused himself and joined Ishitaka, who led him out into the practice yard.

Ishitaka's whisper was tight, half-strangled. "She's gone!"

Only one possibility could elicit such passion and anguish. "Yuri is gone," Ken'ishi said. "To where?"

"I don't know! Her house is empty. Her clothes are gone. I went to the Roasted Acorn, and the proprietor told me that she left town with her father, and that she won't be back for a long time. She wouldn't say how long." Ishitaka's voice was haunted, faint, as if spoken through a screen.

"And she left no word for you?"

"Nothing."

"Perhaps she left in a hurry and there wasn't time. Can she read and write?"

"I...I don't know. She's just a peasant girl. Who would teach her?"

Ken'ishi clasped Ishitaka on the shoulder. "Perhaps she will be back soon."

"Her house was *empty*. As if she were nothing but a sweet, lovely dream. And I can't go asking after her all around town. Word will get back to my father. I once asked him what he thought of samurai marrying peasants, and he laughed at the idea. He said that might be all right for a bumpkin samurai, but not for high-ranked Otomo retainers. What am I to do, Ken'ishi?"

Ken'ishi sighed. He had walked his own lovelorn road for too many days to lie to Ishitaka and say he would feel better soon. If

Yuri was truly gone, Ishitaka would drive himself into the depths of despair. The young, foolish, besotted Ken'ishi had been able at least to say goodbye. There had been no mystery, only the final, brutal truncation of it, like the chop of an axe. But this...

"I have to find her!" Ishitaka's voice grew shrill.

"Brace up," Ken'ishi said. "The men might hear you."

"Yes, you're right. Yes. Brace up." Ishitaka swallowed hard and seemed to gather his courage. "Good night, my friend." He bowed and turned to depart.

"Where are you going?"

"To look for her."

"You won't find her."

"Perhaps not, but it will save me from thinking about how she is not here."

This made no sense to Ken'ishi, but he let Ishitaka go. The nonsensical nature of love would not be countermanded.

"If one were to say in a word what the condition of being a samurai is, its basis lies first in seriously devoting one's body and soul to his master. And if one is asked what to do beyond this, it would be  to fit oneself inwardly with intelligence, humanity, and courage."

—Hagakure, Book of the Samurai

Ken'ishi sat in the great hall of the castle with fifteen other volunteers. Captain Tsunemori sat on the dais to the right of Lady Kazuko and gestured toward the volunteers.

Kazuko looked as if she was sitting upon the upturned edge of a blade, surveying the men gathered here. When her gaze fell upon Ken'ishi, her shoulders seemed to deflate with relief.

Captain Tsunemori said, "My lady, these are the volunteers you requested. All of them claim to be excellent hunters, skilled in woodcraft."

"Thank you, Captain," she said, bowing to him. She turned to the men. "I have no doubt that you are all as skilled as you claim, but I have need of only three of the bravest of you, men of the greatest strength and prowess." Her gaze fell upon Ken'ishi again and held there for a long moment. "You have all heard tales of how my servant Hatsumi went mad. Perhaps you have heard tales of how she is roaming the countryside, howling like a wolf in the dead of night. She is not simply mad, however. She has become an *oni*. We must resume the hunt for her before she causes any more trouble. You well know she evaded us during the previous searches. She can easily hide from a large force, so we will attempt to draw her into the open. We have a witness who has seen her lair."

Captain Tsunemori said, "We need three men for this task. Who will volunteer?"

Sixteen hands rose with a chorus of affirmatives.

"I commend you all for your bravery," Kazuko said, "but only three are necessary. Therefore, we will draw lots." She produced a clay jar. "I have your names all written on wood chips."

Ken'ishi thought it wise of her to prepare the lots in advance. No samurai worth his blade would quail from such a task.

She reached into the jar, her voluminous sleeve obscuring the top half, and drew out a chip. She made a great show of reading the first name: Ken'ishi.

He bowed low, his ears burning at the sound of his name on her lips. Her contrivance was admirable. She knew there was no one else here who had ever faced an *oni* besides the two of them. The next two names were men unknown to him, Yahei and Naohiro, but they looked hardy, with a wiliness in their eyes reserved for men skilled in woodcraft and hunting.

"Thank you all for your courage," she said. "We will leave in the morning."

"Begging my lady's pardon," Ken'ishi said. "You are coming?"

"I will be the bait in our trap," she said in a matter-of-fact tone that brooked no further discussion.

Ken'ishi bowed and clamped his jaw around any protest. What she did not know is that he had faced not one but two *oni*, the bandit Hakamadare and the village *yoriki* named Taro. Both of them had been terrifying, formidable opponents. Silver Crane could cut *oni* flesh. But would these two men stand in the face of the horror that would surely come?

Kazuko stood and departed with swan-like grace.

* * *

A thundercloud whorled across Tsunetomo's face. "I told you, I forbid it. I am your lord." His fan snapped into his palm as he stalked back and forth in their chamber.

Kazuko squared her back. "I have three of your greatest hunters to accompany me. And I will be armed as well. She will not have a chance against four of us."

"I am angry that you defy me." He crossed his arms.

"As this is the first time I have ever defied your wishes, I hope you will find a way to forgive me. In your heart, you know this is the right thing. Hatsumi must be destroyed, and I am the most likely to draw her out of hiding. How is this different than command of the castle troops? You went away to fight. I had to remain here."

Tsunetomo tightened his arms. "I should be going with you."

"Your prowess at arms is formidable, but you are not a hunter. Besides, any day now, word will come that the fortification project is commencing. With Yasutoki away, you must be here to answer that call."

"You sound as if you might be gone for some time."

"I will be gone as long as it takes. Hatsumi is my responsibility. I cannot bear the thought of more peasants dying because we fail to act. Why are you so afraid for me when you would gladly sacrifice your own life in battle? Am I not allowed to make the same choice? I love that you wish to protect me. But I am the wife of the one of greatest lords of Kyushu. How much farther might your prestige reach with a wife as fierce as you?" She gave him a little smirk at that. "You cannot refuse me."

"That also vexes me. I have taught you too well."

She approached him, reached up to stroke his face. "Now that you have seen reason, we must not waste a night together. I leave in the morning."

"You are very forward tonight."

"Do not men say that battle sets their loins afire? May it not also be so for women?"

Tsunetomo seized her hand and drew her into his lap. He stroked her lips with his other hand, his gaze devouring her. "I have indeed taught you too well. And it pains me to say it right now, but I cannot very well bed you before you go on campaign. Carnal liaisons before battle bring on the worst of bad fortune. May our loins catch fire *after* you return."

Feet thumped on the deck above Yasutoki's head. Voices called out the arcane commands of a ship at sea. The lantern hanging from the ceiling timber swayed with the tossing of the ship, casting wavering shadows around Yasutoki's small chamber. The sea breeze wafting through the port chilled him, even here on the cusp of summer. He felt like a doddering old man looking for a shawl.

Tiger Lily knelt at his feet, wringing her hands, looking pale, dark circles gathering under her eyes.

"What is amiss with you, my dear?" Yasutoki said.

Tiger Lily would not look him in the eye. "I am ill, Lord. The sailors tell me it is the tossing of the waves." Her face was pale, sheened with sweat, her eyes bleary.

"You have been vomiting for two days," Yasutoki said with distaste. Such was her illness, he could barely gather himself to bed her.

"I am sorry, Lord. They tell me it will pass."

She was not the only one suffering from this. Several of his bodyguards had helplessly spewed over the side, mortified by the vulgar rebellion of their bodily faculties.

The ship creaked and heaved, chuffing through the waves with a stiff wind from astern. They were making good way to Kamakura. His hope was that they arrived ahead of the emissaries of the Great Khan. He would request an audience with them as soon as possible. His request might not be granted, but he nevertheless yearned to hear news from them, and to give them some from which the Khan would benefit. Would the Khan persevere in his desire to subdue Japan and destroy the Minamoto and Hojo clans? Yasutoki would see the Taira clan rise again, even if half the country had to burn first.

"Was young Ishitaka upset that you had to leave him?" Yasutoki said.

Her face went blank. "I did not tell him."

Yasutoki smiled. "What a fantastically cruel thing to do! The mystery will chew him to pieces."

Her eyebrows rose. "I thought it would be kinder if I...just went away."

"Your age and inexperience betray you. And why would you choose the kinder path? Do you have feelings for our young scion?"

"Of course not, Master. I do as you command."

"You are wise to remember that. When we return to Kyushu, you will have to beg his forgiveness and jump back into his bed."

"Master...I... All I want is you."

"One such as you cannot afford to love. Without fail, it interferes with what must be done."

"One such as me, Master?"

"A whore. A slut. A common slag."

She flinched as if his words were blows.

"Women of the shadows must use every tool—every orifice— to see their mission complete. You will bed those who serve your purpose and discard those who do not."

Her hands were trembling. "Yes, Master."

"Do you not want to have more power than any other woman of your station?"

"Yes, Master."

"Do you not want power over men? Puppets you can manipulate with the tug of a string?"

"Yes, Master."

"Then make them love you. But you dare not love them in return. Or you will not be able to kill them when your master demands it."

"I understand, Master."

"Good girl. Now strip."

Even with insects...
Some are hatched out
    musical...
Some, alas, tone-deaf
                —*Issa*

K azuko rode at the mid-
    dle of their procession,
    behind Ken'ishi and before the other two men. The fresh-
ly flooded rice fields on either side of the road filled the morning
air with a wet, earthy crispness. As they passed an outlying village,
the villagers were still planting. Lines of women carrying baskets
of seedlings, their robes tied above their knees, marched backward
through the calf-deep mud and water to the cadence of drums and
the rice-planting song, bending, planting their seedlings into the
mud, straightening, stepping back, bending, planting, all in perfect
rhythm. It was back-breaking work, but they chanted along with the
song as if it were a festival. The chorus of voices echoed from the
nearby mountainsides.

Somehow, today being the closest Ken'ishi had been to Kazuko
since their New Year meeting, he felt more at ease than he had in
months. Something felt right about it, as if he had returned to where
he had first begun. He welcomed her eyes upon his back. It gave him
strength.

He and the other hunters were armored in breastplate, thigh
guards, and light helmet that covered only skull and cheeks. Kazuko
was dressed in men's robes to minimize attention, but she was not
outwardly armored. However, she did wear a shirt of lacquered iron

scales under her robes, similar to the light coat of scales Junko had given him. All of the hunters carried bows, spears, and swords. And Kazuko wore a *wakizashi* in her *obi*, had a dagger hidden in her sleeve, and carried a sheathed *naginata* alongside her saddle.

In Takeshita village, they found Otsugi, who was beside herself with gratitude. The entire village turned out and prostrated itself around them, weeping and offering prayers of thanks. When the villagers discovered that Kazuko was not, in fact, a man, that she was none other than Lady Otomo herself, a hush of reverence went through them, and they prostrated themselves again like grass blown over by a wind.

In an explosion of obsequious gratitude and hospitality, the village headman offered them food and refreshment that must have taken sustenance out of the mouths of twenty villagers. While the food was prepared, the headman told numerous tales of the Wild Woman's blood-curdling, midnight howls that seemed to swing endlessly from mournful to spiteful, of the disappearances—ten, including the woodsman and Otsugi's brother. Everyone trembled in terror of venturing into the forest. Kazuko listened to his tragic tales in somber earnestness, and vowed to deal with the Wild Woman.

A dozen sets of small eyes peered through the windows and cracks in the walls of the headman's house. Bursts of whispering punctuated the tensest moments of the headman's storytelling. Ken'ishi winked at one little boy, spurring a chorus of tittering.

"Away with you, you crickets!" the headman called good-naturedly, and the children dispersed—for a while.

Heaping bowls of rice, *daikon,* pickled plums, and smoked *ayu* were laid before them. Kazuko and her hunters ate sparingly, knowing the villagers would not waste a single grain of uneaten rice.

When the meal was finished, Kazuko presented the headman with an official certificate exempting the village from taxes for the year. The villagers could keep everything they grew this year. The headman's gratitude overflowed with bowing and weeping.

Kazuko said, "It is the least I can do for a village so terribly beset."

The four of them on horseback, accompanied by Otsugi on foot, left the village to great fanfare. People clutched their prayer beads and besought the Buddha to assist the hunters.

With the tenacity born of decades of unrelenting toil, Otsugi led them up the steep mountain trails. Sunlight slanted through pines, dappling the trail. Communities of birds sang their greetings and disputes and inquiries to one another, sharing news of nearby hawks or foxes, locations of particularly succulent worms, castigating one another for stealing the best nesting materials, and because it was spring, hatchlings screamed their hunger. The scent of pine needles and verdant earth filled the breezes.

After half an afternoon's climb, Otsugi turned around. "This is where I came out of the forest, my lady. The cave is that way." She pointed with a trembling hand.

Just ahead, a stream wound out of the undergrowth and flowed under an old, wooden bridge. They dismounted and tied their horses near the road.

Otsugi bowed low, again and again. "Just follow the stream until you see the...blood on the rocks. May the Buddha watch over you. Then there is a trail that leads perhaps one *cho* up the slope. The cave is there. Even if she is not in the cave, this is the mountain where the howls come from."

Kazuko thanked her, then dismissed her. Otsugi hurried back down the mountain as quickly as her bowlegged gait could carry her.

Yahei withdrew a stoppered vial from a pouch, soaked a bit of cloth with the vial's contents, and dabbed it on his clothes, shoes, and hands. Sour stench roiled off him. He offered it to the other men.

"What is it?" Ken'ishi asked, covering his nose.

"Boiled boar piss," Yahei said. "It covers our scent. If she has truly become like an animal, she may smell us coming, unless we smell like an animal."

"We shall have to spend a month in seclusion to purify ourselves after this," Kazuko said. "But it is a worthy sacrifice."

"Not you, my lady," Yahei said. "If you are the bait, she must smell you."

Kazuko looked relieved at not having to touch the reeking stuff.

"If Hatsumi has truly become an *oni*," Ken'ishi said, "purification will be necessary regardless of what we use to kill her." He thought of the rancid, black ichor that had flowed like tar through Hakamadare's veins.

He took the concoction, applied it as Naohiro had done, and handed it to Yahei.

"You must be careful," Naohiro said, "or else all the local sows will think we've come to woo."

"Or another boar will come to kill the intruders," Ken'ishi said. His two near-lethal encounters with boars sprang to mind, one from boyhood, one from last autumn.

The men laughed, but his comment awoke caution in their faces.

While they strung their bows, slung their quivers, and unsheathed their spearheads, Ken'ishi listened for the *kami,* but their silence told him no immediate danger loomed. Birds sang high in the branches above, hidden by pine needles, but he could not spot any to address. Their knowledge of the area might be valuable, but his ability to speak to animals did not mean they wished to speak to him, especially when was with other people.

Ken'ishi asked, "Is Lady Otomo prepared?"

Kazuko hesitated, then removed her *wakizashi* and tied it to her saddle. "I am ready now. Best if I have no visible weapons."

Ken'ishi said, "We'll be close by. You have nothing to fear. Yahei, you go upslope perhaps half a *cho* and parallel the stream. Naohiro, you go an equal distance downslope. I will stay by Lady Kazuko's side until we reach the location of the attacks, then hide myself nearby. I will whistle like a nightingale when we are situated." He offered the sound from his own lips. "At that point, come closer to her, perhaps half your distance. Understood?"

"Yes, Sergeant," they said.

"Very well." Ken'ishi led Kazuko into the forest.

He was thankful for the carpet of pine needles, which muffled their footsteps. The rush and gurgle of the water also masked their movement. Deeper into the forest, the undergrowth thinned except by the banks of the stream, where bushes and brambles clustered. Ken'ishi crept along the bank, watchful not only for threats, but also for bloodstained rocks. His *zori* squelched in the mud and crunched through sand and river pebbles. His bow was in his hand, arrow at the ready.

Kazuko crept a few paces behind him. Ken'ishi admired the way she moved. Her training since their first encounter clearly had been extensive. She moved like a warrior now, not a young girl.

They followed the stream for perhaps three *cho* when they came upon evidence of the carnage Otsugi had described. Rusty-brown stains slathered the riverside boulders as if painted with a thick brush.

Kazuko clutched a hand over her mouth, then exerted control over herself and surveyed the area.

Ken'ishi surveyed the scene with an eye honed by his wilderness upbringing. The craft of it all came back to him in a flash of instincts. Thick, dried blood glued a few shreds of cloth to the boulders. Splinters of bone lay in the crevices between stones at the water's edge, some teeth, a rib. In the soft earth were numerous bare human footprints scattered in profusion.

A few paces away, Kazuko hissed at him and gestured up the slope. He joined her and squinted up toward where she pointed. In the deepening shadows of the descending sun lay a deeper shadow among some haphazardly strewn boulders, with a faint path wending among the pine boles, beaten into the grass and detritus.

"If she is in there," Ken'ishi whispered, "we might kill her in her den. I'll go check." But first he whistled the nightingale's call to the other hunters, receiving the appropriate responses.

He took a deep breath, and still the *kami* did not speak to him. Perhaps Hatsumi was not in the cave at all. Nevertheless, he must know.

Removing his *zori*, he stole barefoot up the slope with all the stealth Kaa had taught him, the stealth that had once allowed him to sneak up on the *tengu*, close enough to strike, and then retreat, all without his teacher's knowledge. He used long, slow breaths to calm his thundering heart. His experiences with Hakamadare and Taro made him wonder whether an arrow would cause Hatsumi much harm, but all the better if he could kill her at a distance. The stories about her were so wild, who knew what she had become?

As he approached the cave, the smell of decay thickened, mingling with the smell of something he could not identify, almost like a beehive, or a hut that had stood empty for a long time. Only a dozen paces away now, he could see the cave mouth situated beneath a leaning boulder. He would have to crawl on his belly to worm his way inside. The deep shadows within kept their secrets.

Below, Kazuko shielded her eyes from the sun and watched him. He gestured inside.

From his military experiences, he had acquired enough tactical wisdom to know that entering an unknown area with an unknown enemy was not a wise move, but the *kami* remained silent. He trusted them to warn him. But their silence could also mean that she was asleep inside or some other nuance of meaning understandable only to spirits of the air and earth and forest. So he stashed his bow near the entrance, drew Silver Crane, and slid between the rocks, the earth moist between his fingers and toes.

The stench of decay was even stronger within, thick and wet and rancid, and the smell of some creature, too, that was not quite beast. He knew the smell of bears and wolves, and this odor was not in that realm.

As he slipped into the shadows, he allowed his eyes a few moments to adjust to the darkness. The floor of the cave was littered with dried grass. Stains he could not identify covered the grass. Three paces past the boulder he could raise himself into a crouch. Silver Crane glistened in the sunlight from behind him, casting shards of light against the ceiling and walls.

With each step, he listened and heard nothing.

As the darkness deepened, things crunched and dug into the soles of his bare feet, bits of bone and less savory detritus. Perhaps ten paces into the cave, he found a bed of grass nestled against the cave wall. Clumps of earthen roots clung to the grass, but it was a bed much like the one he had used in boyhood. Fox-sized clefts delved deeper into the mountain, but this was the deepest point a human being could reach. And Hatsumi was not here.

He hurried back through the entrance, wormed his way outside, and reached for his bow. Then he heard voices below and the *kami* screaming in his mind.

He dropped low and eased toward the rocks overlooking the path to the cave, then peered down.

Kazuko sat pressed against a large boulder at the edge of the stream. Two paces away, sitting on another stone, was a woman in once-fine robes now ruined with dirt and rusty-red stains. The other woman's hair was a wild mane, matted with sticks and pine needles.

Kazuko's voice came up the slope, tremulous and halting. "—I am sorry, Hatsumi, but I have not come to bring you home. My husband won't allow it. But I am happy to see...you are well."

Kazuko's face had gone white as a winter mountaintop. Her right hand crept toward the sleeve where her dagger lay hidden.

Only Hatsumi's back was visible, hands resting in her lap. She sighed loudly and with great earnestness and disappointment. "I suppose Lord Tsunetomo is unhappy about me breaking the window shutter, isn't he?"

He raised his lips into the song of a nightingale. When no response came, he called again.

Still no reply.

"Did you bring any more escorts with you?" Hatsumi said.

"No," Kazuko said.

He nocked an arrow.

"It was good that you did," Hatsumi said. "Even with your *manlike* martial skills, a lady must be wary of bandits. But we have already had such experience, have we not?" Her gaze began to wander around the area, her nose lifted.

In profile, Ken'ishi could see something wrong with her face. A distortion. A blood-red blotchiness. He drew the bowstring.

"Are you lying to me about more bodyguards?" Hatsumi said.

"Don't be silly, dear Hatsumi. I came to see *you*."

"Then whose shoes are these?" Hatsumi's arm stretched out to point toward the *zori* Ken'ishi had left at the foot of the cave path. Her arm glistened with fresh blood up to her elbow.

He released the arrow, and it flew, hissing and true, into the side of Hatsumi's head.

Her head spun on her neck like an owl's, twisting further than any human head could turn. The red blotches on her face came alive as her eyes found him. Recognition flared in eyes like beads of black hate. The blotches on her face whorled and swelled and tumefied, drawing her lips back from black, razor-like teeth that ringed a circular mouth, like that of a leech. Her torso lifted from her seat, and while her face remained fixed upon Ken'ishi, the rest of her body rotated toward him. Her blood-soaked hands were not hands anymore, but gnarled talons tipped with obsidian claws. A distended belly hung over the remnants of her *obi*.

Another pair of legs unfolded from within her robe, legs that Ken'ishi could not fathom, part spider and part squid, covered in spiny black needles like hairs, and then another pair of legs, legs that parted the cloth of her robes and revealed just how much of Hatsumi's body was still woman and how much was not.

Ken'ishi drew another arrow and released. It flew toward her face. She swatted it away as if it were a mosquito. A long, black tongue extended from that horrid circular hole and licked her puckered lips.

Like the tiny, charcoal-colored spiders that leaped so quickly they seemed to blink from one spot to the next, Hatsumi leaped upon him, wrenched the bow from his hands, and crumpled it like a twig.

His hand found Silver Crane's hilt, and he slashed toward her face. Quicker than sight, she let the gleaming tip *whoosh* past her strangely bulbous nose, then swatted at him with one of those awful claws, an almost lackadaisical movement that would have peeled his face from his skull. But he ducked and scrambled away, interposing the deadly sheen of Silver Crane between them, seeking an entrance to the Void. Something in her gaze transfixed him, kept him mired in fear, unable to release himself into Nothingness.

She came on like a darting scorpion, but stopped short of Silver Crane's point.

His heart was a smith's hammer, his breath a painful desperation.

And then she leaped, but not upon him. Upward, to the wall of rock looming over him, where she clung for a moment like a fly, then thirty paces through the air to the trunk of a thick pine tree. Then down upon him again, those horrid legs foremost. He met her with a slash that severed two of those legs as he danced aside. Noxious ichor spewed over him, and she landed ten paces away. Yellow slaver gathered between her pulsating rows of black teeth. The stench of the ichor brought his gorge into his throat, launching him into a coughing fit, his eyes streaming tears.

Through the haze of tears, she came at him again. He raised his blade to meet her, but then a sear of pain lanced up his leg. One of her severed legs clamped around his ankle, the black needle-hairs piercing his flesh...and *drinking*. The pressure would soon splinter his bones. Hatsumi's claws streaked toward his face and throat. He slashed, but she dodged and then clapped the blade between her palms, arresting its movement and contesting its control. He wrenched and tugged, but her clasped palms held the sword like a stone.

Her leech's mouth pulsed and gnashed, hungry.

Then with a terrific heave, she wrested the sword from his grip and sent it spinning away to clang against the rocks.

The severed limb worried at his ankle, grinding needles into bone, sucking for marrow.

One of her claws snatched his extended wrist.

A shrill *kiai* pierced his ears. The sound of a solid blow came from behind Hatsumi. A flash of Kazuko's face over Hatsumi's shoulder. Kazuko pulled the dagger out of Hatsumi's back and stabbed again. Hatsumi dropped Ken'ishi's wrist and swept a claw around toward Kazuko. The claw ripped through cloth and raked across lacquered scales. Kazuko flew backward to tumble painfully down the slope.

Hideous glee trickled over Hatsumi's face as she watched Kazuko bounce and crash to a halt against a boulder. Hatsumi stood there in indecision, looking back and forth between Ken'ishi and Kazuko.

"No!" Ken'ishi snarled. "Look here, you foul sow!" He braced himself to leap.

Hatsumi faced him, eyes glittering. She sprang toward him.

He lunged for Silver Crane. Somehow it lay closer now than he thought it had been. His fingers closed around the hilt, and he swung blindly behind him. The blade bit something hard and heavy, and lodged.

An ululating howl blasted over him, turning his blood to the frozen slush of a winter river.

Hatsumi backed herself free, and a handspan of his sword point slid from her belly, smeared with blackness.

Her eyes blazed with fresh hatred and pain.

Ken'ishi seized the moment and leaped at her, swinging for her neck.

The cut was true, and her head tumbled from her shoulders to the ground, where it bobbled around the arrow embedded in it.

The satisfaction of a perfect cut filled his breast.

Then her hands reached down and scooped up her head like a *kemari* ball. A squelching, blowing, sucking rhythm spurted gobbets of black ichor from the stump of her neck, as if she were screaming her rage at him without the mouth to form the sounds.

With another tremendous spring, she launched herself higher up the mountainside and fled into the forest.

He watched her only long enough to be sure she was gone before he turned his attention to the needles grinding into his ankle. With the point of Silver Crane, he stabbed the horrid member and slowly, with excruciating pain, began to pry it loose from his leg. The needles came out one by one, wriggling, grating free of bone, pulsing with silent frustration. Blood poured from the pattern of pinholes encircling his ankle. Finally, the last spines came free, and the member hung like an engorged leech from the point of his weapon. With a snort of revulsion, he slung the thing as far as he could and flung himself down the trail to where Kazuko lay against the rocks.

Tremendous forces...
Stone-piled fence all
   tumbled down
By two cats in love.
                     —*Shiki*

The captain had assured Ya-
sutoki that their vessel would dock at Kamakura tomorrow.
They had been becalmed for most of the day, but the captain
knew in his bones the wind would return tomorrow and take them
the rest of the journey.

The man was just the kind Yasutoki relished—half-legitimate
sailor, half-pirate. The kind of man perceptive enough to recognize
power and ruthlessness when he encountered it, and wily enough
to ingratiate himself with it. Throughout the journey, Yasutoki had
noticed a number of clues indicating this captain and crew spent a
significant amount of their time preying upon trade to China. The
predatory looks kept in check only by the stern ferocity of samurai
bodyguards, the areas of the ship forbidden to the passengers—areas
suitable for hiding weapons—and the sailors' general flint-eyed
wariness, as if all of them had secrets to hide. Most of them probably
had prices on their heads and warrants of execution in various
provinces, but these were the kind of men Yasutoki understood best,
the kind of tools he often used.

At the stern, Tiger Lily gazed out over the placid sea and its avenue
of moonlight stretching to the eastern horizon. To the northwest lay
a faint black strip of peninsula.

Belowdecks, the sailors drank and ate with boisterous gusto. The smell of roasting fish and boiling millet wafted up through the glow of lanterns shining up from the hold. Yasutoki and his bodyguards had been served first, given rice instead of millet. The land-legged samurai had finally accustomed themselves to the tossing sea and found enough respite from the relentless vomiting to eat. Tiger Lily, however, had been content with a few pickled plums, saying that her belly was still unhappy.

The night air was pleasant but still calm, and Yasutoki was tired of being aboard ship. He loathed the closeness of so many eyes. The cramped confines of his cabin were hardly enough for him to stretch out when he slept. He was also tired of the sickened cast on Tiger Lily's face. If he had to watch her vomit one more time, he might slit her throat.

The sailor on watch puttered around the deck, checking rigging, knots, and anchor, then spotted Tiger Lily. His coarse, unshaven face turned from his annoyance at being stuck with watch duty into a swaggering, predatory smirk.

Yasutoki stood at the bow and pretended to ignore the man's approach. The lascivious leers the crew lavished upon her flew in the face of all decorum—when they were not deriding her presence as inviting bad fortune—but she kept her gaze demurely downcast at all times, as she had been taught.

The sailor's demeanor bespoke lustful intention to have her right there on the deck while everyone's back was turned. Yasutoki felt no need to interfere. Watching her be ravished in the most bestial way would amuse him as much as watching her defend herself.

The sailor leaned in close and spoke in her ear. She remained motionless, gazing out to sea. His hand clasped her buttock and squeezed, and still she did not move. His fingers lifted her robe and slid between her thighs.

She turned toward him and lifted her face toward his, exposing her smooth, tender throat, parting her moist lips. The sailor's shoulders stiffened. He leaned closer, growling something in her ear. She reached up and pulled out her two lacquered bamboo hairpins, letting her long, lustrous hair tumble over her shoulders. She shook it loose and smiled up at him. His rough hands came up and clasped her shoulders. He leaned down to kiss her. Her hand came up and seemed to brush his cheek. His body stiffened as a wordless, nasal grunt erupted from him. His knees buckled, his eyes turned away from one another, and she guided his limp, wiry bulk over the gunwale. He splashed into the sea. She wrapped her hair back up into a bun and secured it with only one hairpin.

The great splash brought a swarm of sailors boiling out of the hold.

Yasutoki called out to them. "Your man slipped and fell over the bow!" He pointed over the gunwale beside him.

A dozen men rushed to Yasutoki's side, peering over the side, shouting questions.

"Where is he?"

"What happened?"

"I don't see him!"

Yasutoki said, "He was checking the rigging. He fell and hit his head, then went into the water."

Two men leaped over the side and dove under the water. Soon they re-emerged, gasping and sputtering.

"It's too dark!"

"I can't see him!"

Then Tiger Lily's shrill scream from the stern grabbed their attention. "Sharks!" She pointed out over the moon-dappled water. "I saw fins!"

The men in the water began to thrash with panic. "Help! Help!"

The captain roared. "Ropes over the side! Get them up!"

Two ropes went over the side, and moments later, two dripping sailors were hauled onto the deck.

Other men ran to the stern, peering out into the water.

"There!" A sailor pointed. "I think I saw one!"

"I saw two fins, sirs!" Tiger Lily said. "They went under the ship."

Sailors lined the gunwales, snatching up poles and hooks, searching the swirling darkness around the ship. One readied a harpoon.

"We can't risk anyone else," the captain said with a grunt. "If Katsuura was knocked senseless when he went in, he's drowned by now."

"Food for sharks," said the first mate.

The captain barked out to his crew, "Keep your eyes open, but nobody else goes in the water!"

Yasutoki said, "I am sorry about the loss of your crewman,

Captain. Is there any aid I can offer?"

The captain shook his head and bowed. "No, Lord. Thank you, Lord."

"Then I will take my servant and retire." Yasutoki approached the door to his cabin, and snapped his fingers toward Tiger Lily.

She joined him, and they ducked into their chamber.

With the door shut behind him, he lit a match for the oil lamp and said, "That was brilliantly done, my dear."

"Thank you for the distraction, Master. It gave his body time to sink." Her face gleamed like alabaster in the burgeoning glow.

"The 'sharks' were an especially adept touch. Where did you insert the hairpin?"

"His nose, Master."

"You made punching through the bone into the brain look effortless."

"You are...an excellent teacher, Master."

Pride swelled his chest. "Perhaps I have taught you too well. Nevertheless, do not kill anyone else until we reach Kamakura. Avoid the sailors. They already call you a harbinger of ill fortune. Stay in the cabin."

"Yes, Master. Might I entreat to ask a question?"

"What is it?"

"Where did you learn such great skills? Who was your teacher?"

"There is a shadow clan of my family that still exists, a mere splinter after the purging. They have roots now in Koga province, where it was easy to hide. Alas, my teacher, as great a man as he was, is long since dead."

She was trembling now, her face turning paler than usual, yet still a blank mask.

"Sea sickness again?"

"Something else."

"Explain."

She took a deep breath of pondering thought, then let it out. "Rage, Master. For what he said to me, the way he touched me."

He raised an eyebrow. "You hide it well."

"I...have learned well, Master. As I said, you are an excellent teacher."

"If we put this in terms of your own martial art, the mind is not detained by the hand that brandishes the sword.  Completely oblivious to the hand that wields the sword, one strikes and cuts his opponent down. He does not put his mind in his adversary. The opponent is Emptiness. I am Emptiness. The hand that holds the sword, the sword itself, is Emptiness. Understand this, but do not let your mind be taken by Emptiness."

—*Takuan Soho, "The Mysterious Record of Immovable Wisdom"*

R elief drove away Ken'ishi's panic as Kazuko's dagger came up to greet him. Her arm trembled, and she fought to right herself, to catch her breath, groaning and gasping. Blood covered her face, plastered with dirt and leaves. Her robe had been shredded open, and a great rent in her armor exposed her soft, silken under-robe.

She lowered the dagger and struggled up into a sitting position. Blood dripped in a steady beat from her chin. "Is she dead?"

"No, fled," he said. "I think she will come back. We must get ready."

She touched her face. "It hurts." Through the detritus clinging to her face, a gash leaked blood.

"Is anything broken?" he asked.

"I do not think so...."

"Let me help you up." He hooked an arm under her shoulders. She yielded to his aid and stood, shaky and sore.

He called out to Yahei and Naohiro.

"She killed them." Kazuko's voice quavered.

Ken'ishi nodded. "Come to the water."

"She clawed me." Her fingers gingerly touched her cheek. She moved as if in a daze.

"We must clean your face."

"Is it bad?"

"I'll know after it's clean." He took her arm and guided her toward the water.

She squatted in the shallows and splashed water onto her face. The blood dripped faster. "Part of my cheek is numb." Fear glimmered in her gaze. "I think it is bad."

Washing away most of the blood and detritus revealed a deep gash that crossed her cheek from chin to nose. A steady rivulet of blood dripped from her chin. It was the kind of wound that would leave a deep scar.

"You smell terrible," she said.

"Hatsumi's blood. I wounded her." The effluvium smelled as if he had been lying in a bed of corpses.

With tender fingers, he touched her cheek and pinched the gash shut, but when he removed his fingers, the blood flow resumed.

Her eyes searched his face for comfort, and he did not know what to say. Here was a heinous disfigurement upon the face of beauty itself.

With a frown, she pushed him aside and leaned over a pool along the stream bank to look at herself. A sob came out of her, and her hand clamped back a second one. Her breath came in short gasps.

"My lady," Ken'ishi said. "We must bandage it." He wished he knew more about such things, but he knew only how to kill, and precious little about healing.

Blood and tears dripped from her chin into the pool.

He cleared his throat. "And then we must retrieve more weapons from the horses. She will return."

"Yes." Kazuko straightened, her voice dropping low. "This is far from finished."

Ken'ishi produced two strips of clean cloth from a pouch tied to his obi. One he folded into a square, and the other he wrapped around her head to hold the square onto the gash.

By the time he was finished, their faces had somehow gravitated nearer.

He stepped back and offered his hand to help her out of the water.

The *kami* had created a rhythmic buzz in his mind, like the song of cicadas. The air itself seemed to tighten with danger.

"Come!" He snatched up his *zori* and ran barefoot for the horses.

Together they crashed and snapped through undergrowth, dodging stream-side boulders, splashing through the water, sliding in the mud until they emerged onto the road.

Two horses lay in motionless piles of savaged meat. A quick survey told Ken'ishi that the other two had broken their reins and bolted downhill. Relief that Storm had escaped assuaged the thickening sense of doom.

Kazuko's *naginata* lay splintered in the dirt. Her *wakizashi*, still in its scabbard, lay bent at an angle.

For several long moments, they stood over the wreckage of their hopes.

"How are we going to kill her with just your sword?" Kazuko said. "Your arrow did no harm. Killing Hakamadare took both of us working together. We had to cut him to pieces."

"I fear we'll have to do the same to Hatsumi. I took her head, but she picked it up and fled."

"We must entreat the gods for aid."

Ken'ishi thought about the power that Silver Crane had granted him during the invasion, the way the blood of slain Mongols had seemed to feed it. "Perhaps."

His gaze trailed over the ripped horseflesh and puddles of blood. Kazuko's *naginata* blade was still sheathed. He picked it up. The haft was broken and splintered, but when he pulled off the leather sheath, he found the blade intact. "We can fashion a new pole."

A glimmer of hope returned to her eyes.

Then a horrid howl echoed through the treetops and rocky slopes.

"She has reattached her head," he said.

"Then we must hurry."

"We must not draw her down to the village," Kazuko said. "She could hurt more people."

Ken'ishi nodded. "But which direction is most advantageous?"

"While I was talking with her, she sniffed the air several times."

"Like a dog."

She nodded.

"Then we must move with the stream. It'll cover our scent."

"If you are concerned about scent, you must wash off her blood. She will be able to smell you all the way from Hakata."

He knelt in the stream and washed himself, his gaze scanning for signs of Hatsumi, listening for the songs of the *kami*. Then he took a breath and steadied himself, calmed himself, settled himself. He assumed *seiza* among the sand and pebbles of the streambed and let the water gush over his legs.

"What are you doing?" she said.

"Asking questions."

He settled Silver Crane across his thighs and sought the Void.

As the concerns of future and past fell away from him, he found the vast web of silver threads that vibrated with the flow of destiny and time, a web that coalesced upon the sheen of steel in his hands.

Your cut is true, Silver Crane, but Hatsumi is powerful, Ken'ishi thought. *How do I defeat her?*

No reply came.

Ken'ishi grew more insistent. *You follow the bloodline. If I am blood of the Taira clan, you must obey me.*

Vibrations rose from the great depths of some formless abyss and slowly coalesced into thoughts and impressions that formed a whole in Ken'ishi's mind. *If the man dies, another of the bloodline will be found.*

Ken'ishi let his indignation flow through him and seep away. *Until then, you serve me. Now tell me. How do we defeat such a creature?*

Like the flow of time, inexorable, rejuvenating and destructive by turns, there is power in the flow of water.

Kaa, the old *tengu*, used to tell Ken'ishi that mountains were places of power, bridges between the celestial realms and those of men. Ken'ishi had once felt the power of the *kami* of the water, when

Kaa had taught him to swim in a hot spring lake. *Kappa,* like the one he had defeated near Aoka village, drew their power from the *kami* of the water. Perhaps he could entreat such *kami* to lend him their power.

Find water of power, and the man will have his answer.

Ken'ishi bowed in thanks to the sword and roused himself.

Kazuko sat on the bank, staring at him. "Something was happening there. I could feel it. Like the...the rhythm of a loom's shuttle in a distant room."

Ken'ishi eyed her. "Perhaps I should teach you how to commune with the *kami.* You seem to have a knack for it."

Her eyes brightened. "Oh, please! Teach me."

He smiled. "I will, but first we must go upstream."

"Why?"

"We must go higher, where the spirits have more power, where more things are possible. And I was right, we must follow the water." He stood. "And look for saplings as we go. We must find a suitable replacement for your *naginata* haft."

For the rest of the afternoon, they followed the stream up the mountain. The stream meandered back and forth down the clefts and undulations of the slope, through the verdant pine forest, adding its music to the songs of warblers and sparrows. High in the trees, monkeys leaped and chattered. That the birds were singing and monkeys chattering told Ken'ishi that Hatsumi was nowhere nearby. They would go silent at the approach of such a creature.

As time passed, his wounded ankle grew ever more painful. A puffy, scarlet weal encircled it, and the punctures still leaked blood and some pale fluid. A burning sensation spread across his skin in the areas where Hatsumi's blood had touched him, and he could not wash it away. Worry niggled at him that some splinter of her remained embedded in his leg, perhaps bone-deep.

As the afternoon wore on, he found himself growing irritable for no discernible reason. All the struggles of his life, all the heartaches, all the forks in his road that led to even greater miseries, leaped to the forefront of his mind, and he could not put them aside. He grew angry with Kazuko that so many of his troubles were centered around her. His life would have been so much simpler if he had not chosen that particular road on that particular day, or if he had come along only a short while later, when Kazuko and Hatsumi would surely have been dead, and he could have avoided Hakamadare and his bandit gang. How much less trouble he would have experienced. He grew angry that she fell behind. He grew angry that she made too much noise, when his own woodcraft was nearly perfect. He grew angry that she had not banished Hatsumi long before she could degenerate into such madness and evil. He had not asked for his life to be destroyed by love. He had not deserved to be hounded as little more than a criminal or a miscreant from the moment he set foot in the realm of human beings.

Kazuko asked him a quiet question, but he did not hear her words. Instead he turned and snarled at her. "Shut up! This is all your fault!"

She flinched as if he had slapped her. A terrible moment passed as her eyes filled with tears. Her hand rose and touched her bandaged cheek. Her lip began to tremble. Then she swallowed hard and steadied her voice. "Yes, I know. There are a hundred ways I could have prevented this, but I did not because..." She took a deep, shuddering breath, "...because of love and loyalty." Then her voice grew hard. "But if you shout at me again, I will send you away."

Ken'ishi's anger melted, and the realization of its unjustness prompted him to apologize. Had they been in the castle or in public, his outburst would have been a grievous breach of etiquette, punishable by banishment, or even *seppuku*.

Could it be the influence of Hatsumi's blood? Could anger and jealousy become solid things?

As they climbed, the jagged unease hounded him like a pack of wolves on his scent.

At dusk they reached a sharp rise that became a cliff, perhaps the height of five men. The stream cascaded over the lip and plunged into a pool with thunderous, silvery spray. Amid the roar and mist of the falling water, the voices of the *kami* rose in an endless, crashing dance.

"Here," he said. "Can you feel the power here? It's like a swelling of wonder in your chest."

She smiled at the immense beauty of the glade, the sun shining through the scattering mist. "Perhaps..."

"I was so small when Kaa taught me to listen for them, it seems

I've always known how. It is easiest when one's mind and heart are still, like a pool. The voices of the *kami* are like ripples on the pool."

She closed her eyes and took several deep breaths. "I think, perhaps, I felt them. They are like multitudes of bees buzzing in the water. But I only sensed it for a moment...."

Ken'ishi smiled. "Keep practicing, and it will get easier."

She opened her eyes. "Darkness will come soon. Shall we make a fire?"

"Not yet. First we must make you a weapon."

In a stroke of good fortune, he found a suitable pine saplings less than a *cho* from the waterfall and cut one to fashion a makeshift *naginata* haft. While Kazuko kept watch, he trimmed the bark and branches, shaved it as smooth as he could until the light failed, and then slotted one end to mount the tang of the *naginata* blade. Silver Crane simmered with annoyance at being used as a woodcarving tool, but he ignored it. Once, it even cut his thumb. He sucked at the blood and kept working.

"This is not going to be as strong as an oak haft," he said. "The wood is very green and much softer. I hope you might get a handful of blows before it breaks."

Using stones as hammer and anvil, he disassembled the splintered haft and fittings, and drove the iron pins through the wood, through the holes in the tang of the blade. It was during this stage that the unnatural frustrations came roaring back. Every missed blow, every mashed finger, every misalignment of the pins, every time the green wood failed to cooperate with his carving, he cried out with uncharacteristic vehemence. Nevertheless, he forced himself to calm down and keep going.

The final step of construction was to wind his bowstring, salvaged from his splintered bow, around the slotted end of the pole to tighten the wood's grip on the steel tang. By this time, dusk had faded to night.

"Try it, my lady," he said, offering it to her with both hands.

The haft was moist, knobby, and too flexible, but the blade felt solidly mounted. She spun the weapon and made a few practice strikes.

Meanwhile he stripped himself to his loincloth and approached the pool, sword in hand. She gasped and turned her back until he slipped into the water. It swallowed his ankles like the frigid snowmelt pools of his youth in the far north. He found this strangely comforting. Then he waded deeper. The pool was waist deep when he stepped beneath the bone-chilling waterfall. The sensuous richness of moisture flooded his nose with the scent of life itself. The icy cold dashed a headache into his skull, but he lowered his head, held Silver Crane horizontally in both hands, took a deep breath through his mouth, and sought the Void. His skin numbed, even as the tumbling water thumped against his weary muscles, loosening them like the fingers of a hundred blind masseurs. The *kami* were alive with teeming abundance, flowing over him, through him, around him, swimming over his flesh, washing through his mind.

He concentrated on taking one breath after the next, calming the shiver in his flesh, stilling his instincts that cried out to remove himself from such penetrating cold.

Infinite moments passed into numb serenity. He felt only the slick, round stones beneath his bare feet and the hard, sharp weapon resting in his palms. Infinite silver threads filled the universe with possibilities across time and distance, at the heart of which lay Silver Crane. The threads entangled his body and disappeared into vastnesses he could not comprehend. The threads encompassed the trees, the mountain, the water, the *kami,* unseen multitudes of creatures. Every movement of so much as his finger sent subtle vibrations through the web in a dizzying cascade of after-effects.

And here, in this place, at this time, lay a powerful center of possibilities.

Bathed in *kami* and communing with the sword, he could see the threads, the possibilities, but not their likely outcomes.

Other vibrations came from other directions, others whose efforts formed their own webs. From one direction came a cluster of threads that trembled with variations of hunger, rage, and fear, but also yearning, sadness, and the anguish of betrayal. Hatsumi's nexus.

From another direction, closer to him, scents came to him of courage against fear, resolve against danger, and love against duty. Kazuko's nexus.

What if he could manipulate the threads of others through the power of Silver Crane? What if he could determine outcomes that worked in his favor, and then guide others into them?

The man begins to understand.

Ken'ishi's focus intensified. How to accomplish that?

He envisioned a scene with Hatsumi lying dead at his feet, Kazuko unharmed. Then he dragged a fistful of Hatsumi's threads into the scene until they merged. The image wavered, however, with flashes of him lying dead next to Hatsumi, or images of himself mortally wounded gasping out his last breaths in Kazuko's arms.

Crude, inelegant. But understanding grows. Remember that many other threads pass through this place.

Ken'ishi reached out to look at moments up and down the threads of this physical area, seeking possibilities for his advantage. A stout-looking branch weakened by insects. A precipitously-balanced boulder. A sharp rock slick with water. Instances of Kazuko striking in which her makeshift *naginata* haft remained whole. His feet finding solid earth, not loose dirt. As if he watched through the ripples of a pool, the image of Hatsumi's defeat began to coalesce.

But then Kazuko's shout of warning found its way through the roar of falling water.

We hark to cricket
And to human
    chirpings...with
Ears so different
                    —*Wafu*

K en'ishi leaped out of
the water, raising Silver Crane.

Kazuko stood on the bank, her *naginata* interposed between herself and Hatsumi.

Hatsumi lay on her side at the foot of a thick pine tree, extricating herself from a thick branch. Her head was back in place, but now cocked at a grotesque angle. Black venom dripped from her lips, and her horrific, black legs splayed from under her robes, part spider, part octopus.

Kazuko shouted, "Her branch snapped! She was coming through the treetops!"

He plunged across the pool, ignoring the rocks tearing at his feet, and scrambled onto the bank.

Hatsumi tried to right herself, but struggled with one of her legs still pinned under the heavy bough by her own weight.

Ken'ishi charged at her, gathering a powerful *kiai* to focus spirit, sword, and body into the perfect strike.

A spray of glistening, white filaments burst from between Hatsumi's legs and ensnared his arms. Two of Hatsumi's legs seized the filaments, yanked him off his feet, and began to drag him toward her. She giggled like a child with a new toy.

Kazuko leaped forward and slashed at the silken tangle. Her blow severed only a few of the silks, others just clung to the *naginata* blade. She sawed frantically, and still Hatsumi dragged Ken'ishi nearer. He swung himself feet-first and scrabbled for purchase, but the carpet of pine needles slid under him.

Kazuko's blade managed to sever Ken'ishi's bonds. He scrambled to his feet, struggling to free his arms of the sticky fibers.

Hatsumi tried to charge forward, but the bough still trapped her leg.

Ken'ishi snatched a handful of Kazuko's robe and dragged her after him toward the rock face leading to the top of the waterfall. The rocks offered enough purchase for a careful climber to pick his way to the top without much danger. But they did not have time. "Climb!" he shouted.

Kazuko scrambled up the rocks with one hand, *naginata* clenched in the other.

Hatsumi's cries of consternation were turning to rage. The crunching crackle of the bough, splintering under her efforts, echoed down the mountainside. Hampered by the *naginata*, Kazuko's progress was too slow. Hatsumi would be free before they reached the height.

Another tangle of fibers sprayed the rock face, part of it catching his foot, but a quick slash freed him.

Hatsumi moved with a peculiar limp now from her damaged leg, like a spider with a crumpled limb. She leaped and fell short of the rock face. He seized a foot-sized stone and hurled it down into her face. It crashed into her gaping, black maw, striking another howl of pain from her. Her teeth now looked even more jagged. The moment gave Kazuko the opportunity to reach a narrow ledge just below the crest of the rock face. She reached down with the butt of her *naginata* haft for Ken'ishi. He seized it, and she dragged him up beside her.

With no time to convey his plan, he threw his shoulder against a boulder perched at the edge of the ledge. With a roar of strain, he felt the huge rock shift slightly.

Hatsumi peered up at them, grinning that horrid grin, then launched herself up the rock face, grabbing crevices with claws and legs.

Kazuko slashed and stabbed downward. Hatsumi dodged the blows, or swatted them away with her hands, but Kazuko's attacks were herding Hatsumi into the boulder's expected path.

"Come and take us!" Kazuko screamed.

Thanks to the angle of the climb, Hatsumi could not bring her webs to bear.

The gleaming sheen of *naginata* kept her at bay just long enough for Ken'ishi to muster one last sinew-rending heave against the boulder.

With a grinding crumble, the earth underneath it gave way and tipped the great stone off the ledge.

Too late, Hatsumi saw it coming. The boulder caught her full in the chest and drove her down the rock face. In midair, her limbs flailed against it. With her preternatural alacrity, she almost succeeded in casting herself out of its path before it struck the earth, but it crushed the bottom half of her torso against the rocks below. Black ichor squished from the joints of three crushed legs, which now thrashed and spasmed as if of their own volition. Her caterwauling scream tore a jagged hole in Ken'ishi's soul, reverberating through the forest with such anguish that the trees of this mountainside might be forever scarred by its noise.

Ken'ishi and Kazuko pushed more stones over the edge, or flung them down upon her. Hatsumi kept screaming in pain, scrabbling to drag herself away, but she was trapped under the boulder's weight. The fresh stones struck others loose from the rock face, and they began to fall on her, first one at a time, then faster and faster. Each sickening thud of stone against flesh renewed her wail of anguish. Her spasming limbs grew still.

"She is not yet dead," Ken'ishi said, gathering his breath.

"Not until we burn her head," Kazuko said.

When they had defeated Hakamadare together, the *oni*'s body maintained its fierce vigor until they had dismembered it and burned its frightful head. The head had cursed them silently from the flames until reduced to a blackened skull.

As Ken'ishi gazed down upon Hatsumi's shattered, motionless body, he sensed the *kami* of this place crying out in pain at the defilement, at the stain of evil upon the earth, the water, the air itself. It would be up to the *kami* of flame to cleanse and purify this place.

They helped each other down the rock face.

Standing over Hatsumi's monstrous form, he could see she was still very much alive. Her eyelids fluttered, her mouth worked, her limbs twitched and writhed, seeking any opportunity to exact vengeance.

In the falling darkness of the forest night, their task became grim butchery. Hatsumi's head lay separated from her neck, but her eyes would not leave Kazuko. The expression of forlorn sadness, mouthing, *"Why? Why? Why?"* even twisted as it was by her monstrous features, drove Kazuko away for a while to collect herself. "I cannot look at her anymore."

Ken'ishi sent her into the forest to gather wood for the cleansing pyre while he continued his awful task. Kazuko returned with armful after armful, and they piled it upon the dismembered pieces of Hatsumi's body. Black ichor flowed across the ground in shifting rivulets, like sentient tar. Hatsumi's blood clung to Silver Crane, too sticky to sling away. He could only wipe it away with handfuls of grass.

Finally, when they had built the pyre, they set fire to it and stepped away to watch it burn, covering their noses and mouths against the noxious stench that poured forth.

It all brought back for him that day he had saved her life, how beautiful she had been, but how young and fierce with her *naginata,* how soft and kind in her care for Hatsumi. And how the scent of her had driven his heart into a wild gallop. He wanted to reach for her now, to comfort her, to tell her the ordeal was over, that she had done well. But he did not dare.

He said, "You saved my life. I am in your debt."

"I think we are beyond keeping account by now, don't you?" she said.

And so they stood in tense silence.

When the moon had risen high and the flames had settled low, Kazuko sat on the ground away from him, gazing out into the forest blackness, rocking gently on her haunches.

He watched the fire until Hatsumi's skull lay blackened and empty. Stubby horns had sprouted from the bone. Then he stabbed it through with the *naginata,* and planted the butt of the haft into the earth. This would be their trophy, their proof to the countryside, the villages, and Lord Tsunetomo that their hunt had been successful.

The fire would help to cleanse the area of Hatsumi's taint, but only time would heal it fully. Sadness washed over him at the knowledge that he had helped to despoil such a beautiful, pristine place. The presence of evil still lay thick in the air itself.

He said, "We cannot sleep here. Come."

She nodded but would not meet his eyes. The bloodstained bandage on her cheek glowed orange in the ember-light.

Ken'ishi took up the *naginata*, and they hiked back down the mountain in the dark.

Once again I hear
The first frogs sing in
   the pond.
I am overwhelmed by
   the past.
   —*The Love Poems of
      Marichiko*

They reached Takeshita village at dawn, bone-weary and reeking of Hatsumi's stench. Try as they might to cleanse themselves in the stream, they could not shed themselves of it.

Blisters risen and burst turned Kazuko's every step into a low-grade rhythm of pain. Deep, aching bruises had bloomed across her torso. Only Ken'ishi's steadfast, taciturn limp kept her going when all she wanted to do was collapse by the roadside. Even making their painstaking way down the mountain in the darkness, amidst the skitterings of unseen night creatures or unfriendly spirits, was as nothing compared to the horrors of what they had just faced—and defeated.

Villagers, preparing for their day's toils, cried out at the sight of Hatsumi's skull, pierced, aloft on the point of the *naginata*. The headman came out to meet them and practically pulled out his hair in frantic orders to see them given food and rest. There was no shrine or temple here to cleanse them of contact with the *oni*, so the villagers brought them the finest clothes they could muster and sent the ichor-stained garments to be cleaned.

Kazuko sent a messenger on foot to the castle—Takeshita village had no horses—informing Tsunetomo that their hunt had been successful, but at the cost of two of the hunters. She did not mention the wound on her face. How badly would she be disfigured? Would she still be beautiful enough for him? Was she forever marred?

The sense that there was now a dark weight upon her did not diminish when she shed her soiled clothes. It was as if she could feel the malevolent gaze of Hatsumi's skull upon her, even through the walls.

Meanwhile, Ken'ishi ordered the headman to send gravediggers with him back into the forest to retrieve the bodies of the hunters. They would be buried here, with prominent markers to honor their sacrifice in ending the Wild Woman's rampage. Their swords would be returned with honor to Lord Otomo.

When Kazuko heard Ken'ishi was going back into the forest, she wanted to go with him, but he simply pointed at her bloody feet and shook his head.

"Stay here and rest, my lady," he said. "I'll return by nightfall."

But she would not rest until she had made things right here. So she held audience with the villagers to hear their tales of the Wild Woman's evils—from behind a screen where none could see her. She offered reparations of food, tools, and livestock.

In the afternoon, a healer came, brought from a nearby village to look at her cheek. The healer, a stolid, middle-aged peasant woman, peeled away her bandage and failed to conceal her alarm. A sick, twisted whorl in Kazuko's gut wanted to see, but she had no mirror. The healer daubed her cheek with a smelly poultice, covered it with a fresh bandage, and then saw to her blistered feet.

The villagers offered her food, but it all tasted like blood. They even brought her tea, and it too tasted like blood. But that could not be real. It had to be some lingering taint of evil. A tremor of cold fear whispered through her.

Ken'ishi and the village gravediggers returned that evening bearing the bodies of Yahei and Naohiro wrapped in blankets. Kazuko's heart went out to him at how much more pronounced his limp had become from where Hatsumi's spiny appendage had seized his ankle. Ken'ishi had recovered his horse, with all his accouterments still in place. The gray stallion's proud demeanor looked unfazed by having spent the night in the forest.

The bodies were placed in funeral urns and buried at dusk. A Buddhist priest who served several villages in the area came to read sutras over the dead. The village stonecutter extolled how grand would be the markers he made for the two samurai. The villagers would give offerings to their spirits for years to come in thanks for their great deeds.

The reverence and amazement on the faces of the villagers as they looked at Kazuko and Ken'ishi made her even more uncomfortable, because she, for her part, did not deserve them. It was because of Kazuko that Hatsumi had gone mad. That Kazuko and Ken'ishi had survived seemed more a matter of fortune than prowess.

When the headman's wife closed the door on Kazuko's private chamber, she passed into fitful sleep, a sleep of night-sweats and foul dreams, dreams of blood and fire and terror, dreams of cruelty and spite. By turns, her cheek felt numb and hot, burning and dead.

Before dawn, she went outside and found Ken'ishi kneeling on the veranda, keeping watch over her. Neither of them spoke.

The first villagers of the morning found them both sitting on the veranda of the headman's house, awaiting the dawn. She wondered if she would ever sleep again.

An entire retinue from the castle arrived the following afternoon, with an elaborate palanquin, and, to Kazuko's shock, Lord Tsunetomo himself on horseback.

As word of his presence burned like wildfire through the village, the people came out to greet him with prostrations and exhortations of praise for the bravery of his wife and the warriors who had accompanied her.

Kazuko came out of the headman's house to greet her husband, trembling with nervousness, like a child awaiting a parent's decision. She knelt and bowed low.

At the sight of her, he reined up his horse, threw a leg over, and jumped to the ground. A squire leaped from the entourage to take the reins. Tsunetomo came to her, his gaze boring into her.

Where was Ken'ishi?

"Stand and let me look at you," Tsunetomo said, lifting her to her feet. He lifted her chin to look at her cheek, but she could not meet his gaze.

He guided her into the house. Her legs were wobbly. He shut the door behind them.

And then he hugged her, fiercely, ferociously. She collapsed into him and wept for the comfort of it, and for how she had yearned to fall into Ken'ishi's arms for two days and could not allow it.

He laid gentle fingers along her chin. "What of this?"

"Hatsumi was..." Fresh tears burst from her eyes. "She clawed me with her talons. Ken'ishi saved me at the last moment. She nearly killed all of us!"

He appraised her cheek again, his face brimming with regret. "Let us sit. Tell me the tale." He eased her to the floor, and she told him the story.

When she was finished, he said, "You were fortunate to have him with you."

She nodded.

"Where is he?"

"He has been standing guard over me, but then he was gone when you arrived...."

Tsunetomo scowled a bit. A warrior did not abandon his post. He stood and opened the door, revealing Ken'ishi kneeling upon the veranda.

Ken'ishi pressed his forehead to the planks. "Please forgive my absence at your arrival, Lord. I was visiting the village carpenter for a new oaken haft on Lady Otomo's *naginata*."

The *naginata* lay sheathed beside him on his right, with a stout, smooth, oaken haft.

Kazuko bowed to him. "That is very thoughtful, Sir Ken'ishi. Thank you."

Ken'ishi bowed to her in return. "My lord, Lady Otomo saved my life. Without her assistance, I would be food in the Wild Woman's belly. She is truly a formidable warrior, and brave beyond compare. My deep regret, however, is that she did not go unscathed. If my lord wishes it, I will gladly pay the ultimate price for my failure...."

"That will not be necessary," Tsunetomo said. "The lives of a thousand might be worth Kazuko's beauty, but you, Captain Ken'ishi, are worth a thousand and one. The gods have smiled upon me to place you in my service."

"Captain, Lord?"

Tsunetomo smiled. "Command of a few spearmen hardly befits a warrior of your prowess and valor. When we return to the castle, you will be promoted to captain, and begin your study of military tactics and strategy under Yamazaki no Hidetaka-*sensei*, retired general of the Minamoto clan."

Ken'ishi pressed his forehead to the floor again. "Thank you, Lord. Thank you."

Kazuko could hardly contain her pride in him. The profound surprise and humility on his face made her love him even more.

Stubborn woodpecker
Still hammering at
  twilight
At that single spot
                    —*Issa*

Ken'ishi moved into his new house at the base of the castle wall with a strange sense of wonder. The house was a spacious affair, meticulously kept, appointed with fresh *tatami* mats. A wooden wall surrounded a modest contemplative garden, similar to the one enjoyed by Norikage, Ken'ishi's former employer, the administrator of Aoka village. The garden reminded him of his talks with Norikage, and the chafed patch of memory at how they had parted during the invasion. In retrospect, he regretted the intensity of his anger at their last meeting.

While Ken'ishi was called 'captain,' his rank was still significantly below Yoshimura and Tsunemori, whose ranks technically equaled captain of the third and fourth levels, respectively.

Being promoted to captain meant that he not only was given a residence of his own, but that he now had servants, the very concept of which was alien to him. His servants were a married couple, Jinbei and his wife Suzu, with several children. Without being told—Ken'ishi had little idea how to direct them in any case—they appointed his house with food and comforts befitting a retainer of

Ken'ishi's rank.

He had little time to acquaint himself with his servants, however, as he now spent several hours a day studying military history and tactics under the man once known as Yamazaki no Hidetaka. He had retired to shave his head and become a Buddhist monk, taking the name of Jokei, but he was still called Yamazaki-*sensei*. The old general was one of the most venerable men Ken'ishi had ever encountered, well into his seventies but still sharp of mind, and possessed of more wisdom than Ken'ishi could fathom. Decades of service and battle had formed an old warrior's pragmatism and powerful insight into what made men fight—and what made men flee. These connections, previously glimpsed only in disparate bits, but drawn together by Yamazaki-*sensei*'s instruction, fascinated Ken'ishi. He applied himself with rigor to the texts of Chinese generals more than a thousand years dead.

This study was in addition to his practice of spear and *yabusame*. Every day was crammed, sunrise to sunset, with study and practice to such a degree that Kazuko found her way into his stream of thoughts only in the moments between tasks.

Word spread like wildfire across the countryside that Lady Kazuko and a brave champion had destroyed the Wild Woman, thus ending the reign of terror. Since then, Kazuko had secluded herself from the public eye. Scant word of her came out of the castle, only that she was still recovering from the encounter. One night in the Roasted Acorn, Ken'ishi heard a minstrel sing a tune of praise for her courage and prowess. Ken'ishi nodded and clapped his hands with greater enthusiasm than anyone.

His life had moved, overnight it seemed, into a new, unfamiliar realm—one he had only viewed before from the outside, and with distant yearning.

Before he could grow accustomed to his sudden success, however, the arrival of northern warriors, first coming in ones and twos, with their entourages, then in larger and larger groups, assigned by the shogunate to aid in the defense of Kyushu against future attack, set the town into an uproar.

They arrived with letters of assignment from the *bakufu*. According to the letters, they were to be given lodging and stipends according to their rank. The inns in Hita and the surrounding towns filled up quickly until a number of townsfolk were displaced to live with relatives or in the hastily-constructed tent village on the outskirts of town. The province's carpenters and laborers were marshaled into an immediate expansion of the town's living quarters.

Grumbling filled the *saké* houses, from the townspeople at being forced out of their homes and from the visiting warriors at so little preparation being made in advance of their arrival, at being forced to live so close-packed in every available patch of spare *tatami*. Brawls broke out, and men from the castle were assigned to serve as peacekeepers between the locals and the foreign warriors. Tension festered between Lord Tsunetomo's retainers and the newcomers. "They're not Kyushu men!" was an often-heard utterance among the men under Ken'ishi's command. Nevertheless, the order never to brawl with other warriors was still fresh in the minds of most, after the beating Ken'ishi and Ushihara had received over the winter. Lord Tsunetomo made the same edict clear to every visiting samurai, but the memories of some were apparently clouded by arrogance. The deaths of two belligerent locals, slain by samurai "whose honor had been slighted," led to more grumbling, but fewer confrontations.

On a typical evening during the summer rainy season, Jinbei came to tell Ken'ishi of a visitor, Otomo no Ishitaka. Ken'ishi was deep in his study of Chinese military history, as he usually was late into the night, but he had not met Ishitaka in several weeks.

Ishitaka's face was pale and taut as he settled himself with Ken'ishi.

Jinbei said, "May I offer tea, Lords? *Saké?*"

Ishitaka said, "It is a night for tea."

Jinbei bowed and departed.

Ken'ishi said with a smirk, "No *saké?*"

"I must keep a clear head." There was nothing boisterous in the tightness of Ishitaka's mouth. He clutched something in a tight fist against his belly.

"Something must be very serious," Ken'ishi said. "Perhaps word of Yuri?"

Ishitaka nodded. "Her father has dragged her away to Kamakura. A messenger came today with this letter for me." He opened his hand, revealing a crumpled piece of rice paper. The ink had run with the sweat of his palm. "She is...with child. The child is mine."

Ken'ishi took a deep breath and bowed his head. "This is very dangerous ground, my friend."

Ishitaka swallowed hard. "I have considered all the possibilities I can imagine ten thousand times since I read the letter. Perhaps there might be one I have missed. I seek your wisdom, Ken'ishi."

"*My* wisdom! Ishitaka, you have chosen your sage poorly. In matters of love, I am the greatest of fools."

"What am I to do?"

Ken'ishi sighed. "A peasant-born tavern wench is carrying the heir to the Otomo line. Unless Lady Kazuko produces an heir, that is. There has been talk that Lord Tsunetomo would adopt you as his son to ensure a clear succession. Most people look upon that idea with favor. Except now..."

"Now I have produced a bastard child by a peasant girl. I have shamed my family."

"Does your father know?"

Ishitaka shook his head. "I must tell him."

"Even if your father does not disown you, even if your uncle still chooses to adopt you, what will happen if Yuri comes forward with her child? Peasants have no legal standing when making such claims. She could be killed outright for attempting to dishonor the house of Otomo, her child sent to live as an orphan among the unclean."

Jinbei returned with a tea service.

"And the threat to her life would make her claim all the more credible, would it not? Ah, but I don't want any of that."

"What do you want?"

"I want to find her, save her from her father, and claim my child."

"The Otomo clan might well cast you out for that. You could be disowned, cut off. A *ronin*'s life is nothing to be wished for. And with a family to support."

"She says...she says..." Ishitaka choked on the rest of his utterance.

"May I read the letter?" Ken'ishi asked.

Ishitaka handed it over.

Ken'ishi smoothed it out. The script was inexpertly brushed, written in women's script, without Chinese characters, relating what Ishitaka had already conveyed. She ended the letter with: *"In a life filled with cruelty and death, you are the only kind man I have ever known. I wish nothing more than for you to be the father of my child. When Father*

discovers my condition, it may not go well for me. I wait at the shrine to
Kannon every day and pray that you will deliver me."

Ken'ishi handed the letter back. "Your father is a wise, fair man. So is Lord Tsunetomo."

"But this could jeopardize my adoption. I cannot bear to bring this shame to my family."

"How would this be different if Yuri were still here? You brought shame on your family by bedding her, knowing this might be the result."

Ishitaka's eyes glistened.

"I am sorry," Ken'ishi said. "That was too harsh of me. The only honorable course for you that I can see is to confess this to your father, state your wishes, and accept the consequences. You would hardly be the first samurai who took the life of a *ronin* for a woman." The thought of his own father, secluding himself in the wilds of northern Honshu to live the life of a farmer, made him wonder if his mother had played a role in that decision. He knew little of his father, and even less of his mother.

Ishitaka released a deep, shuddering breath. "If she were here, I could show them how beautiful she is, show them my child, and they would love him. Or her, I care not which."

"If the child is a girl, your situation will be simplified. She could not be the heir." Something niggled at Ken'ishi's thoughts, however. "Do you know her father's name? Lord Otomo may order him to return."

"Or her father may kill her to save himself the shame."

"But do you know his name?"

Ishitaka licked his lips. "She never told me."

The *kami* buzzed with warning behind Ken'ishi's ears. "It could be a simple oversight. It could be the girl was afraid of her father, but... something here does not smell right. Do you not feel it yourself?"

"All my thoughts now are to know she is well, and the baby."

Ken'ishi nodded. Nevertheless, the worry remained. Without her father's name, there was no way to track them down.

Ishitaka said, "When my sisters died of fever, my parents were left with only me. They were happy for a son, but Mother doted on my sisters. This knowledge will destroy her."

"Is your mother frail?"

"No. She is very hale and vigorous."

"Is she weak minded?"

"As I said, she is strong, a true samurai's wife."

"If you were to die in battle, what would she do?"

"I'm sure she would weep for me."

"But she would be a warrior's wife."

"Oh, yes."

"Then knowledge of any of this will cause her pain, but not destroy her. And you must accept that. You have already defied what you knew to be the wishes of your parents. But you have undergone your rite of manhood. You are young. You have much time to make recompense. If the barbarians come again, they will not care where your little warrior has been."

Ken'ishi sipped his tea and waited. Ishitaka stared into his own teacup as if the leaves in the bottom might offer a solution.

The lamp slowly burned down, dimming the room. Frogs sang amid a patter of fresh rain on the roof. The air moistened afresh.

"I must think on this," Ishitaka said. "Perhaps if I pray to the gods and buddhas, they will send me an answer."

"Perhaps," Ken'ishi said. "Remember this, however. You are my friend. I know you to be a good and honorable man. I trust your judgment."

Ishitaka gave him a wan smile. "Thank you, Ken'ishi. Good night."

"When you dance, the hand holds the fan and the foot takes a step. When you do not forget everything, when you go on thinking about performing with the hands and the feet well and dancing accurately, you cannot be said to be skillful. When the mind stops at the hands and feet, none of your acts will be singular. If you do not completely discard the mind, everything you do will be done poorly."

—*Takuan Soho, "The Mysterious Record of Immovable Wisdom"*

The following evening, Ken'ishi was riding back from *yabusame* training through town when he spotted a band of performers near the town's central wooden bridge. He spurred Storm to a quicker pace along the irrigation canal. Could they be the same performers as those Kaa had joined at the New Year festival?

Nearing, he caught a glimpse of Kaa's guise as the Raggedy Man, tattered clothing spinning wildly as he cavorted to gong and flute. A throng of townspeople surrounded the performers, clapping and dancing with glee.

As Ken'ishi reined up outside the throng, he bid Storm to remain still and threw himself into the crowd. "Stand aside!"

The throng parted for him.

The performers, with their cymbals and flutes and rhythm sticks, their rainbow attire and gap-toothed grins, all moved together in a chaotic clump. And then with impressive feats of tumbling acrobatics, they formed a great tower of interlocking bodies that brought peals of laughter and applause from the audience. Ken'ishi searched the troupe for the Raggedy Man, but he was gone.

His cheeks heated. His old master was making a fool of him. Kaa had often taunted the boy who would become Ken'ishi with tales of becoming invisible.

One by one, the performers tumbled free of the tower and landed with great aplomb. A wizened old man with a long nose came forward. "Have we offended, samurai?" The mocking tone in his voice put Ken'ishi's teeth on edge.

"The Raggedy Man," he said. "I saw him here not a moment ago. Where is he?"

"We are all raggedy men here, samurai," the man said. The other performers tittered and banged their instruments.

"Perhaps you think I do not know him. He goes by another name, Kaa." Ken'ishi raised his voice. In that moment, he hatched a plan. "I will always be in his debt, but I will not be made a fool! Tell him to show himself to me. I challenge him! If he has the courage!"

The old man's expression flickered with a succession of outrage and amusement. "If we encounter such a man, we will relay your august message." The others snickered anew.

Ken'ishi laid a hand on his sword. "I'll not be mocked by the likes of you. Now, clear out!"

The old man's grin widened.

Ken'ishi turned to the crowd. "Everyone! Go home!"

The townspeople began to disperse, trading glances.

He turned back to the performers, who were gathering up their instruments and accouterments. Ken'ishi stood with his arms crossed as the performers hurried across the bridge to vacate the area and the townspeople filtered away.

But then the touch of the *kami* whispered up the back of his neck. There, in the deepening dusk, were a multitude of footprints of the crowd and the performers. The footprints of the crowd were of *geta* and *zori* and the bare feet of children. The footprints of the performers were...three-toed and clawed, with a single, rear-facing claw. Like those of birds. In the performers' area, the earth bore no impressions of human feet.

The whisper of other worlds raised the hair on his arms. Even so, these beings—they must all of them have been *tengu*—would know his old teacher. Kaa might well have been watching the whole affair from hiding. He would receive the message indeed.

Kazuko took her place behind the screen via a small door in the corner. The room was a small chamber near their quarters, usually used for private meetings. Tsunetomo, Tsunemori, and Lady Yukino had just seated themselves in a circle, and two servants were pouring tea.

Kazuko's screen sat just off to the side of the circle. None of them would be able to see her. The thick bandage plastered to her cheek, held in place by a kerchief wrapped around her head and tied under her chin, distracted her whenever she spoke.

She hated it. And she was coming to hate what lay beneath it.

"Please forgive me, Brother and Sister," Kazuko said, addressing them both honorifically as elders, even though she held the higher rank. "My wound is still too fresh." She could just see their outlines in the lamplight through the gauzy rice paper screen. "I insisted on the screen."

Lady Yukino said, "After all you've been through, my lady, we would expect nothing else." Her voice, normally measured, serene, and elegant, carried a brittleness this evening.

The bonds of family were strong between the two brothers, and Kazuko greatly admired Lady Yukino. The two Otomo couples occasionally met for meals or tea, but those events were always carefully planned, not impromptu. Tonight's abrupt request for a visit over tea bespoke something of great weight brewing. Unfortunately, she could not see their faces through the screen, only vague silhouettes.

Tsunemori said, "Lady Kazuko, we have every hope for your full recovery. Your bravery is a credit to your sex, and a boon to my elder brother."

"Thank you for your kind words," Kazuko said. "My strength returns day by day."

Tsunetomo took a sip of his tea. "I am immeasurably proud of my wife. Have you seen the skull? It is monstrous indeed." The skull was hoisted now upon the point of a lance over the practice ground of Barrack Six, a trophy of Ken'ishi's former unit, and a symbol of martial prowess and valor. It had been purified and blessed by both Shinto and Buddhist priests before Tsunetomo would allow it within the castle.

"I have seen it," Tsunemori said. "The thing seems to be looking at me whenever I pass. I have beheld a thousand heads, but never had such a feeling." Like Lady Yukino, there was a tightness in his voice, urgent news waiting for pleasantries to pass before it could come out. Coming straight to business was rude without first filling the room with harmony. But would harmony make this unknown news any easier to bear?

Tsunetomo mirrored her thoughts. "Our get-togethers outside of clan business are always enjoyable, but there is something amiss, I think. Something serious."

Lady Yukino dabbed a sleeve to her face. Was that the sound of a sniffle?

Tsunemori said, "Ishitaka has been...very foolish. We must apologize for his behavior, Brother. He has dishonored our house. We are so sorry."

Both Tsunemori and Yukino bowed to Tsunetomo, then to Kazuko. Kazuko returned the gesture with a burgeoning sense of dread and curiosity. Ishitaka was a good-hearted young man, if still over-exuberant in his youth.

Tsunetomo returned the gesture, then eased back as he did when preparing for difficult news, as if he were fashioning himself into a bulwark that would stand against any tide. "What has happened?"

Tsunemori said, "Ishitaka is gone, departed. On his way to Kamakura."

"Is this some sort of stunt?" Tsunetomo said. "Why Kamakura?

Does he intend to speak to the barbarian emissaries? The *bakufu?* I have given no leave to make such a journey."

"Nor did I, Brother. His purpose is... He went alone. To meet a..." Tsunemori seemed to squeeze out the next words, "...a merchant's daughter. He got her with child." The last words were a barely intelligible garble of desperation and fury.

The weight of shame filled the room like a choking blanket.

"I knew he had a plaything in town," Tsunemori said, "but that is hardly uncommon."

The trouble with playthings was that they were most often discarded when the amusement abated. Kazuko's heart went out to Lady Yukino. That the girl was a merchant's daughter was worse than if she had been born in the mud of a rice paddy. As merchants made nothing, produced nothing, only profited from the efforts of others, they were superior to only whores, gravediggers, and actors in the celestial order.

Tsunetomo said, "But why not just discard her? An occasional bastard is also hardly uncommon. Send her a few pieces of silver to support the child and be done."

"The young fool!" Tsunemori said. "He says he loves her and wants to raise the child as his own. He may as well have said he wants to marry a common whore!"

A sob slipped free of Lady Yukino.

Tsunetomo said, "This is a grave impropriety. It reflects badly, especially here on the eve of the Council of Kyushu Lords in Dazaifu. What did you tell him of your wishes?"

"I told him to discard her. Claim the child as a bastard if he must, even as distasteful as that notion is, but send the girl away. It was as far as I could go. The house of Otomo is a warrior house! We will not embrace a *merchant's* daughter. But he would have none of that. He told me her father might harm her when he discovers she's with child. I told him that would be the simplest solution for everyone."

"Now, Brother," Tsunetomo said, admonishment in his tone, "fairness and charity to the lowest people, even merchants, is part of the Way. They serve us, and we protect them."

Tsunemori grunted and scratched his chin. "Perhaps it was impolitic of me to say such a thing, but the moment was hot. Merchants are simply a different kind of whore, always chasing their profit and gold. Bah!"

Tsunetomo said, "I was not aware of any merchants in town trading with Kamakura. Having too many dealings with the northerners sits ill with Kyushu men. He must not be particularly wealthy, or Yasutoki would have informed me. He does well keeping an eye on the merchants and their activities. Alas that he were here. We might have a bit more information on this merchant and his daughter. Did Ishitaka give the merchant's name?"

"I pressed him, but he shut his lips like a clam."

Lady Yukino cleared her throat softly. "My lords, if I may speak? My chief concern is for my son's welfare. A mother learns to bear the wanton cruelties of her thoughtless children when they are young. It is through those that she redirects their path to goodness, to realign them with the Way. I cannot bear the thought of never seeing my son again. He was one breath short of declaring himself *ronin* before he stormed out. My husband was one breath short of disowning him."

Tsunemori grunted again. "I'm of a mind to do that still, except..."

Silence stretched for several moments, and then Kazuko realized all three of them had just glanced at her screen. Kazuko's voice wavered just above a whisper. "Except that Ishitaka...may become the heir." Her shoulders slumped. Her head bowed.

Tsunetomo said, "My wife, we must not give up hope that the gods will bless us with a son."

"Of course not, Husband," Kazuko said.

"Nevertheless," Yukino said, "adopting Ishitaka as your son, Brother, would go far toward easing many worries."

Kazuko's guts twisted. If Tsunetomo adopted Ishitaka, that would mean any son Kazuko might bear, even born of the true blood of Tsunetomo, would become the younger sibling. Such confusion had sometimes resulted in war, down through history. The elder son was the designated heir, through law and custom, set to inherit everything. The younger siblings existed at the sufferance of the elder. Tsunetomo had taken Tsunemori into his service, but such arrangements were not always the case among the powerful, and when they were, the arrangements were not always fraternal.

Removing the pressure of having to produce an heir might be a welcome respite for Kazuko, but marriages between powerful families—hers, the Nishimuta clan, and Tsunetomo's, the Otomo clan—were about producing heirs and cementing alliances. Tsunetomo adopting Ishitaka as a son would be tacit, public acknowledgment that his wife was barren and thus of minimal importance to his line. He could not divorce her out of hand, or else risk gravely offending her father, Nishimuta no Jiro, leader of the Nishimuta clan. She did not believe Tsunetomo would be so cruel to her, but the alliances and advantage of shifting politics made a bloody game of Go. She did not wish to believe it could happen, but she did believe it.

And now, abruptly, she realized that everyone in the room had given up on her. And for that betrayal, that admission to herself, she let the tears come. She was to become an afterthought, a hindrance. And now that she was irrevocably marred, she was no longer beautiful. How much of her usefulness would fall away before Tsunetomo set her adrift?

Lady Yukino said, "Perhaps such an act as adoption would entice him to return home."

Even through the screen, Kazuko could feel the pressure of her husband's eyes on her.

Another long, thundering silence. Finally Tsunetomo said, "If we order him to return home, he will refuse. I have no doubt that whatever course he has set himself upon, he must see it through. Perhaps soon he will see the folly of it. The heart is such a fickle thing when you're young."

A flash of anger shot through Kazuko. She was only three years older than Ishitaka. Her heart was as steady and true as could be.

"Here is my position," Tsunetomo said. "We will not speak publicly of his actions, except to say that we sent him to Kamakura. When he returns, if he returns, he may raise the child as his own, but he will not marry the girl. He may keep her as a concubine, but not as a wife. But when he returns, he *will* be married. He is a man of the Otomo clan. It is time. Lady Yukino, you will find a good match for him. Perhaps with the Shimizu clan. You have a good eye for advantageous matches. And as for the upcoming council, we will not speak of Ishitaka. If anyone inquires after him, we will say he is indisposed." His voice carried the force of a decision already made.

Tsunemori and Yukino pressed their foreheads to the floor. "Thank you, Brother. Again, please accept our apologies."

Kazuko breathed a little easier that he had not mentioned adoption, which meant that for now at least he had not made up his mind on that issue. But for how long would that last?

"Then what is the Greatest Happiness? To be without desire and to know what is enough, to be perfectly fair and selfless, not to fight about what is right and wrong with things, to understand the very foundation of one's mind, not to be confused by life and death or good fortune and calamity, to entrust life to life and to exert all of your powers in following that  Way, and to entrust death to death and to be content in that return. Not to envy wealth and honor, not to loathe poverty and low birth, not to be obsessed by thoughts of the differences between happiness and anger or likes and dislikes, but rather following good and bad fortune, or prosperity and decline as one meets them, and calmly enjoying oneself in the midst of creation and change: This is the Greatest Happiness under heaven."

—*Issai Chozanshi, The Demon's Sermon on the Martial Arts*

The letter from Ishitaka arrived in the morning, while Ken'ishi was preparing for the day's military strategy lecture. He had sat quietly while Shunsuke, his squire, shaved his pate and cheeks and styled his topknot, then dressed himself in a crisp, new robe. Nowadays, he looked the proper warrior gentleman.

Jinbei brought him the letter, and Ken'ishi read it with growing alarm and then sadness. Ishitaka had set sail for Kamakura from Moji. He was going to bring Yuri and his child home. He described a terrible argument with his father, after which Ishitaka's status in the clan was uncertain. He had taken no bodyguards or entourage, only his squire.

Ken'ishi could understand following one's heart. Nevertheless, the pangs of love were too often a distraction from the Warrior's Path. A warrior could not devote himself to the discipline and training with the demands and distractions of lovers and wives pulling him down other paths. Ken'ishi had often told himself that this was his reason for withholding his full affection from Kiosé. Whether it was the truth, he did not like to consider.

This had thrown Captain Tsunemori's and Lord Tsunetomo's houses into turmoil, especially now as they prepared to depart for Dazaifu to attend the Council of Lords. The lords of Kyushu were gathering to discuss preparations for the defense against the barbarian invaders. The engineers from Kyoto and Kamakura had arrived in Dazaifu. A stone wall was to be built around the entirety of Hakata Bay, more than five *ri* long. Doubtless there would be much wrangling over the division of costs and labor among the lords and gentry. The Imperial Court and the *bakufu* would foot much of the expense, but the lords were already grousing over the state of their coffers. Taxes would increase, which would further sour the peasants, who would already be forced into a greater share of labor in the construction of the defenses. Life on the island of Kyushu would grow more difficult for everyone.

Concerns of Ishitaka's welfare found their way into Ken'ishi's thoughts many times throughout the day, distracting him from lessons and training. It was on his mind even when he reached home that evening, when Jinbei met him at the door.

"A samurai came by today and demanded to speak with you," Jinbei said. "He would not offer his name, which I thought very strange."

"Strange indeed. What did he look like?"

"He looked...foreign. A kind of features I have not seen before. All these strangers pouring into the province... But he had two swords and a warrior's demeanor. Plain garments, but not poor. Very tall. He asked for you by name."

"If he comes back, I will see him." Ken'ishi received so few visitors, and Jinbei's description stoked his curiosity.

"Very well, Master. Suzu has prepared your dinner."

Having someone to prepare his dinner for him, to welcome him home, to care for the place while he was gone, all seemed so alien to him. How long before he became accustomed to it? Given how long he had spent on his own, was this lifestyle something to which he wanted to become accustomed?

That night, when the songs of the night frogs and crickets were at their height, when the moon shone through the open veranda door, turning his mosquito net into a gossamer tent, he heard the pull-string bell at the front door, signifying a visitor. He waited a moment to be sure he heard the bell, but it did not come again. Silver Crane rested in a rack within easy arm's reach of his *futon*. He took up the sword and slipped out of bed. The *kami* were not just whispering, nor were they shouting in cacophony. They were *singing*. The chorus of a multitude. Singing a welcome.

Jinbei and Suzu were doubtless fast asleep at this tender hour, having not heard the bell in their tiny chamber adjoining the garden.

Then again, Ken'ishi could not be certain he had heard the bell.

He stole through the house. He had never encountered such joy from the *kami* before, and it raised the hairs on his neck, as if something extraordinary hovered just out of sight, awaiting his ability to see it.

Inside the front door, Ken'ishi called, "Is someone there?"

"There is." The voice seemed to waver and shift, as if through a heavy rain, impossible to tell if it was man or woman.

"Name yourself."

"Fear not, you will know me."

His thoughts flashed to the fox he had encountered in the woods on his way to Lord Tsunetomo's castle. The fox had worn the guise of both a beautiful woman and an enormous warrior, both dressed in emerald green. The warrior had left a deep cut over Ken'ishi's heart, and the woman a deep cut inside. Why the mysterious fox had been testing him, he could not fathom, but he felt he had failed both tests.

He gripped Silver Crane's scabbard a little tighter and opened the door.

Standing outside was the warrior that Jinbei had described, but Ken'ishi did not recognize him. The man wore a basket hat. He was tall, gangly, and wore long and short swords thrust through his *obi*.

The night lay silent as a tomb. A low mist clung to the earth. Far down the street, the lantern of the firewatch bobbed like a distant firefly, the only visible light. The castle loomed behind him, the twin towers milky white in the moonshine. A long streak of white zipped across the sky in a brilliant flash that shifted to green before it dissolved into a puff of sparks, as if Hachiman, the guardian of warriors, had just struck with his blade against the fabric of night.

"Who are you?" Ken'ishi brought Silver Crane into view. "I've no patience for strangers in basket hats. Show yourself."

The stranger removed his hat. Without it, he looked even sparer, with gaunt cheeks, a shockingly long nose, and a scrawny neck. His beady eyes were as quick and sharp as the thrust of a dagger. Ken'ishi had never seen him before, but still there was something familiar about him.

"You have made a name for yourself, Sir Ken'ishi. 'Sword' and 'stone.' An interesting combination of characters. Your renown spreads."

"Is not the hour too late for flattery? I would rather listen to the sound of the frogs. State your business."

"My business is simple. It is said that you are the greatest swordsman in this province. I intend to test that."

"I have never said so. And if I were, would I waste time and effort on a man who won't even offer his name?"

The man took two steps backward, cast his hat to the ground, and put his right hand on his hilt. "Refusing is not an option."

Ken'ishi stepped into his sandals, then down onto the earth, keeping his eyes fixed upon this stranger. "Why me?"

"You are Ken'ishi the Oni-Slayer, Destroyer of the Wild Woman, Captain Ken'ishi of the Otomo clan, all worthy names."

"My old teacher once told me that I had to make my own name.

You'll not be able to steal mine for yourself."

The man smirked.

Ken'ishi said, "Would a test with *bokken* satisfy you?"

"Are you afraid to die?"

"I've no wish to kill you. And I haven't been given leave by my lord to die. In fact, fighting is forbidden by Lord Otomo himself. If you defeat me, you will likely be punished."

"That is why I have come to you at this hour. No one need know what occurs between us."

"Then how can you expect to build your name by defeating me?"

"No one else will know, but *I* will. Are you going to draw, or shall I cut you down with your sword still in its scabbard?"

Ken'ishi took a deep breath. The tumultuous chorus of the *kami* rose around him with fury that he felt across his back, neck, and shoulders. The air seemed filled with fireflies darting in and out of existence. He rubbed his eyes once to dispel the dancing, luminous motes. Mist swirled around the feet of his opponent.

The man's patience turned him into a serene, motionless pillar.

Ken'ishi drew Silver Crane. The dancing motes seemed to coalesce around its moonlit sheen.

The man drew his sword.

Even from this shadowed distance, Ken'ishi recognized an exquisite weapon. It was not richly appointed, but its steel glimmered like quicksilver, a weapon to rival Silver Crane in the perfection of its edge.

In the empty street they circled one another, spiraling closer into striking range.

Ken'ishi took another deep breath and allowed himself to descend into the Void.

The man's blade settled into the middle guard stance as they circled one another. The serenity and surety of his stance and movements bespoke incredible skill.

This man was indeed a rival, if not superior, to Ken'ishi in ability. The man's skill far exceeded that of Masoku, Green Tiger's *ronin* henchman. It far exceeded that of Nishimuta no Takenaga, the arrogant constable who had provoked Ken'ishi into a duel. It far exceeded that of Teng Zhou, the Chinese leader of the White Lotus gang in Hakata. Ken'ishi had never encountered such a swordsman before, so calm and collected, so precise in every movement.

But no matter. If Ken'ishi lost, he lost. If this night, this wondrous night, was to be his last, the fireflies were beautiful, and the heavens were aflame with wonders.

Another slash of light in the sky, in the far corner of his vision.

It was then his opponent struck.

The falling star seemed to hang there, waiting for the outcome of the strike before it allowed itself to disappear.

His opponent moved with preternatural speed, the kind of speed found only in the Void between moments of time. Had Ken'ishi not been rooted in the Void himself, his head would have been split like a melon. But he caught the blow, deflected it, stepped aside, and counter-struck. The man's blade caught Ken'ishi's as if expecting the precise counterstrike.

They slid apart, blades interposed.

Ken'ishi slid into the stance Kaa had taught him, blade raised to face-level, edge upturned, point toward the throat of the attacker, like a crane's beak.

The man smirked, stepped in closer, and assumed the same stance.

Ken'ishi never seen another human being use this stance before, and the sight of it startled him out of the Void.

And in that moment, the man struck.

His blade darted toward Ken'ishi's throat. Ken'ishi's desperate parry deflected the sword point into the meat of his left shoulder. Blinding pain exploded in the joint. Ken'ishi's wild riposte slashed across his opponent's right wrist. They staggered away from each other.

The stranger's right hand released his hilt and hung at his side, two fingers dangling from a chunk of palm, blood pouring onto the ground. His left hand still clutched the pommel of his katana hilt. He swung one-handed at Ken'ishi leg.

Ken'ishi swung his thigh out of the blade's path and seized the opportunity. He struck hard with the flat of his blade against the top of his opponent's hilt, just above the hand, driving the weapon onto the ground. Then he jumped forward and kicked his opponent in the belly, away from the fallen weapon. Breath burst from the man's lips, and he toppled hard onto his back.

Ken'ishi laid the edge of his blade against the man's throat.

Like a thunderous gong, Silver Crane's voice rang in his mind. *Blood! Blood! Blood!*

Just a flick of the wrist would spill the man's life irrevocably onto the earth.

The man's sharp eyes narrowed as they gazed up into Ken'ishi's. There was no fear in them. He was as prepared to die as to take his next breath.

Blood! Blood! Blood!

"No," Ken'ishi said. He took half a step back, blinking away the powerful suggestion to open the man's throat to the night.

"Why not kill me? I am a cripple now. A crippled warrior does not deserve to live."

"I have seen whole and healthy warriors who do not deserve to live. You are not only a worthy opponent, you are the superior swordsman. Fortune was on my side today, not skill."

"I am glad to see you are not a fool...Monkey Boy."

Ken'ishi gasped and took another step back. Only one being had ever called him that. "*Sensei!*"

The man levered himself up to an elbow. His nose grew even longer. His skin took on a gray, mottled appearance. And then, in a burst of speed, he leaped to his feet.

Ken'ishi lowered his weapon and bowed.

The man's voice grew harsh, crow-like. "First you challenge me, and now you are so deferential! I'll never understand you upright monkeys." His skin disappeared under a coat of fine, silvery-gray feathers, and his nose and mouth merged into a hard, blood-red beak. His dark, flinty eyes speared Ken'ishi with derision.

Anger flared in Ken'ishi. "For months I have entreated to speak with you. For months you have been taunting me. I need answers to my questions, and if you're not prepared to give them, I would prefer you leave me alone. I've had enough of distractions. I challenged you because I knew you would be honor-bound to respond. I know you, *Sensei.*" Blood soaked his left arm from the deep puncture in his shoulder, dripping from his fingers. "And now I have defeated you, rightfully or no. Your life is mine."

The *tengu* threw back his bird-like head and laughed uproariously, like a murder of crows startled into flight. "My life will remain long after you are food for grubs! You do not know me as well as you think."

"And you will still owe it to me, unless you answer my questions, once and for all. You told me I must make my own name. I've done it! And I've learned a few things about my past—"

"At my allowance! Just like that starving woman I put in your path at the shrine of Jizo. Who do you think brought Tametsugu the sword-polisher back from the Realm of Dreams?"

Ken'ishi stared.

"Always you underestimate my power." He flexed his injured hand. The cleft had healed. "And what did Tametsugu tell you?"

"That Silver Crane is a relic of the Taira clan, a treasure beyond worth. Silver Crane itself tells me that it follows the Taira bloodline. That must mean I am of the Taira clan. But that does not tell me who my father was, or why he left the clan to live as a farmer with my mother on the edge of the wilderness, or who killed them. Or why Silver Crane chose him. It was lost in the straits at Dan-no-Ura, at the bottom of the sea a hundred years ago, and now..."

"And now it has chosen you, Monkey Boy."

Anger rose in him again. "Call me that again, and I shall say pick up your sword and let us finish it. Ken'ishi is the name I have made, *Sensei*."

Kaa sniffed. "You should not be so hasty."

"I...remember the day they died, the day you saved my life."

"A day I have often rued."

"Nevertheless, I know there is honor within you. I defeated you in a fair duel."

"Even the gods can stumble. Even a *tengu* might suffer ill fortune."

In a flare of frustration, Ken'ishi leaped forward and slashed.

Kaa's eyes bulged with surprise. An instant later, he was a palm-sized sparrow dodging the wind of Ken'ishi's passing stroke. "Not very sporting!" came a tiny voice.

"I'm through playing games, *Sensei*. I will always honor you as my former teacher, but I'm not afraid of you, not anymore. Why not just tell me?"

"I swore to protect you. What a foolish day that was. The men who killed your parents might well come after you if they knew you were alive."

"Why?"

"Because of what you represent."

"Why?"

The sparrow became a hawk that lit on the thatched eave of Ken'ishi's house. "Your father's name was Morihisa. He was a swordmaster of the Taira clan, chief instructor at the clan's only remaining school. He was born fifty years after the war that destroyed the Taira and brought the Minamoto to ascendancy. He could have been one of history's greatest swordsmen, except he had been born into a clan that was suppressed. Only those Taira who swore fealty to Yoritomo escaped execution—or so the Minamoto thought. A significant portion of the Taira went into hiding, folded themselves quietly into other houses, or gathered in the wilds of Koga province. They hated the Taira who acceded to the enemy, the 'betrayers.' And your father was among the worst of these 'betrayers,' because the woman he married was a Minamoto. Her name was Hikari. They escaped an attempt on their lives in the capital, which was a testament to his prowess. He slew fifteen men, then fled with his wife into the wilderness. Eventually, these shadow-Taira found him and came for him again. When and how he acquired Silver Crane, I do not know." The hawk preened his feathers. "Now, is knowing all of that everything you wished it would be?"

Ken'ishi's parents' names swam through his imagination, through the smoke-filled memories of his three-year-old mind. Thoughts of who they were, who they might have been had they been allowed to live, how his own life would have been different, dizzied him.

He had built a name from his exploits, but he had a family now. A lineage. His parents' names gave them flesh in his mind, gave them breath and life. His pedigree sprang from two of the greatest bloodlines in history.

His blood joined those lines.

To the men who had murdered his parents, he was a symbol of their defeat, their failure, their surrender to the enemy. To these shadow-Taira, Ken'ishi would forever be the enemy, marked for death.

He knew of only one fellow Taira.

Was Yasutoki one of these shadow-Taira who murdered Ken'ishi's parents? Could Yasutoki have participated? He was old enough.

Ken'ishi bowed to the hawk. "Thank you, *Sensei*."

"You have your name now," Kaa said. "The question is, what will you do with it?"

With that, the hawk leaped into the air, shat upon Ken'ishi's roof, and winged away, dwindling to a dark speck against the wild tapestry of stars.

"One may explain water, but the mouth will not become wet. One may expound fully on the nature of fire, but the mouth will not become hot."

—Takuan Soho, "The Mysterious Record of Immovable Wisdom"

K en'ishi awoke with a start in the early dawn and jumped out of bed, his heart hammering. He felt his left shoulder and found no wound there, no pain. Either Kaa had healed him, or their encounter had taken place in the Land of Dreams and his wound there had not translated into the mortal realm. Nevertheless, the reality of the encounter could not be in question.

He took up Silver Crane and sat upon the veranda overlooking his garden, sword across his thighs, listening to the silence of the frogs, to the trickle of dew on the leaves.

He turned his parents' names over and over in his mind, like a child with a new treasure. *Hikari. Morihisa.* And, like a boy, he tucked his treasures away and cherished them.

All this time, all these years, and the truth now lay before him.

What should he do with it? His fondest wish, the wish he had clung to through childhood, through endless days and nights walking the earth as a *ronin* when his only friend had been a dog, the wish that had sustained him in the darkest recesses of Green Tiger's prison, had been granted. He would never know his parents, but he knew their names. They had been a symbol of hope to build amity between clans steeped in mutual loathing. Ken'ishi was the living, breathing embodiment of that hope. But no one knew or cared who he was. The war and slaughter were a century past. The Taira clan lay in bloody shreds of its former glory, all but forgotten, scattered across islands and provinces, under the watchful eye of its former enemies.

Tatters of cloud turned red, then orange. Today would be a good day to travel to Dazaifu. Ken'ishi was to be among the twenty retainers accompanying Tsunetomo to the Lords' Council. Each lord was to be allowed only twenty retainers and their servants, to prevent any unwelcome displays of force. Ken'ishi's rank had placed him within the circle of Tsunetomo's highest-ranked retainers. Some of the captains were remaining behind to continue troop training and readiness, but Tsunetomo wanted "the best swordsman in the province" with him in Dazaifu.

After the events of last night, Ken'ishi knew his reputation might exceed his prowess. He needed to find another swordmaster under whom to train. *Tengu* were renowned for their swordsmanship, but Ken'ishi still felt terrible unease that his skills had been stagnating for far too long. What would happen when another ambitious warrior, a real one, challenged the famous Oni-Slayer to a duel? Lacking a teacher, he had grown lax in his martial studies.

When they returned from Dazaifu, perhaps he would discuss bringing in a swordmaster, similar to Yamazaki-*sensei*, with Captain Tsunemori.

At the Hour of the Rabbit, Lord Tsunetomo and his retinue gathered in a dual column at the gates of the castle. Servants brought forth the horses. The Otomo banner, two blue apricot blossoms facing each other on a white field, rippled in the morning breeze. Hiromasa, now a lieutenant, lofted the banner, his face as taciturn as ever, but with a fresh pridefulness in his shoulders at the honor of bearing Lord Tsunetomo's standard.

Ken'ishi's squire, Shunsuke, a samurai of modest lineage just a year younger than him, had risen early to prepare Storm and bring him to the gates.

The retinue assembled quickly, as none wanted to be the last one ready to depart. Lord Tsunetomo took his place astride a great black stallion at the head of the column, Tsunemori beside him. With the blast of a conch shell, the assemblage set forth. The servants brought up the train in the rear, hauling several carts.

Riding through town toward Dazaifu, Ken'ishi recalled his journey with the curmudgeonly old peddler, Shirohige, on this very road the previous year. So distant, it seemed like a previous existence. The sheer weight of experience laid upon his soul since that day made that younger man, for all his trials and experiences, seem like a poor, naïve fool. Watching peasants clear the way and line up beside the road, prostrating themselves, gave Ken'ishi a stark sense of wonder at how far he had risen.

How far, then, could he fall?

Dazaifu had changed since Ken'ishi's previous visit. Gone were the profusion of tents and pallets filled with wounded, dying men. Absent were the smells of smoke and blood and fear; in their place now was an officious bustle. The outskirts of the town hosted the encampments of the various lords, as there was no other space in Dazaifu to accommodate them. Looming above it all, the fortress atop Mount Ono stood like a massive sentinel. Built into the mountain to make use of its natural defenses, the six-hundred-year-old fortress' high, thick walls and central keep formed a terraced monolith representing the power of the history and tradition.

Government functionaries in stiff, black caps and starched robes, their arms full of scrolls, hurried up and down the streets. Grim-faced warriors in unfamiliar colors squinted at them as they passed, watchful. Even a ravening enemy just a few score *ri* across the sea did not diminish decades or centuries of war and distrust among powerful, ambitious men.

The council was set to begin in earnest the following day. Tonight would be feasting and drinking, renewing old alliances and forging new ones.

Excitement coursed through Ken'ishi at being part of it all. He would remain vigilant, protecting Tsunetomo at all cost, but the unparalleled event seemed to have infected everyone. The feeling in the air was of great things brewing, auspiciousness, and an earnest importance.

By evening, the Otomo encampment had been erected on the outskirts with the others. Three other Otomo lords arrived and gathered with Tsunetomo and Tsunemori for an evening banquet. The *saké* flowed and the courses of food kept coming. The baggage train had brought plenty for just this purpose, and the stewards had been hard at work preparing it since the tents had been erected.

While the five Otomo lords and their highest ranking retainers banqueted inside Tsunetomo's pavilion, Tsunetomo's men mixed with the other Otomo retainers at the campfires outside.

Ken'ishi's time in Tsunetomo's employ had made it easier for him to interact with strangers. *Saké* certainly helped the conversation and laughter flow. Before long, they were all taking turns sharing their exploits.

They watched a fresh arrival pass by on the road, a lord and his retainers in a dual column with a baggage train following behind.

Then, with a flash of anger, Ken'ishi recognized the lord at the head of this column. The man who had cast him out of his province on pain of death. Kazuko's father. Lord Nishimuta no Jiro. Short and broad, with narrow eyes and a stern countenance, Lord Jiro rode like a block of oak, gaze steadfastly forward.

The *kami* buzzed with danger, and rightfully so. Lord Jiro could just as easily recognize Ken'ishi. And if he did, what would he say to Lord Tsunetomo? *You have a man in your employ who was once a ronin in love with your wife, and she with him. And by the way, he also killed one of my retainers.* Such a revelation might not fall on welcome ears. After all, in spite of his meteoric rise, Ken'ishi had been in Tsunetomo's employ for only half a year.

Should he reveal his prior acquaintance with Kazuko to diffuse any surprise? Perhaps hearing the truth from Ken'ishi, rather than from Tsunetomo's father-in-law, would soften the reaction. Perhaps Ken'ishi should do all he could to avoid Lord Jiro's notice. Might then all awkward questions be avoided? But was that the honorable path? Tsunetomo had not shown himself to be a jealous man, but the cost to Kazuko might be too high.

Ken'ishi turned back to the fire, rubbed his chin in thought, and put away his cup. He needed a clearer head.

The Lords' Council had commenced the following morning, and Ken'ishi had been given the duty of guarding the exterior of the Great Hall of the government offices. The Western Defense Commissioner, a Kamakura appointee named Hojo no Toshitsune, had insisted that the Lords' Council take place at his offices as the Kyushu lords fell under his authority, granted by the *bakufu*. The extent to which this was true had been a matter of speculation while the *saké* was flowing, but no one dared speak any disloyalty or insubordination openly.

This morning, while standing guard outside, Ken'ishi spotted several warriors bearing the *mon* of the Taira clan—a butterfly— upon their robes. They kept apart from the warriors of the other clans. As there were only six of them, Ken'ishi wondered if that was the entirety of their retinue.

After his encounter with Kaa, Ken'ishi had asked Yamazaki-*sensei* for permission to study books from the teacher's extensive library. In a book on heraldry, he found the *mon* of the Taira clan and several bits of intriguing history.

The Taira clan had first gained its name about four hundred years before. It was the name given to members of the imperial family who fell just a bit too far from the tree and became subjects. The Taira were a line of former- and almost-emperors, offshoots of the imperial dynasty who believed staunchly in the preservation of imperial authority. Their blood was inextricably woven with the imperial line.

Ken'ishi's blood was the blood of emperors. This thought had given him pause, and he had chewed on it for hours.

From this line came a man named Kiyomori, whose ambition, exploits, and political acumen raised the Taira clan to the height of power and wealth. Such was Kiyomori's power that he succeeded in banishing his rivals from the imperial court, forcing the sitting emperor, his own son-in-law Takakawa, to abdicate in favor Kiyomori's grandson, Takakawa's infant son. The boy became known as Antoku.

Ken'ishi recalled the powerful visions he had seen while in Green Tiger's captivity: dreams of the boy-emperor Antoku and of the last bloody battle in the straits at Dan-no-Ura, when Taira no Tomomori, the great general of the clan, seeing that defeat was inevitable, tied an anchor rope around his waist and threw himself into the sea, taking Silver Crane with him. Antoku's grandmother, Kiyomori's wife Tokiko, by then a Buddhist nun, had taken the child in her arms and also leaped into the sea.

That war had been the cost of Kiyomori's ambition. One did not rise to such heights without creating bitter rivals and alienating former allies. Kiyomori's exercise of authority turned most of the samurai clans against him, even members of his own clan. The deposed Emperor Takakawa's brother, incensed at the way Takakawa had been cast aside, raised the ire and power of the Minamoto clan to destroy the Taira and restore the rightful imperial line. The Battle of Dan-no-Ura ended that five-year war. The crushing Minamoto victory raised the status and power of Minamoto no Yoritomo to such heights that he seized the title of shogun, established a samurai government in Kamakura, and stripped the imperial court of its power.

The day wore on, heat and humidity bearing down upon them, and Ken'ishi found that the Taira warriors fascinated him. They could well be his distant relatives, a thought at once alien and exciting. He could recall no sense of family, and the thought of Green Tiger as his only known kinsman sickened him.

He filled a crock with water from one of the central wells and took it to the Taira men. They eyed him skeptically as he approached, crossing their arms and squaring to face him.

He took a drink from the crock. "Hot today, isn't it?" Ken'ishi said, then offered it to the man who appeared to be their leader, a tall, middle-aged man with austere features and an old scar across the bridge of his nose.

"You could use a few more sea breezes around here," the man said, accepting the crock with eyes narrowed.

The other Taira men eyed the crock. They had been standing in the heat a long time while the lords wrangled inside.

The man took a drink, then handed it to another man.

"I am Ken'ishi, captain of the first rank in the house of Lord Otomo no Tsunetomo."

The man's brows furrowed. "I am Taira no Yoshisada, captain of the fourth rank in the house of Taira no Kagenari, governor of

Ikishima."

"Ikishima," Ken'ishi said. "You took the first blow of the invasion." The island of Ikishima lay between Hakata Bay and the Koryo peninsula, a natural first target. The invaders had taken it before launching their attack on Hakata.

Yoshisada's face darkened. "Our kinsmen did. I come from Kyoto." The tone in his voice made Ken'ishi think the man wished he were still there. "Taira no Kagetaka was my master's cousin." Kagetaka had been the governor appointed by the *bakufu*. No men, young or old, survived the attack. Most of the women were raped to death or taken as slaves.

"Are you Taira by birth?" Ken'ishi asked.

"Why do you ask?"

"Forgive my rude directness. I was a *ronin*, but my blood is Taira. I encounter so few kinsmen."

The man's eyes narrowed. "Why were you *ronin*?"

This was akin to asking a man what crime he had committed to be cast out of service, but perhaps this was a conversation for awkwardness. "I never had a lord," Ken'ishi said. "I have my blood from Taira no Morihisa."

"Impossible," Yoshisada said. "Unless you're a bastard. Or a liar."

Ken'ishi bristled. "Explain yourself."

"Taira no Morihisa disappeared twenty years ago."

"After someone tried to assassinate him."

"He never had any children. My father studied the sword under him."

"He did have one child. Me. My mother was Minamoto no Hikari."

"I have heard no tales of him having a wife, much less some Minamoto trollop."

Ken'ishi's fists clenched, and he spoke each word separately. "Mind your tongue, friend, lest your own parentage be called into question and your line truncated."

"And why should I believe what you say?" Yoshisada said. "You're wearing Otomo garb. The Otomo clan was among the first to join the Minamoto. They took it upon themselves to rid Kyushu of Taira blood. You're working for the enemy."

Ken'ishi's face heated.

One of the other men stepped forward. "Those battles are long since fought. The only enemy now is the barbarians, yes?"

Ken'ishi glared at Yoshisada. "I brought you water out of kinship. Dash it in my face again and we will exchange more than words."

He turned on his heel and returned to the Otomo men, who had been watching this exchange from across the street.

At that moment the *kami* sent shivers through him so deeply that he laid a hand on his hilt. He glanced behind him, half-expecting attack, but the Taira men were now conversing in a quiet circle. He scanned the street and its throngs of warriors. The colors and heraldry encompassed every Great House on Kyushu. Only his compatriots were paying him much attention.

Then he saw another familiar face, one with eyes fixed upon him, among the men in Nishimuta colors. A man named Sakamoto, chief captain to Lord Jiro. Four years ago, Captain Sakamoto had been the one to lead the escort when Ken'ishi returned Kazuko safely to her father's castle; the one to offer hospitality while Ken'ishi was still naïve enough to believe that Lord Jiro would accede to Kazuko's wishes to take Ken'ishi into service; and the one to cast Ken'ishi out at the end of that devastating evening. Sakamoto knew of Ken'ishi's history with Hakamadare, knew that young Ken'ishi and Kazuko had fallen in love, and knew that Ken'ishi had killed the arrogant constable Takenaga. It had never mattered to the Nishimuta clan that it was a fair and rightful duel.

Ken'ishi met Sakamoto's gaze. Sakamoto's face registered recognition, then turned to inscrutable stone. Ken'ishi looked away and continued across the street to rejoin his compatriots.

By tonight, Lord Nishimuta no Jiro would know of Ken'ishi's presence in Lord Tsunetomo's retinue.

Uguisu sing in the
  blossoming trees.
Frogs sing in the green
  rushes.
Everywhere the same call
  of being to being.
Somber clouds waver in
  the void.
Fishing boats waver in the
  tide.
Their sails carry them out.
But ropes, as of old, woven
With the hair of their
  women,
Pull them back
Over their reflections on the green depths,
To the ports of love.

—*The Love Poems of Marichiko*

The new naginata haft was so smooth, lacking the scratches and wear of long use. Kazuko had erected ten fresh *tatami* targets in her practice yard. It felt good to release the strength of its blade with such wild abandon. Each whirl and slash opened a gleeful crack in her otherwise dark mood.

Since Tsunetomo had gone to Dazaifu with Ken'ishi and the rest of his highest ranked retainers, her mood had soured without clear cause.

That was a lie.

The cause lay plastered to her cheek, concealing the terrible blemish of Hatsumi's hatred.

The bandage hung there, a constant reminder that she was no longer beautiful.

A reminder of the cost of kindness and mercy betrayed.

The *naginata* dipped and thrust and slashed. Bits of *tatami* flew in all directions. Servants replaced the mats behind her as quickly as they could, and struggled to keep up with the savage whirl she became. Her chest burned. Sweat slicked her body, her hands, burned her eyes. Her sodden robes flopped as she moved, spattering sweat behind her.

So unladylike, said Hatsumi's voice in Kazuko's head.

"Burn in hell, you horrid witch!" Kazuko muttered, slashing through a three-roll target that mimicked the resistance of a human torso. To her, it felt like one of Hatsumi's spidery limbs. How many bits had she chopped those limbs into?

With increasing speed, she whirled and slashed until her breath went ragged and fresh blisters formed under the calluses on her palms.

When the mats were gone and she was ankle deep in *tatami* pieces, chest heaving against her armor, she came to a halt. The servants stood far out of the way, silent, eyes wide at the precision of the massacre they had just witnessed.

Throwing herself into martial pursuit to forget her pain, her failures, was nothing new to her, but this time felt different. It was not sadness and despair in her heart, but anger and regret.

She would kill Hatsumi a thousand times before it might be enough.

This morning, she had refreshed her bandage, but before she allowed her new handmaid, on loan from Lady Yukino, to apply the poultice, she studied the wound in her silver mirror.

An angry, crimson slash, as long as her finger. She touched it gingerly. The lips of the gash felt numb, dead, as did parts of her cheek. This frightened her.

Would she ever smile properly again?

Her loyalty to Hatsumi had cost her more dearly than death.

And with a womb as barren as an empty beach, she would have to maintain her place in the Otomo house by other means.

She would have liked to travel to Dazaifu, where she might greet her father, but Tsunetomo had forbidden her to come. It was a place for only the men, he said. In spite of her growing anger and dissatisfaction at her woman's role, she still missed her husband, and she missed knowing that Ken'ishi was nearby.

The Lords' Council had begun four days ago. The fortification project was an immense undertaking, but new edicts had arrived from the *bakufu*. A series of defense posts were to be constructed across northern Kyushu. These posts were, in effect, small garrisons, to be manned at all times. How their construction was to be paid for, how they were to be manned, who would build them in the midst of other massive undertakings, all were questions to be answered at the Lords' Council. And samurai lords were often a fractious, willful lot. She knew this well, growing up around her father.

Then a terrible thought occurred to her.

What if Ken'ishi and her father encountered each other?

The façade of secrets she had kept would crumble.

A chill of real danger swept through her.

She ignored the servants' discomfiture and returned to her chambers, where she called for the *ofuro* to be filled and heated. She needed a bath to drive away this chill.

At the close of the day's council business, the lords repaired to their respective encampments outside Dazaifu.

Ken'ishi had stewed in the summer heat all day about Nishimuta no Sakamoto—until he hatched a plan. Sakamoto would reveal Ken'ishi's presence to his lord, and Lord Jiro would discuss the matter with his son-in-law, Tsunetomo.

But how could he reveal to his lord this dark, incriminating corner of his past, one that so directly involved Kazuko? How could he do so without besmirching Kazuko's reputation, or worse, endangering her life? Lord Jiro would not know of Ken'ishi's tryst with Kazuko that long-ago night. Kazuko would not have revealed that, even to Hatsumi. But apparently everyone in Lord Jiro's banquet hall that night had seen Ken'ishi's heart wide open, regardless of how well he thought he had hidden the truth. Could Ken'ishi lie to Lord Tsunetomo? To save Kazuko's life, he might have to try. Many would say the mere thought was the most dishonorable of paths. Better to cut one's belly open. But that would raise unpleasant questions for Kazuko, and he could not consign her to death. Would he be able to lie convincingly? Tsunetomo was an astute judge of men. On the other hand, Green Tiger was operating directly under Tsunetomo's nose. Tsunetomo was either blind to Yasutoki's deception, which meant Yasutoki was a profoundly skilled liar or Tsunetomo was too willing to believe in the good of his retainers, or else Green Tiger operated with the sanction of Lord Tsunetomo. Would such an upright, stalwart leader of men suffer such a vile canker in his own house?

With all these thoughts twisting him up this afternoon, Ken'ishi had hatched a plan. During what he claimed to the others was a trip to the privy, he had meditated with Silver Crane in the quiet seclusion of a nearby garden. And in that meditation, he had explored the threads of destiny, plucking and weaving and tying. Many of those threads had led to Kazuko's beheading. Many of them had terminated in Ken'ishi's torture and crucifixion. In all of those threads, Lord Tsunetomo suffered such a grave loss of face that his retainers and subjects began to desert him, his lands never to recover. Other threads led to less certain outcomes where their deaths were not the inevitable conclusion, moments of conversation that might leave Tsunetomo trustful of Ken'ishi's confession.

Men's minds were mercurial. Threads of thought and intention could shift subtly in the tiniest of moments and create vastly different outcomes. The fate of ten thousand could hang upon a single man's slice of arbitrary decision.

Ken'ishi's hands vibrated with tension as he followed the palanquins of Lord Tsunetomo and Captain Tsunemori back to their encampment.

The two men were grim and taciturn as they stepped out of their palanquins. The difficulty of the day's wrangling had tightened their lips and deepened the furrows in their brows.

Ken'ishi seized his opportunity, hoping that Sakamoto had not yet let the fox out of the bag. He spoke up as the two brothers were walking toward their tent. "My lords, I am sure you're weary. I apologize for asking to delay your rest just a little longer, but... there is a matter I wish to discuss with you. It is most urgent."

The *kami* commenced a curious hum around him.

Silver Crane's voice clashed in his mind. *The man seizes destiny. Such fine threads you walk.*

Lord Tsunetomo said, "Is something amiss? Has there been trouble?"

"No, Lord," Ken'ishi said, "this is a private matter."

Tsunetomo and Tsunemori exchanged glances, then turned to Ken'ishi after an interminable pause. Finally Tsunetomo said, "Come in then, Captain Ken'ishi."

Ken'ishi bowed low.

The eyes of the all men around him followed him into the tent. Ken'ishi and Tsunemori left their swords on a rack near the tent flap.

Tsunetomo's steward prepared a pot of soothing tea. While they waited for the tea to steep, Tsunetomo related results of the day's deliberations. One of his responsibilities would be to provide men for building the fortification from Hakozaki east to the Shiga spit. He would also have to provide troops to be rotated through the defense garrisons to be built across northern Kyushu. The entire effort would put great pressure on peasants and farmers to not only pay higher taxes, but be removed from their livelihoods for long periods to work on the fortifications. "The alternative, I suppose, is to leave our bellies exposed to the barbarians. Many will not be able to see the cost of inaction, I fear."

The steward poured them tea, and they relaxed onto cushions.

"Captain Ken'ishi," Lord Tsunetomo said, "you look as if you have an unpleasant tale to tell."

Ken'ishi bowed. All day he had turned his words over and over in his mind. "My lord, I must confess something that might have escaped your awareness. There are those here who might not look favorably upon my presence. I have no wish to reflect poorly on you."

Tsunetomo's eyes narrowed. Tsunemori leaned forward, elbow on his knee.

"Four years ago, I was a wandering *ronin*. I came from the far north. I was newly come to Kyushu. I was passing through a village. I accepted the hospitality of the village headman. The village constable, however, found it necessary to abuse me, to impugn my honor, to insult me. Perhaps it was wrong of me, but I could not let the insults stand. I challenged him to a duel, and he accepted. I offered him the chance to decide by first blood. He declined that offer."

Tsunemori said, "By your side of the tale, it was a rightful challenge. The constable behaved poorly. We all have pasts. Few among us manage to go through life without mistakes. Even the Buddha was a human being."

Ken'ishi bowed again. "Later that day, I came upon a noble maiden and her retinue beset by bandits. I helped her *yojimbo* defeat the bandits. And then I saw the gang's leader. You've doubtless heard the rest of the tale...from Lady Otomo."

Tsunetomo stiffened. "You're *that ronin*."

Ken'ishi bowed. "I brought Kazuko safely home to her father. Lord Nishimuta banished me from his domain for the death of the constable. Had I not saved Kazuko's life, there is no question my life would have been forfeit, even though the duel was a rightful one. I have no wish to cause trouble between you and your father-in-law. No doubt he still sees me as little more than a criminal."

Tsunetomo crossed his arms and looked at Ken'ishi long enough to make him squirm. The songs of the *kami* waxed and waned in Ken'ishi's awareness, like the rise and fall of cicadas. "You and Kazuko were acquainted before you came into my service."

"For those brief days, yes."

"No doubt she wanted you to help her hunt down Hatsumi. Her lottery was a sham, at least in part."

Ken'ishi nodded. "I knew it immediately. I felt somewhat responsible for Hatsumi, Lord. I have long regretted not being able to spare both of them from Hakamadare's attack. But my actions brought me to Kazuko's aid that day. Hatsumi always blamed me for this. Had I chosen differently, I might have saved Hatsumi from Hakamadare, and Kazuko would have been attacked instead. Last year, I found myself in Ishitaka's unit during the invasion."

Tsunemori stiffened at the mention of his son.

Ken'ishi continued, "I did not know he was your nephew, Lord. A strange chain of fortune has brought me here. Encountering Captain Tsunemori there in the ruins of Hakozaki. Finding myself in your service, and immensely grateful for it. Both Lady Otomo and I were surprised to encounter one another after all this time. I do not know why fortune has brought me here. But I do know that I am your loyal servant. I swore my life to your service. My life is yours to use as you wish." He bowed low again.

If Tsunetomo took offense at the omission of information, if he saw it as deceit, he could order Ken'ishi's demotion, banishment, even *seppuku*. The outcomes Ken'ishi had tried to weave with Silver Crane's power were all uncertain.

"What do you fear, Ken'ishi?" Tsunetomo asked. "In this moment."

"Finding service with you has been the granting of my fondest wish. I fear that events from my past will tarnish your trust in me. I do not fear to die in your service. I fear to die having served poorly. I fear to die an unworthy death."

Tsunetomo studied him again for another long, tense moment, calculations and emotions flickering behind a stone mask.

Finally Tsunetomo said, "It was...astute of you to discuss this with me before Lord Nishimuta brought it to my attention. I would not have liked to hear from him that I have a criminal in my employ."

Ken'ishi pressed his forehead to the floor. "I deeply regret the timing of my confession. Please forgive me."

Tsunemori eased into the space between words. "No man walks the earth as a *ronin* without questionable deeds. If we dug into the pasts of all the new recruits, who among them would escape flogging? We cannot afford to squander what good swords we have."

Tsunetomo raised a hand, and Tsunemori fell silent.

"Men do not become powerful without making enemies," Tsunetomo said, his voice even. "Thus far, you have proven yourself a worthy retainer. You saved Lady Kazuko's life for a second time. Tales are spreading of your prowess with sword and bow, and increasingly, horsemanship. Yamazaki-*sensei* tells me you have a sharp mind, with leadership potential. All of those together are the reasons you are now a captain, and not just a spearman. I cannot very well turn my back on such a capable retainer, regardless of my father-in-law's wishes. One of the tenets of lordship is responsibility to those beneath. You owe me your service, your life, your loyalty. I, too, owe loyalty in return. If Lord Nishimuta objects to your presence, I will deal with him."

Ken'ishi pressed his forehead to the floor again. "My deepest thanks, Lord."

Tsunetomo said, "I trust that you have no more secrets. Go." The tone of his voice, as if he were still deep in thought, still considering possibilities, gave Ken'ishi pause. Then he bowed his way out of the tent.

Yes: the young sparrows
If you treat them
   tenderly...
Thank you with
   droppings.

              —*Issa*

As Yasutoki familiarized himself with Kamakura and its environs, he was struck by how new everything was. Until Minamoto no Yoritomo had declared it to be the seat of the shogun's authority, it had been little more than a highly defensible fishing town. Mountains on three sides and Sagami Bay on the fourth made Kamakura difficult to reach, even in peacetime. The seven mountain roads into the city were narrow; in many places wide enough for only one man. Kamakura's defensibility made it very attractive to a general who had just come through a long, bloody war, and its distance from Kyoto mirrored the distance Yoritomo had wanted from the imperial court.

Nowadays, Kamakura was a thriving government town, the home of the ten-year-old shogun Minamoto no Koreyasu and the Hojo clan regents who "guided" him, a hive of offices and ministers, a city teeming with Yasutoki's most hated enemies. The entire city had an austere, utilitarian feel that echoed the tenets of the warrior code.

Frivolity had no place here, only serious business. Let the decadent imperial court embrace useless frivolities, and let the warriors see to the business of running the country. In any case, the samurai behaved as such. Much of the Emperor's power had been stripped away during the war between the Taira and the Minamoto, but the imperial court's centuries of prestige and wealth could not be discounted. Powerful families maintained their loyalty to the emperor. The Taira clan had been destroyed protecting the true emperor, Antoku. When the Mongol hordes wiped away the Minamoto and Hojo clans, perhaps the prestige of the emperor might be renewed, the royal bloodline purified and strengthened. The Taira were, after all, the blood of emperors.

The arrogance of Yoritomo rippled down through history. He had built this city as a monument to his own ambition. Young Prince Avenue formed an arrow-straight thoroughfare half a *ri* long, almost forty paces wide, lined by beautifully manicured pine trees, and passing through three *torii* gates, running straight north from the sea to the Shrine of Hachiman. Commoners were not allowed to use the avenue except during festivals. Yoritomo had had the avenue constructed as a prayer for the health and prosperity of his first son, Yoriie. Yasutoki could only smile at the irony. Named shogun at seventeen, Yoriie had held the post for only two years before he was assassinated by his uncle, Hojo no Tokimasa.

"May they all die in lakes of fire and blood," Yasutoki murmured inside his palanquin. He peered through the bamboo slats at the walled compound, surveying the walls, the gates, the number of guards. His bearers maintained an officious pace. The guards would not tolerate idle curiosity.

The barbarian emissaries were sequestered here near the shogun's residence. No one saw the emissaries, and as yet, no one in the *bakufu* had debriefed them either. They were pampered prisoners.

Yasutoki had made subtle inquiries into the possibility of meeting with the emissaries, but the shogunate made it clear no one would be allowed access to or communication with the emissaries without the express permission of the *bakufu*. He had made two passes near the compound in his palanquin, assessing the difficulty of stealing past the guards to speak directly with the emissaries. The sheer number of guards, posted two spear-lengths apart, made the task a daunting one. He did not know the guard organization within the compound, so he could not predict what might happen if he tried some sort of diversion such as a small fire or a murdered guard. And even if he managed to get inside, he had to get back out again. Regrettably, he had let some of his skills stagnate, and he was not so young anymore.

Nevertheless, he must consider the possibilities. Perhaps allies might be found in other members of the hidden Taira, if he looked in the designated haunts.

When he reached the residence the *bakufu* had loaned him just west of Young Prince Avenue, he found a constable from the city magistrate awaiting him. Yasutoki entered the residence from the rear gate and was thus settled before the constable was brought to him. The unexpected guest felt like an intrusion, as he had been looking forward to availing himself of Tiger Lily's pleasures when he returned. However, she did not show herself, as he had ordered her to remain out of sight of guests.

The constable was a young man wearing perfectly pressed robes and a high black cap. Any brush with the law set Yasutoki on edge, but he concealed this. None of his criminal contacts in Kamakura had knowledge of Green Tiger's true identity.

After they exchanged cordial greetings, the constable said, "We must come to my purpose here. Earlier today, a trading ship came into port. Several of the crew had been wounded and claimed they were attacked by pirates. They only managed to escape because a samurai had taken passage aboard their ship. The samurai had not given his name, but his armor and weapons indicate he is of the Otomo clan. He managed to fight off the pirates. He killed eight of them before they fled."

"I am not aware of any Otomo warriors dispatched to Kamakura," Yasutoki said. "Where is this heroic warrior now?"

"Unfortunately, he died of his wounds. The body awaits at the magistrate's offices, and we hoped you would be so kind as to see if you recognize him. Even if he is unknown to you, it is only right that his weapons and armor be returned to the Otomo clan."

Yasutoki's first reaction was annoyance that such a task must fall to him as the ranking member of the Otomo clan. He had more important things to do than identify a dead man. But he was also curious. Otomo clan retainers would not be allowed travel to

Kamakura except on official business.

Movement behind a nearby rice-paper door caught his attention. Too stealthy to be a servant. It could only be Tiger Lily, listening. He would have to chastise her for her nosiness when he returned.

Yasutoki thanked the constable and agreed to view the corpse.

"By the gods and buddhas," Yasutoki said, "I *do* know him!"

The constable bowed his head, covering his nose and mouth with his voluminous sleeve. "Who is it, my lord?"

Within the compound of the Kamakura city magistrate's offices, on the veranda above the justice ground of raked white sand where the magistrate adjudicated criminal cases, the body had been laid out on a table and covered with a white sheet. Flies buzzed around the corpse. The summer heat had not been kind to a body slashed and pierced in several places.

"He is indeed Otomo clan. His name is Ishitaka, the nephew of my master Lord Tsunetomo."

The constable made a sound of recognition. "Forgive the circumstances, my lord. It is a terrible pity. Will you be seeing to the funeral arrangements?"

Yasutoki nodded. As ranking representative of the Otomo clan, it was his duty. "Your assistance would be much appreciated, however, as I have been in Kamakura only a few days."

"Of course, my lord."

Ishitaka's single glazed eye stared at the sky. A blue-black fly lit upon his cracked, pale lips.

The constable said, "All of his personal effects are here as well."

A samurai of Ishitaka's rank would not have been traveling alone. "Was anyone traveling with him?"

"A squire, the ship captain said. The squire, however, was wounded and lost overboard."

Ishitaka should have been traveling with an entire retinue. Why only one squire? "Where is this ship captain? I would like to speak with him."

"We would be happy to bring him here. His ship is still in port."

"I would be most grateful."

* * *

Under Yasutoki's penetrating gaze, the ship captain fiddled nervously with his hands. They sat together with the constable in a private office while the captain related the story of Ishitaka's defiance of the pirates, his heroic fight against them, and his submission to the grievous wounds he had suffered.

A tall, weathered, broad-shouldered man on the verge of sliding into old age, the ship captain bowed low. "He was truly a brave man. Exceptionally good hearted. He saved my life and the lives of my crew." He smelled of the sea as if saltwater flowed in his veins.

"But he traveled with only the squire?" Yasutoki said.

"Yes, Lord."

"Did you hear them discuss the purpose of their journey to Kamakura?"

"No, Lord. Nothing. But you don't often see a man so determined."

But determined *why?*

Yasutoki said, "And this is *all* of his personal effects?" He gestured to the items laid out beside them. Besides armor and weapons, a lacquered case containing toiletry items—a razor, a comb, wax for his topknot—a paper-wrapped packet of coins, a worn, ragged slip of paper.

The ship captain bowed, "It is, Lord. That's all of it. If I could pay him for the lives of my crew, I would. Not only did he save our lives, but he put a sword through the guts of one of the most notorious pirate captains ever to ride the waves, the Sea Wolf of Iyo. That's what broke them to run."

Yasutoki rubbed his chin. Perhaps some clue hid in Ishitaka's personal effects. The captain appeared to be the most earnest of fools, and bereft of any further useful information.

"You have the gratitude of the Otomo clan, Captain, for bringing this to our attention. Otomo no Ishitaka will take his place among the clan's greatest heroes. You may return to your ship."

The ship captain pressed his forehead to the floor and departed.

The constable said, "Shall I have the warrior's possessions sent to your residence, Lord Yasutoki?"

"I will examine them first, Constable. Many thanks for all your assistance."

The constable bowed and departed.

The array of items looked mundane. Except for the slip of paper.

The ink had run from water stains, the paper heavily crumpled as if much handled. He unfolded it and read.

Within moments, he recognized the hand at the brush.

Yasutoki was not surprised when he returned to his residence to find that Tiger Lily had disappeared without a word. The rage simmered in him like the slow creep of a fire across a moist field. She had overheard every word with the constable and known its significance long before Yasutoki had. His absence had given her the opportunity to escape.

His mistakes with her paraded across his mind like some grotesque mummer's dance. Chief among those mistakes was growing complacent in trusting her. He had let her fear subside. She should still be living every day in terror of him, but she had found courage somewhere.

With servants present, he could not release the rage quivering in every limb. Killing them in his fury would be perfectly legal—indeed, it was his right—but it would be frowned upon. It would draw unwanted inquiries. Tsunetomo would be displeased at any indiscriminate killing of his subjects. Back at home, the ramifications of Ishitaka's death would be profound, but he could not think calmly about them just yet. Perhaps tomorrow, he would be composed enough to send a missive home relating the news.

He contacted the local constabulary and informed them that a slave had taken the opportunity to escape. The constable was surprised to hear from Yasutoki again so soon, but he agreed to dispatch deputies to the Seven Entrances to watch for her.

Night fell, and Yasutoki prowled the rooms of his residence. He ordered the servants to bed early. He ordered two of his bodyguards to forget that he left the house at the Hour of the Rat, wearing a basket hat.

Tonight he was not Otomo no Yasutoki. Tonight Green Tiger haunted the streets of Kamakura. Someone was going to die, perhaps many, and the killing would stop only when his rage had spent itself.

Two flowers in a letter
The moon sinks into the
 far off hills.
Dew drenches the
 bamboo grass.
I wait.
Crickets sing all night in
 the pine tree
At midnight the temple
 bells ring.
Wild geese cry
 overheard.
Nothing else.

—*The Love Poems of Marichiko*

T he tension in Kazuko's husband radiated from him. Rather than greeting her in the castle, he closeted himself in more meetings with Tsunemori and his other retainers. This was unlike him. Never before had he returned from traveling and not greeted her with gifts and affection.

She remained in the castle, feeling hurt and alone, anxiously waiting. When he did not take his evening meal with her, she began to think something was truly amiss, but she did not dare seek him out when he was in the company of his highest officers. It would feel like stepping out of place.

He did not return to their chambers until very late. She was still waiting for him in the feeble light of a single lamp. Moonlight spilled across her through the open shutters. A cricket chirped in some dark corner.

He slid the door open and stepped inside, then started at seeing her awake.

"Welcome home, Husband." She bowed to him. "Why have you waited so long to come to me?"

His lips seemed to have something poised to say.

She touched the bandage on her cheek. "Is it this? Do I disgust you now?"

His gaze brushed over her, then returned to the floor. "The last few days have been...trying." He did not move to embrace her, or even approach her. Instead a rare scowl appeared. He seldom let himself appear so displeased. "Why did you never tell me that Ken'ishi was the *ronin* who killed Hakamadare?"

A cold slash went through her heart. Secrets must come out. She cast about the room for an answer, then said, "Because my father branded him a criminal. Quite unfairly. Ken'ishi killed one of my father's retainers in a duel, but by Ken'ishi's account, the man insulted and mistreated him."

"I spoke to your father in Dazaifu. The village headman describes Ken'ishi as a scurrilous ruffian who demanded food at the threat of violence. The constable was doing his duty to protect the village. I might add that your father was most displeased to discover that Ken'ishi was in my service."

"When I met Ken'ishi, he was starving, unwashed. He had been traveling a long time with no money or food. But he saved my life and rid the land of a terrible scourge. Is my life worth less than the constable's?"

"That Ken'ishi still lives proves the answer. It seems, though, that your father's reaction in the balance of crimes versus valiant deeds is somewhat unjustified."

"He was very angry about the constable's death."

"That was not my impression from speaking with him. There was something else." He stood across the room, arms crossed. His gaze fixed upon her. Its pressure bored into her heart, into her mind, mining for long-buried secrets.

Cold dread settled into her belly. Was this to be the moment she had feared from the day of her betrothal? Would a half-truth satisfy him? Did she dare reveal anything at all?

He said, "Why did you never mention that such a great warrior as the *Oni*-Slayer was in my service?"

"Perhaps you should ask him why he never revealed it."

"His answer was the same as yours."

"Then perhaps it is the truth." Her heart pounded harder and harder, like a boulder bouncing down a cliff.

His lips pursed tight, and his gaze still bored into her. "Why did you ask him to accompany you in the hunt for Hatsumi?"

"He volunteered," her voice tightened. The accusation was building in his voice. Should she play the wrongly accused? Protest her innocence?

"But you arranged it."

"In your entire domain, is there anyone more suited to hunt an *oni*? He has killed three now."

"Three?"

"The village constable's *yoriki* took it upon himself to avenge his master's death. He pursued Ken'ishi with such fervor and hatred that he became an *oni* himself."

"How do you know of this?"

"Ken'ishi and I recently spent several days traveling together."

"Several days alone together. Again."

She jumped to her feet. "Enough of this! I have been true to you since the day of our marriage! Jealousy is an evil beast. It peers out through my husband's eyes, and I do not know him." Would he notice her tiny bit of dissembling?

He took two steps toward her, fists clenched at his sides. Then he stopped, trembling. He took a deep breath.

"What do you have to fear from him?" she said. "You are the strongest lord on Kyushu. He lives and dies at your command. When Ken'ishi and I met, he was nothing but a penniless vagabond. Do you think I would dishonor the Nishimuta clan for such a man? Do you think I would dishonor *you*?"

For a long time, he gazed into her. "Those are separate questions. Are they not." At those words, something cracked in his voice, like a stone pillar suddenly giving way, but not collapsing, no, never collapsing. The hardness of his face melted into the hint of sadness, but before it could take hold, he spun away from her.

She reached out to him. "Husband, I—"

His gaze fixed upon a square of rice paper in the door. "He has saved your life, twice now. I have never met a warrior with his strength and humility. If I had a thousand of him, I would be shogun. He has become...important to me."

"I am glad of it, Husband. He is a worthy retainer."

His voice resumed its customary matter-of-fact tone. "I'm assigning Ken'ishi new duties. He will oversee construction of the new fortifications near Hakozaki." He glanced over his shoulder for her reaction.

She remained stolid, unmoved, even though the words sliced a hole in the bottom of her heart that began to bleed. "He will do you honor there."

He nodded, then slid open the door and departed.

For the first time, he did not come to her bed that night. The wound on her face ached until morning.

Tsunetomo returned the next morning while she was picking at her breakfast. He wore the same clothes, and his eyes were red-rimmed and haunted, his back so rod-straight he looked like a wooden doll. He clutched a scroll.

Kazuko put down her chopsticks in growing alarm. The weight of exhaustion and grief had left her feeling fragile this morning, like an empty eggshell. "What is it, Husband?"

"Word from Yasutoki..." He held out the scroll. "Ishitaka is dead."

The last of Kazuko's strength drained from her like water, but she stood and approached him, reaching out. He let her embrace him, and told her a story of Ishitaka's valiant death, saving his ship from a pirate attack on the way to Kamakura. But when it was over, all he seemed able to say was, "He is gone, he is gone."

And with him went the Otomo line's last hope for an heir. She wept against him, for him, for them both.

When they informed Ishitaka's parents, Tsunemori stiffened as if he had just taken a dagger in the side. Lady Yukino clutched her sleeves to her face to muffle her keening wail. Kazuko had never seen her lose control before. Yukino crawled to her husband's shoulder, clutched him, buried her face in his back, and wept against him. He clutched his knees, bowed his head, and closed his eyes.

Kazuko reached out to squeeze Tsunetomo's hand, and he allowed it. She felt deep grief for Ishitaka—he was such a good-hearted man—but she marveled at the ragged sharpness of Yukino's anguish, the anguish of a mother bereft of her last living child. Yukino's body became a limp cloth, boneless, leaking great, crystalline tears. It was said that the love of a mother for her child was like nothing in this world. Seeing Yukino's raw, tortured agony, Kazuko felt fortunate to have been spared it—but only for a moment, because that sentiment quickly drowned in fear for the family line. There was no one now who would carry on the blood. Lady Yukino was too old to bear another child.

She and Tsunetomo offered the best words of comfort they could, but in the end, the grieving parents could only shuffle back to their tower alone, where they would confront their heartbreak both together and, ultimately, alone.

As sad as Kazuko was about Ishitaka's death, she could not help thinking about the increasing tenuousness of her own fate.

SO ENDS THE SEVENTH SCROLL

PART III: THE EIGHTH SCROLL

I cannot forget
The perfumed dusk
  inside the
Tent of my black hair
As we awoke to make
  love
After a long night of love.

                            —*The Love Poems of Marichiko*

"Captain!" Ushihara said. "It happened again!" He bowed low, soaked with sweat in the late summer heat. Dried mud caked his bare feet and legs.

Ken'ishi stabbed his shovel into the earth and brushed the dirt from his hands. "Another death?" He stretched his aching shoulders. Several months of hard labor had brought back the lean hardness of his *ronin* youth. His bare chest and belly rippled with strength and glistened with sweat.

Just down the slope of the embankment, Hakata Bay lapped at the beach. For as far as the eye could see toward the west, toward Hakozaki and Hakata, stood a stone wall in various stages of construction. Traces of cloud streaked the azure sky. A welcome freshet of sea breeze brushed over him.

"Yes, Captain!"

"Where?"

"Looks like there was a village, but all the people are gone now." Ushihara pointed along the beach toward the northeast, toward a spot on Hakata Bay that Ken'ishi knew well.

This was the second time one of the builders had died in the area of what was once Aoka village. One death could be an accident; two could not. "I will investigate."

It was almost a year now since the barbarians had slaughtered most of Aoka's inhabitants, including Kiosé and Little Frog. A lifetime ago, it seemed.

Ken'ishi looked around the earthworks, where men swarmed over the shoreline like ants, moving stones and shoveling earth. Stonecutters worked from bamboo scaffolds interspersed along the wall. Lever arms of wood and bamboo swung great buckets of earth and stone into place. Then he spotted the engineer overseeing this section of the wall, a man named Hojo no Akihiro, hunched above a makeshift table under a cloth shade, poring over a sheaf of drawings and lists.

Ken'ishi approached the engineer, Ushihara close behind. Akihiro was a thin, pensive man, whose opulent robes hung sodden with sweat in the heat. His bald pate, fringed with carefully trimmed gray, shone with perspiration.

Annoyance flashed on Akihiro's face at Ken'ishi's approach. Akihiro often stated, "Every moment that work is delayed reflects badly on our efforts and dishonors us before the shogun." Even though Akihiro had come all the way from Kamakura, one of the shogun's own builders, Ken'ishi's rank equaled his. Ken'ishi's men respected him; they despised Akihiro.

They greeted each other tersely, then Ken'ishi said, "There seems to be trouble along the work line to the east. Another death."

Akihiro waved a hand. "And what of that? Keep the men working."

Ken'ishi said, "Ushihara here says the first death last week has the men in that area frightened."

Akihiro raised an eyebrow. "How so?"

Ken'ishi gestured for Ushihara to speak.

Ushihara said, "I saw the body, Lord. His face was...awful. Eyes wide and staring." He circled his fingers to bulge his own eyes. "Mouth open like he was screaming. His skin white like paper. Not a wound on him. Healthy as a horse the day before. I just got word there's another one."

Ken'ishi said, "I'm going. We cannot let this continue. The peasants are already working double shifts. Fear will send them stealing away back to their villages."

"Then they'll be flogged as deserters!"

"It is harvest season. Their villages are already suffering from their absence. Michizane will serve as foreman until I return."

Akihiro snorted and waved a dismissive hand again. "Do what you think you must."

Ken'ishi retrieved Silver Crane from his tent and Storm from the makeshift stable. Ushihara retrieved his own horse, a swaybacked, old stallion with as much gray in his coat now as brown. Nevertheless, he mounted the horse with the same pride as if it were part of the shogun's private herd.

The two of them took the road toward Aoka village, trotting their mounts at a quick, sustained pace.

In only half an hour's travel along the shoreline road behind the construction of the fortifications, they passed at least ten new shrines honoring the *kami* of the air and sea, honoring the gods who had sent the storm to destroy the Mongol threat. Some of the shrines were still under construction. The Shinto priests were swimming in gold as people poured their thanks into coffers more than happy to accept those thanks. The scent of incense carried up and down the shoreline road.

The farther they traveled from Hakozaki, the sparser the shrines became. Ken'ishi knew these roads well, and soon he and Ushihara rode into the ruins of Aoka village. The charred remains of burnt houses sat untouched. The few structures left standing bore the stamp of desertion, their thatch falling away, their shutters and doors looking ever more weather-beaten, ragged curtains and broken shutters hanging limp in open windows. Near the center of town lay what was once Norikage's administrative office, and near that the ashen ruins of Ken'ishi's humble house, where he had burned the bodies of Kiosé and Little Frog.

Heaviness settled into his heart at this portion of his life that was lost.

The village was not deserted now, however. The fishermen's docks had been demolished, along with all the buildings closest to shore. In their places, great mounds of earth had been built in preparation for the stone walls. But all work had ceased. Stonecutters should have been chiseling blocks of stone. Laborers should have been carrying baskets of earth on their backs. But instead they were standing in sullen clumps, eyes furtive and hooded.

Ushihara served as a workgroup foreman here. "The body is over here, Captain." He spurred his horse toward the ruins of Ken'ishi's house. A group of workers stood near a body covered by a dirt-stained blanket. They bowed low at the sight of Ken'ishi.

He dismounted and approached. "Tell me what happened."

One of the men, a gnarled, leathery man with a sparse set of remaining teeth, bowed and stepped forward. "I found him this morning, Captain. Found him right here, I did. He was with us last night when we went to bed."

"Where have you been sleeping?"

"In some of the houses, Captain."

"Did none of you see him go outside?" Ken'ishi said.

The man shrugged. "We all get up in the night and shake off the dew, Captain."

"But did anyone see him?"

The men traded wide-eyed looks and shook their heads.

"Which houses are you sleeping in?" Ken'ishi said.

The men pointed, one street over, toward a cluster of houses that had escaped fire, perhaps seventy paces away. Ken'ishi knew who used to live there. They had not escaped barbarian blades and arrows.

The distance was too far to walk for a man who was just out to relieve himself.

What could have happened here, on this spot?

He knelt beside the body and threw back the sheet.

The men gasped and jumped back.

The miasma of decay flew free with the sheet. Ken'ishi covered his nose and mouth. One of the men made a sign against evil *kami*. Fat, blue-black flies buzzed lazily. The dead man's milky eyes stared, one straight up at the sky, the other rolled back out of sight. The mouth was wide open, as if in a scream, but the bloodless lips were peeled back grotesquely to expose the teeth. The pale, almost white skin was lined with blue-gray streaks. The fingers were clawed and reaching, as if gripping something. There were no bloodstains, no wounds.

The men milling around had obliterated any discernible tracks.

He stood and sighed. "Ushihara, ride back to Hakozaki and find a suitable priest. Bring him back before nightfall. We must put this man's spirit to rest. Such an evil death will haunt this place, and we have work to do."

Ushihara bowed, "Yes, Captain." He ran back to his horse and was soon away.

Ken'ishi surveyed the area again.

"Do we need an exorcism, Captain?" one man said.

"I don't know," Ken'ishi said. "The realm of the dead is not my knowledge." He composed himself to listen for the *kami*. A pall of dark fear hung in the air, an unquiet stillness. The surrounding forest lay silent. The *kami* offered no alarm. Whatever danger there had been, whatever had killed this man, was apparently gone now.

Gravediggers were working among one of the crews in the area. They kept to themselves as no one else wanted to work with them, given their status as unclean, but they dug the grave and dutifully disposed of the body. Ken'ishi hoped that Ushihara would return soon with a priest, lest the dead man's spirit be trapped in the mortal realm as a hungry ghost.

At Ken'ishi's urging, the men went back to work, but uneasiness kept them looking over their shoulders. A wave of ill fortune swept the area. Broken shovel handles, torn baskets, a stonecutter pulping one of his fingers with a hammer, a section of wall collapsing in a small avalanche of loose earth and erasing several days of labor.

When dusk descended, turning Hakata Bay into a sea of glimmering blood, the workers dispersed to their evening meals with much grumbling and troubled talk. Ushihara, however, had not returned. This was unlike him. Surprisingly, he had become one of Ken'ishi's most reliable men.

With an eye toward inclement weather, Ken'ishi took up a place beside one of the remaining houses with a broad, clear view of the village. Clouds slid across the faces of the stars, deepening the darkness. Sounds of tense conversation diminished in the houses where the workers quartered. Firelight faded to orange glow through the windows. The lap of the sea against the beach subsided. The birds and crickets remained silent. Even the mosquitoes slept. Silver Crane lay quiescent at his side. He leaned against the wall, munched on a rice ball, and watched.

The silence thrummed like a heartbeat, lulling him toward sleep. His limbs seemed to expand and contract rhythmically with the sound of his breathing. Fingers of silver spread through the clouds as if lit from within. The moistness in the air did not smell clean and fresh like rain, but thick and moldy with decay. Mist crept across the ground from the forest at the village edge. Fireflies blinked in the shadows of the forest, bobbing in and out of the mist. The ninth month was not the season for fireflies. He blinked and sat up a little straighter, rubbing his eyes.

His house now stood on its old spot, whole and unburned.

He rubbed his eyes again.

He took up his sword and approached the house.

The same thatched roof. The same weathered walls and shutters. The door stood open. A yellow light swelled within.

The steps up to the door felt solid underfoot. A shadow moved inside.

He stepped inside and found Kiosé lifting the lid from a pot above the crackling fire pit. Steam mushroomed toward the ceiling.

She smiled at him. "Welcome home, dear." Then she stirred the pot with a rice paddle. "Are you hungry? I've been cleaning."

His mouth hung agape, but words would not come.

"Sit down," she said, "you look so weary." Her hair hung long and free about her shoulders, a style he could not recall her wearing.

He took a few steps closer. "Kiosé..."

"It's been too long since we've had a night to ourselves. Little Frog is already asleep."

She was as pretty as any time he could remember.

"Do you...remember me, Kiosé?" Ken'ishi said. Last year, he had lamented to a strange, old man in the forest—Hage, in actuality— that Kiosé's love for him was holding him back. It felt like an anchor. He could not bear to hurt her any more by returning her ardent love with tepid affection. Hage had enchanted Kiosé's memories to erase Ken'ishi from them.

"What a silly question!" She scooped steaming rice into two wooden bowls. From a wooden box she plucked two wrinkled, purple globes—pickled plums—and arranged them atop the bowls.

As she worked, he studied her. He thought he caught sight of an opening cut across the back of her *kimono*. Its placement seemed as if it should be significant, but then it was gone. And her skin was so porcelain smooth now, like...like someone else's whose name eluded him. The more he looked at her, the more beautiful she became, and the greater his admiration grew, as if she drank it up.

"Kiosé," he said, "how is it you're here? It's been so long."

"I've been here all this time, dear." She smiled again and offered him a bowl.

He took it, and the brush of her finger against his was as cold as if she had been walking outside in winter. "But why?"

"You *know* why!" she snapped. Then her voice softened again. "You know."

"Do you remember what happened here?"

"Eat. You're hungry." She smiled again, faintly.

Mist filled the corners of the room now.

As he looked at the rice and the plum, a wild, desperate buzzing filled his mind, like ten thousand mosquitoes trapped his in skull. The rice smelled good. She was so beautiful, and he had not lain with her for so long. He missed her body against his, her little sighs of pleasure, the touch of her lips.

"Kiosé." He reached for her. She edged nearer, coquettishly, but still out of reach.

"There's something I must tell you, Kiosé," he said.

"Mmm?" She edged a bit closer, shoulder toward him, her face obscured by her long hair.

"I...I'm very sorry for what happened. While I was away, I thought about you often."

"And where *were* you?" she said, a harsh accusation lurking there. Again, her voice softened. "Where were you?"

"Searching, I think. Imprisoned. Trying to return."

A distant voice echoed through the door. A dimly luminous fog now obscured the night outside.

"What was that?" he asked.

"Oh, dear. The baby is awake." She turned toward the back of the room, where she gently scooped up a bundle wrapped in a dingy blanket. She gingerly peeled open the bundle, then bared her breast and lifted the bundle to it.

Warmth and joy shot through Ken'ishi. How he had yearned to

hear Little Frog's coarse little voice again. He reached out. "May I hold him?"

Kiosé smiled, "When he's finished." She sang and rocked the bundle against her, walking around the small room. Her waist-length hair swayed with her.

In the distance, voices called, "Captain! Captain!"

Ken'ishi jumped to his feet. "What is that?"

"Just fools lost in the fog," she said. "There, I think he's satisfied for now. Such a hungry baby."

She turned toward him and offered the bundle.

Reaching out, he took it gently, cradling it in his arm. Why had he never held Little Frog like this before? Something crawled across his hand. Instead of warm wriggling baby, the bundle rattled like sticks. Instead of a baby's quiet cooing, the bundle made no sound.

He lifted the flap of blanket aside. Instead of Little Frog's round, pink face, there were only two empty sockets in a small, blackened skull, nestled in a parcel of charred bones.

"He's such a good boy," Ken'ishi said. His voice sounded as if it came from the bottom of a well.

"Handsome like his father," Kiosé said. She clasped her hands over her heart, brimming with pride.

Something brushed across his shoulder blades, stroking his back with affection.

She looked up into his eyes. She was so much more beautiful than...that other person.

Somewhere a baby wailed, as if from a great distance. "Shhh," he said, and rocked the bundle as Kiosé had done.

"I think he is asleep now." She lifted the bundle from his arms and, with infinite gentleness, placed it on the mat. With her back still turned, she said, "You will let me stay, won't you?"

"Yes."

"You make me so happy." She stood and turned toward him. Her knee length hair almost enveloped her, black and silky.

"Captain! Captain!" came voices from the fog.

Ken'ishi stepped into the doorway, but the fog was too thick to see anything. "What are they doing out there in the fog?"

A touch slid up over his shoulder blade. "Come back, dear. We only have a little time," Kiosé said in his ear.

When he turned, she was kneeling across the room from him, unfolding a *futon*. She patted it. "Come to me, my love."

Mist covered the floor, ankle deep. Things black and fibrous slithered in the mist, tickling his feet like seaweed as he crossed to her.

Rather than standing, she seemed to flow upright, rising up to nuzzle his chin. "Why not put that down?"

"What? Oh." He still held his sword by the scabbard in his left hand. "What shall I do with it?"

"Throw it away." A dozen soft hands brushed up and down his back, his buttocks, his legs. Kiosé's hands lay upon his chest.

The sound of a great silver bell pealed through his mind, almost as if meaning were embedded in the echoes.

Obsidian tendrils snaked over his shoulders, between his legs, around his thighs, around his arms, around his neck, so soft, so gentle, caressing, coaxing him down onto the *futon*.

He stretched out on the futon. It was not strange at all that Kiosé had no legs. The hem of her *kimono* floated just above the mist. Her shape knelt beside him, cold, hard hands pressing him down against the mat. The tendrils encircling him cinched tighter, pleasantly.

The tendrils tugged at Silver Crane with increasing strength. He gripped the scabbard tighter. The tendrils' insistence continued to increase, stretching out his arm.

She hovered above him, with no legs to straddle him, leaning down into his face with a screech. "Let it go!" The harsh moment of shrill rage came and went in less than a heartbeat, then she was smiling again. "Let it go. You do not need it anymore."

The peal of the silver bell came again.

"No, I—" He tried to reach for the sword with his right hand, but something pinned his right hand to his side. Her eyes were so dark and deep and beautiful.

Something fell out of her hair, into his mouth. Something sour and wriggling. He spat it out with revulsion. In the darkness he could not see what it was.

The slithering tendrils of black hair cinched tighter, squeezing his chest and throat, cutting off his breath.

"It's all right, my love. Just lie still." Her eyes were cold and empty as a freshly dug grave.

The fire in the firepit turned green.

A blaze of fury erupted in his chest. "No!" With a great heave he tore his right arm free with a sound like tearing cloth.

With his free hand, he shoved against her chest. His hand sank into her breast as if her body was cold *mochi*. He yanked it free, and a deluge of squirming maggots gushed over him. A venomous centipede scuttled across her face and back into her hair. Clamping down on the urge to wretch, he heaved his right arm across his body, reaching for Silver Crane's hilt. Slick black tentacles of hair rose up to ensnare his arm again. Still he could not breathe. His fingers touched Silver Crane's ray skin hilt, encircled it, gripped it. Then, with a stifled roar of defiance, he dragged it free. Its blade caught the green firelight like a glimmering mirror. Shards of emerald light danced across the ceiling, across her corpse's face.

The hair reached for his sword arm, but he slashed at her. She flung herself back as if light as feather and hung there above the swirling mist. A great mane of black hair rose around her head like ten thousand tentacles, each with a life of its own. Her eyes looked like solid droplets of congealed gore, devoid of pupil and iris. Her fingers were black-taloned claws.

He slashed wildly at the hair, and it parted like so much gauze at the sword's razor edge. Then he was free, gasping.

Green flames burst into life at the base of every wall, shooting upward with prodigious hunger, engulfing the walls, licking at the thatch.

As if waking from a dream, Ken'ishi began to remember.

The rice bowl on the floor writhed to the brim with maggots, crawling over not a pickled plum, but a plucked eyeball.

She unleashed a hideous, keening wail that stabbed needles into his ears, into his spine. The nimbus of hair flew around her face as if in a typhoon wind. He raised his sword and charged her.

An explosion of green flame blinded him. He slashed blindly, stumbling over a wooden beam, but kept his footing. His eyes watered, and he blinked and blinked.

Finally, when he was able to see again, he was standing in the cold, charred ruins of his house. Thick fog, gray with the light of morning, surrounded him.

He scrambled free of the debris, gasping, with the sensation of hair still sliding across his flesh.

"Captain!" came voices.

"I am here!" he called.

Moments later, shapes appeared out of the fog, converging on him.

"Is that you, Captain?" called a man's voice.

"It is," Ken'ishi said, turning to survey the blackened timbers and charcoal.

The thick fog muffled all sound, but it bore the light of dawn, not the moon.

Several men ran up, gaping with surprise, carrying shovels and hammers and clubs as improvised weapons. "It is...you, Captain," said one.

"I still walk with both feet in this realm," Ken'ishi said.

Another said, "Gods and buddhas, Captain! You look—"

"Like Taka!" said another, referring to yesterday's dead man.

"What happened?" asked another, eyeing Ken'ishi's naked blade.

Ken'ishi sheathed it and noted the paleness of his arms, the blueness of his veins, the chill that suffused even his bones. "We require an exorcism."

September lightning...
White calligraphy on
    high
Silhouettes the hill
                —*Joso*

Kazuko sat down on a wooden bench in the heart of the *sakura* grove at the base of the castle wall. She had ordered this bench constructed because of her frequent walks. She liked to sit and contemplate here under the dark leaves, often at night, now that Tsunetomo had taken to sleeping in another room. The castle guards did not approve of the lady of the castle wandering outside the walls at night, especially when she demanded to go alone, but they could hardly refuse her.

If her husband knew of these frequent sojourns, he did not challenge her about them. He professed to care about her welfare, but in truth she seldom saw him except at meals, ceremonies, and festivals. He had his business, and she had hers.

Lately, hers had become providing comfort and companionship to Lady Yukino, whose ocean of melancholy over Ishitaka's death remained as deep as the moment the news had come. She still wept daily, even though the mourning period for Ishitaka was several weeks over.

Tonight, clouds blanketed the moon, and a chill autumn wind made Kazuko tug her robes closer. She clutched her loneliness around her like a blanket. Her new handmaiden was a simpering little girl, incapable of interesting conversation. She thought about sending the girl away, but she lacked the energy to seek out another one. Hatsumi, even in her crawling, hidden evil, had at least been a familiar face. Lady Yukino was a chore now, not a comfort. Tsunetomo had all but abandoned her. Ken'ishi was gone.

Kazuko was alone.

This melancholy of hers felt so familiar. She had wallowed in the blackest depths of it in the first months after her marriage. Eventually, she had learned to smile again. But now, any smile reminded her of the unnatural tug on her scarred cheek, the spots of numbness that would never go away, a crack in what had once been perfect, porcelain beauty. She had never thought herself vain until the beauty she had so heedlessly enjoyed was marred. Whenever she appeared in public now, she wore a veil in the fashion of the dark-skinned women from the land of the Buddha.

Some days she could cast herself into martial pursuits, and some days it all felt too much. She did not want to be strong today. She wanted to let herself weep, and that became a battle in her heart. She was a samurai woman. She was steadfast and brave. She was Kazuko the Oni-Slayer, a natural companion to Ken'ishi the Oni-Slayer if ever there was one.

Tonight, the samurai woman lost the battle. She let the tears come, burying her face in her sleeves, at the same time despising her weakness.

Her sleeves were damp when she heard an exasperated sigh beside her.

She started and looked around.

A small voice said, "One might think you were the saddest human in the world."

An old *tanuki* sat beside her on his haunches, preening his white whiskers.

"Mr. *Tanuki,* you frightened me," she said.

"You may call me Hage, lady. That is the name I've worn for a century or two."

"Are you truly so old?" she said. "Are you a god?"

"Young lady, I'm just getting started. And I'm hardly a god, although I daresay a lover or two has proclaimed it of me." He chuckled. "So how do you expect me to enjoy my evening with so much sadness polluting the air?"

"I am sorry to have disturbed you, Lord Hage."

The *tanuki* leaned back with a high-pitched roar of laughter, slapping his knees. "Oh, lady! 'Lord,' you said!"

When his laughter finally subsided, she said, "I wish only to be respectful."

"How about a rice ball instead? Some *saké*, perhaps?" He smacked his lips. "Putting such a title on me is like trying to put a diaper on an ox. You'd find it mighty difficult, and the ox would just soil it."

"I apologize, Hage. If I had known you were coming to my party of despair, I would have brought a picnic."

He slapped his knee again and chuckled. "That's a more suitable spirit, Lady. So tell me about the damp sleeves. I helped an acquaintance of yours once or twice when he was having difficulty."

"Ken'ishi?"

"You two took care of that awful, howling woman, didn't you?"

"Yes." She touched her scarred cheek.

"He didn't bed you, did he? I told him not to."

She gasped at the *tanuki*'s brazen audacity. No human would ever think to ask a powerful lady such a question. But somehow, the fact that he was not human made it easier for her answer. "No."

"But you're both in heat for each other."

"It is a curse for both of us."

"A curse? Bah. For creatures who are open to copulating so frequently, you humans get so twisted up about such things."

"I am cursed, Hage. I am the wife of a lord. My husband needs an heir. I fear the gods have made me barren for dishonoring my family...because of Ken'ishi."

He leaned closer and sniffed her. "Hmm...barren you say?"

"Hage, you have magical powers, do you not?"

"When the mood strikes."

She knelt before him and bowed. "Please do me this favor. Quicken my womb."

He raised a bushy brow and scratched his chin. "As I doubt you're asking me to scamper through your rice patch, so to speak, I must tell you I have no control over your womanhood. The best I could do would be to make you the randiest doe in the forest until morning. I could make you forget your 'curse,' however, if that would please you."

Forget Ken'ishi? Would she if she could? Her yearning for him, and the way she had channeled it, had turned her into a formidable warrior. He had taken her to greater ecstasy than she had ever known, in her heart, in her body. She was a richer woman for having known him. Remove him from her life, and she would be just an ignorant girl.

"No, I do not wish to forget anything."

Hage rocked back and forth on his haunches, pursing his lips, chewing on his whiskers. "You're wiser than I suspected. Wiser than *he* is sometimes. Tell me, what *do* you wish?"

"I wish to make my husband happy, to do my duty, to bear him a son."

He sighed. "Alas, sometimes all there is to do is enjoy the breeze."

She sat on the bench again and tried to follow his advice.

"If one sets up a mirror, the form of whatever happens to be in front of it will be reflected and will be seen. As the mirror does this mindlessly, the various forms are reflected  clearly, without any intent to discriminate this from that. Setting up his whole mind like a mirror, the man who employs the martial arts will have no intention of discriminating right from wrong, but according to the brightness of the mirror of his mind, the judgment of right and wrong will be perceived without giving it any thought."

—Takuan Soho, "Annals of the Sword Taia"

Ushihara returned to Aoka at mid-morning, cursing the fog for his delay. "I'm very sorry, Captain."

Ken'ishi had tried to eat breakfast, but his stomach would not accept food. Every time he looked at a bowl of rice, his memory jumped to the bowl of squirming maggots. So he shepherded the uneasy workers back to their labors, assuring them that he was as hale as ever, that they were safe during the day. Nevertheless, he would not allow anyone to sleep another night in Aoka with Kiosé's *yurei* clinging to the area like the miasma of death around an improperly covered grave. "Where is the priest?"

"He is coming on foot. He wouldn't ride. Said he should keep his feet on the earth." Ushihara shrugged. "Found him at one of the shrines. You want to know how many I had to ask? Most of those snobbish bastards weren't willing to come this far."

Ken'ishi snorted. Such disdain for the dead spoke poorly of these priests' adherence to ways of the *kami*. And they had the audacity to claim that their prayers had something to do with the typhoon that had destroyed the barbarian fleet.

By midmorning the fog had burned away, and the priest arrived in the village. He was a well-fed, jovial-looking man with beady eyes and new, stiffly-pressed robes. When Ken'ishi told him about the worker's death, the priest earnestly set about the proper funeral rites over the fresh grave. Ken'ishi left him to his work, but requested to speak to him again when his work was finished.

Ill fortune continued throughout the day, with broken tools, a barrel of cured fish that turned rancid overnight, and growing malaise among the workers. The *kami* gnawed all day at Ken'ishi's awareness, set into vexation by some evil presence that seemed to have seeped into the ground itself. He found himself growing more and more irritable with the workers. The painful wound around his ankle from Hatsumi's awful tentacle—healed with a spattering of jagged puncture scars—throbbed with a burning ache.

That afternoon, the priest informed Ken'ishi the funeral rites had been completed. The dead man had been laid to rest.

Ken'ishi thanked him and then said, "What do you know of *yurei*?"

The priest said, "They are the remnants of those who die in states of the most powerful emotions. Rage, jealousy, terror. This emotion prevents them from shedding their bonds to the mortal world. They become trapped."

"A *yurei* haunts this place. It is responsible for the death of the man you just laid to rest, and another a few days ago." Ken'ishi then told him what had happened the night before, and of Kiosé and how she and Little Frog been killed during the invasion. The priest's face grew paler with each word. By the end of Ken'ishi's tale, a sheen of sweat had appeared on the man's forehead. "She must be put to rest," Ken'ishi said.

The priest's hands trembled as he wiped the sweat away. "I fear such skills are beyond my knowledge."

"Where do I find someone who has such knowledge?"

"You need an *onmyouji*. Fortunately for you, I know of one. The Emperor has sent his best yin-yang masters to lend their arts to the construction of this wall. With their help, the gods and the *kami* will smile upon this effort." He gestured at the construction.

"Where do I find this *onmyouji*?"

"I would be happy to send him to you." The priest lightly jangled his coin purse.

Ken'ishi swallowed his annoyance and produced a suitable donation. Color returned to the priest's face, along with a broad grin. "Please tell him that the lives of my men and the future of this construction are at stake."

"I certainly will," the priest said. Then he hurried away.

In late afternoon, the *onmyouji* arrived in great splendor. His entourage of servants stretched ahead and behind. They bore him in a magnificent gilded palanquin, lacquered and heavy, bells jingling on it in such profusion that the entire work crew had heard it coming for some time.

When the yin-yang master stepped out, he looked around at the remnants of the village, he looked at the workers, he looked at Ken'ishi, and he sniffed with effete snobbery.

When Ken'ishi approached him, naked to the waist and sweating from labor, his nostril curled, but he looked Ken'ishi up and down with a raised, powdered eyebrow. The man's skin was as pale and soft as a woman's. He wore voluminous robes—they must have been sweltering—decorated with a profusion of incomprehensible symbols that were not Chinese characters, and the high, black cap that was the fashion among lords and nobles. His bony hand clutched a folded fan. His eyes glittered with shrewd intelligence from a spare, angular face.

Ken'ishi had never met a yin-yang master before, but aside from the strangeness of his clothing, the man reminded him of the court nobility he had glimpsed in his brief time in the capital.

He and the workers knelt before the *onmyouji*, pressing their foreheads to the earth. Straightening, he said, "Thank you for coming, *Sensei.* I am Captain Otomo no Ken'ishi, vassal of Lord Otomo no Tsunetomo."

The man bowed slightly. "I am Abe no Genmei, augurer of the second rank to the court of the Emperor. Let us begin as soon as possible." He snapped his fingers at his chief attendant, who immediately snapped orders at the porters and servants to unload and erect an entire campsite in the center of the village.

The chief attendant was younger than Ken'ishi, dressed similarly to Lord Abe, but less ostentatiously, with fewer arcane sigils on his attire and a cap a bit shorter. He had the look of an apprentice.

"Lord Abe," Ken'ishi said, "would you care to accompany me? There is much to tell."

Snapping open his fan, Lord Abe squinted up at the sun and fanned himself. His eyes flicked about the village. "The very air here drips with disquiet." He gestured for Ken'ishi to lead on. "Tell me everything."

Ken'ishi escorted him around the village, telling him the story of Kiosé and Little Frog and of his relationship with them. Leaving something out might disrupt whatever the *onmyouji* was formulating.

"So many intricacies in the flow of the universe, so many twists and turns to fortune and fate. Any detail could be significant," Lord Abe said once between scenes in Ken'ishi's tale. They stood before the ruins of Ken'ishi's house while he told of his brush with the hungry spirit the night before.

Lord Abe's face softened bit by bit as he listened. "Such a pitiable fate. Not even the unclean deserve such a terrible demise."

"What can be done, Lord?"

"I will attempt to exorcise this dim spirit. Do you know the characters of her name?"

"I'm sorry, Lord, I do not. I doubt even she did. She was sold to a brothel when she was very young, then to the innkeeper here. She never spoke of her parents or who gave her that name."

"The sounds alone are sometimes enough. They can echo into other realms. What you must remember is that becoming trapped here has destroyed what was good about her. All that remains are incidental echoes buried in fear and rage."

"How can I assist you?"

"Send all the workers away. Once my servants have made the

necessary preparations, they will also be sent away, except for Koumei, my apprentice. You must stay, as you will be my weapon. Her essence is still very much tied to you. Your return here has fueled her anger, like encountering an old love affair fills the belly with either butterflies or serpents. Unless she is stopped, she would follow you wherever you go, feeding upon your spirit until there is nothing left but a shriveled husk, like the two men she killed."

The hairs at the nape of Ken'ishi's neck stood on end.

"We must have all preparations in place to contain her before nightfall."

The man was insufferably haughty and disdainful, which rankled Ken'ishi, but what choice did he have? There was no one else who could help. The assurance in the voice of the *onmyouji* gave Ken'ishi a bit of comfort, but at the same time the earnestness warned him how dangerous the situation had become.

The ritual began with a five-pointed star drawn twenty paces across. From jars of black sand, the apprentice Koumei drew the star upon the ground near the ruins of Ken'ishi's house, taking meticulous care that every line was arrow-straight.

Meanwhile, Lord Abe told Ken'ishi, "The *yurei* will never depart of its own accord. It must be subdued and forced to leave the mortal realm."

"Will nothing appease her? Is there some way I can convince her to leave, to move on?"

"Can you remove a bloodstain from the earth? The *yurei* is but a shadow of the woman you knew. You cannot appease her. During the ritual, you must obey my commands to the letter. If you disobey me once the ritual has begun, your life, your very soul itself, will be in mortal danger."

"I understand, *Sensei*."

"Now, may I examine your weapon? You must take it with you into the pentagram."

Ken'ishi untied it from his *obi* and offered it with both hands.

Lord Abe bowed and accepted it. The moment he touched it, however, he stiffened, and his eyebrows rose. Then his eyes narrowed at Ken'ishi. "There is more to you than meets the eye, Captain."

"Is that not true of all men, *Sensei*?"

"It is true that every man is an entire universe unto himself, an earthly incarnation of the Nine Heavens, and we walk this universe under the influence of the stars and planets, the *kami* and the Five Elements, the gods and buddhas. We all leave a mark upon this universe, but some leave larger marks than others. Some men leave a mark so large it leaves a scar upon the face of history." His voice was grave as he indicated Silver Crane. "This blade can cut the world in two."

"I know of its power, *Sensei.*"

"Such power in the hands of a mere man.... Do you not feel the burden?"

"I do, *Sensei.*"

"And you bear it willingly?"

"It was given to me to bear by my father, a great warrior of the Taira clan."

"The Taira are no longer so great. 'Twas a terrible pity what happened to them. Echoes of their bloodline honor the halls of the imperial palace. Inauspicious for you to be born under the curse that name has become."

"The best way I can honor my ancestors is to make my own name."

Koumei ran up to them. "The pentagram is prepared, Master."

"Then let us not waste a moment," Lord Abe said.

The disorder of my hair
Is due to my lonely
   sleepless pillow.
My hollow eyes and gaunt
   cheeks
Are your fault.

—The Love Poems of Marichiko

K en'ishi sat in *seiza* in the center of the great pentagram, facing
Lord Abe. Lord Abe sat at one point of the star, facing the
remains of Ken'ishi's house. At each point, a thick candle
burned. Incense filled the air as Koumei circled the pentagram and
waved fistfuls of smoldering sticks. The village was empty except for
Ken'ishi, Lord Abe, and his apprentice, but as dusk deepened into
night, the shadows seemed filled with ten thousand eyes. Even the
waves had diminished to a mutter, as if in anticipation of a great
struggle.

Lord Abe was already deep in a trance, chanting syllables Ken'ishi
could not follow.

Then Lord Abe shouted, "Celestial warriors, descend and be
my vanguard!" As he spoke, the fingers of his right hand made five
precise vertical cuts in the air, then his left made four horizontal.

The feeling of eyes in the darkness intensified, but Ken'ishi could
not look away from Lord Abe.

Lord Abe then intoned a long list of forces, entreating them for
aid. The Five Elements—air, water, fire, earth, and void. A multitude
of gods and buddhas, some of whom Ken'ishi knew and some he did

not. The moon and sun and planets. The seven Northern Stars and their two attendants.

The *onmyouji* intertwined his fingers before him, extended from his chest in a tight, intricate pattern. "I open the Seal of the First Thunderbolt!"

A flash of lightning over the surrounding forest turned it into a stark, black silhouette, and a peal of thunder reverberated in the nearby hills. The rumble traveled through the ground, up into Ken'ishi's legs.

His belly writhed at the memories of last night's encounter with Kiosé, of how nearly he had suffered an awful fate.

Lord Abe changed his fingers to another interlocking pattern. "I open the Seal of the Thunderbolt of Divine Righteousness!"

A distant flare of lightning slashed across Hakata Bay from a starry sky and turned the face of the sea to glimmering silver, the crash and crackle of it arriving moments later.

The fireflies Ken'ishi had seen the night before came into existence at the edge of the forest, like tiny candle flames. And flames they were, not fireflies at all, but tiny tongues of greenish-yellow flame dancing at the verge of darkness.

Lord Abe shifted his fingers to another pattern. "I open the Seal of the Outer Lion, the Exultant and Glorious Celestial Jewel, the Beginning of All Things!"

In the corners of Ken'ishi's eyes, some of the stars sparkled brighter, as if drawing nearer. The air itself hummed. Koumei had taken a position behind Lord Abe, mimicking the finger patterns and humming, but the humming in the air was greater than one voice could produce.

Lord Abe extended fingers and retracted others into a new pattern. "I open the Seal of the Inner Lion, the End of All Things!"

The humming took on a deeper rumble, like a sustained avalanche or great, crashing waves.

Behind Lord Abe, a shadow separated from a building, a human silhouette with long hair. It had no feet. Mist swirled under the figure, seeping into the village from the forest. The silhouette hovered there as if watching. Ken'ishi squeezed Silver Crane's hilt.

Lord Abe's fingers wove a new pattern, all fingers clasped in a double fist. "I open the Seal of the Outer Bonds, where all evil is devoured!"

Mist curled around the foundations of Ken'ishi's house, snaking along the black lines of the pentagram, but not crossing, not yet.

Silver Crane began to thrum in his hands with the hum of the air. *I am the devourer of evil, the drinker of blood, the granter of power.* The sword's voice chorused in Ken'ishi's mind over the growing tumult in the air.

Ken'ishi caught Kiosé's scent on the air, so well remembered. The scent of her hair, of her neck, of her breath, of her sex. As if she were sitting beside him. Her silhouette behind Lord Abe was gone. The hair on his arms and legs spiked. A shadow moved in the corner of his vision.

Lord Abe's fingertips shifted inside his fists. "I open the Seal of the Inner Bonds, where the sacred fire burns!"

A great rush of wind seemed to fill Ken'ishi's breast, swell his limbs with strength, as if he could defeat a thousand men, crush them to pulp in his hands. In his belly, a pleasant heat began to build, suffusing every muscle, every hair. The heat grew and grew, like from a welcome fire in winter, driving away all chill and replacing it with comforting warmth.

Tentacles of mist crept over the boundaries of the pentagram like a tentative octopus. The chill of it glided over his feet and buttocks. The scent of Kiosé was stronger now, but tainted somehow with astringency, bitterness.

Lord Abe wound his fingers into the seventh pattern. "I open the Seal of the Fist of Wisdom, the Divine Radiance That Illuminates All Things, the bridge between realms!"

Another tremendous slap of lightning tore across the hills, rumbling down, and endless fingers of it spread across the starry sky in coruscating claws.

The mist behind Ken'ishi thickened, obscuring the pentagram. He caught sight of a head bobbing from the low mist like the head of a serpent, but swathed in impenetrable black hair, then dipping out of sight again.

The mist rose and boiled, and a crawling presence like a centipede scurried up Ken'ishi's back. Fetid breath washed over him.

Lord Abe had admonished him not to move until ordered.

Silver Crane thrummed in his fingers, sending vibrations up his arms, the earth sending vibrations up through his legs. The vibrations met in his belly, and stoked the flame there.

Lord Abe unwound his fingers into another pattern, this one with fingers spread wide, touching thumbs and forefingers like two adjacent stars. "I open the Seal of the Ring of the Sun, the source of divine perfection!"

A pale arm snaked over Ken'ishi's shoulder from behind, down across his chest, cold as the grave. Small, limp breasts pressed against his back, dead and cold, a bony chin against his neck. Chill breath brushed the back of his head. Great purplish worms, as long as his forearm and fat as his little finger, wriggled out from the earth and squirmed around his legs, nosing blindly up onto his flesh. He clenched his teeth at their clammy sliminess.

Do not move until I order it! Lord Abe had said.

Kiosé's voice whimpered in his ear. "Come away with mc, my love. I'm frightened. Let us be together."

Ken'ishi clamped his lips tight.

"Let's leave this place," she said. "Why don't you look at me?"

Lord Abe clenched his left fist within his right. "I open the final seal, the Seal of the Hidden Form, the form that conceals!"

An eyelid slid open in the middle of Ken'ishi's forehead.

The entire world burst with glorious color, endless rainbows, streaks of light and dark, colors so intense and vibrant they made everything he had seen before during his entire life seem dim and gray and lifeless.

Worms writhed beneath the skin of the arm encircling his chest. Black nails became claws and dug into his chest. Cold seared into him at her touch. Her breath became the stench of a corpse bloated in the sun. Sinuous black hair snaked around his arms, around his body. A pale bone peeked through a rent in her skin. A blind, purple worm with minute teeth chewed a fresh opening and nosed toward him, seeking fresher meat. A cold, leathery tongue traced across the back of his neck.

With his new sight, Ken'ishi looked toward the *onmyouji*, but he was no longer Abe no Genmei.

"I am Fudo, of the Five Celestial Emperors, the Immovable One." The voice was the voice of mountains, of the gulfs of Heaven, of the sea; his expression so fierce and wise that Ken'ishi could only marvel. Scarlet flames roared up around Fudo in a blazing nimbus, but they did not burn him. He sat naked to the waist, his chest and arms thicker and more muscular than a wrestler's. His flaming eyes burned into Ken'ishi's soul, then turned to Kiosé. "Dim spirit! In life, you were Kiosé. This is no longer your place. I order you to leave this place now!"

Kiosé's face split wide into a howl of fury, her mouth black and impossibly wide. A belch of grave wind swirled around Ken'ishi. "He's mine!"

"Leave now!" the god boomed with the power of the cosmos.

"Never!" Her shriek pierced Ken'ishi's ears like needles.

"Then you leave us no choice. Great Warrior, become my weapon! Subdue this evil! Drive it from this place!" The celestial being clapped its massive hands, and the shock blasted over Ken'ishi as if he had been struck himself.

Ken'ishi jumped up, spun on Kiosé, and whipped out Silver Crane. Free of its scabbard, Silver Crane shone with the light of a thousand stars. He gripped it, raised to strike.

He had expected to see a monster. Instead, there was only meek, frightened Kiosé, trembling, eyes wide with terror.

"Oh, my love!" she cried. "What have you become?"

Ken'ishi towered over her, half-again taller than a man. His skin was darkened, mottled as if by a thousand bruises. A great gash above his heart lay open and bloody, revealing four pale ribs. Silver Crane seemed so small in his grip now, like a *wakizashi.*

"Please don't hurt me," she whimpered. "I cannot bear that it's you."

"Strike, warrior!" the celestial being boomed. "It is the only way!"

Ken'ishi had already hurt her too much; with his annoyance, with his aloofness, with his refusal to claim the son he had known was his, with leaving her unprotected to face the barbarians. His tusks gleamed in the light of the god's flames. Innumerable scars crisscrossed his flesh, some from wounds he remembered, others from wounds yet to be.

The force of the god's will, however, drove Ken'ishi a step toward her. Fudo, the Celestial Emperor, would not be denied. She tried to edge away, but the line of black sand, the border of the pentagram, formed an invisible barrier that she could no longer cross.

He raised his shining sword.

"Please, my love. I'll behave. I'll do just as you say. Whatever has made you angry, I'll never do it again! Please, don't hurt me!" She cowered, arms upraised to protect herself.

"Strike now!" the god roared. "Free her!"

She had no feet.

She huddled into a ball.

Ken'ishi slashed, and his stroke opened a diagonal cut across her back.

A cut he had seen on her before.

She screamed in pain and collapsed onto her side.

Guilt washed over him in a bitter deluge. He froze, sword poised to strike again. His skin turned blacker. The cut above his heart began to bleed. He should have saved her. He should never have left.

"*Strike!*" the god roared.

The god's inexorable will seized Ken'ishi's arms.

He struck again, severing her upraised arm. Her arm clattered beside her, just dry bones. Black mist seeped from the stump.

Her wail rose higher.

He stabbed her through the breast.

Her robe burned away from the puncture point like cinders, her flesh peeling away from the ribs, crisping in Silver Crane's luminous heat.

His eyes met hers, and the gulfs of bottomless sorrow and betrayal there turned his insides to water. Tears of blood burst from his eyes.

"I trusted..." she rasped.

Then he cried out and struck off her head. Kiosé's head. The woman who had loved him, cared for him, for three years. It tumbled to the earth a charred skull.

The body collapsed into a pile of bones.

Ken'ishi sank to his knees, gasping. Blood poured from the wound over his heart, soaked his chest. Silver Crane fell from his fingers. His hands were hideous claws now, with bulbous knuckles and cracked, yellowed nails.

"Your third eye sees all," the god said.

He could not bear to look at the god anymore. "Is this what I truly am? An *oni*?" Was it only a matter of time before the inner truth manifested, as it had for Hatsumi, Taro, and Hakamadare?

"Your soul already bears a great burden. So much death and strife, so much struggle and desire. Everything you carry with you, every day. And it is not over."

Ken'ishi gazed up at the stars, wondering if his father was among them, letting the hot, coppery tears stream down his cheeks. The stars were so close now, as if they hovered just out of reach. "Am I to be condemned, then? Is it inevitable that I become this?"

"For some men, the answer would be yes. But your fate remains as fluid as the shifting tides."

Ken'ishi faced the god. "I do not want to become a monster."

"Then look to your soul, samurai. Putting this poor, dim spirit to rest is one of many great deeds. The wound of this place must be allowed to heal."

The god clapped his hands, and thunder pealed again.

The eye in Ken'ishi's forehead slid shut, and suddenly he was on one knee before Lord Abe once again. No more fire, no more coruscating explosions of color. He had returned to his normal size. The stars were back in their places. The night was simply dark again, and Kiosé's white bones lay beside him.

He felt as if he had been struck blind.

He curled up into a ball and let himself weep for the suffering of the world.

"Men do not behave themselves prudently; they blame others and then pray to the gods and beseech the Buddhas for things they themselves are not equal to. This is what men of little caliber always do. Listen,  the gods do not accept improprieties. Men think that no matter what they pray to the gods for, it will be granted, whether good or evil, correct, or perverse. Men's minds are asinine."

—*Issai Chozanshi, The Demon's Sermon on the Martial Arts*

Yasutoki looked at the opulent breakfast laid out before him, and his stomach seethed its refusal. The servant hung back, bowing, and wrung her hands in concern over his welfare. His robes hung looser upon him nowadays, and the bones and veins in his hands were more pronounced.

Tiger Lily's departure had deprived him of Green Tiger's last trusted servant, and the bitterness of the betrayal continued to eat at him even now, months after her disappearance. Seldom lately could he bring himself to eat a full meal. It was as if a burning coal had lodged behind his breastbone. Any time he took food, the coal grew hotter.

He would never have believed her capable of eluding him. She had vanished without a trace. He had trained her too well.

Here in Kamakura, so far from home, insinuating himself into the underworld had taken too long for him to find her. The local gangs guarded their territory as fiercely as those in Hakata, and Yasutoki did not know them or their capabilities. Without a strong arm beside him, like Hakamadare or Masoku, he was too vulnerable. Now, without even Tiger Lily, he was alone; and with too much time spent in the company of nobles, his own skills had grown rusty as a dagger lying in a puddle. Nevertheless, he had made a number of late night sojourns to the pleasure quarter, familiarizing himself with the underworld landscape.

For most of his stay in Kamakura, however, he had felt blind and ineffectual. And worse, the shogunate had steadfastly refused any contact with the Khan's emissaries. They remained locked up tight and under heavy guard.

Yasutoki chafed at this ineffectiveness. His attempts to ingratiate himself with their guards had been rebuffed. Most of his tremendous wealth had been lost in the invasion, as well as his enterprises for building more. He had limited funds for giving persuasive gifts, and while he could call for more from Lord Tsunetomo's coffers at home, such a request invoked the risk of theft along the journey.

Visiting representatives from the imperial court in Kyoto teemed in the noble districts. The imperial court wanted to accede to the emissaries' demands from the Great Khan. The Golden Horde was too powerful to oppose for long. The Mongols had conquered lands farther west than the imagination could reach. Spies from China revealed that Khubilai Khan remained determined to bring "this small country" under the Horde's dominion.

Yasutoki aligned himself with that belief, but not the weakness that engendered appeasement. He did not want appeasement. He wanted the Horde to sweep through every village and hamlet, across every island, and rake the Minamoto and Hojo out like bones from an old graveyard. And in the aftermath, the Taira could reemerge and ascend again.

Many of the imperial nobles still had Taira blood in their veins, but almost none professed it. Their effete lifestyles had made them soft and weak. They, too, should be swept away in the Khan's cleansing fire.

Yasutoki had attempted to circumvent the shogunate's refusal by meeting with various ministers. They had politely received him but still denied the access he wanted. What news of the Khan's plans? How many years to rebuild an invasion fleet after the devastation of the previous year? How long to replenish the tens of thousands drowned in the typhoon?

After so many months of fruitless effort, even Yasutoki—the single most determined man he had ever known—was growing discouraged, wondering if coming to Kamakura had been the right decision. He had been so confident in his powers, in his ability to see his wishes carried out, that the curtailing of those wishes vexed him. Perhaps it should be a lesson in humility. Perhaps he should return to his days as an ambitious young thug, carving out his empire one ruthless play at a time.

These were his musings across the idle hours.

Yasutoki was still sitting before his uneaten breakfast when a messenger arrived, summoning him to the shogun's court.

Such a summons had never before occurred. It suggested a breakthrough with the emissaries. Through the months here, Yasutoki had heard rumors of meetings between the *bakufu* and the emissaries, but the content of any meetings remained secret.

The summons directed Yasutoki to come at the Hour of the Horse, noon, to the parade ground outside the shogun's palace, which lay near the shrine of Hachiman and the tomb of Minamoto no Yoritomo, at the northern terminus of Young Prince Avenue. The summons specifically allowed him and his and entourage to travel upon the grand avenue, which lent weight to the significance of the event.

From his palanquin, as his servants bore him up Young Prince Avenue toward the great shrine of Hachiman, he saw other processions, those of court nobles and samurai lords alike, converging upon the appointed place.

This mass of august personages gathered at the appointed place in the bright, autumn sun. Special ministers of protocol directed the personages to specific locations on the parade ground, a broad expanse of open earth before the shogun's grand palace. The locations indicated the degree of importance the *bakufu* placed on the visitor; the closer the visitor to the palace, the more important. These locations had been carefully marked.

The shogun's palace reared three stories high, with swooping, tiled roofs; thick, wooden pillars; and iron-studded gates. It was the palace of a warrior, not a noble: utilitarian, imposing, an edifice of the shogun's authority—which had been seized at the point of a sword. Near the palace gates, a tall dais stood, festooned with banners of the Minamoto and Hojo clans.

The gathering continued for almost an hour. Parasols bloomed like flowers out of season. Servants scurried here and there.

Yasutoki's place—as representative of the Otomo clan, one of the clans deemed most loyal to the shogunate—was situated respectfully close to the stage, just beyond imperial nobles from the capital. Yasutoki found this interesting, considering that the imperial court and the *bakufu* had long considered Kyushu a troublesome backwater. Perhaps the *bakufu* was wooing greater support from the lords of Kyushu, who maintained a greater autonomy than those on Honshu.

Across the parade ground, Yasutoki noticed three men wearing Chinese-style robes. Two wore long flowing beards and mustaches, their hair lifted into carefully styled buns, fixed in place with combs and wooden pins. The third's head was shaved in the fashion of a monk, and he wore plainer robes than the other two. They sat in a place of higher honor than many of the other lords present, which meant they were, indeed, honored foreign dignitaries.

These must be representatives of the Sung, the kingdom of southern China that had resisted the Khan's dominion for almost fifteen years. Yasutoki had to grant the shogunate respect for their political acumen. Their response to the Khan's emissaries, in light of this new development, was not likely to be conciliatory.

A great drum began to sound from somewhere, deep and sonorous.

Armored guards marched onto the parade grounds and assumed a formation lining the approach to the palace. The ponderous palace gates swung open, and two columns of guards, with spears and full armor, marched out to surround the dais. A solemn procession of nobles emerged behind the guards and mounted the dais, men in high, black caps and immaculate robes.

The last to mount the dais was a boy of ten years, glowing in his resplendent robes, the seventh shogun, Minamoto no Koreyasu. Looking small among the grown men around him, he sat in the center of dais upon a general's camp stool, which was too tall for him.

Beside him stood Hojo no Tokimune, the regent, the true ruler of the country, grim and self-assured in his power but still young and impetuous, only twenty-four. His head was shaved after the fashion of Buddhist monks, because of his adherence to the Zen sect of Buddhism.

The *taiko* drum's rhythm ceased, and the murmurs of the gathering fell silent.

The Hojo chamberlain stepped to the front of the dais and raised his voice for all to hear, "Bring forth the emissaries."

The five emissaries appeared from the edge of the parade ground, escorted by eight guards, four ahead and four behind.

The sight of the emissaries brought back Yasutoki's journey as a young man to China, where he and his father traded with the Mongols, learned their barbaric customs, saw how different they were from the Chinese. The Chinese nobles and ministers he had encountered were as weak and inbred as the imperial court in Kyoto. That the Mongols had conquered them was no surprise.

Of these emissaries, three were Mongols and two were Chinese. Even though they were all dressed in court robes, an innate toughness suffused the Mongols. It showed in their gait, in their stance. They were wolves in silk robes.

Then the emissaries spotted the Sung across the parade ground, and their steps faltered. They traded glances ranging from anger to nervousness.

The Chinese emissaries approached the dais with great solemnity and grace, the Mongols with chin-high defiance.

They all bowed low.

Hojo no Tokimune stepped forward, and his voice thundered over the parade ground. "Emissaries of the barbarian chieftain across the sea..."

Yasutoki's fists clenched at the contempt in the regent's tone.

The regent continued, "We have heard your demands for tribute. We have heard your demands for submission. And we have heard your *insolence*. We will allow you to take our message back to your barbarian chieftain." He nodded to the guards surrounding the emissaries.

The guards seized the emissaries, amid their cries of protest, and forced the emissaries to their knees, arms cranked painfully behind their backs, bending them over at the waist.

One of the Chinese, a fat, shaven-headed man, wriggled free and tried to flee. The nearest guard drew his sword and slashed with a single, backhanded motion. The emissary's head tumbled to the earth. The body staggered forward for a moment, then toppled.

The Mongols struggled, shouting rage and curses, but their captors held them fast.

Then a single guard stepped forward, drew his sword, and, one by one, struck off the heads of the remaining emissaries.

The sizzling rage in Yasutoki's belly increased with each blow. By the time the last one fell, he wanted to charge the dais and slaughter everyone there.

Unfortunately, as thin as he had become, his strength was much diminished.

Murmurs at the brutality of it all rippled over the throng.

Hojo no Tokimune raised his voice again. "These men will indeed carry our answer back to the barbarian emperor. We will bow before no one!"

The twitching bodies emptied their blood onto the parade ground earth, forming a broad, crimson puddle, and as the puddle grew, so did Yasutoki's fury at his helplessness.

On the last long road
When I fall and fail to
  rise...
I'll bed with flowers
    —*Sora, death poem*

K en'ishi clutched his thick coat tighter and tucked his hands under his arms. Snow fell in flakes like drifting butterflies, covering the roofs of Hakata in blankets of white. He had not seen such a snow since leaving the north so many years ago. He had picked a poor day for this particular purpose. The snow was coming down so thick, it obscured sight beyond fifty paces. The streets were empty, the air filled with wood smoke as people huddled at their firepits.

Storm slogged through streets of cold mud, stout of heart, uncomplaining, even as the snowflakes gathered in his mane.

Ken'ishi marveled at how quickly the city had been rebuilt. Just over a year ago, much of it had been little but charred rubble. A crop of newly built homes, shops, and warehouses, especially in the areas nearest the bay, had replaced the devastation.

In a part of town spared much of the damage, he directed Storm up a narrow street. The familiarity of it all came back to him with a host of dreadful memories. He reined up beside a modest gate. The house within the fence looked dark and empty, as did the small, attached stable. Snow collected on a bed of old straw.

Ken'ishi opened the gate, led Storm into the stable to shelter him from the snow, and approached the house, thankful for his *geta* that raised his stockings above the wet snow. He rapped on the door and listened for movement within. Hearing nothing, he rapped again.

"Shirohige!" he called. "Junko!"

Still no response. Hage had told him they had escaped the initial onslaught of the invasion, but much could have happened since.

He tried to open the door, but found it barred from within. He called their names again. "It is Ken'ishi!"

After a time, slow footsteps shuffled toward the door.

A familiar, crow-like voice said, "Ken'ishi, did you say?"

"I did, Junko."

The bar slid aside, and the door opened. An ancient, toothless face emerged, eyes dark and rheumy but full of shrewdness.

"By all the gods and buddhas!" Junko said. "It is you! And you've even gone respectable." She looked him up and down. "Come back to pay me for that armored shirt, have you?" A pink tongue darted out and wet her sunken lips.

Ken'ishi smiled and bowed to her. "Among other things."

"Oh, joyful news! My nethers haven't had any meat between them in far too long!" She stepped back and admitted him. Her tattered, colorless *kimono* hung on her like an overlarge sack.

As he slipped off his *geta,* a tremulous, male voice came from another room. "Is that him?"

The old woman said, "It is, Brother. Hale and hearty as ever."

"Then clap some manners over that awful tongue of yours, hag. We don't want to make him ill. Bring him inside."

She winked at Ken'ishi, waggled her tongue at him lasciviously, and then gestured him to follow her into the house.

Near the firepit, a frail, old man levered himself up onto an elbow from under a tattered blanket. Shirohige's beard was longer, whiter, and matted as if he had not cleaned it in far too long. What little hair remained to him was wispy and unkempt. Dark bags hung under watery, bloodshot eyes. In the year since Ken'ishi had last seen Shirohige, he looked to have aged a decade and lost half his size.

Shirohige's effort to sit up evoked a bout of wet, ragged coughing. When he recovered, he spat into the firepit and groaned. The coals in the firepit were few and dim, insufficient to keep the cold at bay. Shadows and dimness filled the room. In the corner, snow melt dripped into an overflowing wooden bucket.

Shirohige's face was pale and drawn. Dark bags hung under yellowed, watery, bloodshot eyes. "Forgive me, Ken'ishi, but I've been ill. I would offer you tea, but we have none."

Ken'ishi withdrew a bundle wrapped in paper. "We shall have tea anyway." He offered the bundle up to Junko.

Her eyes sparkled as she accepted it, then her excitement waned as she said to Shirohige, "What'll we do for wood to heat the water?"

"Isn't there any of the fence left?"

"There's one more plank."

"Well, go get it. We must offer our guest some warmth."

Junko sighed and hurried out the back door.

"Soon," Shirohige said, "we'll be burning the house down around us to keep warm."

"But why?" Ken'ishi said. "Has business been so poor?"

"There's no business at all." Shirohige coughed again. "The government ordered austerity, as you'll recall. Every copper piece on Kyushu went into building that damned wall. Nothing left for old peddlers like me. People are afraid, and when they're afraid, they sit in their houses and use their old crockery. They patch their buckets, and patch the patches on their clothes. Ah, I used to sell such pretty things."

Ken'ishi remembered the beautiful porcelain crane that he had taken as an omen to travel with Shirohige in search of Silver Crane. "What about the lotus?"

"My supply of lotus dried up before the invasion. There isn't any to be found on Kyushu. No doubt the lotus-eaters are mightily vexed. The Hakata docks are practically deserted. Many of the ships in the barbarian fleet were trade vessels they commandeered from the Koryo."

Ken'ishi thought about the wreckage of hundreds of ships, thousands of drowned men, choking the shores of Hakata Bay. Deaths that weighed upon his soul.

Shirohige brought up a wad of phlegm and spat into the coals again. "There are no vessels to ship anything, even if anyone wanted to buy. The only trade ships from China nowadays are from the Sung, and they're so far south that the routes are slow and dangerous." Shirohige sighed and shook his head. "I had to sell the wagon to buy food."

"Where is Pon-Pon?" Ken'ishi asked.

"We had to eat poor Pon-Pon."

A pang of sadness went through Ken'ishi. The lethargic black ox had pulled the wagon that carried him from Hita town all the way to Hakata. He would never forget the inexorable plod of the ox's haunches—or its earthy wisdom. "That is a pity."

"The meat and the money we made from selling it kept us going a long time. But it's long gone. We even considered putting Junko back to whoring, but there just aren't that many blind men around."

Junko burst back through the rear door carrying a weathered wooden plank, which she took into the kitchen.

Ken'ishi said. "I'm sure your illness will soon pass. Junko still looks very energetic, however."

From the kitchen came sounds of chopping and crackling wood.

Shirohige coughed once and wiped his lips. "She's too evil to die. The Hells wouldn't want her."

"I heard that, you old cripple!" came Junko's shrill retort. "Watch your tongue, or I'll leave you to starve!"

"Her voice is like a band of deaf *oni* minstrels, is it not?" Shirohige muttered.

Ken'ishi smiled.

"But tell me of you," Shirohige said. "You hardly look the part of a *ronin* nowadays."

Ken'ishi told him of his position with Lord Tsunetomo. Junko returned with arms full of freshly split plank, which she arranged in the firepit, along with a handful of twisted straw, atop the coals. Then she fanned it and listened to Ken'ishi's tale of the Wild Woman, and how that terrible victory had granted him the promotion to captain.

She grinned with pride in him. "See? I knew we did well in nursing him back to health. He's become a great man."

Then he told of how he was helping construct the fortifications. "It's because of that I managed this visit," he said. "My lord was generous enough to grant me a few days of rest."

"I won't live to see that project finished," Shirohige said.

"Of course, you will. You must brace up. Spring will come soon."

Shirohige grunted noncommittally. "Where are they getting all those workers, anyway?"

"Workers were brought all the way from Satsuma, peasants from

Shimazu lands. All the domains of Kyushu are required by the *bakufu* to send hands."

"All those damned foreigners," Shirohige grumbled. "Can't understand a word they say." The dialects of southern Kyushu were indeed thick and at times unintelligible, but no more or less so than those of the far north of Honshu, where Ken'ishi had grown up.

Ken'ishi said, "It will take a long time. We had to let the farmers go home for harvest, or there would be no food this winter. Construction will slow down again during planting season."

"A bunch of over-proud samurai thinking they know what's best for everyone. Oh, but they have the sharp swords, so they must be right. Bah! If you ever turn into one of them, I'll disavow I know you."

Ken'ishi bowed, "I try to keep my feet upon the Way, but in truth, I have much to atone for." The scar on his chest began to burn and itch again, as it did more often. He rubbed at it.

"Nonsense!" Junko said. "You have only one thing to atone for, and that's the armored shirt I gave you. So how about we go into the back and—"

"Silence, witch!" Shirohige said, rolling his eyes.

Junko snickered and winked at Ken'ishi. "Riling him up makes the days worth living."

Ken'ishi said, "That's why I'm here, actually. To thank you both for saving my life. I owe you a tremendous debt, far more than a *hyakume* of tea can repay." He reached into his robes and withdrew a ring of coins, both copper and silver.

Two sets of old, rheumy eyes bulged.

It was enough money to feed them both for a long time, but also help rebuild their house, perhaps even buy a new ox. Ken'ishi had not known they were in such dire need when he set out this morning, but upon discovering how hard times had become for them, the amount no longer seemed sufficient.

How much was his life worth?

Would it be worth more if he could atone for the wrongs he had done? Would his burden be less?

They sat and talked for a while longer. He did not tell them about the *yurei* or the yin-yang master who had revealed what Ken'ishi might become. He did not tell them about the way he had had to defeat the *yurei*—slashing Kiosé open, severing her arm, driving his sword through her heart, this woman who had loved him so, and for whom he had felt great affection and tenderness. The memory tortured him most nights. It did not matter that she was already dead. He had killed her himself, once indirectly by his absence, and once directly.

He did not tell them about the way he still yearned for Kazuko, even though he had not seen her in more than six months, did not know if he would ever see her again. Finding her again after three years had reawakened all his old emotions, the love *and* the bitterness. Most days he still wondered how long before the pain subsided again this time.

And he did not tell them about how he had barely restrained himself two days ago from killing one of his men, who spoke of Kazuko's barrenness as a curse upon the Otomo clan, questioning if she was being punished for unknown misdeeds. Ken'ishi had beaten the man senseless, knocked out several teeth, and perhaps blinded him in one eye. Ken'ishi could barely recall how the rage had boiled out of him, but like the searing, molten blood of a fire mountain it came. He remembered Silver Crane poised to strike off the man's head—his name was Ujiyari, he had to keep reminding himself, a warrior with four children and a wife, a devout adherent to the Zen sect. As the man's commander, he had the right, but such behavior was not the Way.

In time, he thanked Shirohige and Junko again. They in turn thanked him for his kindness. He could see their excitement that as soon as the weather broke, Junko would venture out to buy food.

As he untied Storm and led him out to the street, the scar on his chest set him once again to itching, more and more painfully. He pulled open his robes, baring his breast to the winter wind, and looked at the scar there.

The tendrils of red splotch around the long-healed scar had spread, grown darker. They were the same kind of splotches he had seen on Taro's face, and on Hatsumi's.

He indeed had much to atone for.

"Selfish thoughts are born from a mind bent on its own profit. And when you think only about your own profit, you will not think twice about how you harm others. In the end, you will create perversity, generate evil, and even destroy your own body."

—*Issai Chozanshi, The Demon's Sermon on the Martial Arts*

"Captain! Are you well?"

Someone was weeping—a woman.

"Captain! Can you hear me?"

Whose voice was that?

Sergeant Michizane.

Ken'ishi was naked. Sitting with his knees tucked up under his chin, fists clenched against his shins. The air smelled of perfume and *saké*. A small lamp and brazier of coals cast opposing shadows of him against the ceiling. A *futon* and blankets lay in rumpled disarray.

A blast of cold air poured through the door from the hallway, the door that Michizane was standing in.

"He's been like that for hours," said the woman, her hair mussed. She cowered on the floor, covered by her brightly colored robe, except for one bare shoulder. Tears streaked the powder on her face. "I didn't know what to do! He paid for the time, but he's just been sitting there, and wouldn't let me leave." Her face was pale with fear, not powder. She whispered to Michizane as if Ken'ishi could not hear, "He...he said I would be more beautiful with a scar." She traced her finger down her cheek.

Ken'ishi's hands and feet tingled with cold.

"Captain," Michizane said, stepping tentatively nearer, "are you well?"

Ken'ishi glanced at him, then looked away. "Why are you here?" He could not bear to ask the question *Why am I here?*

He knew not where *here* was.

"One of the men came to tell me you were here, and...it's very, very late and..."

"What is the hour?" Ken'ishi asked.

"The Hour of the Tiger. It will be dawn soon." Michizane's voice carried an equal mix of concern and wariness. He was still armed. Brothels required weapons to be checked at the door.

The woman was beautiful. She must have been very, very expensive. Fear glimmered in her eyes, in her tears.

The splotch of scarlet, growing from the scar over his heart like a birthmark, like a writhing octopus, had spread across his chest. The thought back to the masterful skill with which the great, emerald-clad warrior—actually a divine fox-spirit in disguise—had placed that cut, saying that it would be Ken'ishi's undoing. But had the fox meant the cut—or Ken'ishi's heart? He scratched it. It felt raw, like a fingernail peeled to the quick.

Michizane said to the girl, "You may go. I will take care of this. The captain has had too much *sake*."

Her face melted with thanks. She jumped to her feet and hurried out.

"Captain, may I suggest we take you home, right now?" Michizane said.

Ken'ishi cleared his throat of a large, dry lump. "Of course. Thank you for your concern about my welfare. Wait for me outside."

"Captain—"

"I am not drunk." But his back was still turned, keeping the mark on his chest out of sight. "Wait outside. I will join you in a moment."

Michizane bowed. "Yes, Captain." He stepped out and slid the door closed.

Winter wind moaned and hissed across the roof.

Ken'ishi unfolded himself—painfully—and stood. His clothes lay entwined with the blankets. He flexed his hands to return some feeling and found a tightly folded wad of paper in his right.

The paper was important, but Michizane was waiting, and Ken'ishi could not afford any more impropriety. The best he could hope for was to remain silent and try to piece together where the last hours had gone.

The last thing he remembered was a messenger coming to his house in Hakozaki. Could this perhaps be the very brothel in Hakozaki that had sold Kiosé to Tetta, the old innkeeper in Aoka village? Hakozaki was not the city Hakata was; it had only three brothels.

He shrugged his clothes back on, unable to keep from grimacing at the ugly mark on his chest. The sight of it now filled him with cold, penetrating dread.

The messenger had come at about the Hour of the Goat, mid-afternoon. Half a day was lost to him; he had no memory of it. The taste in his mouth told him he had drunk a little, but he was not drunk now, nor was he muddle-headed from the aftereffects. On the contrary, his mind felt uncannily sharp.

Now fully dressed, he tucked the paper into his robe. Perhaps it would offer a clue, but the *kami* whispered of danger if he read it.

He let Michizane lead him home, with assurances that he was indeed well. The starlight made the remaining snow on the roofs glow, and the icy slush sucked at his *geta*. The only thing Michizane said during their walk was, "I miss my wife and daughter every day. I wish I could bring them here. Those we love must live in our hearts, even though they're not here. Right, Captain?" His tone suggested better understanding about what had happened with Ken'ishi than Ken'ishi himself possessed.

After Michizane left Ken'ishi at the gate, Ken'ishi went inside and found that Jinbei had left coals burning in the main room and had prepared Ken'ishi's *futon*. With dawn less than an hour away and Ken'ishi's mind ablaze with questions, he would not be sleeping any time soon.

He fanned the brazier to greater heat, letting the warmth rush up the front of him until he shivered with the pleasure.

The dread in his belly gathered strength, writhing like an eel. Something terrible had happened, something he did not understand.

The terror in that woman's face when she looked at him filled him with shame. What had he done? What had he said?

During their hunt for Hatsumi, Kazuko had told him of the strange things Hatsumi had done. A myriad cruelties exacted on the servants, of which she claimed to have no memory. Wandering about the castle in the dead of night.

His heart thundered its fear against his breast. He would open his belly before he went the way of Hatsumi.

His hands trembled as he withdrew the paper from his robes and unfolded it.

He knew the hand when he saw the first character.

The nightingale weeps,
Her gilded cage a dungeon,
Abandoned by her master,
She sings her loneliness.
At the Sanmon Gate she prays for absolution,
But instead old memories find new life,
And she yearns to make more.

She sings for the blaze of passionate hearts
That melt the snow.
She sings for the world they created,
Where she lives in her dreams.

But someday, a dusting of ashes
Will be all that is left
Of those passionate hearts
And that world will pass away
Forgotten by all but the gods.

In the middle verse, a teardrop had caused the ink to run. The words coursed through him like fire, and his vision glazed with fresh tears. A storm of emotions crashed through him. Pity at her loneliness, anger at Tsunetomo for abandoning her, yearning for her smile, ache for the pleasures of her body, bittersweet memory at the one night they had shared, wishing he could deliver her from all that and see her happy once again.

He held the paper above the brazier. All he had to do was drop it. His heart ached. Or was it the mark on his chest throbbing?

He folded up the paper, then pulled out his *saifu* from his *obi*, untied the string, unfolded the wallet, and slipped the paper inside.

This was a dangerous game, this dance of hearts. If Tsunetomo discovered Kazuko was sending Ken'ishi letters...

A crawling sensation on his breast drove him to peel open his robes.

One of the crimson tendrils beneath his skin wormed its way toward his collarbone.

Then he understood.

"Lord Abe," Ken'ishi said, bowing low in the doorway of the bizarrely decorated room, "thank you for seeing me."

Incomprehensible charts and graphs blanketed the walls of the room, here in Lord Abe's opulent Hakata house. A strange device of nested spinning discs, inscribed with arcane symbols, sat on the *tatami* near Lord Abe no Genmei. Near the door to the garden veranda, shuttered now against the ongoing cold spell, sat a strange device on a brass tripod, a tube angled toward the sky but surrounded by several small arms tipped with arrows and discs. Broad sheets of paper covered the table before him.

Lord Abe set down his brush and frowned. "You took your foolish time."

The servant closed the door behind Ken'ishi.

The yin-yang master's blunt abruptness put Ken'ishi back on his heels. "I...am sorry, *Sensei*," he said. "How did you know I would come?"

"After I saw what you became when the Seal of Hidden Forms was opened, I investigated you. I consulted the Winds and Fortunes, the stars and planets, the *kami*. After all of that, there was no question you would come." Lord Abe's gaze drilled into Ken'ishi with a mixture of admonition and curiosity. "I must say, I have encountered a few *oni* in this world and in my travels to other realms, but I have never encountered a man becoming an *oni*."

Ken'ishi's breast smarted, hot and raw. Even the softest cloth chafed it now like a burn.

"I want to ask you so many questions about what is happening to you, moment by moment," Lord Abe said, "but I suspect you feel you have already wasted too much time. You may well be correct. Nevertheless, it would go far to advance our knowledge of the flow of good and evil."

"I will tell you everything you wish to know, *Sensei*, if you tell me it can be reversed." Ken'ishi's hands became fists as they rested on his thighs. Even as he said the words, however, the cold eel in his belly writhed with anger and protest.

Lord Abe leaned back and narrowed his eyes for a long moment. "I do not know if your condition can be reversed. What I do know is that rites of purification have existed for a thousand years, and with good reason. Evil and death pollute the living, pollute the living world, pollute our hearts. As far as my knowledge reaches, I know of no one who recognized his danger and tried to arrest the infection of evil. Evil is sticky. It clings to places and people like tar. Once one touches true evil, it is difficult to shed and just as caustic. It eats into us and begets more evil. We could spend hours, weeks—lifetimes!— discussing the nature of evil, however. As a warrior, you hold the most dangerous position of any person. Your stock in trade is death and strife. Perhaps you have thought about the weight of death upon your soul that killing bestows."

"I have thought about that very much, *Sensei*, especially after the invasion. I was...responsible for much death." Beyond that, had some remnant of Hakamadare, Taro, or Hatsumi clung to Ken'ishi, lodged under his skin like a splinter, even long after they had been defeated? Had their evil infected him somehow? Had Hatsumi always been on the path to evil, or had Hakamadare's foulness stuck within her?

Lord Abe said, "I sensed this, especially when I saw your weapon."

"You know of its history."

"My grandmother and my aunt were Taira. It is one of the great relics of the Taira clan, long thought to be lost."

"Then you know it is powerful."

"I can sense that by being in the same room, but I do not know what powers it possesses."

The door slid open again, and a servant entered with a tea service. For the first time ever, Ken'ishi saw Lord Abe smile with genuine pleasure.

"You are a lover of tea?" Ken'ishi said.

"I am, indeed. The fields around Kyoto produce wonderful tea, but I find the tea grown on Kyushu much more to my taste. There's a greater earthiness to balance the air and water of its elements, and perhaps some fire as well. It is enough to make my long stint in such...rustic environs bearable. The tea to be found in the capital is more...rarefied."

The servant poured for them, and Lord Abe waited with bright eyes.

Ken'ishi accepted his cup and sipped. It tasted like kindness, and he shuddered.

Lord Abe's eyes bored into him again. "You might be one of the most troubled men I have ever met, but you restrain it all with such a force of will that I cannot fathom where you get your strength."

"As you say, *Sensei.*"

Lord Abe said to the servant, "Tell Koumei I have need of him."

The servant bowed and departed.

The *onmyouji* sipped his tea and rolled his eyes in pleasure. "Now then," he said, beaming, "I wish you to tell me the story of your life."

"My *whole* life?"

"Perhaps you should realize by now, I never mince words. Indeed, your *whole* life. Our lives are fraught with thousands of decisions, some of them momentous and far-reaching, others tiny, perhaps forgotten, but their importance can be just as far-reaching. Our lives are like a weave of those decisions, the shuttle of the loom ever moving. To calculate the most auspicious path for you, the path that might lead you out of this hell of your own making, we must unravel your life. And with that weave unraveled, we might begin to see patterns emerge. There is great magic in patterns. Look at that tapestry there." He pointed to a large sheet of silk, meticulously painted with patterns of horizontal lines in sets of six. "These are the hexagrams of the I Ching, wisdom that has come down from the ancients of China, two thousand years dead. With these lines, the fates of farmers and emperors might be divined."

"Will you divine my fate?"

"As I told you, your fate is more fluid than most men's, but we might find a likely realm, determine whether you maintain the good or fall into evil. To attain the most accurate reading, you must leave out nothing."

"But there is something...someone...I must protect. A reputation."

"I see." Lord Abe gazed into Ken'ishi for several long moments, then nodded slowly. "Already we glimpse the source. Secrets have a way of eating one from the inside, like a rat chewing through a bag of rice."

"Some secrets are more dangerous than a rat."

Lord Abe laughed. "Captain, I come from the capital, where secrets are daily currency, and the prices are high. You have no secret I have not heard before. Let me guess. There is a woman—there is *always* a woman, or sometimes a man. There is a love affair that *must not be revealed.*" His eyes bulged with feigned drama. "*Lives* are at stake!"

Ken'ishi scowled. "You make it sound trivial."

"My dear captain, we *onmyouji* speak often of the Five Elements that make up all things, but there is one element more common than any of them. Love. We humans drink it, eat it, bathe in it. We *wallow* in the want of it, or the loss of it, or the clinging to it. Gravediggers, warriors, farmers, and emperors, love can be our sustenance, or it can eat us from within—like a rat. Every human walking between the Heavens and the Earth has been touched or mauled by love. It is the root of desires, and desires the downfall of men." Lord Abe smiled reassuringly. "Rest easy in my discretion. I come from the capital, after all, where I would be dead if indiscreet."

The door opened again, and Koumei entered, bowing.

"Our scribe has arrived," Lord Abe said with a smile.

"Scribe?" Ken'ishi said.

"You are going to tell me the story of your life, Captain," Lord Abe said. "My apprentice here is going to record every word of it."

Before long, Koumei had assembled his writing desk, stacked several scrolls, and prepared his ink and brush. In large characters, he wrote: *The First Scroll.*

When Koumei gave the nod, Ken'ishi began his tale.

As the ink flowed and the scrolls unfurled, Ken'ishi marveled at his own stories, how he had escaped death so many times, how he had defied fortune and succeeded. And in the doing of it all, faced incredible horrors. The multitude of small weights upon his mind and spirit had grown so numerous, like a choking cloud of mosquitoes, or on some days a swarm of hornets, that he wondered he had not collapsed from it all. The duels, the dangers. Hakamadare. Kazuko. Hatsumi. Taro. Kiosé and Little Frog. Green Tiger and Silver Crane. The weeks of torture, the imprisonment. Green Tiger's cruelties, the horrific execution of the Minamoto historian, Hirosuke, in the sea cave. The fights against Masoku and Fang Shi. The desperate battles against the Mongols. The power Silver Crane had granted him in return for the buckets of blood it had spilled. The gathering of the great storm that destroyed the invading fleet. Ken'ishi still wished he could be sure that the storm had been natural, a fortunate happenstance or the work of the gods, anything but the result of his own efforts in feeding Silver Crane's thirst.

Lord Abe leaned forward with raised eyebrows as Ken'ishi told of Silver Crane's powers.

When Ken'ishi spoke of Kazuko, however, Lord Abe did not even blink. How could this love which loomed within him like Mount Fuji seem so small and insignificant to someone else? How could it not be the most important thing? How many times had he imagined a contrived moment when he and Kazuko could throw their duties aside and be together? And how often had he admonished himself for it?

How much hate and anger had sustained him when he was in Green Tiger's clutches? In the endless weeks of excruciation, how many evil thoughts had taken root in his mind? How many times had he wished himself a hurricane of raging vengeance against Yasutoki and all his minions?

And what of the blood on Ken'ishi's hands? What was the weight of ten thousand drowned souls? Did it matter that they were the enemy? Did they outweigh the hundred thousand townspeople and farmers who did not die under barbarian blades?

Lord Abe's interest piqued again when Ken'ishi told of Hatsumi's fall, and of her destruction. He asked many questions about her strange transformations.

There were so many little tales to tell: of his pledge to Kazuko and hers to him, of the otherworldly sword polisher, and of the *tengu* performers and his duel with Kaa.

Over an entire day, he told his tale. He spoke until his voice was hoarse. The servants kept the tea coming, which helped his throat, but by evening he thought he might never wish to speak again.

"We will continue tomorrow," Lord Abe said.

"Tomorrow is a work day," Ken'ishi said. "I have men I must oversee."

"You will entrust it to your underlings. We must continue."

And so it went for the next several days. Ken'ishi put Michizane in charge. Meanwhile, Lord Abe probed into Ken'ishi's accounts, scribbling his own notes as Koumei brushed steadily, deftly, on the scrolls.

On the sixth day, Lord Abe announced, "I am hopeful that we might be able to reverse your affliction."

Long absent hope surged in Ken'ishi's breast.

"But it will take time. Likely a great deal of time."

"How long?"

"Difficult to say, perhaps years."

The hope deflated. "Years."

"Years of daily purification rites. Years of meditation. Years of study. Exorcisms. Very difficult. You must seclude yourself from the world. And once begun, we dare not stop this process, or else risk undoing it all."

"It sounds as if I must become a monk." He grew angry again. "What good is a monk? Sitting for years in meditation, what do they accomplish?"

"Monks have a purpose, to lead the rest of us along the Way. But we must never neglect the truths of the world. Should lords and emperors do nothing but sit in meditation? Should warriors ignore swordsmanship and archery and forget the martial arts to sit in meditation? Should merchants burn their abacuses and close their shops to sit in meditation? Should farmers throw down their plows? Should carpenters toss away their tools? If everyone gave up their entire lives to meditate, the world would starve and decay from neglect, robbers would run rampant, and enemies would invade with impunity. But each of us must make decisions for ourselves when faced with extraordinary circumstances. Is becoming a monk worth it to save your immortal soul? You would not have to take a monk's vows, however. If we are successful, you might still be able to return to service."

Then a realization sent Ken'ishi's heart into his feet. "I would have to leave Lord Tsunetomo's service."

"I have already sent word to your master that you are very ill, in need of my special assistance."

Ken'ishi could not expect Lord Tsunetomo to keep him as a retainer while in indefinite absence. Everything he had worked for, dreamed of, all was crashing down around him.

Lord Abe said, "You may either remain on your current path and become an *oni* and I will stay far away from you, or you may come with me and I will help you rid yourself of this terrible stain."

"Where would we go?"

"To a sacred mountain some days' travel south of here. It is called Kiyomizu, Clear Water Mountain. You would live upon Kiyomizu, never venturing down, until this cleansing is complete."

"Is there no other way?"

"This is one of those momentous decisions."

"May I have the night to think on this?"

"That is the evil within you, balking! Choose!"

Ken'ishi's chest burned as if splashed with flaming oil. Tears burst in his eyes. "I will go with you."

"The mind was not born
with your birth and will
not die with your death.
This being true, it is
said to be your Original
Face. Heaven is not able

to cover it. Earth is not able to support it. Fire is not
able to burn it, nor is water able to dampen it. Even the
wind is unable to penetrate it. There is nothing under
heaven that is able to obstruct it."

—*Takuan Soho, "Annals of the Sword Taia"*

Ken'ishi knelt in the audience chamber of Tsunetomo's castle. Upon the dais sat the man who had given him the life of his dreams and who possessed the only woman he had ever wanted. The cold eel in his belly still writhed. He could not do what must be done without his lord's permission.

Lord Abe sat beside Ken'ishi, arrayed in court finery, a flower of glimmering silk with a high, black cap and a solemn expression.

Tsunetomo's face was unreadable stone.

Seeing Tsunetomo there after more than six months, this man Ken'ishi so admired for his honor, bravery, and leadership, dumped a furor of mixed emotions into his heart. The lack of warmth in the greeting sent a spike of anger through his heart. And the anger felt *wrong*.

"Lord Abe, you do me great honor," Lord Tsunetomo said. "Your reputation as a powerful *onmyouji* precedes you." His gaze kept passing over Ken'ishi. His face was unreadable, but the lines were carved deeper, his shoulders slumped. The bottomless vigor in his eyes had dimmed. He had not shaved in many days.

Lord Abe said, "I wish that my visit here were of a pleasurable nature. Your *sakura* grove outside the castle gate will be marvelous for blossom-viewing in a couple of months. Indeed, I come before you under the most unusual set of circumstances."

Lord Tsunetomo finally fixed his gaze upon Ken'ishi, as if with great effort. "Your letter, Lord Abe, was somewhat vague. Captain Ken'ishi is one of my finest retainers. What possible affliction could threaten such a man and require the services of a master of the esoteric mysteries?"

"Simply put, Lord Otomo," Lord Abe said, "evil."

Lord Tsunetomo's eyebrows rose. "What?"

"In the course of his defeat of three *oni*, their evil has lodged in his soul like a splinter and started to grow. An accumulation of hardships before he came into your service provided the fertile ground for it to take root. His spirit is in desperate need of cleansing, or else he may well lose himself to the evil that grows within him."

Ken'ishi pressed his forehead to the floor, then straightened again. "It is true, Lord. I wish only honor upon your house. I fear that if I do not undergo the rituals Lord Abe describes, I will bring great dishonor upon you. If you wish it, I will cut my belly to halt the stain now."

His ears thought he caught a tiny, stifled gasp from behind Tsunetomo. From behind the same panel where Ken'ishi had detected a presence on the night he had sworn fealty.

Tsunetomo's gaze softened. "But you have done nothing to warrant *seppuku*."

Had Ken'ishi not done precisely that? He longed unceasingly now for his master's wife. The poem she had written for him haunted his thoughts. The *kami* told him the person hidden behind Tsunetomo was Kazuko. What must she be thinking now? He longed to see her, but knew that if he did, all might be lost for good.

"Not yet, Lord," Ken'ishi said. "I fear I may someday, or worse."

Tsunetomo's expression darkened. "Do not men control their actions?"

Lord Abe said, "Captain Ken'ishi is a unique case. His strength of will and awareness of his true self are such that he has maintained control, until now, but that could slip at any moment. He recognized his condition and petitioned me to help him stop it. Lord Otomo, I ask that you release him to me. If my efforts are successful, I will return him to you better than before. If I am not successful, I will destroy him myself."

"Destroy him?"

"If I fail, he has the power to become a greater force of evil in this land than Hakamadare ever was."

Tsunetomo leaned back, eyes narrowed.

Lord Abe continued, "I admit it is a bit of a gamble. Success is not guaranteed."

Kazuko knelt behind the panel to the rear of Tsunetomo's dais, her hands clutched over her mouth. Seeing Ken'ishi there, his face so tortured, hearing about his affliction, tore a hole in her. Seeing the little flashes of anger in his face, invisible to anyone who did not know him as well as she did, told her it was all true. He was in mortal danger, body and soul.

When word had come this afternoon that Ken'ishi had arrived, elation bloomed that she might get a chance to speak to him. In a dark well of despair, she had written him that poem and sent it by messenger. She had agonized about it every day since, a battle of sentiments that grew worse with each passing day without reply. And he had not answered. But when he arrived with the renowned *onmyouji,* Abe no Genmei, she knew something was terribly wrong.

"Lord Otomo, you could order him to destroy himself now," Lord Abe continued, "but I hope you will not. We *onmyouji* are men of learning and study. We quest for answers to the deepest mysteries of the universe. When I say Captain Ken'ishi is a unique case, I do not use such words lightly. Much could be learned from him, through this effort, of the very nature of good and evil. Such knowledge would benefit all men for a thousand years to come."

Lord Tsunetomo's voice sounded hollow. "And no less share of glory for you, Lord Abe."

Kazuko stared through peephole at her husband. What an incredibly boorish thing to say! And to a man of the imperial court.

Had he fallen so out of sorts?

Lord Abe appeared unruffled. "And what man does not wish his name to ring like a bell through the ages? The question is whether the note is pure or discordant. In truth, I relish the challenge."

Ken'ishi looked ill, his face pale, his eyes troubled. Her heart went out to his, and it seemed she could feel it across the distance, beating with a heat she yearned to touch, but dared not.

His gaze fixed upon the panel where she hid, as if looking directly at her, knowing someone was there.

Tsunetomo said, "How long will this take?"

Lord Abe said, "I cannot guess. To my knowledge, nothing like this has ever been attempted. Perhaps years."

"Years!"

"Alas, possibly," Lord Abe said. "This will be the most difficult task I have ever attempted. It has taken him years to become so afflicted. It will not be cured overnight."

Tears poured down Kazuko's cheeks. Hatsumi's downward spiral had been slow, over the course of years, until one day, it had consumed her. The thought of the same thing happening to Ken'ishi—and worse, that it was again *her fault*—made Kazuko want to retch. But these six months without seeing him had been so lonely and painful. Knowing Ken'ishi was near made Tsunetomo's indifference to her somehow more bearable. But if he was to be gone for years... Or worse, this might be the last moment she ever saw him. The awful possibilities crashed over her like a wave.

"Consider this a pilgrimage, Lord Otomo, for a man who wants to reclaim his very soul," Lord Abe said.

Tsunetomo eased forward on his elbow. "Very well. I will grant your petition. But know this, Lord Abe. This man is...important to me. Should your efforts go awry, I will hold you responsible."

"If my efforts go awry, I expect I will be dead," Lord Abe said with an incongruent grin.

"Thank you, Lord," Ken'ishi said, pressing his forehead to the floor again, his voice choked with emotion.

Tsunetomo leaned toward Ken'ishi. "Captain, I grant this request, but if you fail, if you bring dishonor upon the Otomo clan, I will see you hunted and destroyed like a criminal."

Ken'ishi nodded. "I understand, Lord."

"If you will excuse me," Tsunetomo said, "I apologize for my abruptness. I have business to attend." He stood and swept out of the room.

Kazuko watched Ken'ishi and Lord Abe gather themselves and leave, with her eyes on Ken'ishi's back until he disappeared.

Kazuko found Tsunetomo in the last place she wished to look—Yasutoki's office.

Since Yasutoki's return from Kamakura with news of the barbarian emissaries' execution, he had been changed, and not for the better. His absences had always been welcome, and he had always had an overly lean and hungry look about him, but it had now gone beyond to gaunt desperation. He looked half-starved, and his demeanor had deteriorated to match. Even though he went about his duties, Kazuko saw in him a furtiveness, a selfishness that put her on edge, like a brazen thief with a hand in someone else's purse. She had always despised the man, but now he seemed more of a danger than Ken'ishi could ever be.

In the hallway outside Yasutoki's office, she heard Tsunetomo say, "You're the last man I have left, my friend. Tsunemori is so broken by Ishitaka's death, I fear his courage will never return. The fortification project has taken my best men to the edge of the sea, Yoshimura to Hakata, Ken'ishi to Hakozaki, until today, and the others scattered to the new defense garrisons."

"I am honored, Lord. I have ever been your loyal servant. You are always welcome to seek my counsel."

"Lord Abe no Genmei."

"A snobbish aristocrat with more arrogance than ability."

"And his taking Ken'ishi with him?"

"A well-crafted ruse."

"To what end?"

"To allow Ken'ishi the space for...nefarious dealings. I have heard tales that he visited Hakata this winter."

"For what purpose?"

"Rumors say that he visited a crusty old merchant there, a lotus-peddler. We may surmise much from that."

"Ken'ishi a lotus eater?" Tsunetomo's voice filled with astonishment.

"He has the look now of a man in the clutches of the lotus. If not a lotus eater, then perhaps a peddler to the workers. The construction workers have been pushed hard, taken from their homes and families. We knew it would be hard on them, and the project is far from complete. On such raw feelings, the lotus can be a powerful ointment. Going with the *onmyouji*, free of supervision, could be the perfect cover for such activities. What's more, the criminal gangs in Hakata are no doubt still rebuilding. Men of questionable morals and Ken'ishi's prowess make the perfect kind of—"

Kazuko flung the door open. If she had had a weapon in hand, she would have planted it in Yasutoki's skull. "Silence your vile tongue!"

Tsunetomo spun on her, eyes flashing with anger. "Kazuko! You're interrupting a private meeting!"

She loomed over them, seething with fury. "Enough of this! This is no 'private meeting.' This is you lying down to have this...*creature* drip poison into your ear!"

Yasutoki fixed her with an infuriating smirk.

"What has happened to your heart, Husband?" she cried. "Have you gone deaf to it? How can you give even a moment's thought to Yasutoki's blatant falsehoods?"

"You overstep. Wife." Tsunetomo's voice turned brittle and dangerous. "Lord Yasutoki's perception lets me see sides of things I cannot foresee on my own."

"Even if they malign one so noble, brave, and kind as Ken'ishi?" she said. "Lord Abe spoke highly of him!" She raised her chin in defiance. "And yes, I was listening."

"I heard you behind the panel," Tsunetomo said tightly.

"Husband, you know Ken'ishi is your man, through and through."

"Truly? I fear he has never been *my* man at all. You seem to know him far better than I do."

The words stung like a slap against her cheek, and she hated that Yasutoki was present to hear them. But instead of silencing her, they stoked the anger in her belly. "You are Kyushu's greatest lord, and also its greatest fool!"

Yasutoki almost wriggled with suppressed glee.

She took another step forward. "Minutes ago, I heard your feelings regarding Ken'ishi, and they were not bathed in jealous hatred as I hear from you now. Which is the truth? Are you yourself as two-faced and duplicitous as...*some*?" She glared at Yasutoki. "Where has evil taken root?"

Tsunetomo swung to his feet and faced her, his eyes dark. "Yasutoki, leave us."

A flash of annoyance crossed Yasutoki's smug features. "Yes, Lord." He stood and departed. She slammed the door shut behind him, but no doubt he remained within earshot.

"Evil has taken root all around me," Tsunetomo said, his voice haunted. "I know not where to turn. It is a poisoned bamboo grove that grows faster than I can chop it out. It cages me."

"You did well, letting the *onmyouji* take him. I saw how he has changed."

"I could have had him destroyed." His eyes blazed with challenge, bordering on spite, burning into her.

"I know, Husband. But you are a just and honorable man, and in your heart you know Ken'ishi to be loyal and true."

Conflict and uncertainty flickered in his eyes.

"Why do you still avoid my bed?" she said, stepping closer to him. "Come back to me, Husband, I beg you. It has been far too long. Let us leave the past in the past!"

"The past is when I thought you were innocent and pure. How can I unlearn what I know?"

"Please, Husband. I have missed you terribly." She let the tears flow, because it was true.

He raised a calloused hand and touched her shoulder. Longing splashed his face. He squeezed her arm gently, as if remembering the feel of it. Then he glanced at her face, at her veil.

"Am I so frightening now?" she said. "So ugly?" She peeled the veil away.

"I see your scar, and all I can think about is how long evil festered here, in our house, right under our noses, and we ignored it, pretended it was not here. How much still remains? How much evil must I excise before we can be happy again? Where does it lie? Within you?"

"Or within you!" she snapped. "Jealousy does not become you."

He stepped back from her. "Someday, the greatest house of the Otomo clan will be nothing but ashes on a funeral pyre." He gestured to the castle around them, then slapped himself in the chest.

"Everything that my ancestors and I have built will be dust, because no one will remain to carry it on."

Her anger flared again. "I will bear no more guilt for that. Especially *now*, after you have avoided my bed these long, lonely months. If your house is to die, shall it die steadfast and honorable, or wallowing in suspicion and jealousy?"

She stalked toward him, seized two handfuls of robe on his breast. Her cheeks burned with tears, leaking salt into her mouth. She pulled him down and kissed him hard on the mouth. His lips melded to hers. She pulled away again.

"Be the lord you used to be," she said, "and I shall be your warrior lady. We shall uproot the evil together, and become the stuff of legends. Our names will ring like bells through the ages." She gazed up into his eyes, which were smoldering with emotions she could not sort. "Or else cast me out and be done with it."

For an eternity of moments, he gazed down into her eyes, hope at war with a multitude of fears.

She reached up and touched his cheek.

His fears collapsed like a rotten wall.

He threw his arms around her and hugged her close, his stubbled cheek warm against her forehead. Relief swelled up in her and burst from her eyes in fresh deluge.

In the hallway, a stealthy footstep and a surge of burning hatred.

SO ENDS THE EIGHTH SCROLL

PART IV: THE FINAL SCROLL

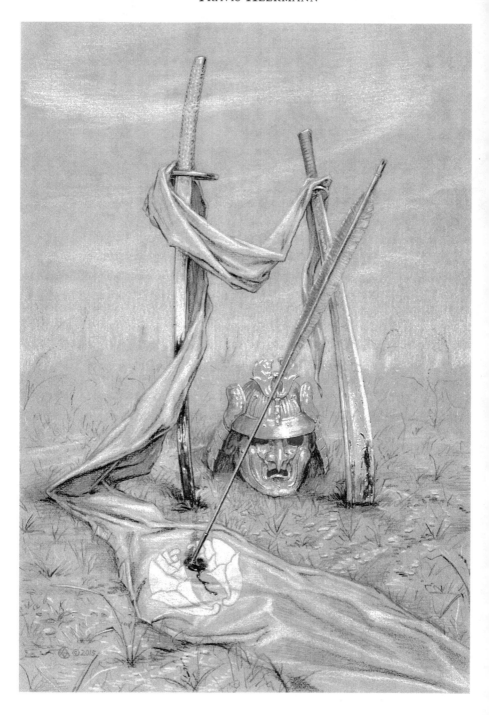

Hear those baby mice
Huddled in their nest...
    peeping
To the sparrowlets
            —*Basho*

Ken'ishi sat, bathed in sunlight filtering through the emerald forest, surrounded by vibrant green lichen clinging to stones that whispered their antiquity. The sound of running water pattering atop his head soothed the fresh aches of his soul. He had grown weary of examining his soul, but he knew its boundaries now—and its darkest corners—better than ever before. The *kami* nibbled at his awareness like minnows, passing around him and through him.

The running water had cleansed his skin of most of the dozens of characters and arcane sigils covering his naked flesh from crown to heel. Its raw energy invigorated him in ways that went beyond the flesh, much like the way he had tried to use the mountain waterfall, clumsily, intuitively, to cleanse himself after his first encounter with Hatsumi.

How many hours he had spent meditating here today, he did not know. How many days since he had climbed Kiyomizu Mountain, he could not fathom. The days from that beginning to now ran together like blood from a terrible wound mixed with water. Finally, the blood stops, and only water flows, but the wound is still open.

He had not set foot upon the plain below since Lord Abe brought him to this shrine, built three-fourths of the way up the western slope. The local peasants brought offerings here, and the priest was honored to have such a dignified grandee as Lord Abe no Genmei in his presence.

Lord Abe had warned him the process would be difficult, but he found it difficult in ways he could not have imagined.

The first days had been spent in meditation. Looking back on them, he thought those days were among the darkest he had ever spent, as dark as the weeks he had spent in Green Tiger's torture chamber. It was as if he were trapped at the bottom of a dark chasm, hemmed in by black, squirming, biting things. He could imagine the stars high above, just a narrow ribbon visible, where happiness might be found, but the biting things only lay quiescent until he moved. Whenever he reached for the finger holds that might let him climb free, the black things swarmed him, hissing and squealing. He could not fight them, could not vanquish them; they were a part of him. He could only accept them, one by one, and in that acceptance, they dissolved like smoke, and he was able to climb a little higher each time.

The biting things were his innumerable failures, the desires he could not relinquish, the wrongs unrighted, the injuries that had never healed, the cruelties he had committed through purpose or indifference, the blood he had spilled.

In these endless meditations, he was forced to gaze deep into the bowels of his own soul and scrape out the corruption that festered there.

The blood of enemies still stained him. Nishimuta no Takenaga, the arrogant constable. Green Tiger's thugs and henchmen. Even the Mongols he had slain were sons and husbands and brothers. They had more family than he himself. He entreated their spirits to forgive him.

Lord Abe brought him many scrolls to read. Treatises on Confucian ideas by the Chinese ancients, Taoist wisdom, stories of the life of the Buddha. He read and chanted special sutras, performed esoteric mantras at hours deemed most efficacious according to the cosmic shifting of stars, moon, and planets.

When Ken'ishi was not meditating or studying, Lord Abe put him through daily rites of purification. When the stars and planets were favorably aligned, he subjected Ken'ishi to exorcism ceremonies. Lord Abe wrote arcane spells upon sheets of pristine white paper, emblazoned with pentagrams, and pasted those papers to Ken'ishi's forehead, where they rested as he painted Ken'ishi's body, front to back, top to bottom, with hundreds of characters in black and red, all the while chanting in deep concentration. The process took hours, after which, even in winter, Ken'ishi would meditate under what Lord Abe called "the purest stream in the world." The waterfall would slowly erase the characters and wash away the evil they drew out.

He was allowed to drink only from the waterfall. He was allowed to eat only one day out of three, and then only rice, plus the fruit and vegetables the local peasants occasionally brought him. Their gifts of food were a hardship to them in these times, he knew, but he could not insult them by refusing. To them, he was simply the Man Living On The Mountain. They did not ask why he was there, but Kiyomizu was a sacred place where one might cross into other realms, so they thought his presence was probably important. The kindness and compassion Lord Abe admonished him to show, especially early on, when the stain of evil still ran deepest, when he was still prone to fits of unreasoning anger, ingratiated him with the peasants. The eel in his belly protested such kindnesses, chewed at him for it, especially in the first year after he came.

Ken'ishi had wanted to maintain his practice with Silver Crane, but Lord Abe had forbidden it. He was allowed to practice with only *bokken*. Silver Crane's power was a corrupting influence. Sometimes, in the depths of his meditations, he sensed the silver threads of the sword's influence passing through him, tugging at him. In the beginning, he had demanded that Silver Crane remain with him at all times. It was *his*.

But Lord Abe placed Silver Crane into a box of fresh pinewood, nestled it in silk, and placed one *ofuda* atop the sword, another atop the box. These paper talismans were written with complex spells and charged with magic. The box was then wrapped in ropes of rice straw and draped with *shide*, white paper cut into zigzag strips, signifying the boundary between the sacred and profane. He would not touch Silver Crane again until he was purified of the evil that had taken root in him.

Swathed in the ancient forest, he reverted to his old ways under Kaa's tutelage, practicing his woodcraft in the ancient forest. By now, he knew even the smallest patch of the mountain, and he still found it a place of wonders.

Near the summit on the south slope, he had discovered an old path choked by bamboo. At the top of it, an ancient, stone tomb, just over waist high, had been carved into a rock outcropping. Two sharp-eyed fox statues, as tall as his thigh, guarded the entrance. The suggestion of red paint remained on the entrance seal. Above the entrance, a bronze plaque read: *Third Empress of Kyushu*, followed by a series of characters Ken'ishi did not know, presumably the woman's name.

Many times he sat before the tomb entrance, pondering the relentless sweep of history and wondering how many hundreds of years had passed since this empress had reigned, since she had laughed and loved. Where had her palace been? What had her domain been like? What would be remembered of her in a thousand years? Would the barbarian hordes slaughter every samurai and impose their domain here, as they had across China and all the way to lands beyond the sunset?

He communed with the pheasants and rabbits, the *tanuki* and foxes, the sparrows and finches. None of the *tanuki* he met were as personable—or as powerful—as Hage. He wondered what the old rascal was doing with himself these days. These *tanuki* preferred to keep to themselves, likewise with the foxes. After two dangerous encounters with foxes, he favored giving them a wide berth anyway. Lord Abe forbade him to eat any of the game animals, with the reproach that any further deaths burdening his soul would disrupt the purification.

Ken'ishi allowed Storm to roam free on the mountaintop. With more fresh grass than the stallion could hope to eat in a thousand lifetimes, he was content to await the day when Ken'ishi might need to ride him into battle. Ken'ishi exercised him often, lest he grow fat with all that grass and nothing to do.

Lord Abe often left Ken'ishi alone on the mountain and returned with news of the outside world. He possessed webs of information gathering, both prosaic and supernatural. So much had happened since Ken'ishi had climbed Kiyomizu Mountain five winters ago.

The fortification had been completed. A stone wall half-again the height of a man now encircled the entirety of Hakata Bay, from beyond Shiga spit all the way to Imazu, some ten *ri*, cutting through Hakozaki and Hakata. A man could climb it, but a Mongol pony could not, and only fifty or so paces lay between the water's edge and the wall. The invaders would not be able to mass large formations of troops. The backside of the wall had an earthen embankment sloping to the top. Men and horses could run right up to the front edge and rain arrows down upon the enemy below.

In the winter of the year Ken'ishi had come to Kiyomizu, the *bakufu* had concocted a scheme to counterattack the shipyards in Pusan and other ports on the Koryo peninsula and wrest them away from the enemy. Thousands of samurai, tired of waiting on their laurels for the next attack, heeded the call for volunteers. Hakata and Hakozaki were turned from trade ports into shipyards, but the number of large ships required proved too costly. The project was abandoned after a few months. Instead of large ships capable of carrying an invading army, a smaller, more agile kind of vessel became the favorite. These vessels were designed to attack the incoming fleet pirate-style. Scores of them had been constructed.

A series of signal beacons had been erected across northern Kyushu, and they were constantly manned. When the barbarians came again, the news would spread with the speed of flame.

And come the barbarians would. It was only a matter of when. Three years ago, the Mongols had finally conquered the recalcitrant Sung empire after an effort of twenty years. This war had been Khubilai Khan's focus, a thorn in his side, a major diversion of resources, and a distraction from the "small country" that had defied him across the sea. But with the submission of the Sung, the Mongols now had command of the largest trading fleet in the known world.

Another embassy arrived from the Khan, went before the shogun, and were promptly beheaded as spies.

Two years ago, the Khan ordered his son-in-law, king of the Koryo, to build him a thousand ships. The shogun's spies reported that fifty thousand Mongols had moved into the Koryo peninsula, along with untold thousands of Chinese and Koryo troops, awaiting completion of the invasion fleet.

Talk in the capital was of war. Talk in Kamakura was of war. Talk across Kyushu was of war. Of course, Kyushu had been living under imminent threat for six years. It was in the air now, in the water, in the crops—that is, what crops remained.

With all the peasants working on fortifications, ships, and others defenses, fields languished. Moreover, two years of drought, followed by two years of blighted crops, had left much of Kyushu starving. Immense quantities of grain had been shipped from the north, but it was only a bandage on a half-severed limb. The peasants were suffering, simmering with growing unrest.

Lord Tsunetomo's domain was hard hit. An entire corner of his domain had rebelled over tax collection the year before. Dozens of half-starved farmers and a handful of bumpkin samurai had to be executed before the rebellion was cowed.

Now, with the fortifications completed, in the burgeoning of summer with rice seedlings growing, people were looking ahead, hopeful for good crops, but fearful the barbarians would burn the crops around them. The farmers could only do their planting and, if the barbarians came, hope their fields were not ravaged.

It had not happened immediately, but perhaps six months into the purifications and exorcisms, the crimson mark on Ken'ishi's chest began to shrink. With that discovery, hope bloomed within him. He might return someday to service, if Lord Tsunetomo would have him. Month by month, year by year, the mark shrank to a few small tendrils around the scar. Kazuko was no longer a specter of aching desire, but a warm, treasured memory that resurfaced only occasionally.

Lord Abe had refused to answer any questions about her for more than three years, and only then after a special divination ritual where he determined if the spike of longing in Ken'ishi's heart was gone.

Diminished, perhaps, but never gone.

According to Lord Abe, Tsunetomo had not divorced her as many had speculated he would do when an heir was not forthcoming. Instead, she had risen to the stature of Captain Tsunemori and was recruiting women of samurai birth for a special unit under her command.

Some thirty women had answered her call, a mix of warriors' wives and women who eschewed the company of men. She had created quite a sensation—although some called it scandal. She trained her followers in the *naginata*, and Tsunetomo's horsemaster, Ishii no Soun, trained them in horsemanship and *yabusame*. Ken'ishi smiled with pride at the thought of her leading such women.

On a night in the sixth month, Ken'ishi sat on a west-facing ledge near the summit of Kiyomizu, looking out across the verdant plain toward the Ariake Sea, across the glimmering patchwork of flooded rice fields where the stars shone. The lights of Setaka village flickered like fireflies. He had fashioned himself a new bamboo flute and played it now. It soothed him, as it always had. The songs of sadness and longing no longer felt right to him, so he played happier tunes, smiling occasionally at his own inventiveness.

Then the corner of his eye caught a flare of yellow-orange light in the distance, a sudden blossom. The flames hung high above the plain, from a hilltop south of Yame village.

He stood and squinted into the hazy, star-studded distance. Farther to the north, another long beacon burned, and farther still, yet another.

A door seemed to shut in his mind.

His days of healing and renewal were over.

Lord Abe was not here tonight. He had been staying as guest of the Nishimuta lord who oversaw Setaka village, Lord Jiro's cousin.

Ken'ishi could waste no time looking for him, either. The lighting of the signal beacons carried only one meaning. The barbarians were coming.

His purification was not complete, but he must assist in the defense. And if he ended up in one of the Nine Hells for his efforts, he would fight his way back out again.

It is time where many threads converge, rang Silver Crane's voice in his mind. *The man's destiny is at hand.*

"Indeed, I suspect it is," he said. "Will you serve me?"

I am here, in this time, in this place. I will serve. Will the man?

Ken'ishi wondered about the cryptic last question, but asking for clarity would bring no response. The sword had always revealed its secrets in its own time.

He approached the sealed box. Five years of exposure had weathered it. Lord Abe replaced the *shide* often, so the boundary papers looked fresh.

Ken'ishi was about reintroduce a dangerous relic back into the mortal world.

That was when the admonishment of the sword polisher Tametsugu came back to him: *At the moment you most desire to use Silver Crane, when deepest peril and greatest triumph are suspended in balance, you must put the sword away.*

Was this that moment? But how could he leave such a powerful weapon here, unused, when the fate of the entire country, thousands of souls, was at stake?

Look to your soul, samurai, Tametsugu had said.

Was one man's soul worth more than those of thousands?

Ken'ishi sensed the sword's amusement at his hesitation, and its thirst after being locked away for so long. Its anticipation of battle tingled over Ken'ishi's flesh.

What would happen to him if he unleashed Silver Crane's full power? How many deaths could he withstand, without losing himself, before he was no longer human? How many deaths would slake the sword's thirst? It had the power to drive him into the thickest fighting before he knew what had happened. It could reshape fortune and circumstance to deliver the thickest bloodletting unto itself, and Ken'ishi would become its pawn.

He untied the rope around the box and lifted the lid.

There it lay, just as it ever had. An unassuming, antique sword.

He picked it up and tied it to his *obi*.

To battle! its voice rang.

"To battle."

"The knowledge of a general is an understanding of human affections. If a general does not have sincerity, righteousness, and human-heartedness, it will be impossible for  him to be in harmony with human affections. It has been clearly understood both in ancient and modern times that when a man does not acknowledge human affections, his strategies will turn into disasters."

—Issai Chozanshi, *The Demon's Sermon on the Martial Arts*

Kazuko sat beside her husband on a campaign stool, never having sat upon a man's chair before. Her armor creaked as she settled herself beside her husband in the half-circle of officers. The armored plates on her arms, legs, and shoulders felt as natural and comfortable as her robes. She had had her *do-maru* modified to fit her feminine contours rather than trying to squash her into a man's shape.

Opposite her sat Tsunemori, grim and tight-lipped, and around the circle, Tsunetomo's other officers, Yoshimura, Soun, Hiromasa.

One was still missing, and there had been no word of him for too many years. She dared not inquire, or else threaten the fragile trust that had regrown between her and Tsunetomo.

The six of them had already prayed together at the temple,

entreating the gods for victory, and now they sat encircled by Tsunetomo's *maku*, broad curtains woven with the Otomo clan *mon* of two apricot flowers, the headquarters of a warrior lord on campaign. The *maku* snapped and fluttered in the morning breeze, erected in the castle's central courtyard. Before them in neat rows sat the unit commanders, armored and prepared for battle.

And now, the ceremonial meal that would send them off to battle, designed by the yin-yang masters to grant the greatest fortune. Servants brought the three courses with great solemnity, presented first to Tsunetomo, then to each of the other officers.

First came dried chestnuts; their name, *kachi-guri,* sounded like 'victory.' Kazuko accepted the tiny dish bearing three chestnuts and ate each of them with focused attention and reverence. Next came *konbu,* the seaweed so common in many meals. She ate each of the three leaves individually, chewing each, savoring the taste of the sea. Third came three *awabi,* raw abalone served in their shells. She chewed the slimy, gristly mass of each only once before letting it slide down her throat. And finally came *saké* served in three nested, porcelain cups. The profusion of threes represented Heaven, Earth, and Man, a sacred, lucky number. She downed the *saké* as a man would, in one gulp.

With the ceremonial meal completed, Tsunetomo raised his voice. "Fortune will be with us now in the coming battles, but there is one thing more." He snapped his fingers and a squire emerged from behind the *maku* carrying a scarlet-laced *kabuto.*

"There are many who say women should not go to war," he said. "They would bring ill fortune, they lack the strength of men, the bravery of men, and a litany of hidebound nonsense." Some of his officers shifted uncomfortably at this. "Lady Kazuko has proven them wrong. I have watched her train with her women, watched them develop as warriors, and watched how she commands them. They will be a powerful force on the battlefield. To honor this moment, I present her with a *kabuto.* And on the *menpo* is the visage of one of legend's most powerful creatures, a symbol of purity and goodness, wisdom and justice—the *kirin.*"

The squire bowed and presented the helmet to her.

It bore two deer-like antlers as a crest, and the face on the *menpo* was indeed that of a *kirin,* a flaming visage akin to both horse and deer, painted scarlet and traced with gold filigree.

Her breast filled with emotion, and tears smeared her vision. In the moment, the beauty of the *kabuto* was second only to the beauty of Tsunetomo's words.

Tsunetomo said, "This *kirin* will bring good fortune. Wear it well, my lady."

She bowed deeply and accepted the *kabuto*. "Thank you, my lord. My heart is full. I will endeavor to be worthy of such a gift." Tears streaked her cheeks.

Then, the ceremony continued. Each of the captains stood, in turn, while their squires tied their swords and fixed their quivers.

Kazuko had no sword, so her squire, a woman named Yuko, presented her sheathed *naginata*.

After accepting their weapons, the captains mounted their horses, donned their helmets, and formed a procession before the *maku*. Kazuko's helmet fit her perfectly. As she closed the *kirin*'s face over hers, a tingle shot through her from head to toe.

Tsunetomo was last, and Kazuko could only watch her husband with pride as he ceremonially girded himself for battle.

These preparations would grant good fortune in the coming days. The previous invasion had been so sudden there had been no time for proper ceremony, resulting in ill omens, and the Kyushu men had suffered for it.

In the fourth month, a disorganized force of Mongols and Koryo had attacked Tsushima, one of the two major islands between Kyushu and Koryo peninsula. Far better organized this time, the warriors there had beaten back the ill-prepared attack. Ever since, the Wolves of Kyushu had waited with weapons close at hand.

Now, two months later, a massive fleet had been seen approaching Ikishima, Tsushima's sister island. From Ikishima, messengers had rushed across the sea to warn the Western Defense Region. When the messengers landed in Imazu and gave their tale, the alarm had spread by flaming beacon.

Tsunetomo's horse was brought forth, and he mounted with the aid of a wooden step, as *o-yoroi*-style armor made it difficult. His squire handed him his *kabuto*, which he placed upon his head and tied under his chin.

Like the previous invasion, a small force of handpicked defenders would remain with the castle; but this time, Kazuko was riding forth to battle. Her warrior-women awaited her. They were as fervent, fierce, and loyal to her as her husband's troops were to him. She had shrugged off the rampant skepticism, bombarding her from all directions, that women could not fight. Tomoe Gozen had long ago disproven such skepticism. Kazuko had won the women's admiration and loyalty. She and Master Higuchi had made them masters of the *naginata*. Captain Ishii had made them into horse archers. Someone had taken to calling them Kazuko's Scarlet Dragons. The name stuck.

All that remained now was to prove themselves in battle.

When Ken'ishi arrived in Hita town after two days' ride, he heard from the townsfolk that Tsunetomo's army was long gone. He visited his old house and found it had been granted to a visiting warrior from Kamakura, who had departed with Tsunetomo's army.

After five years, riding through Hita town gave him a sense of wonder. The people he remembered had gotten older, as no doubt he had. But they looked beleaguered and hungry as well, any mirth long since gone from their faces. The buildings looked in need of repair, weathered and ill-kept.

He visited the Roasted Acorn for a quick meal and news. Except for the castle garrison, every samurai in the province had packed up and set forth with Tsunetomo's army. Scores of peasant spearmen had marched with them as well.

In the castle, he found only a scant forty men. They were puzzled to see his return. Most of them thought Captain Ken'ishi was dead.

Even Yasutoki had gone with the army, traveling in the baggage train to help with planning and logistics.

As Ken'ishi rode down from the castle through the crowded marketplace, he spied a woman whose striking beauty was immediately familiar. She was talking to a vegetable farmer perhaps fifty paces from Ken'ishi. His gaze met hers, and in the instant before she looked away, he saw recognition there. Then she lowered the brim of her straw hat.

Yuri.

The 'lily' who had set Ishitaka's heart afire.

He urged Storm through the crowd, but by the time he reached the vegetable farmer's cart, she had disappeared. The farmer drew back from the mounted warrior looming over him.

Ken'ishi scanned the crowd. "That woman you were just speaking to, where did she go?"

The farmer raised both hands. "I'm sorry, my lord, I don't know."

"Have you seen her before?"

"A couple of times, perhaps. She's new in town, she says, staying with her father, a merchant."

Anger flared up in him. What was she doing back here, telling the same lies she told Ishitaka? And they *were* lies. Ishitaka had died for her. Ken'ishi had assumed her dead somewhere as well, perhaps far away in Kamakura. What could she be up to? A spy? For whom?

"She's quite a looker, isn't she, my lord?" the farmer said with a weathered half-grin.

Ken'ishi sighed. "She is indeed."

Alas, he did not have time to search for her or to get to the bottom of it.

Dazaifu was another two days' ride. In several places, the roads were clogged with troops moving north, many of them Otomo, but other lords from the southern clans as well.

Storm welcomed being pushed so hard. "We have had life too easy these last few years, and I am getting old!" the stallion said. "I do not live as long as you. Let us feel the wind and strike the ground with our hooves!"

Ken'ishi laughed and leaned lower over the horse's mane as Storm kicked up more speed.

When he arrived in Dazaifu, he found the city surrounded by encampments and headquarters, tents clustered around the city like mushrooms around the base of a tree. He searched high and low for Lord Tsunetomo's encampment, asking for news as he went.

The island of Ikishima had fallen once again. All the men had been put to the sword. He did not like to think about what happened to the women. Last time, the women had been lashed together with ropes passed through holes sliced through their palms and bound to the gunwales of the invading ships to protect the invaders from incoming arrows. Ken'ishi's thoughts went back to the Taira warrior who had insulted him in Dazaifu. He said a brief prayer to the gods and buddhas on the warrior's behalf.

This invasion fleet dwarfed the first, they said. Ken'ishi could hardly envision how that were possible. He had never imagined so many ships existed in all the world. The estimates regarding the size of the invasion fleet were scarcely believable. How could the Wolves of Kyushu hope to stand against so many, even with years of preparation?

Where the barbarians would strike next no one knew, but they now possessed a foothold within striking distance of Kyushu and a link for their supply chain back to Pusan.

Ken'ishi found the Otomo clan enclave on the north side of Dazaifu. Lord Tsunetomo and the other Otomo lords had clustered together again, sharing resources.

When he saw Lord Tsunetomo's tent, he reined up and surveyed the area. His heart pounded.

Would Tsunetomo welcome him back? Had Lord Abe kept Tsunetomo apprised of his progress? Who would he encounter?

Yasutoki must also be about. Would he cut Yasutoki down at first sight and finally cleanse his evil from the world? No, not yet. That could wait until all the battles were fought.

He approached the two guards at the entrance to Tsunetomo's tent. He recognized them, but did not know their names.

They also recognized him, shock writ large on their faces. "Captain Ken'ishi!"

Ken'ishi bowed to them. "If our lord is present, would you please announce me?"

One of them bowed and went inside.

The other said, "We thought you were dead, Captain!"

Ken'ishi smiled. "I was, for a while. I'm alive again."

The first guard returned. "Please, come inside, Captain."

Ken'ishi followed him, leaving his sword in a rack near the entrance.

Inside he found Lord Tsunetomo and Captain Tsunemori standing near a makeshift table, poring over a map. Ken'ishi recognized the coastline near Aoka village and north toward Shiga Island, which was connected to the coastline by a sandbar. The two men stared at him as if he had just stepped out of the Land of Dreams.

Ken'ishi knelt and bowed to them. "Lords, I hope you'll forgive the intrusion."

They returned his gesture. The world had passed five years without him, and the two brothers were no exception. Tsunetomo's hair was now mostly gray, the lines in his face deeper. He had lost some of his blockish muscularity, but he moved with the same deliberate grace as ever.

Tsunemori cracked a half-grin. "So, again you come to me as if from nowhere on the eve of battle." He now wore a long beard and mustache. The sparkle in his eyes, absent after Ishitaka's death, had returned.

Ken'ishi smiled. "I hope to be of use again this time, Captain."

"No doubt we'll be able to find some barbarians for you to kill," Tsunemori said.

Ken'ishi felt Tsunetomo's gaze upon him, and he wished the lord would speak.

"I have come to request to join the defense forces," Ken'ishi said. "I am aware that much has likely changed in my prolonged absence. I thank you for the opportunity to do what I have done. I am happy to serve in whatever stead you see fit."

"Have you kept up your swordsmanship?" Tsunemori said. "I don't imagine Lord Abe is much of a sparring partner."

"Two thousand strokes a day with a *bokken*. I have slain many practice posts."

The two brothers laughed.

The look of penetrating wonder on Lord Tsunetomo's face made Ken'ishi squirm. Finally, Tsunetomo said, "Lord Abe informed us of the progress of your efforts, but he would never say when they might be complete. Are you whole again?"

"More whole than in a very long time, Lord."

"You look better than the last time I saw you."

"Thank you, Lord."

"You still carry your father's sword." There was a tone in Tsunetomo's voice Ken'ishi could not identify.

Ken'ishi glanced at Silver Crane's hilt. "I...left everything behind. I regret the necessity. This sword and a horse are all I have now."

Tsunetomo nodded. He went to the back of the tent, where some baggage was stacked. After some rummaging, he hefted out an armor case.

Ken'ishi recognized it, and his mouth fell open.

Tsunetomo's gaze glimmered with hope. He placed the armor case on the ground between them—the same armor case Ken'ishi had received from him so long ago.

"Find Sergeant Michizane, six tents up the path. He will tell you about our plans." Tsunetomo said. "We depart for Hakozaki in the morning."

The sickly orchid
That I tended so...at last
Thanks me with a bud
                     —*Taigi*

"And where would you have us go? Back to Aoka village? We must stay where the mouths are!" Norikage snapped.

Hana scowled at him.

"Besides, my dear, the barbarians are not even here yet. With the wall in place, we shall escape ahead of them."

Hana crossed her arms.

He softened his voice. "When the barbarians come, we'll be first on the road out of Hakata. In the meantime, all these samurai have hungry stomachs and plenty of money."

She sighed. She knew he was right.

Steam boiled around them from the cauldrons of broth and boiling water, exacerbating the heat of the summer day here in their corner shop, even with both counter windows propped open. His sweat-drenched sleeves were pulled up to his armpits. He mopped his brow with a damp cloth.

The small noodle shop he and Hana managed here near the Hakata docks had been an enjoyable, if some sometimes troublesome, decision after their hair's breadth escape from Aoka. He found he enjoyed cooking, and Hana was the best woman he had ever known; kind, motherly, and unafraid of hard work, a fear that often plagued him. This life was a far cry, however, from his days growing up in the imperial court. What would his father say if he knew Norikage was selling *ramen* to sailors, samurai, and conscripted laborers? It amused Norikage to think his father would hang himself from shame. Or fall on a dagger. Or drink poison. Or—

A woman's voice said, "May I have a bowl, please? And two rice balls?"

Norikage mouthed the word *customer* to Hana. He turned toward the counter—and blinked twice at the begrimed vision before him.

Dressed in threadbare peasant rags, hair unkempt under a straw hat, was a young woman whose beauty he had not seen equaled since he was exiled from court. Travel dust had caked around her eyes and mouth. She was perhaps twenty, but her eyes were blank slates of the sort possessed mainly by jaded old whores and people who had given up on the world. But she did not look like a whore. Something in her posture and careful movements bespoke a spirit that was hidden, not broken.

He sputtered, unable to find words.

Hana stepped forward. "A bowl and two rice balls, eh? Can you pay?"

The woman laid a coin on the counter.

Hana scooped it up, gave Norikage a cautionary glance, and went about preparing the noodles.

A small head, just visible with a tiny upright topknot, stepped up to the counter beside the woman. "We eat now, mama?"

The woman nodded.

Norikage produced two rice balls from a basket and handed them across.

She accepted them and handed one to the boy. He snatched it and took a ravenous bite. His cheeks puffed like a squirrel's as he chewed.

Norikage could not help but stare. He had never seen such a beautiful peasant woman. Her skin was porcelain besmirched with dust and sweat. An air of mystery clung to her as well. She removed her hat, but did not smooth her hair as most women did. She left it unkempt, half-obscuring her features.

"Your son looks like a fine boy," he said. "How old is he?"

Her face blossomed into friendly smile. "Five."

"Oh, what an amusing age. Hana and I have a daughter that age. And a son who's three."

The woman smiled wider, but there was an emptiness in it.

Then a gruff voice called through the other window. "Hey, Norikage, you skinny fart. It's time."

A burly, bald-headed man leaned into the other window, palms on the counter. He wore a sword with a battered, old scabbard thrust into his *obi*. Behind him stood another man, taller, thick-muscled, and low-browed.

"Is it already time, Master Shokichi?" Norikage chuckled nervously, his innards clenched like a fist.

Hana turned away, white-lipped with suppressed contempt.

Where the hell was Ken'ishi when Norikage needed him? He could dispose of these ruffians without a second thought. He often wondered where the *ronin* was nowadays, regretting their falling out. Meanwhile he counted out coins, placed them in a bowl, and handed the bowl to Shokichi.

Shokichi grabbed the bowl with a clinking rattle, glanced at the contents, and handed it back. "You're short."

Norikage laughed nervously again. "No, I'm sure I counted thirty."

"Sixty." Shokichi smiled, revealing a mouth fill of blackened, splintered teeth. His breath smelled like rancid fish.

The fist in Norikage's innards twisted tighter. "Sixty! But—"

"Perhaps you didn't hear the news. Barbarians are coming. How do you expect us to protect you from them for thirty?"

These scoundrels would use their mothers as shields when the Mongols came. "Please, Master Shokichi, if I give you sixty, I won't have enough to buy ingredients. I'll be out of business."

"Shut up, before I double it again," Shokichi growled, thrusting his hilt forward.

Norikage's fingers trembled as he counted thirty more coins into the bowl. How would he buy fish and rice tomorrow?

Shokichi scooped out the coins, dumped them into a black-and-white striped drawstring pouch, and tossed the bowl back onto the counter. "You're safe and sound for now, Noodle Man."

The two thugs laughed and sauntered off.

Hana threw herself into Norikage's arms, whispering, "What are we going to do?"

Norikage just petted her hair gently.

The woman at the counter said, "Who were those men?"

Norikage cleared his throat of a lump. "Just some local characters."

A spark appeared in the woman's eyes. "Who do they work for?"

"I had best not say. It's not wise to—"

"Tell me."

The force in her voice drew the whispered answer out of him. "Green Tiger."

The corner of her mouth twitched once. "You said you have children. Where are they?"

"Playing in the back," Norikage said, suddenly fearful without knowing why.

"My son has not played with other children in too long. Would you...allow this, while I perform an errand? I will be back before my noodles are cold."

"What are you going to do?"

She smiled again, a vision so sparkling that it disarmed him. "I won't be long."

He swallowed hard. "Very well."

The woman ushered the boy to the side door, whispered something to him as she handed him over to Hana, then she put on her hat. He noticed that she carried a straight wooden staff in the fashion of a pilgrim. Hana took the boy's hand and led him into the back of the house where their children were playing. She gave Norikage a puzzled expression, but he could only shrug. The woman was already gone.

Norikage finished preparing a bowl of noodles for the woman and placed it on the counter. He leaned out and searched for her up and down both streets.

Suddenly she was sliding back onto the bench before her bowl of noodles. She took up her chopsticks and began to eat. Even when she ate, her movements were meticulous, immensely graceful, as if every mouthful were a choreographed dance.

Norikage wanted to ask her where she had gone, but he could not peel his gaze away from the single spot of blood on her cheek, a ruby on porcelain.

When she was finished, she said, "I hope Ishimaru behaved himself. We should be moving along now."

Norikage called for Hana to bring out the boy.

The woman bowed and pressed her son's head into a bow as well. "Thank you for the delicious meal. It was a feast," she said.

The boy said, "It was a feast."

Then she placed her hat upon her head, took her staff in one hand and her son's hand in the other, and led him away.

It was not until she had disappeared that he noticed a drawstring pouch beside her empty bowl. He picked up the pouch and thought to call after her until he recognized the striped pattern. It was much heavier than sixty coins.

He tucked the pouch away and scratched his head.

"Fundamentally, a man's mind is not without good. It is simply that from the moment he has life, he is always being brought up with perversity. Thus,  having no idea that he has gotten used to being soaked in it, he harms his self-nature and falls into evil. Human desire is the root of this perversity."

—*Issai Chozanshi, The Demon's Sermon on the Martial Arts*

L ord Tsunetomo was true to his word. At dawn, his army marched for Hakozaki. Ken'ishi took command of his former unit.

Michizane's first glance at Ken'ishi when he arrived at the tent had been a strange mix of surprise and consternation. Michizane had assumed command on Ken'ishi's departure, and now he would be expected to relinquish it and serve as a second. Because Ken'ishi had not been formally demoted, he still outranked Michizane.

In the light of the campfire before Michizane's tent, Ken'ishi bowed.

After several moments of shock passed, Michizane recovered enough to speak. "You recovered your smile, it seems."

The men gathered around.

Michizane said, "I can see it in your eyes. Are you here to take command?"

The men stared in amazement.

"I am," Ken'ishi said.

Michizane slumped a bit at that.

"But I will need the help of a wise and seasoned warrior gentleman to reacquaint me," Ken'ishi said. "For five years, I have been practically a monk."

In truth, being thrust back into command frightened him. He had imagined himself just wading into the enemy without regard to tactics or strategy. It was clear this time, however, that the Wolves of Kyushu had prepared extensively for the barbarians' return.

Michizane nodded and scratched his chin, took a deep breath, let it out. "Don't worry, Captain. We'll let Ushihara be your warrior gentleman." He turned to where Ushihara hung back among the men.

Ushihara blinked and farted with surprise. "Me?"

The men laughed.

Michizane stepped closer. "Welcome back, Captain."

They spent the rest of the evening together, with Michizane relating the state of affairs. The enemy had taken Ikishima, but any further movements were unknown. Spies had been dispatched to observe the enemy fleet, but none of those ships had returned.

Now, on the march, Ken'ishi glimpsed in the distant vanguard of Tsunetomo's army a unit of *naginata* cavalry that could only be Kazuko's. He could not discern her, which was just as well. Seeing her would complicate things again. It had been five years, but would his feelings be any less immediate? He hoped so, considering how much time he had spent facing those demons in his soul.

As the army took up its position near Hakozaki, everyone was nervous that the enemy would arrive before the defenders were assembled. But two days later, Tsunetomo's army had erected their encampment and taken up their positions, and still no barbarians. Atop the wall, wooden shields were propped up to protect the defenders from incoming arrows. Defenders could shoot from behind them, and horsemen could shoot over them. Great barrels of arrows and spears were placed at intervals along the wall.

Like the barrels, the beach was dotted by boats as far as the eye could see. These were open-decked and single-masted, almost large rowboats, with room enough for fourteen men rowing shoulder to shoulder and one man on the rudder. Michizane had told him these boats' purpose, and Ken'ishi remembered Lord Abe telling him of their construction. The paint on all of them was fresh.

The defenders took shifts through all hours of the night and day. The barbarians would probably not attack at night, as ships were too difficult to maneuver in the dark and were incapable of stealth, but the unexpected horrors of the last invasion created an aura of fear and reverence that reason would not penetrate.

Ken'ishi thought Kazuko would hear of his return and seek him out, but he did not see her. Perhaps she felt as he did. Better to leave the past buried.

Early on the morning of the second day, a signal beacon blazed to life north of Imazu, and the signal spread. Horns and drums echoed up and down the lines and across the water.

The first ships appeared on the horizon. The hazy distance obscured their numbers, but the sails just kept appearing.

Ken'ishi jumped up and shouted, "To me!"

Michizane next to him waved his *naginata*. "Go, go, go!"

Ken'ishi and his fourteen men jumped off the wall and pelted across the beach toward their boat.

They were taking the fight to the invaders.

Alarm bells rang in a spreading wave across the city of Hakata. Inside his noodle shop, Norikage's innards clenched. Was today to be the day the barbarians finally came?

Stepping out into the street, he looked out over the bay. A flaming beacon flared to life around the bay toward Imazu, then another one on Shiga spit.

He staggered a little. It was happening again. Memories of Aoka village flooded back. The riders. The smoke. The blood. Little Frog's terrible death. And Kiosé's. The wild, terrified flight into the forest with Hana.

He hurried back into the shop and gathered up his family to flee south. They gathered up whatever possessions they could carry on their backs.

Hana kept calmer than he did. His voice kept rising sharp and shrill, with endless second-guessing about what they should take versus what they could carry for long.

The children cried.

Townspeople crowded the streets, but he did not hear any panic. They had known for years this day would come.

When they finally had filled their carrying racks with food and clothing and a handful of valuables, Norikage and Hana herded the children outside.

Standing outside their door was a boy, the one with the strange woman from a few days earlier.

The boy stood there silent, lips pouched, cheeks streaked with tears. He clutched a note in both hands, and held it up to Norikage.

"Where's your mother?" Norikage asked. He saw no sign of her in the crowded streets, only a river of flight, channeling south.

The boy stepped forward, thrusting forward the note.

"Your name is Ishimaru, yes?" Norikage said.

The boy grunted insistently, sniffling, thrusting the note higher.

Norikage took it, already suspecting what it said, a feeling of dread building in his belly.

You have a good family. Please do me this favor. There is something I must do. If I still live, I will find you and come for him. Ishimaru is a good boy. Better than his mother.

The note was written in woman's script, and near the end, the hand trembled in the characters.

Norikage folded up the note, tucked it into his robe, and looked at the boy. Grimy face, shaved head, and little topknot. The boy's eyes bore the mark of hardship, and of fearlessness, defiance, and quiet intelligence.

Ishimaru was slightly older than Little Frog had been when the barbarians came.

Norikage offered his hand. Ishimaru took it.

"When facing a situation where you might die … you should be the first to volunteer and never retreat a single step. There are situations when it's right to die, though, and situations where you  shouldn't die. To die where you should die is praised as a righteous death. To die where you shouldn't die is disparaged as a dog's death."

—*Izawa Nagahide*

The waters of Hakata Bay were calm, the morning breeze cool as Ken'ishi's men rowed for all they were worth. A slight breeze in the sail boosted their speed, but it was the beat of the drum that propelled them.

"One! Two! One! Two!" the men chanted as they rowed.

Ken'ishi held the rudder, studying the faces of the men who were now following him into battle, most of whom he had not met until two days ago.

All of them were armored, which meant that if they went into the water, the interlaced steel plates of their *do-maru* would drag them down like stones and drown them before they could remove it. Best not to go into the water, then. They carried a smattering of weapons—swords, spears, *naginata,* even a few with bows whose job would be to pick off the enemy from below.

Their boat ran alongside four others. A flotilla of five boats would board a single incoming ship, slaughter everyone aboard, and then flee before any other enemy ships could close. Hakata Bay swarmed with these small boats.

Ken'ishi's boat was third in the flotilla under the command of Shoni no Kagetora. Kagetora was a gruff veteran who looked more at home on the sea than on land, several years older than Ken'ishi. When Kagetora had introduced himself, he thumbed his chest and announced he was the great-grandson of one of the revered sea captains who fought with Minamoto no Yoshitune, brother of Yoritomo, against the treasonous Taira at Dan-no-Ura.

Ken'ishi's boat was just one among hundreds. The boats that had launched from Imazu and Shiga had already engaged the nearest enemy ships. The clamor of butchery drifted across the water, screams and the clash of arms. Smoke and flame bloomed from an incoming ship, then another, as the successful samurai set them afire.

The further out to sea they went, the higher the waves became. Their course pointed them into the gap between Shiga Island and Genkai Island, the entrance to Hakata Bay, a breadth of about two *ri*. Invading ships filled that breadth and stretched beyond to the northern horizon. Hundreds of them. He clenched down the memories of that wild, awful, wracking day almost seven years before, when a similar fleet came ashore and disgorged thousands of bloodthirsty Mongol horsemen. The day Kiosé and Little Frog had died.

The drums beat, and the men chanted, and the enemy ships neared. His flotilla was more than two *ri* from Hakozaki now, crossing a line between Shiga and the end of the wall north of Imazu, about to cross into open sea.

The enemy ships were easily four times the size of his small craft, with gunwales above the water half-again the height of a man.

In the boat ahead, Shoni no Kagetora shouted, "Strike the sail!"

Several of his men leaped to obey, folding up the bamboo-ribbed sail and removing it from the mast altogether, while the others kept rowing.

Ken'ishi repeated the order to his own craft.

The approaching ships loomed large, two-masted, with broad ribbed sails, gunwales that swooped to a high forecastle, and even higher terraced poop decks. On those high decks, archers waited for range. Red and gold pennons proclaiming ship designations fluttered high above the sterns.

Their flotilla passed several vessels already engaged or burning. The sides of the boarded ships ran crimson with gore. They also passed the sinking wreckage of a few defense boats, or boats drifting where all the men lay dead, bristled with arrows. Scents of blood and smoke and sweat drifted on the sea breeze. And horses.

The men jumped at a sudden peal of thunder across the water. The corner of Ken'ishi's eye had caught a sudden burst of flame and smoke near a flotilla ahead. The boat nearest the occurrence foundered, the gunwale splintered as if by a tremendous fist, dead men slipping over the side. A puff of smoke and crash of thunder exploded near another defense boat, but too far away to cause damage.

These must be the Mongols' "thunder-crash bombs." They had rained fire and terror onto the defenders at Imazu with these devices during the prior attack, blowing men, horses, and structures to bits.

Catapults rested upon the upper decks of many of the oncoming ships. Men in fur-trimmed armor and pointed helmets swarmed around them. A catapult jumped, and a little black ball arced toward a defending boat, trailing smoke. Just before it reached the water, the ball exploded, spraying splinters and pieces of men across the water.

Dense flocks of arrows flew from the invading ships, stretching to impossible ranges.

"Our bows can't do that!" said a young man.

Michizane said, "We like to look glory a little closer in the face!"

The men laughed and rowed harder.

Their flotilla passed through the first ranks of engaged ships, into a new wave. Kagetora's lead boat angled toward the nearest oncoming ship.

"Prepare mast pins!" Ken'ishi shouted. Two men situated themselves with hammers on either side of the mast.

The approaching ship drew nearer. All around them, flotillas of five swarmed other ships. Thunder-crash bombs arced and burst. Flaming arrows arced. A great machine on the high aft deck cast flaming spears at the incoming boats. One of those spears pinned two men together against the gunwale of their boat. Another punched a hole through the bottom of a boat, which foundered quickly.

Two other craft of their flotilla swung around to angle for the opposite side, and the last aimed for the bow. Ken'ishi guided his craft next to Kagetora's. Kagetora had ordered Ken'ishi to stick close until he "got his sea legs."

The deck above swarmed with men. Arrows blasted toward them from the upper decks, splashing in the water, piercing wood or flesh or lodging in armor. The drum beat faster. Ken'ishi whipped out Silver Crane to deflect incoming arrows, one hand still on the rudder. The men rowed for all they were worth. Kagetora's craft took the brunt of the arrows but kept going until it slammed against the side of the ship.

"Strike the mast!" Kagetora roared. An instant later, the mast toppled against the gunwale of the ship like a felled tree, and the samurai swarmed up it. War cries and clashing blades rang out.

Ken'ishi shouted orders to ship the oars and prepare weapons. Momentum carried his craft into the side of the ship with a thud. "Strike the mast!"

The two men hammered pins out of the mast mount and toppled the mast onto the gunwale above. Ken'ishi charged up the wooden bridge, Silver Crane high. Behind him came his men in a roaring fury.

The bowmen would stay behind to secure the boat to the ship with grappling hooks and then take up their bows.

The men aboard this ship were not Mongols. Their faces most closely resembled the White Lotus Gang he had faced in Hakata. Their swords were straight and two-edged. Their bronze, bell-shaped helmets were topped by red silken plumes. All of them wore coats, reaching to their ankles, of small steel plates that interlocked like the scales of a lizard. Similar curtains of interlocking plates draped their necks.

Silver Crane rang in his mind. *Kill them. Oh, yes.*

Ken'ishi leaped off the tip of the mast and used his downward momentum to add force to his first blow, snapping an upraised sword and cleaving half through a bronze helmet. The man's eyes crossed as he toppled.

Silver Crane sang its joy into the threads of time and fortune.

The face of the first man Ken'ishi had killed in seven years, after five years of ragged effort to expunge the residue of death and evil from his essence, fell away from the edge of his sword with a wet slither.

His men crowded around him, past him, smashed into the Sung like a savage whirlwind. Men fell on both sides.

He stared at the pool spreading around the man's unfamiliar helmet. Was the mark on his chest tingling again, or was it just his fear-fueled imagination?

Naginata spun and slashed and sheared through the lamellar armor like paper. Severed limbs flew. Blood slicked the deck. Chinese swords darted and thrust. The Sung fought with wide-eyed ferocity, but when the other boats of Ken'ishi's flotilla disgorged their boarders up the far side, catching the Sung in the rear, their will evaporated. They died to the last man.

Ken'ishi blinked in the sudden silence, rousing himself from his strange stupor.

His men raised their bloody weapons and cheered.

"Quickly!" Kagetora said. He cut the head off the ship's captain and tossed it over the side, into his boat.

Sixty-odd Chinese heads left their necks. A few of the men wrangled over ownership of the trophies, but Ken'ishi and Kagetora roared reminders that enemy ships were bearing down upon them.

Ken'ishi assessed casualties. Two of his men dead, three lightly wounded. Freshly blooded, their will to fight burned hot in their eyes and clenched teeth.

Then a thunderous explosion, a hundred times greater than any previous, ripped across the water. An enemy ship, perhaps two hundred paces distant, erupted in a boiling cloud of smoke and flame, sending shattered planks and bodies arcing through the air for fifty paces in every direction. A cascade of smaller explosions followed. With five attack boats secured to the sides of the sinking ship, no one was left alive.

"What could do that?" Ken'ishi said.

"Perhaps that's what happens when their stores of thunder-crash bombs explode all at once," Kagetora said.

The men stared in awe for several heartbeats until Ken'ishi roused them. They emptied barrels of pitch across the deck and then retreated to their boats. Ken'ishi waited with a lit torch for the last man to go over the side. Then he tossed the torch onto the pitch and jumped down the mast, barely escaping the blast of blistering heat as flames whooshed across the deck.

Kazuko waited with her bow resting across her thighs. Her *naginata* was sheathed and slung behind her.

Her Scarlet Dragons lined up around her atop the fortifications near Hakozaki.

She gazed over the heads of the defenders and the wooden shields, across the water toward the oncoming ships. She stopped counting at eighty ships that had charged past the picket lines of defense boats. These ships were fanning out toward landing points around Hakata Bay. The strategists estimated that each ship carried sixty to eighty foot troops, or thirty to forty Mongol horsemen and their ponies. Would it be eight thousand Chinese infantry hitting the beach, or four thousand Mongol horsemen? The numbers made her head spin. The gates of the afterworld would swing wide today.

Her chestnut mare waited patiently for her command, unlike the fiery stallions that men demanded as warhorses. Choosing mares instead of stallions for her Scarlet Dragons had sparked yet another round of scoffing and skepticism. Mares lacked the bravery of stallions, the men said, the strength of stallions, the aggressiveness of stallions.

To all of that, Kazuko had said, "Nonsense. Not all men are brave, or strong, or fierce. The men who are, become warriors. As did these women who are brave, strong, and fierce. And so are the mares we choose to carry us."

Today would be their first battle.

Some of the ships paused between a hundred fifty and two hundred paces from the beach and turned broadsides. The others maintained their course toward the sand. From the paused ships, strange contraptions flung metal balls toward the shore in high, smoke-trailing arcs.

Then the balls exploded with deafening thunder, blowing shields, wall, and men to bits.

The Dragons' horses squealed and reared, but the women held in the saddle. With firm grip on the reins and some soothing words, Kazuko comforted her mount.

Captain Ishii no Soun, her husband's master of horse and archery, rode up. "My lady, we must withdraw for now until the enemy has spent their infernal devices."

Up and down the line, mounted warriors were struggling with their mounts. The hail of explosions kept coming.

"Understood, Captain," she said and withdrew across a road that paralleled the shore.

Storms of arrows shot back and forth, most of the defenders' arrows falling short of the Mongols' superior range.

The bombardment continued. At first the noise and explosions drove the *ashigaru* defenders, trained peasants, back from the wall, but when the ships opened their holds to disgorge their assault forces, the samurai commanders shouted courage back into the frightened peasants. The explosions began to evoke less fear.

Kazuko looked around at her Dragons. Their faces were fierce and determined. The scarlet ribbons around their light helmets fluttered in the breeze. Their desire to get into the fight, to prove themselves, simmered around her, but she knew enough of strategy and tactics to hold here.

Then the ships hit the beach. The enemy poured out onto the sand and charged the wall. The defenders sleeted them with arrows, and still they came. More arrows arced from the ships over the heads of the assault troops, driving the defenders behind their wooden shields. Bodies littered the beach like seaweed washed ashore. The defenders sent hissing clouds of flaming arrows into the ships. Crews scurried to extinguish the flames.

War cries and the screams of the dying echoed from all directions, along with the smell of blood and the acrid stench of the brimstone smoke on the sea breeze. Wave after wave of the enemy spewed onto the blood-drenched sand, crossing over their fallen comrades. Defense reinforcements came from the rear to fill holes in the lines. A few brazen samurai, hungry for battle and glory, shouted challenges from atop the wall toward enemy commanders or taunted the enemy troops. She even saw one leap down onto the beach to meet the charging enemy head on. She never saw him again.

How much time passed while she held her Scarlet Dragons in check, she could not remember. But then a hue and cry sounded, a horn from the east.

Something told her it was finally time to act.

She raised her signal fan and called out to her troops. Four abreast, they galloped toward the noise and, in the chaos, spotted a mass of Mongol horsemen on the road, their swords bloodied. They had broken through one of the gates to the beach.

Reinforcements were coming, but the defenders needed time to seal the gap, and a force of Mongol horsemen on the road would disrupt the reinforcements sufficiently to grant the enemy a foothold on the beach.

Kazuko had never seen the barbarians before. Their ponies were small and shaggy, much like the men on their backs. They wore pointed iron helmets fringed with studded leather. Their armor comprised a coat of studded steel plates sewn together and trimmed in fur, reaching just above the knee. Each of them looked like a knot of hardwood, wrapped in hair and steel and leather.

But an arrow through the eye socket would kill them. And she had defeated the two most fearsome *oni* that Kyushu had ever seen.

Her Scarlet Dragons, however, had not. It was time to see how ready they were.

She shouted, "Shoot!"

The Scarlet Dragons formed around her and loosed arrows into the throng of Mongols. Horses screamed and two men fell. Spotting the new threat, the Mongols spun and gathered themselves to charge, at least thirty in number.

"We will lead a fox chase!" she shouted to her troops. "Break when I command!"

The annals of ancient Chinese generals had taught her that cavalry was most effective when it charged, not when it was the target of a charge. She would try to maneuver the enemy into the path of oncoming reinforcements. Already units of *ashigaru* spearmen were gathering to stem the tide of the Mongol breakthrough.

The Mongols charged.

Kazuko ordered, "Shoot!" one last time before wheeling her horse and spurring it away.

The Mongol ponies were nimble, but more heavy-laden, and lacked the stride of the Dragons' taller horses. Kazuko and the Dragons were able to pull away. Passing an intersection, Kazuko spotted Captain Soun leading his unit of heavy lancers, a new type of unit developed and practiced over the last couple of years. They had been waiting in the rear, just like the Scarlet Dragons, for a purpose such as this.

Speeding past the intersection, she raised her war fan to him, and he raised his to her.

Captain Soun's heavy cavalry timed their charge perfectly. The lancers plowed into the Mongol flank amidst the screams of horses and men. The Mongols held firm, however, facing the new threat with blades and war cries and dogged resilience.

With her pursuers tied up, Kazuko reined and spun her mount again, shouting, "*Naginata!*"

The Scarlet Dragons slung their bows, drew their polearms from special holsters along the saddle, unsheathed the blades, and lined up to charge.

They had drilled this dozens of times. The weapons switch went smoothly, and they lined up like veterans. This *naginata* had a longer haft and a longer blade than the one she had first practiced with, the better to fight with from horseback, but she had learned its advantages and disadvantages as well.

Kazuko raised her war fan. "Forward!"

The horses jumped forward into a trot, then a canter, then a barreling gallop. Kazuko couched her naginata with both hands, clutching the reins in her teeth, pounding toward the enemy.

A few of the Mongol horsemen saw them coming, but there was nothing they could do except curse in their coarse barbarian tongue.

The massive impact almost drove her out of the saddle, numbed her hands and arms, knocked the breath out of her. Her mare slammed a Mongol pony onto its side. She lost her grip on her weapon, but was able to snatch it again as it hung impaled through the torso of an enemy horseman. She gasped for breath and let the falling body pull free of the weapon.

The Scarlet Dragons shrieked their *kiai*. They were the hammer, and Soun's heavy lancers became the anvil, and the Mongol horsemen were ground into bloody meat between them.

Kazuko brought her weapon down on the neck of a pony with all her might. With the added leverage of height and the length of the haft, her blow severed the pony's head in a frightening gout of blood. Its rider tumbled off, and one of her sisters impaled him against the ground.

He was the last.

In this first experience with a mass melee, the sight of so much blood—great awful deluges of it—the stench of punctured guts and loosed bowels, the screams of dying ponies, twisted her belly into a watery knot. Tears hazed her vision. She would not throw up before her sisters. She would not show weakness. She was a warrior, just as they were.

The women's voices rose into a cheer, and then came the men's howl of victory.

Kazuko and Captain Soun nodded to each other.

Captain Soun spun his unit and galloped back toward the gate where the Mongols had broken through. A block of quick-legged spearmen seemed to have plugged the breach.

There was no time to congratulate themselves any further, however, as the ships that paused to launch their thunder-crash bombs now rowed toward shore with contingents of fresh warriors lined up on the decks.

"It's hard to hold back and not move. That is why the ability to hold back is important. You shouldn't act impulsively. If you make moves at random without perceiving an advantage,  you're likely to lose. A noble man controls the frivolity with gravity, awaits action in the state of calm. It is important for the spirit to be whole, the mood steady, and the mind unmoving."

—*Kaibara Ekken*

With the bombardment abated, Kazuko led the Scarlet Dragons back to the wall. They rode back and forth behind the defenders, launching volley after volley of arrows into the relentless hordes of the enemy. When their quivers were empty, they refilled them from the barrels and then returned to the front.

The Scarlet Dragons never paused to shoot. They had trained in *yabusame,* just as the men had. They galloped pass after pass, raining arrows into the crowds of stymied foot soldiers on the beach, and their aim was true. The fighting at the lip of the wall was ferocious and bloody. Someday perhaps she might forget what swords and spears and *naginata* did to human flesh. The peasant spearmen, armored only with breastplates and thigh guards, fought as bravely as born warriors. Their homes and families were at stake, too, and they knew it.

By late afternoon, the wall's height had been effectively reduced by mounds of corpses at its base. The invaders charged over the bodies of their brethren, only to join them. At least, thus far.

Kazuko lost count of the number of times she had emptied her quiver, but she kept telling herself, "One more run, just one."

And then horns and gongs blared from the decks of the ships. The men on the beach pulled back toward their ships. The defenders chased them with arrows. The gangplanks retracted, oars extended, and the landing ships clawed back toward deeper water.

Cries of weary triumph echoed up and down the lines.

Kazuko sobbed once with relief. Tears flowed. She started to wipe them away, until she saw the blood caked thick around her fingers. Fortunately none of it was hers, although she had pulled two arrows from her shoulder guards and one from her saddle over the course of the day. The gods had seen fit for her to live one more day.

Her lathered mare, gasping for breath, trembled with exhaustion.

One of her Dragons had fallen from an arrow, Kyoko, a beautiful woman of twenty-two whose warrior husband had died of a fever after stepping on a sea urchin. She had sworn to uphold the family name. Three others had been wounded and would be out of action for a while. That left the Scarlet Dragons with twenty-seven, including her.

Kazuko wanted to fall out of the saddle from exhaustion and sleep where she lay. Never had she imagined such weariness was possible—weariness of limb, weariness of mind, weariness of the heart.

So much death. How many men had she alone killed today? War turned men into monsters, ground down their spirits until naught was left but a hollow shell that must either be unfeeling or tortured.

Captain Soun rode up beside her, looking just as weary, spattered with blood. "You fought well today, but we are not finished."

The sun sank toward the distant mountains beyond Hakata. The ships had withdrawn to perhaps three hundred paces from the shore and dropped anchor. The *ashigaru* and camp servants were hauling carts full of corpses to a mass grave dug behind the lines.

Captain Soun pointed toward Shiga Island. Smoke rose from dozens of fires across the island and the sandbar leading to the mainland. Ships were landing there even now.

Shiga Island was small, less than one *ri* north-to-south, slightly narrower east-to-west. The sandbar formed the perfect beachhead for the invaders to unload their troops. With little room to maneuver or build deep ranks, the spit was too narrow to mount an effective defense. The wall did not reach all the way to the sandbar. The Mongol horsemen would simply be able to ride around behind it and strike deep into Kyushu.

"I see you understand," Captain Soun said. "We are to take positions and block the Shiga spit. There are some Shoni men holding the spit for now, but if they're flanked or broken tomorrow, we will lose the northern end of the wall, and the enemy will have roads south."

"Understood, Captain," she said.

"Follow us. We're leaving now."

As he rode away, she petted her mare's neck. "Just a bit farther tonight, my stout-hearted friend."

Drunk with victory, Ken'ishi and the rest of his flotilla charged yet another ship. This time, he let his worries disappear under the waves. He plunged himself to the neck into bloody battle, and with Silver Crane's power, spun a cyclone of blood and entrails.

Michizane's *naginata* lay a fearsome swath of death about him.

The Chinese armor was thick, however, perhaps more effective than that of the samurai. Two of his men had broken their swords against the thick steel lamellar. When this melee finally ended, one of Ken'ishi's shoulder guards had been hacked away by a double-bitted axe with a haft as long as a *naginata*'s.

Four more of his men lay dead.

They had stormed up the mast-bridge ahead of him this time and met a hissing storm of lethal darts fired from strange, horizontal bows. The darts were shorter than arrows, but the bow mechanisms were made of spring steel. The darts pierced the samurai breastplates as if they were paper. The strange bows took longer to prepare and fire, however, and the samurai soon overwhelmed them. Nevertheless, yet another unfamiliar weapon gave them pause.

While the men collected more heads, Ken'ishi climbed the ship's tallest mast and surveyed the progress of the battle.

Dozens of enemy ships burned. Dozens more drifted uncontrolled, tied up by little boats that attacked like swarms of ants around an invading wasp.

Scores more invading ships, however, perhaps more than a hundred, had pushed past the picket of defense boats into the bay and reached the shore. Fire and smoke bespoke hard fighting up and down the wall around Hakata and Hakozaki.

The barbarian fleet just kept coming. Out here, on the verge of the open sea, Ken'ishi could see as if to the edge of the world itself. Shielding his eyes against the glare of the hot afternoon sun, he clung to the mast and rigging with one arm and both legs. Still more ships filled the waves between him and the horizon, trailing white foam, their decks thronged with men and war machines.

They had changed course.

Battles between the defense boats and the first lines of ships dotted much of the entrance to Hakata Bay. The ships still coming in from the open sea had turned east.

At that moment, a thick weariness washed over him, and he swayed for a moment. His mouth was parched, dry earth. No more ships were approaching.

He shimmied down the rigging and ordered a brief rest. The men pulled out rations of dried fish and drank from the ship's stores of fresh water. Standing amid the ubiquitous, headless dead, they rested, bandaged their wounds, caught their breath.

Ken'ishi climbed the rigging again.

The rest of the fleet continued toward the east, but now he saw their destination. They had landed on Shiga Island and on the north side of the sandbar connecting Shiga to land. Black clusters of men and horses swarmed over the narrow spit like angry ants, coalescing into massed units. More ships were heading east, up the coast toward Munakata.

There was no wall protecting Munakata. The Shoni clan was prepared with troops there, but they would have to fight the invaders without the advantage of fortifications.

He tried to discern how the defenders were faring around Hakozaki, but could see nothing except that the ships were still close to shore.

And then he spotted a contingent of some thirty ships that had withdrawn from the shore and were heading this way.

"We must get out of here!" Ken'ishi called down to the deck.

"Why?" Kagetora said. "We're winning!"

"Because they're coming back." He pointed at the oncoming vessels.

Kagetora shielded his eyes and followed Ken'ishi's gesture.

As Ken'ishi climbed back down, he said, "That could only mean they have failed to breach the wall. Our defenses are holding, but by the time those ships reach us, they'll be ready for revenge."

"Then we'll fight!" said another man.

Ken'ishi said, "We've fought well today. But we succeeded only because we were able to isolate individual ships and bring them down, like wolves on a lone stag. We cannot stand against a full assault."

"You fear to die?" the man said, frowning.

"I'll not die a dog's death," Ken'ishi said. "Best to take our trophies back to our lords and fight again tomorrow." Then he added with a smirk, "Besides, if we take any more heads, our boats will sink beneath us."

The men laughed.

Kagetora agreed with Ken'ishi's assessment.

They set fire to their most recent conquest and oared themselves out of the path of the oncoming ships. Five of the ships tried to pursue, but they were like lumbering oxen trying to catch a fox.

It was sunset when Ken'ishi's flotilla reached shore, a day of blood and victory behind them, but the battle was far from over.

Kazuko and the Scarlet Dragons reached the defenders' camp on Shiga spit an hour after sundown, where they found several hundred samurai and *ashigaru,* bloodied and weary, but steadfast. The land leading toward Shiga spit shifted from forested hills to scrub and sand dunes. The defenders camped among the dunes, bathed in the light of their cookfires.

All along the spit were anchored the invading ships, and their campfires formed an open, blazing path all the way to the island, where more fires burned. Both armies camped in full view of the other, with nothing between them but a few hundred paces of open sand.

The ships themselves were of at least a dozen different types and sizes, two- and three-masted Sung traders alongside smaller but more nimble Koryo vessels. Out on the water, the deep-drafted behemoths waited quiescent, lanterns glittering like fireflies across the expanse of sea.

Inside Kazuko's armor, her clothes felt like sodden rags, bunched up in uncomfortable places; but thoughts of comfort must be put aside. They would all be sleeping in their armor tonight.

With the horses picketed and munching on sacks of millet, Kazuko could rest for a little while. Eventually, the Scarlet Dragons' baggage train caught up with them, and the servants were able to prepare a meal of fresh rice for the exhausted fighters.

The women kept their campsite away from the men. Lord Tsunetomo and his other officers had thought it most prudent. Men did dangerous things in war, bestial things. All knew but no one spoke of what would happen to the women if captured by the enemy. Moreover, there were still many who believed that bringing women to war would bring ill fortune, especially if any of them had their moon's blood. Keeping the women separate would reduce the chances of unpleasant encounters. If moon's blood had come for any of her women, they did not tell Kazuko, and she did not ask.

In war, there was blood enough for all.

After she and her sisters had eaten, after their mounts had been cared for, she crossed the hundred paces of starlight and sand between her camp and Soun's heavy lancers. She wanted to talk to him about the day's events. Yamazaki-*sensei* often said that after-battle reflection was as important as the planning.

As she approached the campfires, the men gossiped about the days various victories and near defeats. For the first day, their defenses had held. They had turned aside every attack except at Shiga Island and Genkai Island, which both lay now in enemy hands.

And then she heard a name she had not in almost five years.

She approached the man who said it.

He started as she stepped out of the dark. "Lady Otomo!"

He and all the men around him knelt and bowed.

"Did you say 'Captain Ken'ishi?'" she said.

"Yes, Lady," the man said. "He has returned. He commanded one of the boats today."

Her heart flipped over, and she chided herself for it. "That is good news. His strength is much needed. How did the boats fare?"

"We lost some, but won more. They were not expecting us to fight ship to ship. If not for them, we'd have had it much harder on the wall today."

"And what of Captain Ken'ishi?"

Another man said, "I heard he took more than a dozen Chinese heads today, all by himself."

So many in one day was all but unheard of. He had not let his martial prowess slip while he was away.

"Don't worry, fellows," said the first man. "We'll have all the heads we can carry tomorrow."

Another man said, "I heard that the Takezaki men captured a general on one of the ships and brought him back for interrogation."

She nodded in appreciation of all these exploits, but there was still a lump in her throat she could not swallow. "The gods and fortunes have smiled on us today. Now, where is Captain Soun?"

"Among five kinds of warfare, war for justice and war for defense are used by noble men. War out of anger, war out of pride, and war out of greed are not used by noble men; they are used by small men."

—*Kaibara Ekken*

Yasutoki dragged the watchman's dying body behind a stack of barrels and wiped the blood from his dagger on the man's robe. The man lay limp in the dark, gasping like a gaffed fish, clutching weakly at Yasutoki's clothes, a second mouth squirting a dark stain onto the storehouse's earthen floor.

Another guard paced back and forth at the opposite end of the storehouse, clinging to the puddles of lantern light.

Yasutoki, on the other hand, moved through the shadows between the stacks of bagged rice and millet, barrels of salt fish, bales of seaweed, and baskets of early-season vegetables.

One of the advantages of being Tsunetomo's advisor was that he knew the location of all the defense force storehouses. He knew their guard schedules and their contents. He also knew the locations of the guard posts around Hakozaki. The guards at three of those posts now lay dead, in no particular order or strategic location. His attacks had to appear random.

Yasutoki was pleased with how his skills were re-emerging after many years of stagnation. And oh, his dagger was sharp. The last guard had died without a whimper.

His first attack earlier tonight had nearly gone awry. The poisoned *shuriken* had missed. If the target had not been more confused than alarmed, he might have cried out before Yasutoki hit him with another. Fortunately, the guard's companion had been pissing behind a house, and returned just time to have his throat cut from behind.

When the defenders of Kyushu discovered that "spies" had murdered guards all over Hakozaki in the dead of night, a new level of fear would sweep through them.

Yasutoki would not be able to make contact with the Khan's generals or offer any sort of intelligence, but he was still the Great Khan's loyal saboteur.

He would only be able to get away with such deeds easily on this one night, however. After as much mayhem as he intended, he would have to lie low for a while. After tonight, guards would be tripled or quadrupled. No one would sleep. Vigilance would be at its height.

Until it flagged, as it always did. People could not remain so vigilant for long. Complacency was inevitable. And in that complacency, he would re-emerge to strike again.

No one could predict what would break an army's will. The pressures and hardships were so numerous that any smallest thing, piled high upon so many other difficulties, could destroy an army's morale.

Now, four days into the fighting, the defense had been so fierce the onslaught had drawn to a stalemate. Tsunetomo's forces, including Kazuko and her horse women, had stymied the Mongols at Shiga spit. Ken'ishi and his boatmen had taken to nighttime raids against anchored ships.

Another Mongol force had sailed north and attacked Munakata, but the defense forces there had driven them back yet again. There were rumors that Koryo ships had been spotted near Moji and Dan-no-Ura, but one could not believe everything.

Yasutoki made his way like smoke and shadow toward the lit portion of the storehouse.

Between target locations, he replenished the poison on each of his *shuriken*.

At the Hour of the Ox, in the darkest depths of night, his associates would finish the job he had started at two other storehouses. But he had to act before the guard shifts changed.

In the seven years since the destruction of his underworld empire, Green Tiger had managed to reclaim a few pieces of his old territory, enlist a few choice henchmen, and now had a comfortable stream of coin finding its way into his hidden coffers. But he was ready to give it all up again to see Mongol rule. The Golden Horde was brutal and merciless to its enemies, but those who submitted could find ways to excel within the new order of things.

This watchman looked like a simple-minded peasant. Yasutoki had of course approved the use of peasants as guards, instead of warriors. Their lack of education and discipline made them easy targets.

A quick flick of his wrist, and two *shuriken* pierced the guard's throat and face. The guard stiffened and then fell limp, allowing Yasutoki to dart forward and slash his throat.

It was almost the Hour of the Ox.

He untied a jar of oil from his black obi and poured it over a stack of rice piled against a wall, taking care to splash some onto the wall as well.

Then he took down the lantern, set the oil aflame, waited to make sure the flame caught, and then faded into the dark city. He paused a safe distance away to watch the storehouse burn. Before long, flames and smoke bloomed from the roof.

He found an area on a low hill that afforded an excellent view of the town, climbed to the crest of a house roof, and lay down to watch.

The firewatch appeared with a cacophony of clappers and gongs to raise the alarm. Fire was a worse enemy to any city than a barbarian horde. Especially when few townspeople remained in Hakozaki to fight the fire. The women and children had fled south in great, weeping caravans. The men and older boys remained, most of whom had been impressed into defense units and labor gangs. After a day of hard fighting, many of them had collapsed with exhaustion near their posts on the wall.

The response to the fire would be slow.

And then a flickering glow appeared across town. Another fire.

Yasutoki tingled with satisfaction.

All that remained was...

The third storehouse erupting into flame.

For almost an hour, Yasutoki watched all three conflagrations, watched the fire crews scurry helplessly, watched samurai on horseback shouting ineffectually, watched great quantities of food disappear in columns of smoke.

The Mongols out on the sea must be watching this and smiling with wonder.

Pleasures like this allowed Yasutoki to forget the painful coal in his belly, for a while.

It was a good night.

Finally, with dawn drawing nigh, he made his way back to Lord Tsunetomo's encampment and to his tent.

He had slipped out a hidden flap in the rear of the tent, out of sight of his two bodyguards. But on his approach to the tent now, he saw that both of them were gone. Abandoning one's post at a time like this warranted execution.

He circled to the back of the tent, keeping to the shadows, and slipped inside. In the gloom, two dark lumps lay across each other in the center of his tent. He froze at the thick scent of blood.

He whipped out his dagger with one hand, *shuriken* with the other, dropped low and slid around the tent in a circle, searching the shadows.

No attack came.

Gray dawn lightened the walls of the tent, filtering inside.

Yasutoki put away his weapons and lit a lamp.

His two bodyguards lay arranged like cordwood. He tipped one's chin back and found the throat had been slashed almost to the spine. The other had taken a blade through the eye socket. The center of his tent was a great pool of purpled, half-congealed blood. These killings had taken place at least an hour ago.

His brain reeled. How could he explain these two dead men in his tent when he was supposed to have been here with them?

Then he noticed that one of the reed mats, similar to tatami, in the corner beside the tent flap lay in slight disarray. The blanket looked twisted, as if by footprints. Leaning over the blanket, he saw something else that turned his blood to ice.

A single kernel of rice.

The assassin had waited here for him to return. Long enough to grow hungry and eat a rice ball, only to be driven away by the approach of dawn.

The camp would come to life soon. Before it did, and before the day's next attack came, he had to construct an explanation for these deaths. He could not move them far, and he could not hide the massive bloodstain where they lay.

"When on the battlefield, if you try not to let others take the lead and have the sole intention of breaking into the enemy lines, then you will not  fall behind others, your mind will become fierce, and you will manifest martial valor.... Furthermore, if you are slain in battle, you should be resolved to have your corpse facing the enemy."

—*Hagakure, Book of the Samurai*

"We hold the bay," Lord Tsunetomo said, "but they hold the sea."

Captain Tsunemori said, "Captain Ken'ishi, your boats have kept many wolves from our door."

Ken'ishi bowed. "Mine is but one of many." He could not help but think about how many of his men had died on their forays, how many replacements as well, and the thousands who had perished in scores of boats.

At this moment, he had no idea how he was keeping the weariness at bay. Four days of fighting. Four days of blood. His entire being felt chafed raw and squeezed empty.

The cloth walls of the *maku* hung slack in the pre-dawn stillness.

Captain Tsunemori laughed. "You are the most modest samurai I have ever encountered."

"It was not always so," Ken'ishi said. "My time with Lord Abe has...changed me."

"At least it has not slackened your sword arm. You've brought back enough heads to populate a village."

Ken'ishi could not find a way to be joyful about that, even though it was the Warrior's Way to present one's lord with the trophies of his prowess. But Lord Abe had called each person a universe. Ken'ishi had destroyed a great many universes. "We have lost many boats as well. The barbarians' are skilled with their thunder-crash bombs. Success often depends on what kind of troops our target is carrying, Mongols, Koryo, Jin, or Sung."

"And your assessment of the reason?" Lord Tsunetomo said. His voice sounded as if he already knew the reason.

Ken'ishi had been present for all of the strategic planning since he rejoined Tsunetomo's forces. He had striven to absorb as much as he could, as well as recall Yamazaki-*sensei*'s wisdom. "The Mongols are the toughest. They are steppe-bred barbarians, fanatically loyal to their Khan. The Sung are well-equipped. Their armor is thick, and they are seasoned and hardy after twenty years of fighting the Mongols. But they still live in the shadow of their defeat. After they surrendered, the Khan offered them amnesty if they would fight for him, but they still bear the stain on their honor, the defeat in their hearts. The Jin and the Koryo have long been subjugated. They are here because they were ordered to fight, like the Sung. The Mongols are here because they wish to be."

The Jin were the people of northern China, subjugated by Khubilai Khan's uncle, Ogedei, and grandfather, Genghis. The King of the Koryo could hardly refuse his father-in-law Khubilai Khan's demand for troops and ships.

Tsunetomo nodded in agreement.

The *kami* had been a dull, unceasing roar in Ken'ishi's mind since the first ships appeared, like the constant, crashing waves of winter, such that the sudden blare of intensity staggered him.

A guard slipped into the enclosure. "My lords, Lord Yasutoki is here."

Ken'ishi's jaw clenched.

Yasutoki entered the enclosure, eyes flicking around its occupants, brushing over Ken'ishi as if he were not present.

"My lord," Yasutoki said, "something terrible has happened. The two *yojimbo* stationed outside my tent have been murdered!"

Lord Tsunetomo jumped to his feet. "Murdered! Were you attacked?"

"No, my lord. Thank the fortunes, but I was out of my tent."

"Where were you?"

Yasutoki looked embarrassed. "Forgive me for my rudeness, my lord, but my innards have not been well these last few months. I visited the latrine late last night, and I was away from my tent for a little while. When I returned, my guards were dead."

"Show me," Tsunetomo said.

Ken'ishi's presence annoyed Yasutoki, and this amused him.

At the entrance of Yasutoki's tent lay two bodies, dragged just out of view. At this hour, no one would have been around to see. These men had been among Tsunetomo's most trusted guards. *Yojimbo* duty was reserved for warriors of special merit.

One glance told Ken'ishi these men were expertly killed. But why would Yasutoki kill his bodyguards? Some nefarious scheme relating to his efforts as Green Tiger, most likely.

"Could this be related to the fires?" Tsunetomo said. "Or the murders of the other guards?" As soon as word had spread of the storehouse fires and the murders scattered all over town, guards had been quadrupled at all the posts. Fire crews were still working to contain the blazes. One had gotten away and threatened an entire district.

"I do not see how," Yasutoki said. "The storehouses are a far from here.... Unless..." He hurried inside the tent. Tsunetomo, Tsunemori, and Ken'ishi followed him.

Yasutoki opened a lacquered document case with trembling fingers, to reveal dozens of small pigeon holes...that all lay empty. His eyes bulged. "My lord, I have been pilfered!"

"Spies," Tsunetomo said.

The *kami* buzzed, restless. Undoubtedly Yasutoki was not only capable of murdering the guards last night, but setting the storehouse fires. This was the kind of machination at which Green Tiger excelled. But why would he harm the defense forces? Was he not in just as much danger as everyone else? Had something changed in the five years of Ken'ishi's absence? How much gold would buy Green Tiger's service as a saboteur?

Ken'ishi wanted to leap forward, lay the edge of his blade against Yasutoki's neck, and force him to confess everything to Lord Tsunetomo—and take his head at the first lie. But Yasutoki still held a higher station. Ken'ishi could not publicly accuse him. And there was still the matter between Ken'ishi and Kazuko, of which Yasutoki knew far too much. If time had mended some of the rents in the fabric of Kazuko's life, Ken'ishi could not readily put her in jeopardy.

The scar on his chest itched. His fingers ached to squeeze Silver Crane's hilt and strike.

The implications of Yasutoki's story rang false.

The *yojimbo* were not fresh kills.

The storehouse fires had been set between midnight and the Hour of the Ox. The guardposts around town had been attacked at roughly the same time. The new guards arriving for their shifts had discovered the murders.

Yasutoki was suggesting someone had killed his bodyguards and stolen all of his documents, including the guardpost and storehouse locations, and then had time to go wreak havoc, all while Yasutoki was in the privy.

Not even a pile of shit like Yasutoki could remain in the privy that long.

"Spies in our midst," Tsunetomo said, scratching his beard. "Saboteurs." He spat. "I must inform the other lords. Yasutoki, your first task is to have the remaining storehouses moved. Distribute the food and supplies to other locations. We cannot afford another such loss."

Ken'ishi bit his tongue and tasted blood. How could a man as wise and stalwart and honorable as Tsunetomo be so blind to the evil right beside him? Ken'ishi swore that Yasutoki would not survive this. The stain of Green Tiger's existence would soon be cleansed from the world, but only after the barbarians had been cast back into the sea.

At sunrise the assault recommenced, but this time the focus moved to Shiga. Fifty ships moved into position northeast of the bulk of the defending army. The enemy was trying to open a pathway for its forces; the sandbar was a perfect site to offload troops in great numbers. The Hakata defenses were too strong, but if they could break through the defense lines east of Shiga, outside of Hakata Bay, they would have open paths south and east, just as they had seven years before. Signals came via flag and fan and drum, passed along the shoreline toward Hakata and beyond to Imazu.

Ken'ishi was given command of a hundred peasant spearmen and twenty-five mounted samurai. The thunder of the Mongol bombs echoed across the distance, and he chafed to be in the battle. But it was Silver Crane's impatience, not his. The foot troops marched with the speed of cold tar. The sword's hunger, pulsing and thrumming through him, drove him to wish he could simply spur his horse forward and throw himself into the teeth of the enemy. But his troops were mostly frightened fishermen and farmers, like the men he had known in Aoka village, a unit knitted together by desperation and leadership. Bravery would inspire them—as long as it was visible. Michizane was a fine leader, but they did not look to him like they did to Ken'ishi.

Stories of his successful assaults on the ships were spreading. No matter what he did, people found it worthy of rumors. At fifty heads, he had stopped counting.

The march distracted him from what evils Green Tiger might be hatching in their very camp.

Aoka village was alive again—with encampments. It had become the rear echelon where supplies and weapons were stored. Exhausted and wounded men, pulled off the front lines for rest, watched with wan faces and empty eyes as Ken'ishi's men marched past.

With less than a *ri* before they reached the beaches under assault, the crackling explosions of the bombs grew louder.

Captain Tsunemori pelted into Aoka from a northern road through the forest. A splintered arrow protruded from his bloodstained thigh, and his eyes blazed with urgency.

"Go, go, go!" he screamed, waving his war fan to follow him. "Otherwise we will fall!"

When Ken'ishi's troops emerged from the forest onto the scrub and sand dunes stretching toward Shiga, a spike of desperate fear shot through his belly.

Fifteen enemy ships had reached the shore. Even now, men and horses were pouring forth behind a stubborn line of Sung infantry. The attack had pried a hole in the defenders' formation and opened a space for the enemy to gain a larger toehold. Cavalry rode back and forth behind the lines, firing arrows into the Sung ranks, but without visible effect.

Ken'ishi's men were puffing with exertion, but he must get them into battle. His samurai disdained the peasant spearmen, anxious to join the fray, but he could not leave these peasants alone. Their sergeants would not know how best to engage the enemy. Ushihara led a company of fifty. He was brave and strong, like an old, scarred bullock, but not a tactician.

The desperation on Tsunemori's face to rejoin the battle burned in his eyes. "Slow, yes, but steady. Do not spend your troops before they reach the battle."

Behind the defenders' lines among the cavalry units, a unit of warriors wearing brilliant crimson armor harried the attackers with bow fire.

Lines of spears and *naginata* rose up behind rows of spiked bamboo barricades just high enough to impale any horse that pressed close. The fences provided little cover from arrows but prevented the Mongol horsemen from charging full into the defenders' ranks. Bodies littered the sand on both sides. Storms of arrows flew back and forth.

For half a *ri* eastward, ships tried to land, tried to disgorge their cargo onto the beach, but the defenders were there, spear points glimmering in the morning sun and driving them back to the water.

The scale of the slaughter gave Ken'ishi pause. After five years of meditating on the nature of life, taking it had become a weightier matter than ever. Hundreds, thousands of universes dying before his eyes, some of them foolish, some wise, the strong and the weak, brave and cowardly, all dying together.

Strike now, or you will die! chimed Silver Crane.

But after four days of grueling, blood-soaked battle, it grew easier to watch men die again.

Tsunemori pointed. "There! If those horsemen flank those Shimazu men, the southwest flank will crumble!"

Ken'ishi could see, beyond the chaos of melee, a mass of Mongol horsemen, fresh from newly-landed ships, forming up to swing wide and flank attack a block of Shimazu *naginata* troops. The Shimazu were fending off a unit of Sung spearmen. There was just enough space on the beach to allow the Mongols' maneuver. That hole must be plugged.

"Spearmen!" Captain Tsunemori shouted. "Follow behind us and fill that opening! Horsemen, with me!" With a great cry, they barreled across the sand. If they could swing around the southwest tip of the infantry lines quickly enough, they could strike while the Mongols were still in disarray.

Tip the cup, and I will drink. Silver Crane's voice rasped across Ken'ishi's bones and teeth.

He whipped it out. "Then give me power," he muttered so no one else could hear, and spurred his horse.

Clouds of grit flew from pounding hooves.

They reached the gap just in time to meet the enemy horsemen's maneuver. The Mongol commander's face twisted into a sneer at being denied his crushing blow.

In the previous invasion, the Mongol horsemen had moved like flocks of birds, in perfect unison. Their favorite tactic had been to swoop in close, loose great clouds of arrows, draw the samurai forces into attack, and then retreat. The samurai, in their zeal to engage, would invariably give chase, and find themselves overextended. Then the horsemen would sweep in and crush them into bloody paste.

The narrow confines of the sand and dunes, funneled between beaches and sea, were too constricted to allow this maneuver. They were surrounded on three sides—by the sea, by their own troops, and by the defenders' barricades. Ken'ishi saw the Mongol commander's recognition of his situation, then his roar of command to meet Tsunemori and Ken'ishi's charge.

The Mongol unit outnumbered Ken'ishi's by four to one, but the constricted space would negate the enemy's superior numbers.

The cavalry units slammed together, a horrific carnage of horses and men. Screams of rage and pain filled Ken'ishi's ears as he slashed left and right. Horses stomped and bit and screamed, crushing each other and any men who fell into the sand.

Storm roared his challenges to the Mongol ponies, taunting them for their stunted ugliness.

Silver Crane shattered blades and sundered armor, cleaved helmets and split flesh. As the blood flowed, strength surged into Ken'ishi's limbs. The sky and the air filled with silver veins that pulsed and flowed like the blood of destiny itself, entwining men, horses, stones, and sky.

Mongol blades licked at him, touched him, but he felt no pain.

He hacked and hewed, and his fury drove the Mongols back. His men surged forward, sensing their advantage. Slashing *naginata* laid open swaths of meat, man and horse. The sand turned to crimson mud. The horses fought for footing.

The Mongol commander traded blows with Tsunemori, *katana* to saber. With a savage snarl, the Mongol launched himself off his horse, grabbed Tsunemori, and dragged him to the earth. In his heavy *o-yoroi*, injured, Tsunemori slammed into the ground like a bag of grain. The Mongol pulled a dagger, stabbed at him. Tsunemori caught his wrist.

Ken'ishi spun Storm and spurred toward them, but the surge of battle crossed his path. He hacked his way through two more Mongols, but lost sight of Tsunemori on the ground.

When the crush parted, the Mongol commander jerked his dagger out of Tsunemori's throat, raised it, brought it down again two-handed into Tsunemori's face. Tsunemori's arms fell limp to the bloody sand.

Rage exploded white-hot in Ken'ishi's breast. He leaped out of the saddle and plowed into the Mongol commander, bearing him off Tsunemori's body. Grabbing the Mongol was like trying to wrestle with an oak bough, but the power surging through Ken'ishi was mightier than any tree.

One hand hooked into the neck of the Mongol's armor, the other clutching his belt, he lifted the writhing knot of fury into the air above his head.

And then he brought the Mongol down across his knee.

The wet *crunch* sounded even above the clamor of battle.

The Mongol's legs went limp as sackcloth. Ken'ishi let him slip to the sand, but instead of fury, the barbarian's face blazed with terror. Even so, he clutched for a weapon that he might take Ken'ishi's life with his last breath.

With a single stomp, Ken'ishi burst his head like a melon.

Power surged away from him in waves, like a boulder dropped

into water, driving the space around him wider. Friend and foe alike fell back.

In a single bound, Ken'ishi was back in the saddle.

With the loss of their commander, the Mongols broke and fled.

Ken'ishi spurred after them, heedless that this was exactly the tactic they had used years before.

He roared after them, Silver Crane trailing blood as it pierced the sky.

He caught one fleeing horsemen and severed his head.

The rest fled through the ranks of their foot troops, putting the infantry in momentary disarray. However, the Koryo spearmen closed ranks again behind the Mongols, and formed a bristling wall of spear points. Ken'ishi hauled Storm to a halt just out of range of the spears. The Koryo spearmen, pouring sweat in their heavy armor coats, similar to those of the Sung, lunged forward, thinking to spear this lone warrior's horse, but Storm drew back.

Ken'ishi leaped from the saddle and lunged into them, feeling the invisible silver threads entwining his body, the spears, the limbs and heads of his foes. He swept their spears aside, plowing through their ranks like a charging boar, slashing right and left.

For a split second, he wondered that he had not sought the Void. He no longer needed it. Its realm of endless possibility was superfluous. He needed only slaughter.

Behind him, somehow, he felt his comrades sense the enemy's surprise.

A lone warrior charging a fully armed and armored unit?

The dance of Ken'ishi's sword and body placed him without fail between every enemy spear thrust. Every step was perfectly timed to move him out of harm's way and into range for another lethal attack of his own. His feet moved with the precision of a dancer. Men fell around him like scythed grain.

Hooves pounded across the sand from behind him.

Encircled now by ten hostile spear points, he whirled and slashed, severing spear hafts and limbs and necks.

Fresh screams filled his ears again as his troops crashed into the Koryo spearmen.

This hammer blow shattered the enemy's courage. A dozen died under the furious cavalry onslaught, and the rest broke and ran.

The momentum shift filled the air like an oncoming storm.

The enemy infantry across the spit, seeing their flank collapse, started to fall back, to contract and protect both flanks again with the sea. The defenders pressed their advantage and charged past their barricades.

In an endless cascade of moments, the enemy fell back with increasing speed, like an avalanche gathering momentum.

The collapsing lines retreated into the narrowing spit, and all became chaos. Bottlenecked, the infantry units fouled each other, panicking the crowded Mongol ponies.

Seizing the moment with a roar of triumph, Ken'ishi and the defending commanders led a devastating charge into the rear of the retreating enemy.

It was there the gods flung open the gates of every Hell to catch the deluge of blood.

Ken'ishi waded through the deepest of it.

The defenders tore through the invaders, leaving hundreds of dead in their wake. The retreat continued westward across the sandbar. Ships that had been safely behind friendly lines now lay exposed on the beach. The defenders stormed them before they could retreat from shore. They butchered the crews and burned the ships.

The enemy commanders struggled mightily to rally their troops and managed to stem the retreat only a few hundred paces from Shiga Island, where the spit narrowed to only fifty paces.

When the advancing defenders encountered this solid block of spears, Sung halberds, and fresh arrow fire, they withdrew out of range.

By midafternoon the engagement had settled once again into a stalemate, but the invaders had lost nearly all of the spit. Fourteen ships burned along the sand. The defenders still held the shore east.

Ken'ishi collapsed at the head of the defenders' lines, drenched in blood from crown to toe.

Four men carried him to the rear. He was only vaguely aware of the shock of his bearers as they talked about someone's wound. His flesh was raw and painful, as if the blood burned him, but he had no strength left to wash it off.

Then he saw the hole the size of a spear point in the side of his *do-maru*.

I will not forget
This lonely savor of my
    life's
One little dewdrop
                    —*Basho*

Kazuko saw them carry Ken'ishi away from the front lines. Other wounded men were carried back, but he was the only one who looked as if he had bathed in blood. It dripped from his wild mane like rainwater. His half-lidded eyes told her he still lived.

After so long, seeing him like this unleashed a tumult of emotions she would need time to sort.

She swallowed the tear-fueled lump in her throat and assessed her own losses. Attrition had reduced the Scarlet Dragons to just over half of their previous number. They were only eighteen now. All of them hard, bloody veterans after almost two weeks of fighting. Six of her women lay wounded back in the village behind the lines.

They had acquitted themselves well today.

An uneasy stalemate descended over the beach, the spit, and the sea. The enemy had formed what looked like an impenetrable block of spears and stubborn fury near Shiga Island, daring the defenders to try to push them back again. The defenders had likewise formed a similar formation.

Ships hovered offshore, withholding further bombardment. Hundreds of their thunder-crash bombs had rained down upon the defenders. How many of them could the enemy have brought in ships' stores?

As Kazuko rode through the ranks of spearmen, she heard men speaking.

"Did you see what that Otomo man did?"

"I can't believe it!"

"He gave us the day."

"What a glorious death!"

"Was he wounded?"

"Looked dead to me."

Kazuko bid her Dragons to remain on the beach and take whatever rest they could, then spurred her horse toward the column of wounded being withdrawn to the deserted village. She forgot her own weariness in concern over Ken'ishi's welfare.

She followed at a distance until they carried him into an old inn, where she dismounted and followed him inside.

The stench of blood and waste filled the inn like the dregs of a battlefield and a privy.

His bearers settled him onto a bloodstained *futon*. His blood-caked eyelids were closed.

His right hand still clutched his sword.

She shed no tears for him, not yet, not until she knew. In truth, she hardly recognized him. Something in his face had changed. It looked thicker now, more brutish. Or perhaps it was just the blood.

She wanted to wash him clean, to bind his wounds, or if necessary, to wash him for burial, but she did not dare.

Finally the men removed his breastplate—she saw the rent in the side, just below the ribs—and then she saw the wound. Ragged lips drooled crimson. A spear thrust. Where it was not painted with the blood of the slain, his skin was pale, almost gray.

His sword fell from his fingers and bobbled on the guard away from him.

A moment later, the fingers twitched as if reaching for it, then subsided again.

The healer, across what had been the inn's common room, marked by his drawn face, bloodstained robes, and rolled-up sleeves, was tending another wounded man.

Kazuko called to him. "Save this man."

The healer looked up. "Eh? I have many men to save, my lady."
"This man is the hero of the day. Save him, and it will go well
with you. Let him die at your peril." Then she spun and departed. It
was a cruel thing to say to a healer, but she did not care.

Ken'ishi thought he remembered Kazuko's voice, like the sound of
music, but when he awoke, all that surrounded him was suffering and
death. His side throbbed with a deep ache that made the multitude
of other pains as candles to the sun. Bloodstained bandages wrapped
his torso.

Silver Crane lay beside him, sheathed. Fresh chips in the lacquer
and bloodstains on the mother-of-pearl cranes made the scabbard
looked rougher than ever. He managed to grasp the scabbard, pull it
close, and clutch it to his chest.

He dreamed of silver elixir pulsing through his veins, knitting a rib,
suffusing his flesh with vitality.

His eyes drifted open and closed.

He dreamed of thirst that could not be slaked, hunger that could
not be sated.

Food came, and went uneaten. He had all the sustenance he
needed.

He dreamed of storm clouds crackling with silver lightning, of
silver threads fluttering like spider silk on a nascent wind, of ripples
in the sea coalescing and building upon each other until waves the
size of mountains brushed the sky with silver foam.

Summer rains pattered on the inn's veranda. The veranda used to
overlook the bay; now it looked at the earthen embankment behind
the wall. The rain trickled over the thatched roof that used to be
redolent with the scents of *saké* and cooking, but now trapped the
stench of death within, hot and thick.

He dreamed of a great whirlpool, larger than Shiga Island, and in
the bottom of it lay an open cave mouth, and he gripped the rudder
of a defense boat, alone. The sight of the cave mouth, waiting as if
to devour him, filled him with terror. The mouth was dark, sucking,
suppurating.

Hands held him down.

Liquid that was salty but not seawater—coppery—splashed into his mouth.

The mouth below him. Swallowing the sea. Thousands of men swirling with him in the maelstrom, bobbing on the spinning surface, reaching, helpless, spinning, spinning, spinning toward oblivion.

Ken'ishi's periods of wakefulness grew longer. He did not know how many days he had lain here, but the defenders still held the coastline. They had not been forced to retreat south.

He awoke to find a bowl of rice and a cup of water beside his *futon*. His mouth desert-dry, he reached for the water, but the *kami* wailed in his mind at such stridency that he dropped it as if it were scalding. The warning of the *kami* subsided. He tried to work his mouth enough to moisten his parched tongue, but found nothing there. He would eat the rice after he had found a drink.

Then he noticed the white paper *ofuda* pinned to the front of his robe, a spell that bore Lord Abe's stamp.

For the first time since he came here, he thought he might walk. He rolled onto his side, lifted onto his hands and knees, levered himself upright, stood up, each movement painstakingly slow. The thudding ache in his side grew warm.

The healer rushed toward him. "Let me help you, Captain." The healer was a small man, wizened and leathery, but he possessed the strength to lift Ken'ishi upright. "Be careful now. You mustn't re-open your wound. It has been a difficult week for you."

"A week?"

"Eight days have you lain here. Fever, delirium, strange ravings, like evil nightmares. An *onmyouji* came!" The healer spoke of the *onmyouji* with fear and reverence.

"Lord Abe," Ken'ishi said.

"He looked very worried about you. Do you know him?"

"He has been my teacher for a long time. All of this is no doubt... very disappointing to him."

"Of course. War is a terrible thing."

Ken'ishi let the healer think that was his meaning as they tottered toward a bucket of fresh water near the kitchen. Ken'ishi took up the dipper, and the *kami* did not rebel this time. What about his water cup had set them off?

The water was so cool and sweet he almost laughed with the

pleasure of it.

Back at his futon, he picked up the cup again. Its contents had long since soaked into the deteriorating *tatami*. He sniffed the cup. The *kami* cried out again. It smelled wrong somehow, at once flowery and acrid.

"Has anyone been near me today?" Ken'ishi said.

"No, Captain."

"Who brought me this food and water?"

"I did, Captain." Puzzlement grew in the healer's tone.

"Who hired you to poison me?"

The healer's eyes bulged, and he stepped backward, waving his palms in protest. "What? No!"

The other wounded men watched this exchange with growing interest.

The healer said, "I've been taking care of you, Captain!"

Ken'ishi handed him the poisoned cup.

The healer sniffed the cup, and his naked eyebrows rose in alarm. "Someone tried to poison you!"

With a groan of pain, Ken'ishi scooped up the bowl of cold rice and sniffed it, too. It carried the same strange scent. "Shall I kill you now, or wait until you tell me who hired you?" He expected only one name.

Suddenly Silver Crane was in his hand. How had it gotten there? His hand clutched the hilt to draw.

The healer nearly collapsed with fear. "Please, Captain! I don't know!"

"Tell me about this cup and bowl." His voice did not sound right. Deeper.

"I brought it to you, uh, just after noon, when you looked like you might awaken."

"And no one else has been here."

A man across the room spoke up. "There was someone here, Lord. A woman." The speaker wore a rough, homespun robe. "She went over to your blankets and fussed with them a bit while you were sleeping."

"Who?"

"I don't know, Lord. I never saw her before. Short and ugly. Looked like a servant."

Green Tiger was wont to have others do his dark deeds for him. Had he hired or forced a peasant woman to poison Ken'ishi? Did anyone else want Ken'ishi dead? Tsunetomo could certainly rest easier if Ken'ishi were killed in battle.

No. Such thoughts were the pinnacle of disloyalty and dishonor.

Tsunetomo had no officers to spare.

The images of Tsunemori's last moments flooded his mind, and all he could do was sigh. The lords of Otomo falling, one by one, to the arrows of fortune.

This poisonous mystery pushed him to the limit of his strength. Grief stole the rest of it.

The healer rushed forward. "Lord, are you—?" He hesitated before getting too close.

Ken'ishi still held Silver Crane. "Weary and sick with grief. Tell me of the battle."

The healer cleared his throat. "Our forces drove the barbarians all the way back to Shiga Island. And then, a few days ago, the enemy withdrew from Shiga and Genkai. All of their troops and ships have retreated to Ikishima."

Ken'ishi sighed again at the good news, easing himself back down. A certainty niggled at his mind. "They will come back."

"I don't know what the lords and generals say, but I think the barbarians are waiting for something. So many rumors..."

"Tell me of the rumors."

The healer rubbed his neck. "I hardly know where to begin. Rumors of barbarians coming ashore from here to Satsuma. Their forces still outnumber ours, but Hakata has proven a tough nut to crack. Why wouldn't they look for other landing sites?"

Horses needed a beach to land. Hakata was the best location, but it was hardly the only one on Kyushu.

The healer continued, "Anyway, there are reports of enemy ships all up and down the western coastline."

"Scouts," Ken'ishi said.

The healer shrugged. "No doubt you're right about this not being over."

"Not until we've destroyed them all." When the words came out, Ken'ishi experienced a peculiar mix of anticipation and dread.

"It will take until the end of time to kill them all," the healer said.

"I will bring you fresh rice and water."

Ken'ishi leaned against the wall behind his *futon*. Feeling warm wetness at his side, he looked down.

Fresh blood leaked through his bandage.

Deep, still silence
Seeping into the rocks
Cicada voices

—*Basho*

The thrumming buzz of the cicadas lulled Kazuko into the land between waking and dreams, rising and falling like the breath of the forest in the hot afternoon. Thousands of cicadas, entire cities of them, hid in the trees around Aoka village. That they sang now in the midst of this enormous strife made her think about how wide the gulf was between the natural world and humanity's desires and efforts.

The defense forces had withdrawn from the open beaches when the enemy fleet withdrew.

Somewhere, out on the sea, a deadly dance continued between the defenders' scout ships and the enemy ships sent to drive them away. The scout ships usually returned, and when they did, they reported hundreds of enemy ships—it was impossible to determine exactly how many—were gathered around Ikishima. No doubt the island had been pillaged by now, all the men slaughtered, the women enslaved and mutilated. From there, the barbarians had been plotting their next assault for over a month.

In the meantime, Kazuko was grateful for the respite. It gave her Scarlet Dragons the opportunity to recuperate. The next time they fought, they would be at full strength.

The pause granted time for Ken'ishi to recover as well. She had seen him the day before, teaching sword techniques to a group of young men. He still moved with some stiffness, but his wound had apparently healed.

Enemy ships roved the western coastline, searching no doubt for possible landing sites and causing a local panic at every appearance, but none had yet tried to land. The defense forces were too few to protect every sliver of beach on Kyushu. As long as the enemy fleet remained at Ikishima, the defense forces would protect the north.

In spite of the weeks of rest, tension among the defense forces remained high. She saw it on faces all around her. The inescapable summer heat and humidity of the eighth month drove her into the breezy shade, where she had erected her own *maku*, a cloth enclosure where her women could withdraw from the eyes of men on the fringe of what had been Aoka village.

The army's idleness was not always a boon. One night two Shimazu warriors had tried to sneak into one of the women's tents. The warrior women promptly subdued them. The following day, the men had been allowed to cut open their bellies.

The sound of an approaching horse emerged from the cicadas' drone.

Tsunetomo's voice rose above the tents and enclosure walls. "My lady wife!" The urgency in his voice roused her instantly.

She hurried outside to meet him. "What news, Husband?"

Astride his horse, he was fully armored, his face dark and grim. "A second barbarian fleet! They attack Takashima!"

The island of Takashima lay in Imari Bay, some fifteen *ri* west of Hakata Bay. Imari Bay's shoreline was less hospitable to a mass landing than Hakata, but Takashima would be an even closer toehold than Ikishima from which to strike. Helplessness splashed through her. How could they hope to drive off an enemy of such magnitude?

She moved to Tsunetomo's stirrup and clutched his thigh, gazing up into his handsome face. Tsunemori's death had carved the lines in his face even deeper. She hardly saw her husband nowadays. The imminence of battle and death filled their thoughts and pulled them away toward their respective duties. They had not lain together as husband and wife since leaving home.

He reached down and stroked her cheek with his callused fingers. His eyes softened for just a moment. Then he said, "It is two days' ride to Imari Bay, four days on foot. The cavalry will march ahead. We leave within the hour."

* * *

Yasutoki watched the Otomo cavalry ride west, joining columns of other clans hurrying to reinforce the defense forces at Takashima. The *ashigaru* spearmen of several lords would choke the roads behind the cavalry, minus several thousand men left to defend Hakata Bay and Shiga.

He had no intention of obeying Tsunetomo's orders to remain here and continue to organize the defense supplies. This battle might decide the war, and Yasutoki intended to help decide it. He did not dare reveal himself to Tsunetomo, however. Such insubordination at a time like this would likely warrant execution, or banishment at the very least.

Would he have to kill Tsunetomo at an opportune moment? Would such a move sufficiently disarray the Otomo forces?

A second invasion fleet was a stroke of genius on the part of the Great Khan and his generals. However, why it had not struck simultaneously with the first fleet, Yasutoki could not imagine. The defense forces could not have withstood two concurrent attacks.

He would leave his servants behind, don peasant's clothes, and travel with the cavalry baggage train. The servants of the baggage train would not question his presence riding with them.

With so many men killed, finding an unattended horse was easy. He would have to move quickly, however, or be stuck behind endless columns of peasant spearmen.

On the road to Takashima, Ken'ishi was back in full armor for the first time since the battle on the spit. The rent in his *do-maru* had been repaired.

Far ahead in the vanguard rode Tsunetomo and Kazuko with her Scarlet Dragons. Ken'ishi found himself with excuses to ride near the rear of the column. His feelings were too mercurial lately to trust himself for long in her presence, and she seemed content to keep him at a distance. Except that every night when he lay down to sleep, she was back in his thoughts. Some days those thoughts were pleasant.

The men around him had not stopped staring since his wound had healed. If they whispered about him, it was not within his hearing.

Once, however, he did hear a man say, "Maybe so, but he's on *our* side."

Even Michizane and Ushihara, while cordial toward him, kept their distance now.

He understood. It was natural. Even he felt it. He was different from them now. On many days since the battle on Shiga spit, his heart ached for what he had lost since coming down from Kiyomizu. The tendrils around his scar were spreading again. How long before he lost himself completely, he did not know, but it was inevitable unless the barbarians gave up their invasion soon. Some days, he did not care. On those days, he simply wanted the gods to place the entire barbarian horde before him so that Silver Crane could scythe them down like a rice harvest and soak the earth with their blood.

He remembered little of the battle of the spit except the rapture of it, not unlike the time he had sampled Shirohige's lotus. The warmth showering him in a waterfall of blood, and the scent of raw meat filling his nostrils.

When he caught himself thinking such thoughts, he took a deep breath and meditated. He had learned to do it even on horseback, allowing Storm to keep up with the rest of the column on his own.

A voice riding alongside roused him from such a meditation. "Sleeping already, old sot?"

Ken'ishi jerked awake.

The man riding beside him was thick-bodied, beady-eyed, jowled, but clad in a full suit of antique-looking *o-yoroi*.

"Hage?" Ken'ishi asked.

The man winked at him, a younger version of the old fellow Ken'ishi had first met in the forest near Aoka village.

"What are you doing here?" Ken'ishi said.

"Same thing you're doing here. Protecting my home."

"But—"

"But-but, tut-tut. I am a creature of surprises."

Ken'ishi glanced at the men around them. The column trotted two abreast down the road toward Imari Bay. None of the men before or behind appeared to be listening.

"Don't worry, old sot. They think we're talking about the weather. A few other *tanuki* are mixed in here. Even some foxes. We're not utterly without care about what happens in the human world. Especially when our entire way of life might change. Have you seen the furs those barbarians wear? The last thing I want is to become a hat. Try to get over your surprise so we can have a two-way conversation."

Ken'ishi finally smiled. "I'm happy you're here, Hage." How long had it been since he smiled?

"I'm not. I've a feeling this is going to make the slaughter at Dan-no-Ura look like children at play."

"You were at Dan-no-Ura?"

"I've been many places. Now listen, old sot. You're starting to worry me. I'm happy you're not dead from your wound. But...you smell bad."

"I haven't bathed in weeks." Aside from a quick dip in the sea.

"That's not what I meant. You don't smell like unwashed human. You smell like unwashed...something else."

Ken'ishi took a deep breath. "I know."

Hage's gaze held upon Ken'ishi for a long time.

"I am still myself," Ken'ishi said.

"I'm unsure that's desirable. You would be much better off if you were someone else."

The double-edge of Hage's words rattled around in Ken'ishi's thoughts for a moment, until he caught the twinkle in Hage's eye. Then he laughed.

They rode together in companionable silence for a while. Then Ken'ishi realized what a comfort Hage's presence was. Then he realized that his only true friend in the world was a *tanuki*. Then he laughed again. It felt good to laugh.

Ken'ishi heard the battle before he saw it. It was late afternoon when the distant crackle of the enemy thunder-crash bombs echoed over forests and hills. Tsunetomo's cavalry was still a *ri* distant.

When they finally rounded the skirt of a forested hill, they came upon a pitched battle raging across a patchwork of rice fields, the only flat places available in a valley between forested mountains. The valley stretched down toward the rocky coastline of Imari Bay. Hundreds of ships choked the bay, but not floating separately. The entire fleet had been lashed together, hull to hull, in lines and blocks forming great floating walls. Beyond these walls, the dark hulk of the island of Takashima lay like a smoking wreck. Dozens of plumes of black smoke rose from the island, smudging the clear, blue sky.

From this elevated vantage point, Ken'ishi could see the wreckage of small boats littering the sea between the lashed ships and the shore—the remains of hundreds of defense boats. No enemy ships burned, but instead pounded the shore with thunder-crash bombs.

The tactic that had saved Hakata Bay did not work when the enemy ships were bound together to create an immense floating platform, where the high bows and sterns were the only point of attack and men could move freely from ship to ship to repulse boarders. One look at the profusion of wreckage made Ken'ishi doubt that many of the defense boats remained in Imari Bay.

On the distant beach, ships disgorged wave after wave of troops.

Orders rippled down Tsunetomo's column to form ranks. Drums thundered and conch horns blared.

Between the cavalry reinforcements and the shore, lines of spearmen and archers faced close-packed lines of Sung infantry. Beyond those, masses of Mongol horsebowmen poured swarms of arrows into the defenders. Bodies littered the battlefield in all directions.

Tsunetomo marshaled all of his cavalry, some two hundred warriors on horseback, holding his iron war fan high. Upon it, the writhing red dragon of his house encompassed the apricot blossoms of the Otomo clan.

The column deployed from the road, several clans' worth of cavalry fanning out into large units, and together they marched closer to the battle. The muddy rice fields sucked at their horses' hooves, an entire valley's crop trampled.

Hage rode alongside Ken'ishi. "Let's stick together, eh, old sot? We've made a fine team before."

Ken'ishi smiled and nodded, his breast filling with joy and anticipation of battle. Silver Crane thrummed at his hip.

"But if you ever grab my tail again," Hage said, "I'll turn you into a toad."

"I saved your life then."

"It was undignified!"

"Vow never to turn me into a woman again, and we shall be even."

Hage laughed, eyes sparkling. In his antique-style armor, wearing a *tachi* of even older style than Silver Crane, he looked like a warrior from a long-ago century.

Crossing the valley toward the battle took longer than Ken'ishi expected. The horses sank to their knees in the soft mud. The terrain would hamper any full-out charge. Only two narrow roads afforded easy approach to the battle, too narrow for the cavalry to make an effective mounted assault.

The rear defending units spotted the newcomers' arrival, and a cry of jubilation echoed through the valley. Drums pounded and horns blasted out with renewed vigor.

The too-familiar stench of battle and death wafted toward Ken'ishi, even two hundred paces from the fighting.

Silver Crane's thirst crawled into Ken'ishi's belly and coiled there. His breast tingled with pleasure, like warm, sensuous fingers stroking him, trailing down to his groin.

The force of Mongol horsemen crashed into the left flank of spearmen. Even slowed by the mud, they plowed into the *ashigaru* like an axe, splitting them, pummeling them under the muck. In moments, that flank would crumble.

"There!" Tsunetomo roared, pointing with his fan. The Otomo cavalry surged toward the collapsing flank.

The Scarlet Dragons swung wide. Ken'ishi knew this maneuver. They would use the Mongols' own tactics against them, harrying the corners of the enemy unit with arrows, then charging in with *naginata* if the opportunity presented. The Mongols would not dare swing to attack the Dragons with a mass of heavier cavalry bearing down on them.

The mud made keeping ranks difficult. Their front grew ragged as they approached the rear of the collapsing block of *ashigaru*.

At Ken'ishi's side, Silver Crane began to sing with joy, the music of clashing blades, the rhythm of a thousand heartbeats pounding as one. This rhythm seeped into him, drawing his own heart into this cadence.

Now was the time for arrows, and he joined his comrades in emptying his quiver at the Mongol horsemen, even as the spearmen were ground to bits under hooves and swords.

But the appearance of Tsunetomo's cavalry was too little too late. The courage drained from the nearby *ashigaru,* and they began to fall back.

Faces ablaze with bloodlust and victory, the Mongols crushed the last of the spearmen into the mud and charged toward Ken'ishi and Tsunetomo's cavalry. Ken'ishi hurriedly slung his bow, drew Silver Crane, and aligned Storm to meet them. The rest of the men dressed their ranks and moved toward the enemy horsemen.

Then with a roar from Tsunetomo, they charged forward.

Ken'ishi's vision became a narrow tunnel, and at the end of it, a single enemy warrior snarled at him. His sword arm tingled with Silver Crane's thirst and with power. Storm's hooves slurped through the mud, and he huffed with the effort, lurching with each step.

The two units crashed together with far less force than if the field had been dry, more like a slow melding of lines and combatants. Screams and war cries filled the air like thousands of battles before and after. Ken'ishi's first adversary was driven backward off the saddle by Silver Crane's powerful, one-armed thrust.

As Silver Crane began to bite and sting, to sever and hew, its voice rose in his mind. *I am the Way to power, unto the end of the world!* Its voice seemed to drown the screams of the dying or swallow them like elixir.

The silver threads of destiny coalesced in his vision, glimmering into the expanse of future and distance in an infinitely complex weave, through the men struggling for their own futures, through the earth, into the sky, through wisps of cloud. The intricate pattern of it all formed in Ken'ishi's mind.

And then, he saw it all.

The defenders would lose this battle.

The Mongols would gain a foothold on Kyushu, here on the shore of Imari Bay, and their sheer numbers would sweep the defenders before them. From here, they would crush Hakata and overrun Dazaifu.

The barbarians would subjugate Kyushu, and from there launch attacks on Honshu, working their way east, *ri* by *ri*, until the capital, and finally the *bakufu* in Kamakura, knelt at the Great Khan's throne.

The throne of skulls Ken'ishi had seen once in a vision.

Tsunetomo would die, spitted on a Sung halberd.

Ken'ishi would die, pierced by a hundred arrows.

Kazuko would die, raped to death by a thousand leering barbarians.

No.

With a fist, he seized a handful of threads, invisible to everyone else, and tore them asunder.

A thunderclap echoed across the battlefield that was not from a bomb.

The man takes his destiny in his fist and shakes it at the gods.

Every muscle in his body trembled with power, filled to bursting with the excess of it.

The Mongols fell before him like dogs before an enraged boar, spilling blood and entrails in every direction.

All around him, Tsunetomo and his comrades fought and struggled, hand-to-hand, face-to-face, shoulder-to-shoulder with *tanuki* and foxes they thought were men. The *tanuki* fought with tenacious strength, and the foxes with deceptive dexterity. In the clouds of silver filaments, Ken'ishi knew them all.

Silver Crane drank and drank and drank.

And its power grew and grew and grew.

Ken'ishi seized another fistful of threads, twisted and wrenched, and the world tore open in a deafening fusillade of thunder and blinding light.

The sky darkened. The cottony wisps of cloud turned to smoke-like smudges, thickening, coalescing.

But no matter how many Mongols and Sung he laid low around him, more surged up from the rear.

A cry of alarm vaguely registered in his mind.

He shook an enemy from the tip of his blade and pulled his awareness back from the abyss of slaughter. Across the field, another mass of perhaps fifty Mongol horsemen swung toward the Scarlet Dragons, driving a wedge between the Dragons and the rest of Tsunetomo's forces, a wedge that spilled out wider until there was no path for the women to reconnect with their comrades. Several women already lay motionless in the mud, bristling with arrows.

Kazuko's *naginata* flashed in the graying light, pointing toward a hill.

At the base of the hill, a red-painted *torii* arch stood among ancient trees, beyond which stone steps climbed into the foliage out of sight. A shrine lay at the top of the hill.

Even from this distance, Ken'ishi could see that Kazuko knew she was cut off. Her only options were to retreat or be annihilated. But if she retreated, her unit would be pincushioned with arrows before they reached the shelter of the forested shrine hill.

With the hundreds of enemy troops between Ken'ishi and her, he would only be able to watch it happen.

"The dragon is a creature with the ultimate positive energy, so much so that it can fly in the sky without wings. Yet it usually remains curled up in supremely still waters. This is how a man with a heart of true martial courage constantly cultivates himself."
—*Kumazawa Banzan*

Barely in time, Kazuko saw the second mass of Mongol horsemen pounding across the fields toward her, loosing storms of arrows as they came. Two of her women went down, then two more. The power of the short, recurved Mongol bows could punch an arrow through a *do-maru*.

The second unit of enemy horsemen filled the gap between the Scarlet Dragons and Tsunetomo's heavy cavalry, expanding like a wedge, pushing the Dragons farther away from their comrades, threatening to envelop and destroy them. The only direction to go was away.

The arrows kept coming. She saw Mongol bowmen clutching three arrows in their drawing hands, firing in quick succession with only a heartbeat between each shot.

She had to get her women under cover. They would be cut to

pieces. To die now would be a dog's death.

With her *naginata* waving high, she pointed toward a shrine hill perhaps four hundred paces away. "Fall back!"

The women obeyed her without question, turned, and spurred away. Only twenty of her Dragons remained. But first she had to move faster. She guided her mare up onto a dike between rice fields, where the ground was solid. The horses were mud from hoof to hock, but the moment they climbed onto the dike's footpath, they leaped to greater speed. She spurred her horse toward the hill. Arrows disappeared into the mud around her. The mare's eyes shone wide, and Kazuko leaped her over irrigation canals and gates. They quickly left their pursuers behind, except for a few who followed onto the dikes. Without their overwhelming numbers, individual Mongol riders, savage as they were, posed far less threat than a massed onslaught.

A Scarlet Dragon's horse screamed in pain and tumbled off the dike into the mud with several arrows in its back and rider.

Kazuko spurred her mount to greater speed. The others had formed a single-file line behind her.

The pursuers fanned out along several other dikes to prevent her from circling back toward Tsunetomo's heavy cavalry. Arrows sliced toward the Dragons from several directions now.

Two more women went down, each loss a stab in Kazuko's heart. She had to get them out of range. Three more. They were down to fifteen.

And still the enemy came, harrying them with arrows.

In the distance, the first mass of barbarian horsemen still held Tsunetomo's heavy cavalry engaged.

The Dragons were on their own.

They were twelve when they finally emerged from the maze of rice field paths and galloped toward the bright-red *torii* arch at the base of the hill. She hoped the *kami* would forgive her for bringing death to their doorstep.

From the *torii,* stone steps made a path straight up the hillside. In the distance, the shadowed red of another *torii* sat at the summit of the steps.

The pursuers paused fifty paces away and loosed another swarm of deadly shafts. Their aim was lethal. Five more of her Dragons or their horses went down. Some were only wounded, but the pursuers would make quick work of them. Yuko shoved herself from under her fallen horse, snatched up her *naginata,* and braced herself to face the enemy.

"Get under the trees!" Kazuko called.

But Yuko twirled her weapon in defiance of the enemy. "Up the hill, my lady!"

Within heartbeats, the Mongols fell upon her. She took one out of the saddle with a perfectly timed swipe that split his chest like a melon, then another.

Kazuko's quiver was empty.

Ten paces away from Yuko, a Mongol drew his bow and took aim.

Yuko saw it coming, with only a moment's resignation on her face before the arrow shot through her skull.

The remaining handful of Dragons spurred their mounts up the steps. Two more women screamed and fell at the foot of the steps. The clatter of hooves echoed in the tunnel of lush greenery that smelled moist and alive. The canopy shielded them from further arrows.

Five horsemen came into view in the mouth of the *torii.* Two of the women who still had arrows fired downward, taking one of the enemy out of the saddle.

The horsemen leaped the bodies lying in the *torii* and charged up the steps, two abreast, eyes gleaming with savage anticipation.

Kazuko's horse stumbled, almost lurching her out of the saddle.

It was then she saw the arrow protruding from its hindquarters.

With a nicker of pain and exhaustion, the mare's rear leg buckled. Kazuko leaped off before the horse could fall and crush her. The mare stumbled into the greenery and fell. Kazuko spun her *naginata* and faced the oncoming foes.

Firing arrows uphill under the low-hanging canopy was difficult, but the barbarians' marksmanship sent another of her women crashing onto steps with an arrow through the eye. The riderless horse plunged off the steps into the woods, crashing through the underbrush as it went.

Up and up Kazuko and her last two mounted women climbed; up and up the four Mongols pursued.

"To the top!" Kazuko shouted. They would fight from the level ground above. The advantages of a higher position and the length of their polearms might be enough. She plunged up the steps.

Reiko, a stocky, square-shouldered woman of nineteen, and Yukie, a twenty-eight-year-old widow of the previous invasion, spurred up after her, then spun atop the steps to face the oncoming enemies under another *torii*.

The Mongol ponies whinnied and kept coming.

Reiko said, "It has been an honor, Lady."

The two mounted women traded glances, squared their mounts, and plunged back down toward the enemy.

Their charge sent two Mongol ponies and riders sprawling. *Naginata* flashed and slashed. One of the mounted men tumbled away, missing half his face.

The last man hopped up to plant both feet in his saddle and then launched himself at Reiko. His powerful swing caught her in the shoulder guard and knocked her sideways out of the saddle. He plowed into the horse, and the horse tripped over Reiko, and all three went down in a grinding tangle of panicked mare.

One of the unhorsed men leaped out of the bushes and stabbed Yukie through the side of her *do-maru*. She grunted in pain, but reined back, pulling herself off his sword point, then splitting his skull with the last of her ebbing strength.

The horse knocked over by the Mongol's leap thrashed back onto his feet, cut and bloodied. Both the Mongol and Reiko lay broken and twitching against the steps.

Clutching her side, Yukie turned her horse back up the steps and gave Kazuko a wan smile.

Then the last Mongol staggered out of bushes to Yukie's left and plunged his sword into her thigh. The startled horse leaped aside, throwing off Yukie's feeble return stroke.

Kazuko ran back down, only twenty steps from them. The Mongol sword split the head of Yukie's horse, and it flopped onto its side. The side of Yukie's head slammed against the edge of a step and her face went slack, eyes staring.

Kazuko stopped five steps away.

The Mongol yanked his sword out of the horse's head, then spun on her, his face a vicious sneer. He looked her up and down and licked his lips, said something that sounded like a taunt in his own tongue. In his eyes, she saw all the things he would do to her, all the things he would cheer his fellows to do.

She leaped forward with a shrill *kiai*, dredging all the power she could muster. He raised his sword to block her blow. The *naginata* blade severed his wrist and, through armor and all, cleft him diagonally from shoulder to hip.

Gasping for breath in the sudden silence, she blinked and steadied herself, then assessed her plight.

All the horses were dead, fled, or injured beyond help. Yukie and Reiko were dead. The rest of her Dragons lay scattered between here and the ongoing battle below. The forest muffled the din of battle. Doubtless the rest of these Mongols waited at the bottom of the hill.

Alone, she had no way to reach friendly lines. She could not see whether Tsunetomo's army held the field or lay crushed and broken under the enemy's relentless onslaught. And night was falling.

"The courage of bloodlust makes no distinction between reason and force, justice and injustice. It is nothing but ferocity, overcoming others, and not being afraid of anything. Like the ferocity of tigers and wolves, therefore, it can perversely impede the human path. Being brave and having no fear resemble the courage of humanity  and justice, but having no discrimination between reason and force, justice and injustice, merely inclined to bloodlust, the behavior of tigers and wolves is very lowly. The ones with status start rebellions, the poor ones become bandits."

—*Nakae Toju*

Ken'ishi gulped dipper after dipper from the bucket of water. He thanked the woman with the bucket and marveled for a moment at the bravery of the women in the supply train. If the defenders fell, the women would get the worse of it in barbarian hands.

With the fall of darkness, the armies had withdrawn.

The infantry reinforcements were two days behind, and after two days of riding and a day of battle, the horses were spent. The enemy controlled the valley. The defense forces had been pushed back into the hills but controlled the roads out of the valley. Fortunately, enough fresh troops had occupied the area that the defenders had not been routed.

On a tree-covered hilltop, Ken'ishi and Tsunetomo gazed across the valley toward the shrine hill. Between their position and the shrine lay hundreds of enemy cookfires, clustered on the dikes between rice fields. Clouds gathered against the stars, thickening. A steady breeze ruffled the branches and leaves.

"We cannot reach her," Tsunetomo said.

Ken'ishi had seen the handful of Scarlet Dragons disappear up the shrine hill. He had seen the enemy horsemen pursue.

He had not seen the horsemen come back down. But in the chaos of battle, he could not be sure of the outcome.

"I'll go, Lord," Ken'ishi said. "I shall find her and bring her back to you." Both of them knew Tsunetomo could not go after her. Tsunetomo dared not leave his troops. His death would cut the heart out of them, and it was the Otomo troops who had prevented disaster today.

Tsunetomo turned to him. "She is a warrior. She may well be dead already. Am I to lose you, too?"

"I am only one man."

"One man who fights like a thousand."

"Then no one will be able to stand against me in the dark. Alive or dead, I will bring her back. If she's alive, she will boost our men's courage."

For several long moments, Tsunetomo gazed out over the sea of enemies. In the silence, Ken'ishi watched the emotions—too many to sort—crossing Tsunetomo's face.

Hands clasped behind his back, Tsunetomo said, "Very well, Captain."

Ken'ishi bowed and left him there.

He spotted Hage sitting with several other disguised *tanuki* around a campfire.

The group of them watched him approach, some with amusement, some with wonder, some with fear.

He pointed at Hage. "You, come with me."

Hage raised an eyebrow. "Now, won't this be interesting."

Yasutoki walked into the Mongol encampment with his hands in the air. Behind him walked the perimeter guard with a spear pointed at Yasutoki's back. The Mongols chewed their meat and drank their fermented mare's milk and watched him with a mix of suspicion and interest.

The guard brought Yasutoki before a tall, barrel-chested man, enormous for one of his breed, swathed in iron and leather, with long drooping mustaches and flint-hard eyes.

The guard said in the Mongolian tongue, "This man approached me in the dark. He spoke in Chinese. He says he is a servant of the Great Khan. He says he wants to speak to a commander."

It was strange for Yasutoki, after all these years, to hear so much of the barbarian tongue. He spoke it as best he could recall after so long. "Forgive, Great Leader. Skill with Chinese better."

The commander spoke in Jin Chinese. "Then in Chinese you will tell me why I should not kill you as a spy."

Yasutoki bowed and told the story of how he had visited the lands of the Golden Horde as a boy with his father, how his father had met Khubilai Khan soon after he claimed the title of Khan of Khans after his uncle Ogedei. Yasutoki had been so impressed by the strength and majesty of the Great Khan that he applied himself to learning the Mongol tongue, as well as Jin Chinese. He told of how he had been the Khan's agent during the previous invasion and how he wished to offer his services now.

After so long, he could not be sure that his Chinese would be well understood.

The commander's face was implacable, shrewd, and ruthless. "I am Batu, *zuun* of this hundred."

Yasutoki bowed. "You may call me Green Tiger."

Batu laughed. "A tiger is sick?"

The men around him laughed.

Yasutoki maintained his composure. "Today there was a great warrior. He killed many of your men. He fought with only a sword."

Batu's face darkened. "I know this man. Killing him will be a great victory. And a great pity that such a warrior must be cut down."

"I have come to give him to you."

Batu's eyes narrowed.

"Today, there was a group of women warriors," Yasutoki said. "Some of your men chased them up that hill across the valley."

Batu grunted to continue.

"The leader of that group is the wife of one of the lords who face you. Her husband is among the most powerful lords. Kill his wife, and his spirit will be weakened. The great warrior is going alone to bring her back."

"We searched that hill. No one up there still lives."

"Nevertheless, the great warrior is going alone, and on foot. He will be an easy target. And if the lord's wife still lives, you will have her as well. She is renowned for her beauty." Kazuko and whatever remained of her silly women warriors could have evaded a search. "But you must hurry, or they will escape you."

Batu wet his lips. "Very well. But you are coming along. If you lie, you will be the first to die."

Yasutoki bowed low. "Of course, *Zuun* Batu. I am at your service."

"You won't have to hold on to me this time to maintain the shape," Hage said, in *tanuki* form, balanced atop two enormous, furry melons. "I have been storing up my power. My jewel sack is full to bursting, and the *kami* here are thick as lice on a boar. They seem to be gathering."

"I have felt them," Ken'ishi said.

Ken'ishi and Hage had paused in the shadows away from camp, where he told Hage his plan.

Hage said, "With this much power in the air, I will be able to change her, too, and we'll all three scamper back here without a scratch."

"Let's waste no more time," Ken'ishi said.

With a disquieting familiarity, Ken'ishi shrank into the shape of a *tanuki.* The world around him was suddenly much larger.

In the shape of *tanuki,* they crossed the valley toward the shrine hill, giving the enemy encampment the widest possible berth. The night darkened as they slunk along the dikes, concealed among the trampled rice stalks.

Hage paused to sniff the air. "This valley is filled with the stench of humans and horses."

With such short legs, the distance to the shrine hill looked so much farther. Nevertheless, their small size and natural stealth allowed them great speed.

At about midnight they paused in the grass near the final dike. Between them and the *torii* lay open ground, which was littered with dead horses and dead women. The barbarians had taken their dead comrades away.

The breeze ruffled the fur on Ken'ishi's back, thick with the smell of blood and mud from behind them. The *kami* roared in chorus, but there were so many he could not discern if they were warning him of danger. The nearest enemy encampment lay some four hundred paces distant.

But Kazuko was alive and atop that hill.

"Come!" Ken'ishi said.

The two *tanuki* slunk out of the grass and darted for the shadows of the underbrush at the foot of the hill. In his zeal, Ken'ishi surged ahead.

"Wait, Ken'ishi!" Hage called. "Something is wrong!"

An arrow shot out of the darkness, hissed past Ken'ishi's ear so close the fletching brushed him.

The arrow speared Hage and sent him tumbling like an ill-formed ball. The *tanuki* emitted a bloodcurdling, hissing-squeal.

"Hage!" Ken'ishi's voice was high and childlike.

Ahead, he heard a quiet snickering of congratulation from the bushes in a tongue he did not know. They were shooting at the *tanuki* for sport, or perhaps for food. They were, after all, an army on campaign, and food could be hard to find.

More arrows shot toward him, as fat as bamboo stalks to his *tanuki* eyes.

He charged across the open ground, still on all fours, zig-zagging around more arrows, rage boiling up in him, turning the night crimson in his vision, boiling away the magic that Hage had imbued in him. By the time he reached the base of the hill, he wore the shape of a man again, and Silver Crane was in his hand.

The entire forest at the base of the hill began to move. Storms of arrows poured toward him. Silver Crane wove an intricate dance of glimmering steel that sliced and deflected the swarm of arrows as they came. Then he leaped upon the nearest foe to come out of the bushes and cleaved him from crown to crotch with a single blow. His roar of fury echoed like the call of a beast against the hillside.

Look to your soul, samurai, echoed behind the wrath in his mind, but Silver Crane reveled in its thirst.

In a trice, they surrounded him, and just as quickly he descended once again into the blood-hazed fugue of the afternoon. His entire being became steel, with a puppet of muscle and bone to wield it. His edge sliced lives away in great frothing buckets of gore.

He seized fistfuls of destiny threads again and wrenched them for all he was worth.

The clouds in the sky coalesced. The stars disappeared.

The tenacity of his foes kept them coming. Their swords licked and hacked. All of them wanted to be the man to bring down this invincible enemy. Such a man could become a *tumen,* one who commanded ten thousand. Ken'ishi could smell their anticipation of the kill. Surely one man could not stand against a hundred battle-hardened warriors and prevail. Every one of them believed it.

Ken'ishi did not see the kills anymore. All was a crimson haze. He did not feel his wounds. But instead of blood, starlight glow seeped from the wounds until they closed up again.

He did not tire.

He did not stop.

Kill them all.

"Kill them all," he said, over and over.

Black clouds boiled in the sky.

A slash of lightning sundered the night.

Wind rose, stiff and wet and insistent.

The story in the threads of destiny said that he could not have stood against this many men, no matter what his prowess. These men were to have lived through this day, some of them to have fathered children. Except that their threads had now been severed. Silver Crane's tiny manipulations had given way to an outright re-weaving of the fabric of fate.

He smote them and they flew back into their own throng, each taste of blood feeding the sword's power.

And then there was only one man left, tall and thick-muscled, with thicker armor than the other men, with long, drooping mustaches.

A sudden tumult of wind howled across the field, making both men stumble for a moment to regain their balance. Fat droplets of rain pattered against the earth.

Ken'ishi and the Mongol rushed at each other, traded tremendous blows, drew near and gazed into each other's eyes, blades crossed between them.

Ken'ishi kicked him in the knee and felt it snap under his heel. The Mongol commander grunted with pain as his leg collapsed. A swipe of Silver Crane sent the Mongol's sword hand spinning away.

He did not need the quiet purity of the Void anymore. He had all the power he could imagine. The world itself lay at his feet.

He took the commander's head in a single blow.

The burgeoning rain pattered into the lakes of blood around him, began to wash away the blood covering him. The earth would drink it all.

The forest hissed in the howling wind.

In the distance, the enemy army roused itself, but it was not coming toward him. The sudden storm threw them into an uproar.

Then he could hear his heartbeat again, feel his breathing, feel the rain on his face. His mouth was full of death.

"Hage!" he called.

The skies opened up and poured rain.

He leaped over dozens of bodies on his way to where he thought Hage had fallen, but found no sign of the *tanuki* anywhere. He called again and again, but the only reply was the wind.

Then he looked toward the top of the hill, silhouetted against spatters of lightning.

I scream as you bite
My nipples, and orgasm
Drains my body, as if I
Had been cut in two.
—*The Love Poems of Marichiko*

The massive camphor tree in which Kazuko sat in a high crook swayed with the growing breath of the wind. Warm rain lashed her face, almost like the spray of blood. The ancient tree stood sentinel over the shrine below. The *torii* atop the steps opened into a flat clearing before a rock face, which had been pried open by the unstoppable growth of the great tree, the wood almost flowing around the stone. A thick rope of rice straw encircled the base of the tree, and she had prayed to the *kami* of this mountain to protect her.

Earlier, a scout party of Mongols had searched the hilltop. The closeness of the rock face had allowed her to scurry up the tree and hide among the thick boughs. Fortunately, the scouts had not thought to search the canopy. She still clutched her *naginata* across her knees.

Across the stony glade, the shrine itself sat with its *shide* papers, disintegrating in the rain, and its bright red bell rope. She considered climbing down to take shelter under the eaves, but the wind would drive the rain underneath to keep soaking her. And the Mongols might return. She had just heard a frightful clamor of battle and slaughter below.

A figure appeared under the *torii*. A man in armor, calling her name.

In an instant she recognized him. "Ken'ishi!"

His gaze swung upward, and a thrill of joy shot through her.

"Kazuko, is it you?" he called.

She called his name again and shimmied down the tree as fast as she could. He put his sword away and ran toward the tree.

They reached its base together, and he threw his arms around her so tight she could not breathe. The armor between them was stiff and sodden.

But she did not care.

He was here, and she would live.

Giddy with joy, she laughed and drew back from him. In the lightning, she could see the streaks on his face that must have been blood.

Seeing him like that, ensanguined, his eyes glimmering with heat, touched her in a way she was not ready to name.

Her *menpo* was long gone, and she had no veil.

His finger traced the scar, and his touch sent fire through the numbness of her cheek, deep into her veins where it throbbed with a life of its own.

Her breath caught.

Their eyes met.

The only way she could think to tear her gaze away was to hug him close again and bury her face in his neck.

Instantly she remembered the smell of him. It was still there, masked by the stench of blood and battle and death, but still there. She noticed her hands trying to squeeze him against her, but the armor stymied her.

She pulled away.

His hands fell to his sides, clenched.

She said, "What of the enemy?"

"They were waiting below, like they knew I was coming." He gazed up into the roiling clouds. "The storm..." His voice trailed off, as if he sensed something she could not. "They won't come again."

He sank to his knees, as if all his strength had drained way.

"Ken'ishi! What is it? Are you wounded?"

"I...was. Not now." He looked up into her eyes, and they were both young again, and no one existed in the world but them. "I'm so tired."

"Let me help you." She knelt before him and reached to unlace his armor.

"No, the enemy—"

"If they find us here, let them kill us. There will be no more armor here, in this place."

He seemed to relax more with each piece she removed: his shoulder guards, his *do-maru*, his thigh guards, his forearm and shin plates, until all he wore were a soaked, bloodstained robe and trousers.

His shoulders shuddered with his breath. His chin fell to his chest. His hands fell palm up against his thighs.

The continuing flickers of lightning illuminated his arms and face. When had he gotten so many scars? They all looked healed, but she could not conceive how he had gotten so many.

Still so much blood on him.

Rainwater sluiced down the rock face, gushing outward in a cascade not far away, splashing into a natural channel in the rock.

She took his hands and helped him to his feet. He roused from some inner torpor then, as if remembering she was there.

He began untying her armor as well, and she helped him. Her heart swelled with each piece that clattered to the earth. Soon she was left in only a robe and trousers as well.

She took his hand and led him toward the small waterfall. They shed their sandals as they walked.

She guided him under the water. Beneath the waterfall was a natural depression in the stone, forming an ankle-deep pool. The waterfall was warm, and even with the thundering of her heart, she felt the *kami* pouring over him. Blood ran from his hair in dark streaks, darkening the pool around him. Untying his obi, she let his robe fall open, baring his hard-muscled chest and the livid scar on his left breast, surrounded by what looked like a birthmark she did not remember. And so many more scars. She wanted to kiss each one of them.

His voice was a croak. "All for you."

He let her peel off his torn, stained robe. The dried blood of untold foes was caked thick under his clothes. With her gentlest touch, she washed it from him while he stood weaving as if about to collapse at any moment, running her fingers through his hair, over his hard shoulders, across his back, across his breast. He trembled under her touch. The front of his trousers stood out before him. She untied his *obi*, and his trousers fell around his ankles, leaving only a strained loincloth to cover him. She gently lifted each of his feet from the trousers, then she washed the blood from his thighs, from his calves, feeling the heat building under his skin.

The heat bloomed within her as well. Each droplet of rain across her breasts was a shock, her nipples exquisitely erect, her thighs hot and sensitive.

She could not see his downcast face.

His voice was ragged. "We...we..."

She touched the deep scar on his breast, over his heart. Streaks of stubborn crimson surrounded it, and would not be washed away.

He seized both of her wrists.

She gasped at his strength, but his grip relaxed before hurting her.

His palms went to her shoulders, slid down her arms. Then his hands dropped to her *obi* and untied it.

She shrugged out of her robe, then her under-robe, until she stood naked to the waist, her breaths short and quick.

Standing there under his gaze, shrouded in shadow, she had no wish for comforts, no *futon*, no fire, no shelter. Her heart thundered in time with the sky, with a primal need.

His hands fell to her waist, and a brief tug let her trousers slide down over her hips.

They were no longer the man and the woman they had been when last they faced each other this way. Scars crisscrossed their bodies and souls. But suddenly she felt like the virgin of that first night, unsure what would happen next, but knowing without question that it *must*.

She hooked her fingers into his loincloth and pulled it down, then stood and faced him.

He took her face in infinitely gentle hands, hands full of carefully restrained power, and stroked her cheek; and then he kissed her.

A rush of molten fire blazed through her from crown to toenails. Her knees weakened, but he caught her.

The next ripple of lightning revealed a bed of spongy, green moss not far away.

They took each other's hands.

More naked than at any time she could remember, she gently pressed him down onto his back and settled herself atop him, guiding him inside. He convulsed with a gasp beneath her, driving himself deeper. The intensity of his gaze sent heat gushing through her.

She moved on him, fell upon him, kissing him, tumbling into a shrinking point of ecstasy, that place she had not experienced but one night before.

A serenity filled Ken'ishi's face, wonder, joy, as if what they were doing was what they had waited their whole lives for.

When he cried out and bucked and she felt the hot flood inside her, her own pulsing ecstasy exploded as well, shattering her into pieces only the gods could reassemble.

Light stroked the black sky like fingers, and he did not stop. He seized her and rolled on top of her. The mossy earth cushioned her against his driving thrusts, each one sending spasms of pleasure through her. The rain fell into her face, mixing with tears of joy.

But then a strange tension crept through his body. His face turned away from her.

With each thrust he whispered, "No no no no..." in a haunted voice.

Ken'ishi closed his eyes against the appalling images flooding his mind, images the pleasure only blurred. Beneath him, this porcelain goddess, more beautiful to him now than ever, clutched at him and gasped and cried out in waves of pleasure. It was as if he were one with Amaterasu, the Sun Goddess herself, shining in heaven, and only her light kept him from drowning in shadow.

Terrible thoughts, slaughter and drowning and trackless rivers of blood, chewed and writhed at the edges of his awareness until the only way to escape them was to lose himself in the bliss of Kazuko's body.

She clutched at him with her deepest core, seized his hips with both hands, and pulled him deeper.

When he could not bear to gaze upon her beauty, she took his face in her hands and forced him to look, as if she knew his anguish, for the anguish had been hers as well. She understood his pain, as no one ever had. And she forgave him for all of it.

She pulled him down close to her, clawing at his back until he could bury his face in her hair, in the scent of her neck, and her warm lips kissed his face with tenderness he had never known existed.

Her cries drove him harder, until a tsunami of ecstasy exploded out of him again.

And in the aftermath, as he subsided and rolled off her onto the wet, spongy moss, she pulled him close again in the rain and stroked his hair, whispering soothing things he would not remember.

When the afterglow faded into the tumult of the storm, they found a rock outcropping that kept off most of the rain and wind, and piled their clothes there for comfort, and huddled together for warmth. They made love again, this time for the sheer, exuberant pleasure of it.

Neither of them spoke. Neither knew what to say.

In the early morning, they made love again, this time languorously, savoring every moment, but with a looming sense of the inevitable, that with the coming of morning, this night of dreams and nightmares would be over.

Then Ken'ishi dressed and armored himself while Kazuko huddled under the rocks with her robes covering her nakedness.

He drank from the cascade of rainwater, relishing the surging caress of the *kami* filling him with their power and wisdom.

And then hearing their warning.

He spun in time to see a figure across the glade, a pale smudge against the foliage. A face painted with shock. A face he knew.

"Yasutoki," he growled with a voice deeper than any man's.

The smudge of face disappeared.

"Stay here!" he said to Kazuko.

With Silver Crane naked in his hand, he charged the foliage where Yasutoki had stood. The criminal would not survive to see the dawn, and his death would save the lives of ten thousand, and perhaps erase a bit of the debt upon Ken'ishi's soul.

Kazuko called after him, but her words were lost in the deluge.

At the edge of the foliage, no sign of Yasutoki remained.

Ken'ishi pelted through the *torii* and down the steps. Something sharp stung his arm. He stopped to pluck out a small blade, a *shuriken*, and tossed it aside. Dizziness washed over him. His limbs turned to lead and sackcloth.

The wound in his arm released a silver glimmer before it sealed like a pair of lips.

In the silver weave of fate, Ken'ishi saw the truth. Yasutoki had brought the Mongols to kill him. Yasutoki had been a traitor all along, in more ways than his double identity as Green Tiger. Even now, he would return to Tsunetomo and tell of the tryst between Ken'ishi and Kazuko, for no other reason than to destroy Tsunetomo's spirit once and for all. Without the spirit of their leader, the Otomo troops would collapse and be swept away like chaff before the Horde.

Down the pitch-black tunnel of slippery stone steps he pounded and stumbled, but he kept his feet, Silver Crane aglimmer with lightning.

He burst through the bottom *torii.*

No sign of Yasutoki.

Nothing moved between Ken'ishi and the rain-hazed distance. The cookfires of friend and foe were extinguished, and the dark mounds of the surrounding hills kept their secrets.

Clustered around the *torii,* however, were the bodies and pieces of the Mongols he had slain.

Suddenly the walls of denial crumbled, and death deluged his mind. The storm—no, a typhoon bigger than the last one—had seized the enemy fleet in its pitiless swells and was even now grinding it to bloody splinters, pounding it with rain and wind. The threads of destiny yanked taut in his imagination, and he saw the entirety of the enemy fleet, more thousands of ships and men than he could count, numbers so large they lost their meaning.

Yet another enemy force had already landed farther west and had been moving east to rendezvous with the army at Takashima, crushing all resistance in its path. Eventually, the defense forces would meet them and the fighting would continue for a while, but without their supply lines, the enemy armies would wither like a tree with its roots severed.

These images blasted through his mind, through the silver weave of his own making.

The ships that had brought them bobbed and struggled against towering waves, only to be crushed under them. The ships lashed together for defense in Imari Bay were being torn apart and pounded into splinters by the very defenses that had preserved them. Hundreds at a time, smashing themselves to flotsam. Thousands of souls— helpless in those ships' holds—cast into the waves, only to drown as they sank to the bottom of the sea where sharks would feast and crabs would gorge upon dead men's eyes and soft, fleshy morsels.

The carnage that had choked Hakata Bay in the aftermath of the last storm would be nothing compared to this. Thousands of dead men would wash ashore for weeks to come across the entire north coast of Kyushu.

The defense forces would scour northern Kyushu and the other coastal islands, catching tens of thousands of stranded invaders in their sweeps. Bereft of supply lines and reinforcements, those men would never see China again.

All these things he had blocked from his awareness by driving himself into this woman he worshiped, losing himself in the softness of her.

Kill them all, Silver Crane had said.

And Ken'ishi had killed them all.

The sword was an endless loop, a bottomless well of destruction and power, gorging itself upon death and feeding its infinite power to its wielder, a circle ever building and tightening until the wielder was ultimately destroyed, like a man trying to grasp at lightning.

All of these men were dying at his wish.

All of this knowledge flooded over him at once.

He could not breathe.

But he was going to lose Yasutoki to the darkness.

Until another thread, one scarred by cruelty and tragedy, appeared from a weave as complex as Ken'ishi's. And just ahead, it intersected Yasutoki's.

The night grew darker and darker until the blackness overtook him.

There goes a beggar
Naked, except for his
  robes
Of Heaven and Earth
                —*Kikaku*

Yasutoki fled through the lashing rain, glancing over his shoulder as he tried to follow the dikes in the dark, stumbling often into the muck of the rice paddies. The world was incomprehensible shadows amid sheets of rain. The downpour drenched his clothes, slowing him down. Mud sucked one of his *zori* free, and he ran on with only one sandal.

The time for intrigue was over. He would find Tsunetomo. Ken'ishi must be destroyed. The two of them could no longer both exist in the same realm. Yasutoki had never flinched from killing a man, had never believed that killing any particular man was beyond his power. Yet when he saw the blazing fury and strength in Ken'ishi's eyes, his bowels had turned to water, and all he could do was flee.

He had never fled in the face of peril before.

It angered him.

Nevertheless, the force of Ken'ishi's pursuit would not allow Yasutoki to turn and face his enemy. This rain had doubtless weakened the poison from his *shuriken,* and his only other weapon was a *tanto*. And in this darkness, he would not be able to see his pursuer, nor could his pursuer see him.

A flash of lightning split the sky wide open, revealing a figure before him, standing on the dike as if waiting for him.

He gasped and skidded to a halt. The after-flicker of the lightning revealed a figure, but it was not Ken'ishi. The build was too slight and the figure wore a conical straw hat.

All he saw in the flash was two piercing eyes peering from under the brim of the hat.

The figure's drenched robe and peasant's trousers clung to womanly curves.

What was a woman doing here? In this weather?

A woman with a wooden staff.

He could hardly hear his own voice through the roar of the rain. "You're looking for me."

The woman remained still.

He flung two *shuriken* at her face, but she remained on the path.

Had she dodged or had he missed? The darkness made him unsure.

She gripped her staff with both hands.

"What do you want?" he shouted.

Between flickers of lightning, she moved.

Suddenly she was upon him.

He fended off a blow to his skull with his left wrist and felt something *crack*.

Then the staff came apart in her grip, and steel flashed from within. He caught the hidden blade on the guard of his dagger. The rasp of steel on steel. He tried to reach for another *shuriken* in his sleeve, but his fingers would not grasp.

The staff swept against his ankle, but he moved with the blow, shifting his weight out of the path of the sweep in a technique he had learned decades before. A moment of astonishment grabbed him that his body still remembered the training of his youth, even as he realized the technique now used against him was just as familiar, and may well have been taught in the same training hall.

A whisper-thin touch across his breast, and the pain an instant later as the blade's edge stroked him like a lover. The front of his robe fell open and blood flowed.

He regained his stance and slashed at her face.

She dodged—barely—and his up-sweeping hand knocked off her straw hat. He tried to glimpse her face, but the darkness and rain obscured her.

"Bah!" he snarled. It did not matter who she was. Someone had sent her to kill him—a rival gang lord, perhaps, and the dancer-like precision of her movements bespoke a long, thorough training.

He kicked at her, but she danced away.

In the distance between them, he managed to fling a *shuriken* at her. He had only one left. The throw had felt good, but the darkness denied his eyes.

His skills were too rusty. He prepared for another flash of lightning; in that moment he would strike—

Agonizing pain exploded deep in his knee. A *shuriken*—his own *shuriken*—protruded from his kneecap. The leg crumpled under him.

And then the lightning flashed, and he saw her face.

He did not need to say her name.

He raised his dagger in defense, a weak, desperate gesture.

Steel licked through the rain, and his severed arm jumped free halfway from his elbow. It splashed into a puddle beside him. He snatched for the dagger with his left hand.

Another *whish* of steel, another jolt of hot, gushing pain. His other arm spun away through the night.

Her fist twisted into his robes and dragged him up to his knees. The *shuriken* ground deeper into his knee joint with pain that stole his breath. His strength gushed from the stumps of his arms.

He stared up into Tiger Lily's face. It had once been so beautiful. But now it was nothing more than a soulless, porcelain mask. Only her eyes lived now, and their sustenance was hatred. In them, he saw every cruelty he had ever enacted upon her, every "correction," every "night of play."

He had indeed trained her too well.

She raised her straight-bladed sword, point down, glimmering with runnels of bloody rain water, and jammed it between his lips, splintering his front teeth, filling his mouth with blood and metal and agony, splitting his tongue, prying his face toward the sky.

And as he screamed around the cold steel, she pressed the point deeper, where it slithered into his throat and went all the way down.

* * *

Kazuko dressed herself, waiting for Ken'ishi to return. She donned her armor and took up her *naginata.*

The last few moments she saw him kept repeating in her mind.

Unmistakably, he had said, "Yasutoki."

But the voice had been like that of Hakamadare.

"Stay here!" he had said.

Had his eye glinted like a red coal as he looked over his shoulder at her?

She thought she had seen someone at the edge of the forest, but she could not be sure it was Yasutoki. His presence here made no sense. Vast, unknown truths lurked beneath all of this, of which she knew none.

She waited for Ken'ishi to come back as the blackness of night faded to dismal gray.

He did not.

The storm lashed the hilltop. Somewhere nearby, a tree branch cracked and fell.

Ken'ishi might need help. She hurried down the hillside, trusting the forest to conceal her from any enemies. From her concealment, she tried to fathom the breathtaking carnage littering the earth at the foot of the hill. Surging sheets of rain drowned visibility beyond a hundred paces. The valley had become a sea of muddy rainwater, broken only by the lines of raised dikes and the bodies of the dead.

She picked her way among the corpses at the foot the hill, looking for him, but they were all barbarians and the scant handful of her Dragons. She wept for her brave women.

How far had Ken'ishi pursued his prey?

Safety must lie to the southeast, where the defense forces were gathered before the storm started. She dared not stay here. But she might become lost without sight of any landmarks.

Even atop the dikes, the mud was deep and the going slow. At times, she felt like she must be walking across the surface of the sea itself. The wind slapped at her like the hand of the gods, driving the rain against her flesh like pellets.

Bodies littered her path. More of her Dragons, a handful of dead Mongols and their ponies.

And then a familiar face.

Yasutoki's dead visage stared up at the sky, rain filling his gaping mouth.

Ken'ishi had caught him. A sliver of justice in a world of suffering.

But where had Ken'ishi gone from there?

She already knew the answer.

She wept again, this time for him, but kept moving.

After what seemed like hours of slogging through the mud and storm, the dark hulks of the southern hills came into view, and she turned toward them.

She wandered like a ghost through abandoned encampments, exhaustion sucking at her limbs. Finally she found the road they had traveled from Hakata. For a *ri* she followed it until she found a village, and there were tents erected in the shelter of trees.

When they took her to Tsunetomo, the astonished joy on his face lit fire to hers, and she embraced him with the most bittersweet happiness.

Something cool and wet touched Ken'ishi's cheek, at once familiar, but so long gone it could only be a dream.

It pressed into him, insistent, nudging him.

A warm, wet tongue licked his cheek, his eye, his forehead, his nose. The scent of a dog's breath came into his nose.

He pried one eye open.

A rust-red snout and little black nose nudged him again. "Get up, fool," said a voice Ken'ishi had not heard in far too long.

He rolled onto his back. His armor felt made of anvils, constricting his breath, pinning him to the earth.

Warm rain sluiced out of the gray sky, wind like the breath of the gods driving the rain against his skin.

The dog licked his face again.

He reached up and ran his fingers through Akao's warm, rain-soaked ruff. Akao climbed onto Ken'ishi's chest and plastered his face with more warm, soft tongue. The smell of wet dog, rich and earthy, came even through the rain. Tears stung his eyes, washed away in the rain. Laughter bubbled out of him, quickly stifled for fear this might not be real.

Akao bit into the laces of Ken'ishi's breastplate, trying to tug him into a sitting position.

"How can it be you?" Ken'ishi said, his voice cracking and thick with joy, his heart so full it could not be contained. He was sixteen years old again, and his truest friend was with him.

Akao grinned, tongue lolling. "In this time, in this place, anything is possible."

Silver Crane lay half-buried in bloody mud beside Ken'ishi. He did not want to touch it.

"You should get out of the rain," Akao said.

Ken'ishi rolled onto his hands and knees, levered himself upright. He staggered to his feet.

"Do you have any food?" Akao said. "I feel like I haven't eaten in a lifetime." His sharp eyes darted around the field of the dead.

Ken'ishi half-smiled and half-sobbed. "I'm sorry, old friend, but no."

The dog's nose dropped to the ground, and he snuffled among the dead, moving away from Ken'ishi. "With all this water, I can't smell anything," Akao said with disgust.

The rain poured down, thick with fresh-smelling *kami*, thick with both life and death. The wind howled like a ravenous thing. Muffled thunder rumbled in the distance, and it was not barbarian bombs.

Akao stopped and his dark, earnest eyes looked deep into Ken'ishi's. "Are you coming?"

Staggering after Akao, Ken'ishi longed to curl up in a warm place and dry off.

Silver Crane lay quiescent for now, sated and spent. But only for now.

His voice was thick. "Not yet. There's something I must do first."

Akao grinned at him. "Very well. Do what you must."

Then the dog turned away and picked his way through the bodies. Ken'ishi watched him go until he had faded into the rain.

"Wait, don't go," he said, and sadness filled him.

He did not know how long he stood there, smelling Akao in his nose, feeling his thick fur in his fingers.

Another crack of lightning roused him to action. He picked up Silver Crane, wiped off the mud, and sheathed it.

Suddenly his belly clenched, doubling him over. A torrent of black, wriggling things spewed from his mouth and nose, tasting of death itself, like ten thousand tarry, bitter, leeches, seething, squirming out his nose and plopping into the mud. He heaved and heaved, spewing a shiny mound before his knees, more than any man could hold.

In the rain, the blind, squirming things began to dissolve like blood clots.

He spat again and again, wiped his mouth and tried to breathe, trembling and weak, spent in ways only his spirit understood.

Finally, he knew what he had to do.

He would not go back for Kazuko. She would find her own way home. The certainty, the finality of it struck him like a hammer.

In this sprawling field of storm-drenched dead men, it was not difficult to find a peasant spearman of roughly Ken'ishi's size and build. He traded clothes and armor with the dead man, the simple breastplate of *ashigaru*. Everyone in Lord Tsunetomo's army knew Captain Ken'ishi's armor. Then he cut off the dead man's head and carried it with him for some distance, thanking the man's spirit for fighting well and for the use of his head.

He would regret not saying farewell to Storm. The stallion had been as fine a mount as any warrior could desire.

When he reached a populated village, he would buy a jar of *saké* and drink to Hage.

More than ten years ago, he had passed Mount Kurama. It lay to the northwest of the capital. It was said to be a home of the *tengu*. Perhaps they would know what to do with a thing like Silver Crane. Its power did not belong in the hands of human beings. Perhaps they would help him finish what Ken'ishi and Lord Abe had begun. Besides, Mount Kurama was near the capital. Perhaps Lord Abe would be willing to help him reclaim his humanity once and for all.

He hoped Kaa was not still angry about their duel.

Without even a last look at the carnage he had wreaked, he carried Silver Crane into the lonely rain.

EPILOGUE

Live in simple faith...
Just as this trusting cherry
Flowers, fades, and falls.

—*Issa*

"Why this the Ronin Shrine, Mama?" the little boy asked.

Lady Otomo no Kazuko squeezed her three-year-old son's hand.

The *sakura* blossoms fell around them like velvety pink and white snowflakes, blanketing the earth. The castle loomed above, silhouetted against the sunset sky. Captain Michizane, her chief *yojimbo*, hung back a respectful but watchful distance.

They stood before the shrine she had had erected in the *sakura* orchard. Incense sticks lent bittersweet aroma to the air. She checked the *saké* cup before the battered, rusted *do-maru* with the fading laces, and found it empty. The rice ball from two days ago was also missing. Good that she had brought another.

She spotted a *tanuki* footprint embedded in a nearby patch of moist earth.

"Why, mama? *Ronin* dangerous, Father say."

Wiping a tear, Kazuko knelt and stroked his plump cheek. "Sometimes *ronin* are wild, desperate men, Tsunemaru. Sometimes they are heroes." She kissed her son on the head, her son in whose face she saw the one she loved, her son who had become the love of her life. "The waves of life can toss people in many directions, some easy, some difficult. The *kami* of this shrine watch over them...."

Ken'ishi's armor had been found, but not Silver Crane. And she had a piece of him still, right here with her. His eyes looked at her with adoration every day.

"...Wherever they are."

SO ENDS THE FINAL SCROLL

AFTERWORD

I started writing the story that would become the Ronin Trilogy in about 1998, fueled by a passion for samurai films like *Ran, Seven Samurai, Yojimbo,* and *Lone Wolf and Cub.* That decision launched me into an overwhelming research effort, which propelled me into further research, which drove me to start learning the Japanese language, which ultimately led me to moving to Japan, Fukuoka Prefecture, where I lived for three years, which led me to even *more* research, much of it first-hand, including the fortifications around Hakata Bay, the museums, the shrines, and more.

If you're curious about how far down the research rabbit hole goes, be assured it's more like a wormhole. It goes *all* the way down, and beyond is a new galaxy.

When I started this journey, I found what I thought was plenty of research material in printed form, encyclopedias, library books, etc. Those were the days when the Internet was still in its infancy and the best research sources were only available in Japanese. Now, however, the sheer volume of digital information that is readily available astonishes me, and it continues to expand. More and more sources, both scholarly and otherwise, have become available in English, digitally and in print. (I could do the research in Japanese, but that doesn't mean I *want* to.) If I had had this much information available in 1998...I probably wouldn't have started at all. I'd have been paralyzed by overload.

One of the challenges with a work of this nature is that historians disagree on a myriad of small details like exact dates, the order of the events, who was there and what they did. The disparate sources I consulted often spanned many decades of scholarly research, and, like scientists, historians often change their conclusions when new evidence arises.

In the case of the Mongol invasions of Japan, the archaeological research is ongoing, much of it happening under the waters of Hakata Bay. That research offers new insights not only into the culture of 13th-century Japan, but also into the Mongols and their Chinese and Korean subjects. These archaeological discoveries allow new and ever-changing suppositions, which were unavailable to George Sansom in the 1950s when he was writing *A History of Japan to 1334*, one of my most comprehensive sources.

Over the course of writing this novel, I discovered more up-to-date research sources, some of which contradicted information I had already used in previous volumes, or which contradicted areas where I had applied artistic license. Tying the perspectives of so many sources together is a challenge. Relying on only one source might give the perception that the Battle of Takashima, for example, took place largely at sea, whereas a different source might imply that most of the fighting must have been on land. It is easy to become myopic and overlook the fact that the Mongols' second invasion was of breathtaking scope, with purportedly 3,500 ships in total and more than 100,000 men in the Sung fleet alone. I have tried to get it all to jibe as best I could. In every case, however, the story's needs were the final arbiter.

Astute readers of some previous editions of *Sword of the Ronin* will also note that I have changed the name of Tsunetomo's castle town from Oita to Hita. This was an error I felt obliged to correct. Oita and Hita are both real, modern day cities on Kyushu, but the geographical locale I intended was situated more properly in the location of modern-day Hita. I hope those readers will forgive the inconsistency.

The end result, I hope, is that the reader experiences the kind of wonder that I do when history meets fiction: trying to figure out where the real history begins and ends. The historical record is full of stories of incredible heroism and astonishing courage. I hope the reader will seek out those boundaries and explore them further.

Travis Heermann
June, 2015

GLOSSARY

ashigaru – literally "quick legs," called such due to their minimal armor, peasants enlisted or conscripted during times of war to serve as spearmen or archers, forming the bulk of a warlord's forces.

awabi – raw abalone served in the shell.

ayu – *Plecoglossus altivelis*. Fresh water fish indigenous to Japan and Korea, often called "sweetfish" because of the sweetness of its flesh.

bakufu – literally "tent government," but came to mean the dwelling and household of a shogun, or military dictator. Generally used to refer to the system of government of a feudal military dictatorship, equivalent in English to the term 'shogunate.'

biwa – short-necked fretted lute, often used in narrative storytelling, the chosen instrument of Benten, goddess of music, eloquence, poetry, and education in the Shinto faith.

bokken – wooden practice sword, designed to lessen damage. Swordmaster Miyamoto Musashi was renowned for defeating fully armed opponents with one or two *bokken*.

bushi – synonymous with "samurai," military nobility, warrior gentleman.

cho – unit of distance, equivalent to 119.3 yards (109.3 m).

daikon – literally "big root," variety of large, white radish with a mild flavor.

daimyo - literally "great name," feudal lord of Japan, vassal of the Shogun.

do-maru – literally "body wrap," style of armor constructed of lacquered metal plates and leather, lighter and closer fitting than the *o-yoroi* style.

eta – one of the Unclean, a class of people typically relegated to such jobs as leatherworkers, gravediggers, and prostitutes.

futon – padded mattress flexible enough to be folded up and put away during the day.

geta – elevated wooden sandals.

Go – a board game for two players, originating in China more than 2,500 years ago, noted for being rich in strategy despite its relatively simple rules. Players place black and white "stones" on the intersections of a 19 x 19 grid, the object being to use one's stones to capture a larger total area of the board than the opponent.

hamen – the temper line of a sword blade.

hara – the belly or stomach, believed to contain the soul or the "center of being."

hyakume – a unit of weight, 100 *momme,* corresponding to about 13.2 ounces (375 g).

jitte – literally "ten hands," also called a *jutte,* weapon consisting of an iron bar and U-shaped guard, designed to catch and hold sword blades, often used to disarm unruly samurai, typically 12-24 inches long (30-60 cm).

kabuto – helmet, comprising many different styles, secured to the head by a chin cord, often adorned with crests.

kachi-guri – dried chestnuts.

kai-awase – a game played by wealthy nobility, wherein the insides of seashells were painted with pictures (*e-awase*) or poetry (*uta-awase*). The object of the game was to find the most appropriate matching shell, such as the visually related or thematic match to a picture or the second half of a poem.

kami – sometimes translated as "god" or "deity," but also referring to the ubiquitous spirits of nature, the elements, and ancestors, which are the center of worship for the Shinto faith.

kappa – supernatural river creature or spirit, about the size of a child, with a turtle-like shell, a beak for a mouth, a flat saucer-like indentation on its head that must remain filled with water when it is on land, or else it loses its power. Their behavior and feeding habits range from pranksterish and lecherous to predatory and vampiric.

katana – style of sword, of later design than the *tachi*; also the long sword of a pair used with a *wakizashi*.

kemari – an ancient game wherein the players strive to keep a leather ball in the air using various parts of their bodies.

ki – spirit, life, energy.

kiai – battle cry or sharp cry meant to focus technique, awareness, and fighting spirit, sometimes to startle an opponent or express victory.

kimono – literally "thing to wear," traditional garment worn by men, women, and children, typically secured at the waist by an *obi*. Straight-lined robe that reaches to the ankle, with a collar and wide sleeves.

kirin – creature of folklore resembling a scaly horse engulfed in flames, with either one or two antlers, cloven hooves, and scales. Said to be a good omen, signifying luck, justice, wisdom, prosperity, and fertility. Often conflated with the European unicorn.

koi – catch-all name given to many species of carp, a fish that symbolizes warrior spirit, perseverance, courage, and prosperity.

komadori – *Erithacus akahige*. Japanese robin.

kozuka – small utility knife fit into the side of a *katana* scabbard.

maku – curtain erected around the headquarters area of an army on campaign.

menpo – metal mask, armor covering the face from the nose to the chin, often fashioned into fearsome shapes.

miso – a thick paste made by fermenting soy, rice, and/or barley, used as seasoning. Very healthy. Miso soup is an excellent hangover cure.

mochi – rice cake made from pounding short-grain glutinous rice into a thick, sticky paste.

momme – unit of weight, approximately equal to 0.13 ounces (3.75 gm).

mon – emblem in Japanese heraldry, similar to coats of arms in European heraldry, used to identify individuals and families.

naginata – a polearm with a stout, curved blade 12-24 inches (30-60 cm) long, with a wooden shaft 4-8 feet (120-240 cm) long. Sometimes called the Japanese halberd.

nodachi – also called *odachi*, lit. "great/large sword," averaging 65-70 inches long (165-178 cm), typically used from horseback.

nori – seaweed.

obi – sash used to secure robes, of a myriad of lengths and styles. Typically men's *obi* are narrower than women's.

ofuda – a paper talisman, written with spells and charged with magic.

ofuro – a deep, steep-sided wooden bathtub, but also sometimes referring to the room where bathing is done.

oni – supernatural creature from folklore, translates as demon, devil, ogre, or troll. Hideous, gigantic creatures with sharp claws, wild hair, and long horns growing from their heads, mostly humanoid, but sometimes possessing unnatural features such as odd numbers of eyes or extra fingers and toes.

onigiri – rice ball.

onmyouji – practitioners of a form of divination based on esoteric *yin-yang* cosmology, a mixture of natural science and occultism.

oyabun – literally "foster parent," but most often used to refer to the boss of an organized crime family.

o-yoroi – literally "great armor," heavy, box-shaped armor, used primarily by high-ranking samurai on horseback, consisting of an iron breastplate covered with leather, lacquered iron scales, woven together with silk or leather cords, and rectangular lamellar shoulder guards.

ramen – noodle dish consisting of wheat noodles served in broth, often with pork, *miso*, green onions, pickled ginger, or other toppings.

ri – unit of distance, equivalent to 2.4 miles (3.9 km).

ronin – a samurai with no lord or master, having become masterless from the death or fall of his master, or after the loss of his master's favor or privilege.

saifu – A cloth, drawstring wallet used by men of means to carry money, papers, or small personal items.

saké – fermented beverage made from rice.

sakura – *Prunus serrulata,* the Japanese cherry blossom. Blooms brilliantly for a few days in the spring, but does not produce fruit. Deeply symbolic of the samurai's life in its extreme beauty and quick death.

sama – an honorific suffix appended to names to indicate the addressee's superiority in station.

seiza – literally "proper sitting," kneeling position with legs folded under, sitting on calves and heels.

sensei – honorific title given to teachers and mentors.

seppuku – also called *hara-kiri,* literally "belly cutting," ritual suicide performed by disemboweling oneself.

shide – white paper cut into zig-zag strips. When attached to a rope made of rice straw, they signify the boundary between the sacred and profane. Most often used to denote sacred trees or holy sites.

shugenja – also known as a *yamabushi,* an ascetic, itinerant follower of Shugendo, a practice of magic, augury, and exorcism claiming ties to both Buddhism and Shintoism.

shuriken – literally "hand-hidden sword," any small, concealed bladed object, used for throwing, stabbing, or slashing. Common types include weighted spikes and thin, bladed plates.

soba – buckwheat.

sumi – traditional ink, made from soot, water, and glue.

tachi – style of sword, earlier design than the *katana,* with a more pronounced curvature, usually worn with the edge hanging down, in contrast to the *katana,* which was worn with the edge facing up.

taifu – literally "great wind," hurricane, root of the English word "typhoon."

taiko – a large drum, used for marshaling troops, as well as sending warnings and messages great distances.

tanto – single-edged dagger.

tanuki – *Nyctereutes procyonoides.* Mammal indigenous to Japan, sometimes translated as "raccoon dog," member of the dog family (*Canidae*). Resembles a raccoon in having rounded ears, dark facial markings, and brown coat, but its tail is not ringed. Its limbs are short, brown or grayish in color, and its body low-slung. In folklore, *tanuki* are tricksters, said to possess magical powers and the ability to change shape. *Tanuki* are said to keep their magical powers in their scrota.

tatami – mat used for flooring, made of a core of rice straw wrapped in soft rush straw.

tengu – supernatural creature from folklore, having both avian and human characteristics. *Tengu* were long believed to be disruptive demons and harbingers of war. However, this image evolved into one of protective, if still dangerous, spirits of the mountains and forests, said to be masters of swordsmanship.

torii – a gate most commonly found at the entrance of or within a Shinto shrine, where it symbolically marks the transition from the profane to the sacred. The presence of a torii at the entrance is usually the simplest way to identify Shinto shrines.

tsuba – round or square guard above the hilt of a bladed weapon.

uguisu – *Cettia diphone*. A song bird known as the Japanese bush warbler.

wakizashi – a short sword, usually paired with the longer *katana*.

yabusame – a style of mounted archery developed in the early Kamakura period by Minamoto no Yoritomo to train samurai to shoot from horseback. A rider gallops his mount past three diamond-shaped wooden targets, each approximately eighty yards (73 m) apart, sized and placed to replicate firing at an enemy's face and upper chest, just above the breastplate where armor is light or nonexistent. Special "turnip-headed" arrows are fired at each target in succession. In modern times, it is believed that the whistling sound emitted by the arrowheads drives away evil spirits.

yojimbo – bodyguard.

yoriki – literally "helper, assistant," in the case of this story, the deputy to a provincial constable.

yurei – literally "dim spirit," supernatural entity from folklore, analogous to Western ghosts. A person who dies in a state of extreme negative emotion, such as revenge, love, jealousy, hatred or sorrow, may be trapped in the earthly realm as a *yurei*.

zori – flat, thonged sandals made from straw or wood.

BIBLIOGRAPHY

Benedict, Ruth. *The Chrysanthemum and the Sword.* New York: Mariner, 2005.

Bryant, Anthony J. and Angus McBride. *Early Samurai: 200-1500 AD.* Oxford: Osprey, 1991.

Chozanshi, Issai. *The Demon's Sermon on the Martial Arts.* Trans. William Scott Wilson. Tokyo: Kodansha, 2006.

Cleary, Thomas. *Training the Samurai Mind: A Bushido Sourcebook.* Boston: Shambhala, 2008.

Hamill, Sam. *The Sound of Water: Haiku by Basho, Buson, Issa, and Other Poets.* Trans. Sam Hamill. Boston: Shambhala, 2000.

Hearn, Lafcadio. *Shadowings.* Tokyo: Tuttle, 1971.

Kure, Mitsuo. *Samurai: An Illustrated History.* Boston: Tuttle, 2002.

Miyake, Hitoshi. "Religious Rituals in Shugendo: A Summary." *Japanese Journal of Religious Studies.* 16.2-3 (1989): 101-116. Web.

Miyamoto, Musashi. *The Book of Five Rings.* Trans. Bradford J. Brown, et al. New York: Bantam, 1982.

Yagyu, Munenori. *The Life-Giving Sword: Secret Teachings from the House of the Shogun.* Trans. William Scott Wilson. Tokyo: Kodansha, 2003.

Ogasawara, Nobuo. *Japanese Swords.* Trans. Don Kenny. Osaka: Hoikusha, 2003.

Ratti, Oscar and Adele Westbrook. *Secrets of the Samurai: The Martial Arts of Feudal Japan.* Edison: Castle Books, 1999.

Rossabi, Morris. *Khubilai Khan.* Berkeley: University of California Press, 1988.

Saito, Takafumi and William R. Nelson. eds. *1020 Haiku in*

Translation. Trans. Takafumi Saito and William R. Nelson. North Charleston: BookSurge, 2006.

Sansom, George. *A History of Japan to 1334.* Stanford: Stanford University Press, 1958.

Sato, Hiroaki. *Legends of the Samurai.* Woodstock: Overlook Press, 1995.

Soho, Takuan. *The Unfettered Mind.* Trans. William Scott Wilson. Tokyo: Kodansha, 1986.

Turnbull, Stephen. *Essential Histories: Genghis Khan and the Mongol Conquests 1190-1400.* Oxford: Osprey, 2003.

—. *The Mongol Invasions of Japan 1274 and 1281.* Oxford: Osprey, 2010.

—. *Mongol Warrior 1200-1350.* Oxford: Osprey, 2003.

—. *The Samurai Sourcebook.* London: Arms and Armour Press, 1998.

—. *Samurai Women 1184-1877.* Oxford: Osprey, 2010.

Yamamoto, Tsunetomo. *Hagakure: The Book of the Samurai.* Trans. William Scott Wilson. Tokyo: Kodansha, 1983.

Yoshikawa, Eiji. *Musashi.* Tokyo: Kodansha, 1981.

CONTRIBUTORS

This book would not have been possible without the generous support of this amazing army of people.

Spearman
Joe Aliment
Tyler Gleason
Helen
Lore Preuss

Archer
Colette Black
Martin Dick
Catharine Dixon
Thomas Albert
   Fowler
Philip Harris
Patrick Hester
Erica Hildebrand
Lynda Hillburn
Elaine Isaak
Aren Jensen
Greg Little
Rhel
Derek Williams
Frank Wuerbach

Archer Duo
Matthew Porter
Henry Lopez
Elton Mottley
Josh Vogt
Alice Wong

Ronin
Stanley Anderson
Scott T. Barnes
Jason Batt
Michael Beddes
Rose Beetem
Craig
Arthur "Buck"
   Dorrance
John Evans
Carolyn Fritz
Lorraine Heisler
Angie Hodapp
Chandra Osborn
Diann T. Read
Chris Richardson
Holly Roberds

Kyle Simonsen
Christopher Vogler
Amber Welch
Amber Wendell
Richard Wulf

Bushi
Gerard Ackerman
Danielle Burkhart
Guy Anthony
   DeMarco
Doug Dandridge
Fantomas
Mark Innerebner
Zach Jacobs
Korey Krabbenhoft
Nicholas
   Lapeyrouse
Theresa Oster
Pretentious Moniker
Stacy Roberds
Suzanne Stafford
Kimberly Dahl
   Vandervort

Ronin Duo
Samantha Cleland
Julia Dvorin
Aaron Michael
    Ritchey
Peter Sartucci
Karen Sundstrom

Bushi Duo
William Miskovetz

Bandit Chieftain
Bree Ervin
Robert Fraass
L. K. Hart
Kim Hosmer
Kevin Ikenberry
Leigh
Kristin Luna
Ann M. Myers
Ashley Oswald
Ruth Phillips
Logan Waterman

Samurai
Tony Aliment
Dawn Christensen
Shelda Cline
Brandi Michelle
    Corsillo
Bob Darcy
Kevin Derouin
Paul Duncan
Amanda Ferrell
Brian Fishback
Susan Malcom
    Holland
Peter J. Mancini

Joseph Narducci
Michael Nave
Sheldon Peters
Daniel Read
Steven Rief
John Shoberg
Emerson Small
Jeanne Stein

Infantry Sergeant
Chad Bowden
Kelsie Gardner
Norajane McIntyre
Steve Meyer
Josh Seybert

Cavalry Sergeant
Jason Burns

Samurai Duo
Eric Cogbill

Cavalry Captain
Bob Applegate
Rich Chang

Samurai Band
Todd Ahlman
Chris Bertolotti
Rachel Brewer
Maggie Christensen
Casey Heermann
Dorothy Heermann
Alexis Safwat
Michael
    Severtsgaard

Samurai Vanguard

James Sams
Mistina Bates-
    Picciano
Tenebrae
Kelly Washington

Sensei
Gina M. Vick

**Lord of the
    Underworld**
Scott Baldwin
Cody Heermann

General
Patricia Vandewege

PERMISSIONS

ABOUT THE AUTHOR

Author, freelance writer, award-winning screenwriter, poker player, biker, roustabout, and graduate of the Odyssey Writing Workshop, Travis Heermann is the author of numerous short stories appearing in such places as the Fiction River anthology series, Cemetery Dance's *Shivers VII*, and *Historical Lovecraft*. In addition to the Ronin Trilogy, he is also the author of *Death Wind, Rogues of the Black Fury,* and *The Wild Boys*. Aside from his fiction work, he has contributed to almost thirty roleplaying supplements, including the *Firefly Roleplaying Game, Legend of the Five Rings, d20 System* products, and *EVE Online*.

He spent three years living in Japan, where much of this story was researched and conceived, and now lives in a much larger world than before.

Find the author online!
Email: travis@travisheermann.com
Web: www.travisheermann.com
Blog: www.travisheermann.com/blog
Twitter: @TravisHeermann
Facebook: www.facebook.com/travis.heermann